DEBT BOMB

A NOVEL

MICHAEL E. GINSBERG

North Carolina

Debt Bomb

© 2021 Michael E. Ginsberg. All rights reserved.

This is a work of fiction. All of the characters, names, incidents, organizations, and dialogue in this novel are either the products of the author's imagination or are used fictitiously.

Published in the United States by BQB Publishing
(an imprint of Boutique of Quality Books Publishing, Inc.)
www.bqbpublishing.com

Printed in the United States

ISBN 978-1-952782-08-4 (p)
ISBN 978-1-952782-09-1 (e)

Library of Congress Control Number: 2021935109

Book design by Robin Krauss, www.bookformatters.com
Cover design by Rebecca Lown, www.rebeccalowndesign.com
First editor: Caleb Guard
Second editor: Andrea Vande Vorde

PRAISE FOR DEBT BOMB

"A timely and fast-paced spy thriller by a former U.S. intelligence official, *Debt Bomb* is a sobering reminder of the national security threat posed by the ballooning U.S. national debt and the silence of Republican spending hawks in the Trump years. With this debut novel, Mike Ginsberg may be destined to be an American John LeCarre."

—John Bellinger, Former Legal Adviser
to the National Security Council

"A deftly crafted thriller that kept me turning pages—through politics, money, and murder—to the ending I didn't see coming."

—Chris DeRose, New York Times Bestselling Author
of *The Fighting Bunch*

CHAPTER 1

After nearly two decades as an accountant, Andrea Gartner had fatally wielded ledger books more times than she cared to remember. She was well acquainted with watching entire lives unravel before her, tears streaming down the faces of grown men annihilated by simple balance sheets charting their financial ruin in ink redder than blood.

Today, she found herself in that painfully familiar spot once more.

She fixed her eyes on the man sitting opposite her, Cam Davis, owner of the largest chain of furniture stores in Columbia, South Carolina. She was the only thing standing between him and the end of his financial life as he knew it. His devil-may-care attitude—the source of so much of his business success—had now left him teetering on the precipice of bankruptcy.

"You have an existential debt problem," said Andrea.

Telling the cocksure, self-styled Mattress King of South Carolina he was flirting with financial ruin was terrifying, but what Andrea truly feared was him ignoring her dire warnings. She prayed she wasn't about to watch another client whistle past the graveyard of fiscal reality.

"A *what* problem?" asked Cam incredulously. "Come on. I sold more furniture last year than my next two competitors combined."

"I've been through your books," she replied. "Your finances are a house of cards. You're a hair's breadth from complete bankruptcy."

Cam didn't act like someone about to go broke. Everyone in

Columbia knew he was one of the most generous people in the city. Every Christmas, he donated hundreds of mattresses to homeless shelters. When his alma mater, the University of South Carolina, made the playoffs in any sport, he'd give away free sofas to the first fifty customers in his stores the next day. He sponsored Little League teams and 5K races for charity. His heart was big. His wallet was even bigger and seemingly always open.

She glanced out the window. The Mattress King's red Ferrari with "MTRSKNG" vanity license plates was parked next to her battered ten-year-old Toyota Camry. His thousand-dollar sports coat and Rolex contrasted sharply with the peeling wallpaper and army surplus furniture of her office. Even his cologne smelled expensive.

"You can't be serious," said Cam. "I've got twenty stores in Columbia. And twenty more across the rest of the state. If I need cash, I'll borrow it. No bank is going to turn down a loan application from the Mattress King."

Here we go again, she thought. *He's not getting it, and I'm not getting through to him.*

Andrea turned her computer screen so Cam could see his balance sheet for himself. "Your Highness, you have maxed-out credit facilities with the two largest banks in Columbia." She dragged her finger line by line through his balance sheet. "You have a five-million-dollar loan with the largest bank in Columbia and you're six months behind on payments. You're also behind on lease payments for your three largest stores. Personally, you're carrying five-digit balances on four separate credit cards."

Cam waved his hand dismissively, the gold bracelet on his wrist jangling against his Rolex. "I have the highest-grossing furniture stores in Columbia. I'm getting ready to build more throughout the state. If I don't have the money now, it'll come. I'll be fine. Stop worrying, will you?"

Andrea pursed her lips. "Cam, we've been working together for years," she said earnestly. "You were one of my first clients, and you're still one of my favorites. I've bought four mattresses since moving to Columbia, all from Cam's Discount Furniture. So I'm going to give it to you straight."

"Give me what straight?"

"I hate debt, and you are neck-deep in it. You've got the Sword of Damocles hanging over your head. An unexploded grenade in your hand waiting to have its pin pulled. Pick your metaphor. And someone else is in control of dropping the sword or pulling the pin."

Cam laughed. "Aren't you being a little dramatic?"

"If someone out there wanted to destroy Cam's Discount Furniture," said Andrea, "all they'd need to do was stop loaning you money and call in your loans. Your stores would be liquidated and out of business in a week."

"I sold twenty million dollars of furniture last year. There has to be cash somewhere."

Andrea shook her head and ran her hands through her hair in frustration, mussing the extra curl and bounce she'd given it by blowing it dry a little longer this morning. "The minute the money comes in I have to allocate it to paying interest on one of your loans. The money goes out faster than it comes in. This isn't about your revenues. It's about your spending."

Andrea suspected no one had ever talked to him like this before.

"What are you saying?" Cam's air of confidence was beginning to fade.

"You need to sell some stores. Or close some."

"Close stores?" asked Cam, wide-eyed.

Andrea nodded. "Take the proceeds and pay down some of your debt. Sell your mansion. Sell the Ferrari. Take the kids out of private school. Clean your slate. I'm telling you, if you don't do this now, in six months, the banks will do it for you. It'll be a lot less painful and humiliating if you do it on your own terms."

"Forget it," Cam scoffed. "We'll figure something else out. I built this business from the ground up. It's my life's work. And my kids' inheritance. I'm not selling any of it. Things can't possibly be as bad as you're saying."

"You said it yourself: you outsold the other two furniture stores in Columbia combined," she said. "There isn't more room to grow. Not enough to pay back your creditors. If you don't sell some of your stores, they'll all get foreclosed, and you'll have to declare bankruptcy. Do what I'm telling you and you can still save some of your business."

"I'll get another loan." Cam leaned forward and placed his hand on Andrea's desk. His face reddened as he dug in against her advice. "I'm not selling any of my business, you hear me?"

"No one is going to loan you more money," Andrea said quietly. She put her hand on top of his and could feel the tension in his fingers. "You have to sell some of the business. It's the only way to save at least some of your stores. Your only other option is to declare bankruptcy."

Cam forcefully yanked his hand free. "I started with nothing!"

He stood up from the chair and paced the room, his hands gesticulating wildly. Seeing Cam's tall, muscular frame angrily march around the room exacerbated Andrea's inferiority complex. She was five foot five and ten pounds overweight.

"Everything you see—my stores, my Ferrari, my mansion, my kids' private school—I earned it," Cam seethed. "I'm not giving it up just because things are a little overextended. We'll find the cash some other way. How could you ask my family to give all this up?"

If only he knew, Andrea thought. She glanced at the picture of her family on her desk. Six months after that family portrait was taken, her father was diagnosed with prostate cancer. A year later he was dead. He'd left them a financial mess and medical bills they couldn't pay. Andrea was fifteen at the time. Her mother had sold their house and pulled Andrea and her brother out of their private school. Alone and adrift in a public school, unable to break into the existing high school cliques, Andrea would spend hours sobbing in the girls' locker room. Her college dreams were dashed because there were no funds to pay for it, so she resorted to working multiple jobs while her friends partied every weekend.

Andrea had never forgotten the searing experience of losing everything she'd known. That was why she became an accountant, to help other families the way she wished someone had helped her.

Cam put a cigarette in his mouth and fumbled with his lighter.

"I thought you quit," Andrea said.

"I have." He lit the cigarette and took a deep drag, then puffed a cloud of smoke into the air. "But I keep some around for emergencies."

Andrea had never seen Cam react this emotionally. He was one of the most self-assured businesspeople she knew. If he considered this an emergency, maybe she was getting through to him.

"You earned it. That much is true," she said. "But you didn't just earn revenue for your business. You also earned the opportunity to borrow money against your success and the trust of lenders that you'd pay back what you borrowed. You took advantage of that trust. I'm telling you, as your accountant, you can't pay it back. As soon as your lenders realize it, they'll collapse your entire empire."

Cam sat back down in a huff, taking deep drags of his cigarette. Sweat glistened on his forehead.

"Don't beat yourself up about this," said Andrea, trying to comfort him. "You think you're the only person who's fallen into this trap? You're not. It's a common story. Every accountant has experienced some version of it. An entrepreneur starts small, hand-to-mouth, and hits it big."

"It's the American Dream!" exclaimed Cam. Cigarette ash fell to the floor when he threw his hands up for emphasis.

"Right, but then suddenly everyone wants to lend him money to grow his business and expand his lifestyle. More stores for the company. Fast cars, yachts, and beachfront condos for the owner. The business grows, but the debt grows faster. Before long, a company with a great product and business model is drowning in debt and goes under. Toys "R" Us sold eleven billion dollars' worth of toys a year. Eleven billion dollars! And they still collapsed under a mountain of debt."

Cam glowered at Andrea with gritted teeth, still fuming.

"I know how easy it is to get addicted to debt," she continued. "You think you're the only one? Look at the federal government. America has forty trillion dollars of debt. The average person has no idea how much we're borrowing every day just to keep the government running. Your debt is peanuts compared to that. What's happening to you will happen to the country if we don't do something soon. If America's lenders demand repayment, we're hosed. The thought scares the bejesus out of me."

"For goodness' sakes, Andrea, every time I come in here you bring up the national debt," said Cam. "Blah, blah, blah, the national debt monster is going to come and bite us all. You've been saying that for years, and has the debt monster bitten us? Even once?"

"Not yet, but it's coming," said Andrea. "Trust me. It's coming."

"When? Next century?" Cam threw his hands in the air. "You've been saying that since we started working together. That was in 2008! It's now 2027, and nothing has changed! All you do is warn about the debt boogeyman, but nothing bad has happened. While you're busy predicting doom and gloom, the stock market is hitting the stratosphere and the economy is going gangbusters. Now you're warning me the same debt monster is going to eat my business. Why should I believe a word you say? Your Chicken Little act is getting old. You're all talk, no action."

Andrea clenched her jaw. Who the hell was Cam Davis to tell her she was all talk and no action?

"That's not true," she protested. "I spent four years as the chairman of the Richland County Republican Party. And then I was Third Vice Chairman of the South Carolina Republican Party. I've supported Debt Rebel candidates promising to reduce the national debt for as long as the Debt Rebellion movement has been around. And the only reason I got involved in Republican politics in the first place was because I was worried about the debt! I've seen debt destroy peoples' lives. I don't want it to destroy the country too."

"Please," Cam said dismissively. "I'm a businessman. I know the difference between talk and action. You debt scolds are all talk. Has the national debt gotten one dollar smaller since fearmongers like you started screaming about it?"

"I've spent years researching what it would take to run for Congress and deal with the debt myself," she blurted before she could stop herself. "And I've cultivated relationships across the state to make it happen. Is that action enough for you?"

She folded her arms across her chest and stiffened her back. Surely this would impress Cam as bold action. But even as the words were leaving her mouth, she knew she was getting far out in front of her skis. All she had ever done was idly muse about running for office with her husband, Ryan. Now here she was, practically declaring her candidacy with a client.

"Seriously?" Cam's voice dripped with disbelief.

"I'm dead serious," said Andrea, too dug into the argument to walk back her confident declaration.

"I know your personality." The corner of Cam's mouth curled into a smirk. "You're an accountant, not a politician. Politics would eat you alive."

Andrea threw her head back in exasperation. "Everyone tells me the same thing! 'You're too nice.' 'You're too honest.' Even my husband says politics is too tough a business for a quiet homebody like me. First you tell me I should take action, and then when I propose action, you say I'll suck at it."

"If it will get you off my back, then go ahead and run for Congress," said Cam.

"I will," Andrea shot back. "And maybe I'll win."

"Go ahead," said Cam. "Scare other people for a change. Let the rest of America enjoy your national debt neurosis."

"Fine, I'm running," said Andrea. "You satisfied?"

They stared at one another across the desk.

She sat stunned and angry with herself. How could she have let him goad her into running for Congress? She tightly folded her arms across her chest again, feigning confidence in her abrupt decision.

Cam finally spoke. "I'm glad you're finally doing something about the national debt instead of nagging me every time I come in here. Tell you what, I'll make the first donation to your campaign."

"Don't you be making any donations," said Andrea. "Use that money to pay down your debts. If you don't sell some stores, cut back your lifestyle, and pay down your debts, you'll lose everything."

"Not a chance," said Cam. He emphatically extinguished his cigarette in the ashtray on Andrea's desk. "I've made it this far. I'll figure out something."

He got up from his seat and walked to the office door.

"Cam, this is it," she warned. "If you leave now without doing anything I've suggested, your entire furniture empire is as good as gone."

Cam hesitated, his hand gripping the doorknob.

Is it going to happen again? Is yet another client going to ignore my advice and run headlong into financial ruin?

Cam turned and smiled, his confidence back. "Don't worry, the banks and lenders love me," he said with a cocky grin. "I'll work something out with them. I always have."

Then he opened the door and walked out. The office windows rattled as the door slammed shut behind him.

Andrea laid her forehead on her desk.

Why can't I persuade clients to fix their bottom lines and clean up their debts?

It wasn't as if she hadn't prepared to make the case to Cam. She'd even practiced making her arguments just before he had arrived. Fat lot of good it had done. By the end of their conversation, he was as unconcerned about his finances as ever, and she had backed herself into running for Congress.

If I can't convince a man on the cusp of bankruptcy to take my advice, how am I going to convince anyone to vote for me so that I can fix America's finances?

She stood up and looked at her reflection in the full-length mirror on the wall beside her desk. Her plain, professional pantsuit and unremarkable shoes practically screamed to the world she was the typical unassuming accountant. Two kids, a modest suburban rancher, and the ubiquitous sensible family sedan or minivan in the driveway. Accountants like her weren't meant to play in the big leagues, and Cam's dismissive attitude confirmed every bit of the inferiority she felt.

But the terror of America's looming debt crisis had been

building inside Andrea like the pressure between tectonic plates on a fault line. Cam's insults had just jarred the plates loose and unleashed an earthquake within her. Most people were completely unaware of how many lives crumble before the nondescript personalities who work within the antiseptic office walls of an office like hers. They could never conceive of a taciturn, bespectacled accountant morphing into death, the destroyer of worlds.

Her piercing ice-blue eyes, the ones her husband Ryan said reminded him of Steely Dan's Josie, the Roman with her eyes on fire, stared back at her in the mirror. Ryan always said her eyes were the clue that there was much more buried within this humble accountant.

But all she saw in her eyes was failure. Failure to persuade her clients to follow her advice. Failure to get anyone to take her concerns about the national debt seriously. She'd seen Cam's fate on this day. In his impending doom, she also saw the fate of a country.

CHAPTER 2

Acorn shot out of bed at six a.m. to the buzzing of the same alarm clock he'd been using since high school. He hated crowds, and by eight a.m. the Metro subway train he took downtown to his Capitol Hill office would be a sardine can as riders jockeyed for space to grip the handholds.

Even though he lived only ten Metro stops from his office, he hated the commute. Trains had a fifty percent chance of having broken air conditioning, a disaster during the hot summer months. He had to go down three levels of escalators to get to the train platform. And he had to pay five dollars one way for the privilege.

Acorn dressed in his customary suit, draped the lanyard with his Capitol access badge around his neck, and smiled at himself in the mirror. At forty-four years old, he sat at the pinnacle of staff power in Washington as the chief of staff to Congressman Lewis Mason, the chairman of the House Debt Rebel Gang, and damn did he look the part. The badge gave him a feeling of importance and superiority. Other people lived by the rules; he made them.

His self-satisfaction was well-placed. He'd begun his Washington career fresh out of college as a lowly staffer in a conservative think tank. But he had no patience for climbing the greasy pole slowly. He was on a mission. Within two years he had set up his own think tank dedicated to balancing the budget and cutting the national debt. He stormed cable news and built himself into one of the go-to talking heads in Washington on the budget and the debt. Lewis Mason had taken notice and hired him to be his chief of staff at the tender age of thirty-six. His political rise had been meteoric even by Washington standards.

On the way to the Metro station, Acorn made his usual stop at the small Tivoli Gourmet shop outside the station for chocolate chip scones. The thought of digging into a scone always lightened the burden of his unpleasant commute. He approached the pastry counter and said, "The usual."

"And what is that?" the counterman asked.

"Huh?" Acorn took his eyes off the case of pastries and peered at the man. It wasn't PJ, the proprietor of the Tivoli Gourmet whom he'd known for the twenty-two years he'd been living and working in Washington. Today's counterman appeared to be Chinese, probably in his early twenties. Acorn had never seen him before.

"Greetings, my friend, I'm Frank Palmer," Acorn said, using his real name. "You new here?"

"Yes, I'm a student at Marymount down the street," the counterman said in perfect English without a hint of an accent. "I've started working here mornings. Today is my first day."

"Good to meet you," said Acorn, but his antenna went up. PJ had never mentioned about hiring new help. The only other time PJ wasn't there was when he was at the hospital with his daughter after the birth of his first grandchild.

"Where's PJ?" asked Acorn.

"Meeting with a supplier. Can I help you?"

Meeting a supplier? That was not like PJ. He'd been in business for twenty years. Suppliers came to him.

"Two chocolate chip scones, please."

"We don't have any today."

"Two chocolate chip muffins, then."

"We don't have any of those either."

"I've been coming here every weekday for ten years, and there's never been a day you didn't have chocolate chip scones or muffins. First PJ's gone, and now this."

"Can I get you something else?"

"How about a cheese Danish."

"May I suggest the red velvet cupcake?"

"I don't do cupcakes for breakfast."

"This cupcake is more like a muffin and less like a dessert," the man said.

"I think I'd prefer the cheese Danish. Do you have any?"

"I think you'll like the red velvet cupcake," the man insisted. "I strongly suggest you try it."

Acorn had pressed hard enough. He knew what the counterman's insistence meant.

Crap. Over the years, Acorn had half-convinced himself that his minders had forgotten about him. Every day that passed, he became more convinced he would make it to a ripe old age safe and sound.

"I'll take the cupcake," said Acorn.

"I know you'll like it." The man carefully picked the cupcake in the left column and third row of the display tray and handed it to Acorn.

Acorn paid for the cupcake and left the store. He sat down at a nearby bus shelter and glanced around to see if anyone was nearby. Seeing no one, he unwrapped the cupcake from its paper.

The paper was blank.

He took a bite of the cupcake. The man was right. It wasn't bad.

He took a second bite.

Ouch! His front teeth had bitten something hard.

It was a small coin with a Chinese character on it.

Acorn stared at it. Exactly as he feared. He was now an active agent.

He crumbled the cupcake to check if it contained any other

signals but found nothing. Only crumbs. He brushed them to the ground and the flock of pigeons camped around the Ballston Metro stop ravenously descended on them.

Acorn glanced about. No one seemed to be paying him any attention.

Twenty-two years he'd been living and working in DC with nary a peep from his minders. Now, with no warning, his minders had activated him.

Why?

The why would have to come later. For now, he needed to be on alert for his instructions.

He furtively made his way to the subway entrance, discreetly scanning everyone he passed as he'd been trained. He reflexively hunched his shoulders, hoping it would make him less conspicuous. He spotted the man who distributed copies of the *Express* mini-newspaper to Metro riders at the station entrance.

"Morning," said Acorn.

"Morning," the man replied. Usually, he gave Acorn the copy on top of the pile, but today he fumbled through his stack as though looking for a specific copy. He finally pulled one from near the bottom of the stack.

"Here you go." He handed Acorn the paper. "Have a great day."

"Thanks," said Acorn. "See you tomorrow."

"As always."

As he turned to leave, the man slipped something heavy into Acorn's pocket. Acorn slid his hand into his pocket as he headed down the station escalator and felt the mysterious gift. When he pulled it out, he saw it was a TAG Heuer wristwatch. He quietly slipped it onto his left wrist.

Acorn sat on one of the benches on the platform. Usually he'd turn to page two of the *Express* to read about the hearings happening on the Hill, but now he turned to the sports page. It featured a picture of Washington football players heading into their team headquarters, "the Temple," in Ashburn, Virginia. The caption read: "Washington players prepare to enter the Temple." Someone had highlighted "prepare to enter the Temple."

There it was: *prepare to enter the Temple.* Exactly what Acorn didn't want to see. But he was devoted to the Cause, had handed his life to the Cause, and he was going to see it through.

He wrestled an American Express credit card from his wallet where it was tucked into its own pocket behind his driver's license. The card had seen the light of day only three times in the twenty-two years since Acorn became an agent. The first time was when he put it in the wallet, and the second time was when he transferred it from an old wallet to a new wallet. Today was the third time.

The front of the card appeared to be a typical American Express card, but the back didn't have the usual magnetic stripe. Instead, there was a list of stock phrases his minders used as instructions listed in two columns, the code on the left and the translation on the right. Next to "prepare" it read "await instructions." Next to "enter the temple," it read "cave."

Acorn slipped the card back into his wallet. He understood the message.

The train to Capitol Hill arrived, and he took a seat feeling a torrent of conflicting emotions. His pulse quickened in anticipation of his coming mission, but paranoia had also set in. He scanned every face, wondering if they were friend or foe.

Memories of his parents overtook him, and conversations he hadn't thought about since his childhood emerged from the recesses of his mind. His parents had prepared him for this moment. They'd been gone for a decade now, having failed to fulfill their dreams of bringing capitalism to its knees. His mother and father had gone to work for China after the fall of the Berlin Wall, though Acorn was convinced they'd never emotionally recovered from the Soviet Union's collapse.

His parents were Harvard physicists, but they'd never quite made it in the scientific world. Despite their talents, their struggle to win research grants left them serving only as post-doctorate research fellows in an academic laboratory, at the mercy of their boss's willingness to obtain grants to keep them employed. They were consumed by bitterness at the system that hadn't rewarded them and barely recognized their years of toil and sacrifice.

Over the years, their bitterness turned to hatred. Their hatred wasn't merely ideological; it coursed through their veins. Capitalism had left them nearly broke, living in a ramshackle house on the outskirts of Cambridge while their classmates had gone to Wall Street and made millions doing nothing but moving money around. The "velocity of money," they'd called it. Meetings, phone calls, balance sheets. Five-star business lunches. "What the hell are they actually doing?" his father would say. His father and mother were the ones inventing things and making things while the students who partied into the wee hours and happily coasted on gentlemen's Cs in college were considered Masters of the Universe. Under Communism, the roles would be reversed. There would be no Wall Street money boys to swoop in and reap the profits from the scientists and engineers who created the value.

It wasn't until Acorn was a Harvard undergrad studying chemistry that he understood his parents' vision. In his senior year, a colleague at the *Harvard Independent,* a campus weekly, bragged about his new job at some Wall Street firm.

"What do they make?" Acorn had asked.

"They make *money,*" his colleague had replied with a smirk.

In that instant, something within Acorn snapped. His hatred of a capitalistic society was no longer ideological. It was visceral.

Personal. Everything his parents had been spouting all those years was true. No one made money. People only passed it back and forth.

"People like us—the scientists and engineers, the workers and laborers—are busy designing, creating, and assembling the computers that Wall Street guy will use, the skyscrapers he'll work in, the cars he'll drive, the planes he'll fly in, and the flat-panel HD televisions and surround sound he'll install in the screening room of his country estate. We'll fix the HVAC there too. Hell, we'll even create the plastic in his pens and the carbon fiber composite in his golf clubs. And he won't think a thing about it. He certainly won't appreciate what it took to create all these modern goodies. Without us, that guy would be sick, cold, hungry, and bored. But he'll be the one who gets to enjoy them because he'll have the money while schlubs like us toil away in labs for peanuts," his father had said. "Never forget: financial wizards get rich. Scientists, engineers, and laborers get paid."

That was the devil at the heart of modern capitalism, and Acorn hadn't forgotten. The producers, the labor, the workers got the crumbs while the capitalist got the bread even though the producers and workers baked the bread. For every billionaire tech entrepreneur, there were a thousand scientists toiling in the bowels of company labs and academia, begging for funding while their CEO made seven figures.

His parents had become Chinese agents because China was the last, best hope for ending the United States' domination as a superpower. Once the Soviet Union was gone, China was the only country big enough, strong enough, and aggressive enough to bring down the capitalists.

If Acorn wanted capitalism to go down, he'd need to work for China. And he wanted capitalism to go down to honor his parents and complete their mission. Thus, Frank Palmer, secret red diaper baby, immediately upon his college graduation followed his parents into the service of the Chinese, who christened him "Acorn," a seed that would grow into a tree strong enough to bring down American capitalism.

"Next stop, L'Enfant Plaza," announced the Metro train.

Acorn snapped out of his reverie. He was two stops away from his Capitol South Metro stop, but his focus was no longer on his daily routine. He awaited the next message from his minders, the message that would explain the mission in store for him.

CHAPTER 3

T he clicking of her heels on the fine marble floor echoed through the hallways of the Longworth House Office Building as Andrea hustled to meet with the House Debt Rebel Gang, the small group of Republican congressmen who had made debt reduction their singular crusade. With a sheaf of papers tucked under her arm and her longtime friend and college roommate, Rachel Samuels, following her, she felt confident and anxious all wrapped into one. She'd barely made it to the Capitol with only ten minutes to spare thanks to the terrible DC traffic and parking.

Cam Davis had lit a fire in Andrea.

He'd struck it rich, concluded he was invincible, and over-extended his finances. Sure enough, just as Andrea warned, his banks called in their loans and collapsed his entire furniture empire only a few weeks after their meeting. Humiliated and unwilling to face the world, he'd drowned himself in his backyard swimming pool. She was horrified at the sight of another family ruined by debt, and on her watch.

Cam's carefree attitude about his crumbling finances was no different from the country's see-no-evil view of the national debt. She could not bear a similarly tragic ending. His carefree attitude about his crumbling finances was no different from the country's see-no-evil view of the national debt. Someone had to scream about America's debt crisis from the rooftops. So Andrea Gartner, small-town accountant, pulled the trigger and declared her candidacy for Congress in 2028. It was her congressional race that brought her to Washington on this crisp November afternoon, almost exactly one year from the 2028 election.

To win, she'd first have to get the Republican Party's nomination. If she were the Republican nominee, she'd have at least a fifty-fifty chance of defeating the incumbent Democrat in what was still a competitive congressional district.

And to win the Republican nomination, she needed the endorsement of the House Debt Rebel Gang and its kingmaking chairman, Congressman Lewis Mason. Whoever the Debt Rebel Gang endorsed would be virtually guaranteed the nomination. Without the Gang's endorsement, her campaign would be hopeless, so Andrea had come to Washington hoping to convince Mason and the Debt Rebels to endorse her.

Andrea turned to see if Rachel was keeping up. "You back there?"

"Sweetie," said Rachel with her southern flair, hurrying down the hall behind Andrea, "I spent ten years up here as a chief of staff to two different congressmen. I've run these halls more times than I care to count. You think I wore flats by accident? Turn around and keep going. We're almost there."

As they rushed down the hall, Andrea caught a glimpse of the House office building's ornate decor. The walls were marble with brass mail slots built into them. Antique decorative molding framed the elevator doors. Every congressperson's office had an American flag and the member's state flag out front. The doors were adorned with bronze plaques with the member's name and the state seal of his or her state. The plaques weren't your everyday office nameplate. These giant bronze ornaments undoubtedly cost a fortune.

Andrea was glad to have Rachel by her side. If Andrea was the fresh-faced novice, Rachel was the grizzled political veteran. Andrea secretly admired people who'd worked their way to senior positions on the Hill. Deep down, she felt inferior among them. They were real Washington insiders. She was just another person at the end of the bar with an opinion.

She reached the conference room door with about five minutes to spare. The staffer outside the door told her she'd have to wait before going in.

Rachel caught up.

"Their staff guy says they're running a little late," explained Andrea, as they both struggled to catch their breath outside the conference room. "We ran here for nothing."

"Oh honey, I'm not surprised," said Rachel. "I could count on one hand the number of Hill meetings I've been to that started on time."

As her breathing settled, she motioned for Andrea to join her in a small vestibule across from the conference room that used to be a phone booth. No one had bothered to fill the hole in the vestibule wall and the stubs of telephone wires protruded from it.

"Just some last-minute advice before you go into the lion's den," Rachel said. "Don't forget, just because you care about the debt doesn't mean these guys are going to like you. You might get a rude reception in there."

"You've got to figure they'll like my debt-cutting message. That's their jam, isn't it?"

"Maybe. But you know what they did to me. They trashed my boss as too 'Establishment' and unwilling to fight the tough spending cut battles. They ran some gadfly, called me and my boss 'Establishment losers,' and got the voters to boot us out of office."

"You sound so cynical," observed Andrea.

"I can't help it," said Rachel. "These guys ended my political career. That poppycock salesman Mason swaggers around Capitol Hill calling himself the 'Chief RINO Hunter.'"

'Republicans In Name Only,' muttered Andrea in disgust. She was well acquainted with this epithet from her days in the South Carolina Republican Party's leadership.

"That's right. And anyone they decide has deviated a scintilla from what they think is true conservatism they brand as a RINO and purge as a heretic. If you're mild-mannered and seek consensus and compromise instead of fighting endlessly, good luck. They're going to call you a squish."

"But I'm a grassroots activist, not a politician. Why wouldn't they endorse me? The only reason I'm running is the national debt. These guys are the House Debt Rebel Gang, for goodness' sake. I'm a one-trick-pony, and it's their trick! They should eat me up."

"Don't be so sure," cautioned Rachel.

"What do you mean?"

"If you aren't part of the Debt Rebellion, you're ripe for purging. All this branding people 'Establishment' and 'RINOs' and whatever else is a great way to push rivals aside and get ahead. Toss around a few pejoratives, brand someone a scarlet Moderate, designate yourself the tribune of True Conservatism, and watch your fortunes rise and your rivals crumble."

Andrea loved the way Rachel said *RINO* in her southern accent, drawing out the *i* into an *ah,* so it came out *Raaaahno.* But she realized their conversation was getting loud and looked around to see if anyone was listening.

"Shhh! People can hear us. Rachel, don't let your anger cloud your judgment. Your boss didn't stop the spending. The Debt Rebellion was the only group talking about the debt."

Rachel shot Andrea an exasperated look. "*Was* talking about the debt, sweetie. *Was.* Past tense. President Roberts promised not to touch Medicare and Social Security, and Mason didn't say 'boo.'"

"Forget Mason," Andrea said. "There are thirty congresspersons in the Debt Rebel Gang. If I can't get Mason, there are twenty-nine others I can get."

"You think any of those lemmings are any better? Congressman Stokely just said 'Deficits don't matter anymore'! Heck, some of these people were making money off this Debt Rebellion stuff the whole time."

"What are you talking about?" Andrea asked.

"Frank Palmer, for starters."

"Mason's chief of staff?"

Rachel nodded. "Yeah, him. That little shyster got rich off of claiming the mantle of Debt Rebellion leadership and raking in donations. Talk about a racket. Those unsuspecting activists who really cared about the national debt had no idea. These guys shouldn't be in Congress. They should be defendants in a RICO case."

"Rachel, listen, I know you're still mad about your boss losing. But this is not about him, or you, or me. I put aside my accounting practice to do this. It's unconscionable we'd make our kids pay for our retirements and health care and all the rest. Your kids, my kids, everyone's kids: that's why I'm doing this. They have to be able to see that, right?"

"I just know what makes these guys tick. Especially Mason. Don't be so sure they'll find your 'I'm a homespun activist who only cares about the national debt' act all that compelling."

The door to the hearing room opened.

"Andrea Gartner?" the man who had opened the door said.

Andrea stuck her head out of the vestibule. "Yes?"

She recognized Frank Palmer from the pictures in the Debt Rebellion's emails. He was almost six feet and slightly built. He seemed nervous, his sandy hair somewhat disheveled, and his brown eyes darted back and forth behind round, rimless glasses.

"Greetings, my friend, I'm Frank Palmer, Congressman Mason's chief of staff. The Debt Rebel Gang is ready to meet with you now."

Andrea nodded, praying no one had heard her conversation with Rachel. She was nervous enough, and Rachel's tirade was only making things worse. She had one foot out of the vestibule when Rachel grabbed her arm and pulled her back in for one last piece of advice.

"Before you go in there, remember that no one died and appointed these guys the arbiters of conservative purity." Rachel stared into Andrea's eyes and wagged her finger. "You might be a soft-spoken consensus builder, but you're a rock-solid conservative on the debt. After all their talk, these guys did nothing about the debt under Roberts. Whenever you think you might be getting in trouble, just remember that when it comes to reducing the debt, these guys are full of it."

Andrea nodded, but her friend's reassurance wasn't much help. Her pulse and breathing accelerated. Then she remembered the last thing her husband said when he dropped her off at the airport: "Your whole family is rooting for you, honey. Go in there and make us proud."

She took a deep breath, exhaled, and headed into the meeting.

CHAPTER 4

T he Debt Rebel Gang gathered in a small but ornate wood-paneled hearing room in Longworth every Tuesday morning. The room ordinarily was used for full public committee hearings, but various groups of congresspersons liked to use it for private meetings because of its grand feel.

Members of the Gang were seated on the raised dais in the front of the room. Their haughty faces and lordly postures left no doubt they enjoyed flexing their muscles in front of supplicants like Andrea coming to kiss their ring and win their endorsement. Draped over the dais was a flag featuring an upright elephant wearing boxing gloves, the Gang's logo.

"Head in and take a seat at the witness table," said Frank Palmer. "A few of the members are on a brief break. They will be here shortly. Can I offer you anything?"

"No, I'm fine," Andrea replied, swallowing her words from nerves.

"Okay. Chairman Mason will be here in just a moment."

The room took Andrea's breath away. The three-tiered dais was made of fine polished mahogany. Carved into the wood paneling above the dais was the seal of the United States, with the intricately detailed olive branches and arrows in the American eagle's talons and the American motto, "E Pluribus Unum," etched crisply into the banner above the eagle's head. Between the lights on the walls hung oil paintings of past Speakers of the House, Appropriations Committee chairs, and other notables. Overhead a massive bank of klieg lights sat arrayed to spotlight hearings. Expensive flat-panel screens flanked each side of the dais. It reminded her of the Lyric Theater in her Baltimore hometown, which had seemed like the biggest thing she'd ever seen when she was a kid.

She was relieved to see the witness table wasn't too high for her short frame. On the table were four bottles of water for candidates. Each bottle had the logo of the US House of Representatives printed on it.

Unbelievable. Congress has its own custom water? They couldn't get pallets of water from Costco like everyone else? Andrea's accountant mind reflexively tallied the cost of this one room and concluded it had probably cost millions of dollars to outfit. She shook her head at the extravagance but couldn't help but be awed by the imposing scenery. Here she was, Andrea Gartner, anonymous accountant to anonymous local middle-class lawyers, doctors, and families, about to address thirty powerful members of Congress.

Cam's words echoed in her ears: *You're an accountant.*

By now thoroughly intimidated, she timidly seated herself at the witness table as the thirty members of the Debt Rebel Gang stared down at her from the dais.

Hundreds of candidates for Congress had been coming in week after week from all over the country vying for the Debt Rebel Gang's endorsement. Today, the candidates from South Carolina's Second District came to make their case.

A door on the left side of the dais swung open and a middle-aged man of average height and stocky build with narrow eyes, thinning light brown hair, a bulbous nose, full cheeks, and round black-rimmed glasses theatrically entered the room.

Lewis Mason, Congressman from Kansas.

He hurriedly climbed the stairs of the dais, put down a pile of papers, and seated himself in the chairman's seat. He quickly adjusted the microphone and wasted no time starting Andrea's endorsement interview. "We've had a chance to read your résumé and background."

No "thank you for coming," no opening statement, no nothing. It was like the old *People's Court* on television she watched when she was home from school on snow days, where Judge Wapner would greet parties with a brusque "I know you've been sworn and I've read your complaint." These guys were all business.

"Andrea Gartner, South Carolina. Why are you running? And why should we endorse you?"

Andrea hesitated and took a sip of water, followed by a deep breath to steady her nerves. She leaned into her microphone. "That's a fair question, Congressman Mason. I've been a leader in the South Carolina Republican Party for years," she said, unnerved by the entire Debt Rebel Gang staring down at her. She couldn't believe the words coming out of her mouth. They were nothing like what she practiced. "This is my first time running, but I've gotten a lot of campaign experience from my leadership positions in the local and state party organizations. Professionally, I'm an accountant with a degree in economics from the University of Pennsylvania. I've been in private practice for fifteen years and I've been married for ten years with two children . . ."

She could see from the Gang members' bored expressions she was getting nowhere. She took another sip of water. *You've got this*, she told herself. *Stay focused.* She felt a wave of control, of inspiration, of her spine stiffening. She took a breath. Now she was ready.

"Mr. Mason, Gang members, honestly, I'm running for one reason only." Her voice was firm now. "The United States is utterly dependent on members of the public and foreign countries to buy our debt. If they decide they don't want to loan us money and we can't finance our debt, the country goes broke. We won't have a dime to spend. No Social Security. No Medicare. This thought terrifies me. And we're doing this on the backs of our kids and grandkids. If we don't cut our deficits and pay down our national debt, they will be paying for all the things we're spending money on now. No one is speaking for them. I want to be their voice. Believe me, Congressmen, I have lived this. My father died when I was young and left my family in a pile of debt. I don't want other families to go through the same hardships. This country needs financial help. I have two kids at home, and I'll be damned if I saddle them with debt they have to pay tomorrow so I can get free government goodies today. There is nothing—absolutely nothing—I hate in this world more than ruinous debt."

Andrea began gesticulating for emphasis as she built momentum.

"You're the only people who have raised this issue. You inspired me to run. I'm an accountant. Balancing books is what I do. With me on your side you'll have as credible an ally for debt reduction as you can possibly imagine."

The Gang members had no reaction whatsoever.

What am I doing wrong? she wondered. *Cutting the debt is these guys' calling card. Their raison d'être. What gives? Keep going. Maybe they'll come around.*

"Congressmen, if you—"

"Thank you, Ms. Gartner, but I'm afraid we can't endorse you this election cycle," interrupted Mason.

The words sent a shock through Andrea's body. She'd barely gotten two minutes to state her case and the Debt Rebel Gang had already rejected her. And the way Mason emotionlessly dismissed her only added to the shock. All those years of helping candidates who were worried about the debt, and she got three sentences in before these guys rejected her?

"Come again?" Andrea said.

"We're endorsing Dan Morgan."

Seriously? Dan Morgan? That ridiculous opportunist?

She'd known Dan Morgan from her local Republican work. When cutting spending was all the rage, Dan Morgan was a deficit cutter. When Republican-controlled Congresses were spending like drunken sailors but conservatism demanded absolute support for President Roberts, Morgan was there. You could always count on Dan Morgan to get a double dip of the Republican flavor of the month.

Ryan and Cam were right. Politics was a dirty business. And once again, she'd gotten the short end of the stick.

Mason continued, "Dan Morgan has been an unwavering supporter of the Roberts Agenda. You spent your time blasting the debts and the deficits at a time when President Roberts needed all the support he could get. We need a team player, not a Johnny-one-note. Dan's reliable. You aren't."

"But reducing the debt was your signature issue. You all inspired me to get active and fight to reduce spending and debt. I'm here because of you," Andrea said, her voice rising to a crescendo. "I'm an accountant, and what America needs right now is an accountant!"

The look on Mason's face said it was time for the impudent suburban grassroots nobody to shut up and leave things to the political professionals.

"Ms. Gartner, Dan Morgan is a true outsider," reiterated Mason. "You're a professional and a Penn grad, the very definition of the elite. No thanks. We've made our decision."

Andrea fished in vain for words. Mason's summary dismissal had shattered her equilibrium. She fought to restrain the tears welling in her eyes. Blood pumped through her vessels as her frustration and anger built to a boil. Her grandfather used to get like this when some *momzer*, "bastard" in the Yiddish he spoke at home, angered him. Someone cut him off on the road? *Momzer.* Someone tried to rip him off on a home repair? *Momzer.*

But Andrea couldn't control her anger with the precision of her grandfather. Instead of releasing a litany of curses, she'd become tongue-tied, unable to fight back. She'd failed, like she failed with Cam, like she always failed. No matter what she'd done for the party, she wasn't good enough for the Debt Rebel Gang.

Out of words and on the verge of tears, Andrea couldn't summon a response. That was when she noticed him: the congressman in the back row of the dais on the far right. He had said nothing and sat expressionless. No comments, no questions. Not even a head nod. But his perfectly coiffed and parted silver mane, chiseled face, and ramrod-straight frame gave him a gravitas that stood out from the other members of the Gang.

It was Congressman Earl Murray. While everyone else was finishing Andrea off, he remained silent. Now and then he wrote in his notepad or whispered something to an aide seated behind him. Andrea had made eye contact with him a couple times but had gotten no reaction. She half-wondered if he was sleeping with his eyes open. His silence was surprising. He was running for president in the crowded 2028 field. Many pundits thought he had no chance. Why wouldn't he take the opportunity to get a little speechifying in?

Angry and frustrated, Andrea decided the time had come to leave. "Just so you all know, I never thought of myself as 'Establishment' or 'anti-Establishment' or 'RINO' or 'True Conservative.' I just thought I was a little accountant and volunteer who cared desperately about reducing the national debt. But if you all insist on assigning me to 'Team Establishment,' I'll play for it."

"What do you think you're going to do?" Mason chortled. "One little accountant can't cut the debt without being on my team. And one little accountant definitely can't make a difference on her own. It's why we're up here and you're down there, begging for our support."

Andrea was about to let loose *momzer* and a whole litany of her grandfather's choicest Yiddish insults—maybe she had a little of him in her after all—but she hesitated. She was afraid to create an enemy. She didn't know when or how, but something told her she would be facing Mason again.

She stood and hustled out of the room, her back hunched and her hand over her face to hide the tears preparing to burst forth. Rachel leaped from her seat in the gallery and followed her out.

The sound of her heels against the marble floor echoed like machine-gun fire as Andrea charged down the hallway. She bolted past the security guards at the entrance of the building and headed into the small park next to Longworth. She stopped beside a bench and kicked the nearby trashcan, then punched at the air. In a huff, she sat on the bench, put her head in her hands, and began to sob.

Rachel finally caught up, sat down, and put her hand on Andrea's shoulder. "Look at me, Andrea."

Andrea looked up, eyes puffy and red.

"Quit your crying. That was incredible. Did you hear yourself in there? You spoke truth to Lewis-freakin'-Mason. I didn't know you had it in you."

"Who cares?" asked Andrea. "I didn't come here for a moral victory. I've spent a decade helping candidates who said they were conservatives who wanted to cut the debt. For what? To be rejected in one stroke because someone says I'm . . . 'the Establishment'? I thought I was safe from that. I'm a deficit-cutting activist, not a politician. But it was all a waste."

"No, it wasn't," said Rachel. "These guys obviously went in wanting Morgan. Once they decided he was the anti-Establishment good guy, they had to make you the Establishment bad guy. Mason and Morgan are two of a kind. The kind who zip to the head of any parade and pretend it was their idea."

Andrea suddenly felt angry. "No one cares about the debt, and no one ever did. It's all about power. Jockeying for it, getting it, keeping it. Who was I to think I could break into this world? No one wants to hear from the candidate peddling castor oil."

Rachel grabbed Andrea's arm and stood up. "Get up. C'mon, get up. I want to show you something."

"All right, all right, take it easy. Don't pull my arm out of its socket, okay?"

Rachel led Andrea one block north to the Capitol South Metro station and they descended the escalators into the underground station. When they reached the bottom, Rachel let go of Andrea's arm.

"Look at that." Rachel pointed to the wall that was filled with ads. "What do you see?"

"Rachel, have you lost your mind? It's a wall."

"Not the wall, sweetie, what's on the wall."

"The ads?"

"Read them and tell me what you see."

"I see seven different ads on one wall and seven different ads on the other."

Rachel sighed, exasperated. "And who are they for?"

"TechOps Consulting's government IT solutions. Six Sigma Industries' mechanized armored vehicle manufacturing. A senior citizens' lobby demanding protection for Social Security. A college association demanding more grants for higher education. What's your point?"

"My point is that every one of these ads is about spending

government money. Keeping that sweet government money flowing. Do you see any ads talking about cutting spending?"

"No."

"Of course not. The whole economy around here is based
on government spending. No one around here gives a fig about
cutting spending. Not even the Debt Rebel Gang."

Andrea rolled her eyes. "Don't you think I have a pretty good
idea of that after today?"

"That's why you need to keep at this. Someone has to warn
people of the consequences of what they are voting for so that no
one can look back and say, 'If only we had known better.'"

"The guys who were supposed to be warning everyone just gave
me the boot, so that someone isn't going to be me," said Andrea.

"Don't be so sure. There's one more thing I want to show you."
Rachel pulled out her iPhone. "I videoed your entire session with
the Debt Rebel Gang," she said with a wide, slightly devious grin.

"Holy crap," said Andrea. "What are you planning to do with
that?"

"Sweetie, if the Republicans nominate Dan Morgan instead of
you, I'm going to press 'send.'"

"To whom?"

"Everybody," said Rachel. "Mason isn't the only person who
can play this game. I spent ten years on the Hill. And ten years
running campaigns. I know all the tricks."

Andrea's eyes were wide as she stared at the phone. "Pretty
devious, Rachel."

"They want to run you out of town as 'the Establishment,'
you've got the ammo to show the world just how committed they
are to their debt reduction principles," Rachel said. "If they take
you down, you can fight back."

Andrea appreciated Rachel's enthusiasm, but her own enthusiasm was draining away. "I'm so tired of fighting. If those

congressmen and their voters want to stick it to elites, or the Establishment, or whatever, let them take their anger out on someone else. I've had just about enough."

CHAPTER 5

A ndrea's campaign for Congress was a desultory march to certain defeat. She could barely bring herself to continue campaigning. People she'd known for years, people she thought would support her, turned on a dime when the Debt Rebel Gang rejected her. All her years of toil for the party hadn't earned her an ounce of goodwill once the Debt Rebel Gang branded her the handmaiden of the hated Establishment. She felt like the housewife who lost the lottery in the famous Shirley Jackson short story. One minute she was a valued member of the Republican community, the next minute she was being stoned to death.

Her innate lack of confidence, her paranoia that no one liked her or would support her when push came to shove, roared out of the cage she'd put it in after she began her run for Congress. So four months after the meeting with the Debt Rebel Gang, when the nominating convention finally came and Andrea lost to Dan Morgan, she felt relief, as if she'd been released from a prison of her own making. All she wanted to do was shut the world out and bury herself in doing someone's taxes.

On the morning after the convention, Andrea was lying on the bed savoring the first campaign-free day. No events. No fundraising calls. She could sleep late and watch the sunrise.

Then the phone rang.

Seriously?

Andrea rolled toward the nightstand to see who it was. She

recognized the number. It was Ty Washington, a reporter from the local ABC affiliate. She answered the phone.

"Hey, Ty, the campaign's over. What are you doing calling me so early?"

"Did you know you are all over the internet and Twitter?"

"Huh?"

"There's a video of you reaming out Lew Mason," said Ty. "It looks like it's been out since yesterday afternoon. It's already gotten half a million views."

Andrea shot upright and pressed the phone to her ear. She began to bite her lip slightly and rub her forehead. A vein in her temple was throbbing. *Get me out of the spotlight.*

"Ty, I don't know anything about this, so I've got nothing to say right now," said Andrea.

"Okay," replied Ty. "But I'm warning you, this is not going to be the last call you get on this. This thing is blowing up."

"Thanks, Ty. I guess we'll be talking later."

Andrea threw off the covers and dressed quickly. She called Rachel.

"Isn't this great?" said Rachel giddily. "You've gone viral!"

"Jesus, Rachel, you could have warned me about this."

"I was afraid you'd tell me not to release it," said Rachel. "I thought it would be better to ask forgiveness rather than permission."

"What do we do now? After what happened with the Debt Rebel Gang I wanted out."

"Too late," said Rachel. "Let's see what happens. Your political career may not be dead yet."

"That's what I was afraid of," said Andrea.

"Check your campaign inbox," said Rachel. "You have a following."

Andrea opened the inbox. It had exploded with hundreds of emails. Many of them were from suburban women like her, angry about how she had been treated and even more frightened about the debt.

"They're stealing our children's future!" wrote a mother of two from Phoenix.

"I had no idea how bad the debt was," wrote a lawyer from Memphis.

"I have a hundred women who want to start a real movement to cut the debt," read an email from a doctor in Philadelphia. "We need your help!"

"It's amazing," said Andrea. "There are emails from all over the country. A lot of them are working moms like me. You think we could start something here?"

"Absolutely," said Rachel. "I have it all figured out."

"What?"

"I'm setting up a political organization. We're going to call it 'Suburban Ordinary Moms Against the Debt.' And you are going to lead it."

Andrea thought for a moment. "The acronym is SO MAD?"

"Genius, isn't it?" Rachel proudly stated.

Andrea paced across the room. "My husband is still asleep. I should ask him first."

"Remember, ask forgiveness, not permission." Rachel laughed. "You want to stick it to Mason and his Debt Rebel Gang?"

"With a samurai sword," Andrea replied.

"Then let's do this."

Andrea took a deep breath. She thought about all the time it took to run the Richland County Republican Committee. Every other weeknight there was some event she had to attend. Not to mention the weekend campaigning and fundraising calls.

"Rachel, I can't sink the time into this like I did for the local committee. My family needs me at home. And I have to get back to work. We need the money."

"We can raise money to pay your salary if you want," said Rachel.

"No way," Andrea replied. "If we're doing this, we're doing this as a true grassroots movement. No one is going to make money off this. I'm not taking a salary. What we raise goes to the cause and nothing else."

"I figured you'd say that," said Rachel. "I'm one step ahead of you. You can go back to your accounting practice. All we need you to do is be the face of the organization. Make videos. Make speeches. Rally people to the cause. I'll handle the rest. I know the entire Republican PR universe. I've got this."

"If you handle the organizing and I can keep my practice going, I think I can make it work," Andrea said. She glanced at her family picture on her nightstand. "Okay, I'm in."

CHAPTER 6

With Rachel's encouragement fresh in her mind, Andrea got to work making SO MAD videos. She followed the same routine for a month. Every morning, Andrea would record a SO MAD video in her basement, passionately telling moms across America why the national debt threatened their children's future. Rachel would post it online and work her magic with her PR network. Every morning, Andrea would watch the view counts grow as the videos went viral. One thousand views. Five thousand views. Ten thousand views. Rachel wasn't kidding when she said she could make SO MAD happen.

Thanks to Rachel's organizational skills, SO MAD had built a following in just one month, with a mailing list of nearly fifty thousand people. Over one hundred thousand people regularly watched her videos where she talked about the threat the national debt posed to the country. The videos about how the debt would destroy economic opportunities for children had suburban moms up in arms.

Rachel's PR savvy had made Andrea Gartner a visible voice too. Andrea frequently did television, radio, and print interviews. Politicians suddenly called to woo her. Except the Debt Rebel Gang. Not one of them came calling.

But just as Andrea had insisted, her SO MAD work wasn't paying the bills. So she returned to her accounting practice, located in a tiny suite in a nondescript suburban office building. How underwhelming it all was. Stuck in her mind was that finely appointed congressional office building. Instead of a marble floor, her building had worn brown carpet, torn and patched in places. Instead of flags outside her office door and her name in bronze, there was a plastic nameplate. The building management was so cheap it hadn't even replaced the whole nameplate, only the letters. The faint outline of the name of the previous occupant, "Jake's Doggy Day Care," could be seen underneath. Instead of the fancy restaurants around the Capitol, there was a hot buffet and salad bar on the first floor. Going to work in her sterile office every day while thinking about the palatial congressional offices was torture.

Some elitist I am. Look at my elite office!

Adding insult to injury, she'd already lost her receptionist to a higher paying job. Ryan was helping in the afternoons before he headed to his night shift as a psychologist at a local hospital.

One afternoon, a little more than a month after the convention and five months after she met with the Debt Rebel Gang, Ryan poked his head into Andrea's office. "Honey, there's someone in the waiting area who wants to see you."

"Don't I have an appointment in a couple minutes?"

"Your three-o'clock is out there," said Ryan. "He said it would be okay if you took a moment to meet with this other guy."

Andrea huffed. "You're asking clients to wait until I talk to some random visitor? What are you doing? The clients pay the bills, not random visitors."

"Sorry, I wasn't thinking. I'm a psychologist, not a reception-ist. I got distracted."

"What could possibly be going on in the waiting room of an accountant's office that could have distracted you?"

"Your visitor is important."

"Is it Publishers Clearing House with one of those oversized million-dollar checks?"

"No."

"Then my clients are more important."

"Andrea," said Ryan softly but seriously, "you need to come out here. Remember that congressman guy who you said didn't ask you a thing in your big endorsement meeting?"

"Earl Murray?"

"Yeah, him. He's standing in the waiting room."

What?

Andrea leaped from her desk and charged into the waiting room. Sure enough, there was Congressman Murray, standing in her small waiting room with the worn *People* magazines and the half-green, half-brown plant in the corner. Two young people with lanyards stood a few feet behind him. Staffers, Andrea figured. She nervously fixed her hair with her hand and could feel the butterflies growing in her stomach.

She turned to her three o'clock. "I'll be with you in just a moment."

Her three o'clock looked up, nodded and, unbothered, returned to staring at her smartphone screen.

"Ms. Gartner. It's good to see you again." Congressman Murray extended his hand.

"Congressman Murray. I . . . I apologize for the state of my office," she stammered, struggling to keep her voice from cracking from nerves. She felt herself swallowing her words but somehow managed to get out a greeting. "Please, have a seat. Can I get you some coffee or water? You don't need your taxes done, do you?"

Murray laughed warmly. "No, I'm good on my taxes. A water would be great, though."

Andrea nervously turned to Ryan. "Can you get Congressman Murray a bottle of water?"

"Sure, no problem," said Ryan, smiling.

Andrea turned back to Murray. "How . . . how can I help you?"

"I heard you lost the nomination for Congress," said Murray.

"Word travels fast," said Andrea.

"I saw you didn't take it lying down, though," said Murray. "I've been getting angry calls all month from your SO MAD followers about how the Debt Rebel Gang is ignoring the debt."

"I guess we didn't call it 'SO MAD' for nothing," Andrea said sheepishly, so nervous she couldn't look Congressman Murray in the eye.

Murray grinned. "A hundred thousand pissed-off suburban moms angry about the debt definitely got my attention. I think they were inspired by your performance at the endorsement meeting. As was I."

"Really? I didn't persuade a soul. Three minutes in and the Debt Rebel Gang was endorsing Dan Morgan."

"Those guys?" Murray rolled his eyes. "They go in whichever direction the anti-Establishment crowd points. You were right. They used the debt issue to gain power and dropped it like a hot potato after President Roberts got elected. You, on the other hand, were a real truth-teller."

Great. That and a dollar would get me a cup of coffee. Where was he in the hearing when I could have used him? He sat on that dais like an Easter Island statue.

"How can I help you, Mr. Murray?"

"I want you to come work for my presidential campaign. You're exactly what I need on my staff."

Andrea did a double take. He'd spoken words she'd dreamed of hearing for years. A presidential campaign? There would be no better perch from which to argue for reducing the national debt. And to most everyone's surprise, including hers, Murray was likely to win the Republican nomination for president.

But now that she'd heard Murray make the offer, she felt terrified. She was reestablishing her accounting practice. A nice, stable income. Leaving that for the political world? With no guarantee of a job if Murray lost the presidential general election as most pundits were predicting?

Ten years ago, Andrea would have jumped on the offer. But with two kids, a mortgage, and all the expenses of raising a family, she just couldn't.

"Honestly, Mr. Murray, I have a full-time job, and between my accounting practice and SO MAD . . . well, it's just too much for me."

"Then come work full-time for me," said Murray. "I'll pay you what you need."

So much for that excuse. Andrea tried another. "Mr. Murray, with all due respect, I didn't like the person I was in that room five months ago. I'm not persuasive and I get upset easily. I couldn't convince a couple hundred people in one congressional district to support me. How am I going to tackle the fiscal problems of the entire nation?"

"Not persuasive?" said Murray in disbelief. "Andrea, your SO MAD group has over a hundred thousand followers on social media. And they're there to watch your videos. You're a goddamned grassroots hero. I need you."

Andrea paused for a moment, marinating in Murray's offer. "Really? You didn't say anything at the endorsement meeting five months ago. Not one word about the debt."

Murray leaned toward Andrea and spoke in hushed, conspiratorial tones. "Look, I need to get elected if I want to deal with the debt. I won't win if I harp on the debt. You should know by now that no one wants to cut it, not even the Debt Rebel Gang or the rest of the Debt Rebellion."

"Then what's the point of all this?"

Murray put a hand on Andrea's shoulder. "This is where you

messed up. We need to run a quiet budget-balancing campaign. I'll never get past Republican primary voters if I spend my time railing about Roberts's deficits."

"If I was messing up so bad, why didn't you say anything in the Debt Rebels meeting?"

"Because it was worthless. Those guys wouldn't listen to me. What good would it have done me to chime in?"

See? They're all out for themselves. Murray had watched her flailing at the endorsement meeting and sat there like a stone because it was better for him. *Thanks heaps, pal.*

"What's going to keep you from cutting me loose like you left me out to dry in the Debt Rebel Gang meeting?"

"Mutually assured destruction, Andrea. Your plans will be my plans. We hang together or we hang separately. But we'll succeed. Before I got elected to Congress, I owned a bunch of auto dealerships. Very successful. I'm a car salesman, Andrea. I know how to make a sale."

Andrea wanted to say yes. A far cry from how she felt after she lost the nomination for Congress, when all she wanted was for politics to disappear from her life.

"Come on Andrea, join the campaign. You've got the financial brains. I've got the political brawn. Let's save America lots of money."

"Ah, you're a Pet Shop Boys fan." Andrea smiled and nodded knowingly. "Maybe I misjudged you."

"Keep it quiet. They're British. Can't have the Gang find out I like their music."

Andrea laughed. She was warming up to Murray. The guy had a sense of humor and good taste in music. But she couldn't overcome the raw hurt of losing the congressional nomination and her fear of losing the stability her accounting practice provided.

"Mr. Murray, thank you for the offer," she said. "I truly appreciate it. But I think I belong in the accounting world."

Murray glanced at the half-dying plant in the corner. "Tell you what, Andrea. How about a compromise? Why don't you just work on some budget plans on your own and send them to me? I'll need those in case I win. And you're an accountant, after all."

"I'm only an accountant, Mr. Murray," she replied. "And I need to keep my practice running. We need the money. I can't go traipsing off on the campaign trail."

"No problem," said Murray. "You can write the budget plans from this office, or at home, or wherever. But there is one more thing."

"What's that?"

"Suburban moms," Murray said. "If I want to win, I need them. And you've rallied them. And I need their votes. Cut some videos supporting me. Make my campaign SO MAD's cause."

Andrea was intrigued. She could continue to publicize the debt issue, stay at home, and work with someone who might just do something about the debt.

She instinctively glanced at her husband, who was waiting behind the receptionist desk with a bottle of water, captivated by the conversation before him. He silently nodded yes.

Andrea turned to the congressman. "Okay, Mr. Murray."

Murray smiled and shook her hand. "That's wonderful. You won't regret this. My staff will be in touch." He and his staffers began to make their way out of the office. As he was walking through the door, he tripped on a carpet seam.

"I'm so sorry, Congressman." Andrea's face flushed with embarrassment. "Are you okay?"

"I'm fine. No worries. Just so you know, they don't have carpet seams like this in the White House," said Murray with a wink.

Andrea saw Murray out the door. He seemed different to her. He was a politician who saw something more in her than manual labor for knocking on doors and stamping envelopes. How could she say no to him?

"The guy's pretty good, Andrea," Ryan said.

"He wants me to be his campaign budget policy person."

"Isn't that your dream job?"

"Once upon a time. Now it's a pay cut and angry mobs if I start slashing the budget."

"Don't chicken out. Do it."

"Really? What happened to 'you're not meant to be in politics'?"

"Well, obviously Congressman Murray disagrees. And he knows more about politics than I do. Now you'll be able to vent about the debt all you want to people who might do something about it. And I might be able to watch television in peace."

Ryan had a point. Venting her spleen at the politicians doing nothing about the national debt wasn't solving anything. Going to work for Murray at least would give her a chance to present her debt-cutting message to Americans.

She tried to shift into her clinical, analytical accounting mindset, creating a pro and con ledger in her mind. If Murray lost, at least she would have gotten someone to talk to the country about the seriousness of the national debt. And if he won, who knew? Maybe she really could prevent the coming debt crisis and protect her children from the unfathomable debt being piled on their shoulders.

But if he lost, she'd have to restart her accounting practice. Again. Would her clients really come back to her after she closed up shop for two different campaigns? And what about her family? Presidential campaigns were frenzied affairs, the province of twenty-somethings pulling all-nighters hopped up on Red Bull. She had a husband and kids. And how are Americans going to react when Murray and I start pushing to cut Social Security? It would make the Debt Rebel Gang's rejection seem like a walk in the park.

She simply could not escape how the Debt Rebel Gang had chewed her up and spat her out. Her debt-reduction politics had just gotten her rejected by her party. She didn't think she could handle being rejected again. Maybe Ryan thought she was chickening out. Easy for him to say. The Debt Rebel Gang hadn't humiliated *him*. She'd reached her compromise with Murray, and she was going to stand by it.

CHAPTER 7

A corn was waiting in line for dinner in the cafeteria of the Longworth building when the TAG Heuer watch began vibrating on his wrist.

For the five months since the *Express* newspaperman had dropped the watch in his pocket, it had done nothing but tell Acorn the time of day. Now the Ministry was breaking its silence.

Acorn got out of the line and went to a quiet corner of the cafeteria's seating area. He glanced around and made certain he was alone. Hunching his shoulders to hide his wrist, he pushed the small button on the side of the watch that would have started the stopwatch's sweep. But this was no ordinary watch. A window opened on the dial face to reveal a small digital screen. Across the screen ran the same three words.

Enter the temple . . . enter the temple . . . enter the temple . . .

It was the same phrase written on the back of his fake American Express card. He briskly walked out of the cafeteria and headed for the parking lot, avoiding eye contact to prevent being stopped by anyone who might want to chat. He jumped straight into his car and drove four hours west, deep into western Virginia, toward a favorite location, the Homestead resort, picking up a cheeseburger for dinner at a little drive-thru in Staunton. He might have hated rich peoples' playpens like the Homestead, but his trips there were always on the taxpayers' or donors' dime. A luxurious trip that depleted the pockets of the capitalist donor class was a win-win in Acorn's book.

But today Acorn stopped at an abandoned drive-in theater

twenty miles east of the Homestead. He'd driven past it every time he'd traveled to the resort, but this was the first time he'd gotten out and gone into the woods just behind the rotting wood frame of what once was the screen.

It was dark by the time Acorn arrived. He pulled out a flashlight and scanned the darkened woods. Fallen leaves and branches rustled under his feet as he crept into the forest. He carried the bag with his cheeseburger dinner in one hand. He could swear animals were watching him.

Then he saw it: a small dome of earth about two hundred yards into the woods with an earthen door and a small blue sign that read "Utility Entry Port." It was obviously the work of some smart-ass Harvard grad. Only the Harvard daily paper, the *Crimson*, was politically correct enough to call a manhole a "utility entry port."

Opening the door and climbing down some stairs, Acorn entered a small chamber. It was no natural formation. The walls were unnaturally sharp and jagged, clearly carved by someone, and were beige-brown, the color of the natural rock of the area. They glistened with condensation, giving the cave a dank, damp feel. Small drops of water dripped from some of the pointy edges of the walls where the condensation would bead up and drip onto the floor.

Inside was a modest flat-screen television, about seventy inches wide. The engineers had taken care to insulate the wires to protect against electric shorts caused by the condensation. His minders must have been here recently. He'd been working with them for longer than flat screens had been around.

Acorn had arrived early. His minders expected timeliness. He opened the bag and began eating the cheeseburger.

At 10:01, the appointed hour, he pushed a red button on a panel to the right of the television.

A small Chinese woman appeared on the screen in a room as drab and unexpressive as she was. She was standing in front of a plain black metal desk. There were no family photographs on the desk and no artwork on the gray cinderblock walls. The place looked like a prison from Communist central casting.

Acorn had heard of Xu Li, the mythic head of the Chinese Ministry of State Security, known to all its agents as simply "the Ministry." The one-word name gave the organization and its agents an additional hint of menace, not that it was needed.

Acorn recalled nights when his father would come home pale white in a daze and go straight to his room without even acknowledging his family. "Your father must have crossed Madame Xu," his mother would tell Acorn. "One must never cross Madame Xu." They spoke of Madame Xu in hushed and reverential tones, and only at home. Once, Acorn had mentioned Xu Li in a conversation with his parents in a restaurant and they had taken him home and spanked him so hard his rear end swelled. But he'd never seen Xu Li himself. As a child, Acorn imagined her as a James Bond villain, living underground, traveling to and from the government compound in an underground train with food testers to protect her from poisoning.

Even after Acorn had reached adulthood and joined the agent ranks, he had never seen or heard from Xu Li. Eventually, he began to think Xu Li was a creation, a myth, a way of terrifying agents into staying in line.

Acorn's hands trembled. Could this be Xu Li across from him on the screen? She had such a piercing, cold stare. Her lips were straight, not quite a scowl, yet more sinister. At least a scowl was straightforward, a clear signal of anger. Xu Li's visage was almost emotionless yet terrifying, laden with purpose, precision, and focus.

The woman on the screen looked Acorn up and down, only her eyes moving as she took his measure, inspecting him as one might inspect produce before buying.

Acorn bowed deeply and silently, too tongue-tied to speak. His mother's words—"One does not cross Madame Xu"—and the image of his father's ashen, gaunt face after meetings with Xu Li filled his head.

"I am Xu Li," she said in impeccable English. "You have gotten our message, Acorn."

My lord, it is Xu Li. And she knows who I am.

"No one leaves the Chinese Communist Party," he replied.

"You have been raised well by your parents," Xu Li said. "Do you know why you are here?"

"Of course, Madame Xu," said Acorn. The truth was he had no idea what Xu Li had in store for him.

"I hope you lie better in operation," said Xu Li. "Your shaking hands give you away."

"Madame Xu, forgive me, I did not expect to see you. To be honest, I thought you were a legend, not a real person."

"We set it up that way," she answered. "I suppose I cannot fault you for this."

Acorn exhaled and took a closer look at Xu Li. She had a menacing air about her despite her slight statute. Her hair was short. She wore a plain baby blue Mao-style suit. But there was something about her nondescript nature, her absolute blandness, coupled with her intense stare that enhanced the fear she struck within Acorn. He could see why she enjoyed such a ruthless reputation.

"Are you eating, Acorn?"

Dammit! Why didn't I put down my damned dinner?

"Yes, Madame Xu. I humbly apologize. I was trying to recover from the long trip and be fresh for our meeting."

"Then perhaps you should have eaten before our meeting. What is that you are eating?"

"A cheeseburger."

"Ah yes, the cheeseburger. The perfect crystallization of American gluttony, selfishness, and decadence. Meat from pastures created by destroying rainforest, and cows fattened on the grain that could feed hundreds of starving children. The artery-clogging that makes you Americans the fattest people in the world. What would your parents say?"

"I think they would be proud of every way in which I blend into American culture to accomplish Ministry operations."

Xu Li smiled wanly. "Good answer, Acorn. Your parents were devoted Communists and two of our best agents. Dedicated to bringing down capitalism and knocking the American government from its perch. I suppose the Ministry can forgive you this one decadent Western vice. After all, you've handed your life over to us."

Bullet dodged.

"This congressman running for president . . . Mr. Murray," Xu Li continued, getting down to brass tacks.

"Earl Murray?"

"Yes. You know him, correct?"

"Yes, Madame Xu. He is a member of the Debt Rebel Gang."

"Ah yes, your boxing elephant gang." Xu Li derisively referred to the Debt Rebel Gang as the "boxing elephant gang" after its boxing elephant flag. "Is Mr. Murray really interested in solving the American debt problem?"

"I don't know." Acorn considered saying he knew what Murray's plans were, but he was terrified of getting caught in another lie.

"You are supposed to know. We did not work so hard and bury you so deep in American society to have you not know."

"Madame Xu, I've burrowed into the very heart of American politics. I built my balanced budget think tank from scratch. All the ferment from the Debt Rebellion? I had a big hand in stoking that."

"Yes, I read all your think tank's reports, Acorn. I'm well aware of your efforts to stir the masses with your anti-spending, anti-Establishment propaganda."

"And without establishing my anti-spending, anti-debt bona fides, Lew Mason would never have chosen me to be his chief of staff and right-hand man running the Debt Rebel Gang," said Acorn proudly. "That was no mean feat. It took years of preparation."

Xu Li said nothing. She merely nodded her head slightly.

"Murray is famous for keeping his cards close to his vest, Madame Xu," continued Acorn. "He barely has said anything in our Debt Rebel Gang meetings these last two years."

"Silence means uncertainty, Acorn. And uncertainty is the enemy. We need to know what Mr. Murray is planning to do."

"Why is that?"

"Because the timing of Operation Pripyat depends on it."

"Operation Pripyat?" Acorn felt embarrassed he didn't know what Xu Li was talking about, and terrified he was supposed to know.

"We have not briefed you on it yet. Mr. Murray is not the only one who holds information closely."

"I'm ready, Madame Xu. Please, tell me my role." Abject deference always played with the Ministry, which prized absolute and total loyalty.

"The Ministry has been planning Operation Pripyat for twenty years. It will be the greatest and most glorious triumph of the Ministry and Communist China. We will bring down American capitalism and the American government without firing a shot."

"How will Operation Pripyat achieve this?" Acorn tried not to sound skeptical.

Xu Li walked around a small desk that was behind her and seated herself. Her face radiated disdain. Acorn had heard Xu Li had little respect for her non-Chinese agents, viewing them as untrustworthy, disloyal to their societies, and lacking the disciplined thought processes that only native Chinese agents possessed.

"The American government owes the world forty trillion dollars. It owes China and her friends four trillion dollars. It runs annual deficits of a trillion dollars. All covered by money borrowed from lenders, including China and her friends. Two million dollars a minute."

All true. But where is she going with this, and what does it have to do with me?

"What does the American government use all this money for?"

Acorn pondered momentarily, then rattled off the government expenses that came to mind. "Health-care benefits, Medicare, Medicaid, Social Security retirement benefits, the American military, education grants, running the government. How many reports did my think tank put out on this?"

"Careful, Acorn, we do not regard insolence highly in the Ministry. As I said, I read your reports."

"My humblest apologies, Madame Xu. But you must know I know what the American government spends on. Guns and butter, all day, every day. Defense, intelligence, and an endless array of medical, old age, and social welfare benefits."

"And if that were to stop?"

Acorn opened his mouth to speak and then caught himself. His eyes widened.

Good lord. It was brilliant.

Xu Li smiled. "It looks like you are starting to understand.

We have been watching as the American government addicted itself to debt. All the while we have been preparing to collapse the American government by cutting off its ability to borrow money. You could say we have been waiting to get the Americans by, how do you say it . . . ?"

"The balls. To get the Americans by the balls."

"Ah yes, the balls. So charming, you Americans."

She's right. Cut off America's ability to borrow money and it will be forced to slash its budget. That will slash Americans' Social Security and Medicare benefits, slash America's defense spending, and, most of all, slash the nation's pride. It was simple, it was elegant, and it would bring down the United States.

Xu Li cleared her throat. "Back to Mr. Murray . . . do you think he'll be able to successfully push his debt-cutting agenda?"

Acorn felt a rush of excitement. Xu Li was asking him for his views. For the first time in his many years as an agent, what he thought mattered. He was about to say something that was highly important to the head of the Ministry.

"No. He won't even win his race for president. When he loses, any influence he has will disappear."

"I see," said Xu Li, lacking conviction.

Her response made Acorn nervous. Frightened of having expressed the wrong opinion to Xu Li, he changed the topic. "Where did you get Operation Pripyat? It sounds Russian. They are not part of this, are they?"

He didn't want anything to do with the Russians. He didn't give a damn about restoring the imperial glory of Russia or the Soviet Union or whatever the kleptomaniacs in the Kremlin had in mind. Xu Li might try to give Operation Pripyat a Boris-and-Natasha look, but Acorn couldn't believe she would allow any operation this audacious be anything but the Ministry's show.

Xu Li laughed. "It sounds Russian because it is Russian. And no, the Russians are not helping us. We have no time for their substandard capabilities. Why do you think the only things they attack are weak neighboring countries and defenseless old defectors living in the English countryside? They don't stand a chance against anyone with an ounce of sophistication and capability."

"If the Russians aren't involved, why 'Operation Pripyat'?"

"How old were you when Chernobyl exploded?"

"Chernobyl? The nuclear reactor? I don't remember when it happened."

"It was 1986."

"Then I was two."

"So you remember nothing."

"You remember anything from when you were two?" Sometimes Acorn could not contain his irritation.

"Watch yourself, Acorn."

"I am sorry, Madame Xu." Acorn bowed deeply.

"Pripyat is the town that was next to Chernobyl. The reactor employees and their families lived there. The radiation forced the Russians to evacuate the town. It is now the abandoned, quarantined symbol of a nuclear meltdown."

"What does a 1980s nuclear meltdown have to do with America's national debt?" asked Acorn.

"Sometime within the next year, an American bond auction will fail. You need to make certain the American government won't be able to borrow any money after that."

My Lord, this really is going to melt down the United States. No government borrowing meant no government spending. No government spending meant catastrophe for the United States. And he, Acorn, would be the key man implementing the plan in the United States. He pictured himself in a history textbook as the man who brought down capitalist America.

"That is all I have for you, Acorn. You will know when it's time to go into action, and you will know what to do."

He hated the Ministry's cryptic nature. Why can't the Ministry just tell me what they want me to do and when they want me to do it? Sure, he wanted to overthrow capitalism and take down the American government, but the CIA probably told its agents exactly what they wanted them to do. Xu Li was treating Operation Pripyat like some kind of Choose Your Own Adventure.

But one did not question Xu Li. He had already made one mistake in the conversation and wasn't about to make another.

"Yes, Madame Xu. I will be ready."

CHAPTER 8

"**M**om, you down here?" Aaron hollered down the basement stairs. "Michelle and I are going to the park to play."

"Honey, I'm busy working," Andrea replied. She had been putting together budget drafts for Congressman Murray for weeks, and her thirteen-year-old son had made it his mission to interrupt her every hour.

"Geez, Mom, could you be any more obsessed?" Aaron poked his head down the stairs. "We never see you anymore ever since that congressman guy showed up at your office. The only things left in the refrigerator are mustard and ketchup. How am I going to be able to stay on the basketball team if I'm eating Chick-fil-A every night?"

Andrea laughed. "If you don't want Chick-fil-A, there are frozen steam-in-the-bag veggies in the freezer."

"You idiot!" whispered ten-year-old Michelle, who apparently had joined her brother on the stairs. "Now we're not going to get Chick-fil-A for dinner anymore and we'll have to eat steamed broccoli."

Andrea smiled to herself.

Footsteps pounded down the stairs, and Michelle and Aaron made themselves known.

"What have you done down here?" Michelle uttered as she glanced around the basement.

Andrea had been so absorbed in developing draft budget proposals she had been oblivious to the mess she'd created.

Rejected drafts littered the floor. A small trash can overflowed with paper and candy wrappers. Diet Pepsi cans and empty Doritos bags were scattered on the floor around her desk chair. The only clean spot was the area in front of the SO MAD backdrop where she recorded her videos.

She immediately regretted not locking the basement door, embarrassed her children had seen this mess.

"And you tell me to clean up my room?" said Aaron.

"I'm just working on that budget stuff I told you about," Andrea said. "If you're so worried about the condition of the basement, maybe you would like to help with the laundry down here on occasion." The threat of laundry duty would surely end this unwanted conversation.

"You're going to save the country from inside this mess?" Michelle's high-pitched voice exuded doubt.

"That's the plan. I'm putting together the different budget proposals Mr. Murray asked me to give him. If he wins, he might use one of them."

"Did you save NASA?" asked Aaron. "Because I'm going to fly in space one day."

"I'm trying," she said. She wanted to add, *But every rocket we pay for to launch people into space might cost someone their prescription benefits,* but decided against it.

"You both doing all right?" asked Andrea. "I have a meeting in fifteen minutes."

"We just wanted to tell you we're going to the park," said Michelle.

The local park had a lighted basketball court and playground, a favorite spot for the children. Another time Andrea might have insisted they be home at seven and text her updates. But she was so lost in her own work that she'd unconsciously suppressed her usual overprotective instincts.

"Sounds good, kids. Call if you need anything."

The kids raced up the stairs and Andrea got back to work. She had prepared three different budgets for Murray. One was a gradual set of cuts that would put the country on a course to pay down its debt in fifty years. Another paid down the debt in twenty-five years. And one was a draconian, slash-and-burn emergency budget that paid down the debt within eight years, two presidential terms. Murray wanted that option in case he became convinced none of his successors would continue his debt-reduction efforts and would turn on the spending spigots again. Andrea christened it "The Nuke" because she considered it the financial equivalent of dropping a nuclear bomb.

In the quiet before her call with Murray, she sat back in her chair, folded her hands behind her head, and smiled. She was pleased with her budget plans. But she felt growing frustration. She watched the news every evening to see if Murray had mentioned the national debt on the campaign trail and so far, he hadn't. What was he waiting for? If he wasn't going to talk about the debt, what was the point of her work?

Andrea was raring to go when Murray joined the online meeting.

"What did you think of the draft budget plans?" she asked.

"Looked good to me," Murray replied. "They're exactly what I wanted."

"I'm looking forward to your telling the country the hard budget truths," said Andrea.

Murray gazed at Andrea through the video chat. She recognized Murray's faraway look from the Gang meeting. Something was on his mind.

"Congressman?" she asked, trying to prompt some conversation. "May I ask you a question?"

"Sure."

"When are you going to release these budget plans?"

Murray sighed. "Not during the campaign, Andrea. After it. If I win."

"You're not going to use them in the campaign?" Andrea drew her face close to the screen to fill Murray's screen with an incredulous look. "I spent weeks holed up in this basement living off Doritos and Diet Pepsi and you're not planning to use my work?"

Murray cocked his head and peered over his reading glasses. The jocular visitor to her office was gone, replaced by the steely-eyed, calculating politician. The type of guy she hated.

"Andrea, if I push budget cuts, I'm going to lose," said Murray. "We're going to lose."

"Not you too." Andrea threw up her hands.

"You need to trust me on this. I promise, I'm using them. But didn't you learn anything from your experience with the Debt Rebel Gang?"

Oh Lord, here it comes, the politician condescending to the un-schooled rube.

"People are mad all right, but not about the debt," said Murray. "If I start talking about cutting their Social Security and Medicare, I will lose. And what do you think will happen if Zack Hunter wins and opens the spending spigot?" Zachary Hunter was Murray's Democratic opponent in the presidential election.

"But somebody needs to condition people to prepare them for the cuts someone is going to need to make. If Hunter does Medicare-for-All, and pays off everyone's college debt and medical debt, we're going to go bankrupt in a week. I'm telling you, Americans will listen. They know Hunter is talking about paying for things with unicorn farts and pixie dust."

Her foot twitched under the desk. Yet again, someone was

ignoring her advice. Cam Davis disregarded her, with tragic consequences. The Debt Rebel Gang disregarded her. And now Earl Murray, the one politician she thought took her seriously, was disregarding her. She was back to being an unimportant suburban nobody.

"Listen, I'm frustrated too," said Murray. "Believe me, it did us no favors when the Debt Rebel Gang admitted they weren't really concerned about the debt after all their balanced budget caterwauling. Even the talk-radio babblers confessed no one ever truly cared about the debt, that it was all a ruse to stir up anger and get their favored candidates elected. What do you think that did to our credibility? Even if I try to make the case, no one will believe us. At this point, I wouldn't either."

Acid burned the lining of Andrea's stomach. Her powerlessness was literally consuming her. Was she such a nobody that she couldn't make a genuine case to the public to cut the debt despite the Debt Rebel Gang's cynical leveraging of the debt issue to gain power?

"The bottom line is this: In order to lead, we have to win," said Murray.

Andrea grimaced through the pain of her acid reflux. "Isn't it supposed to be the other way around?"

"Maybe, maybe not," replied Murray. "If you want to drive the conversation, you have to win the election. Elected officials control the debate. Election losers stand on the sidelines shaking their fists and yelling at the clouds."

Andrea took a sip from an open can of Diet Pepsi.

"If I win," Murray said, "I'm going to attack the debt hard with the budgets you've been putting together." He pointed at Andrea for emphasis.

"In other words, you're going to trick the American people

into thinking you're not worried about the debt and then start cutting spending and all their government-provided goodies," she snapped.

"Delusion is a two-way street," Murray said. "If the American public has deluded itself into thinking the country can incur debt forever, we can delude it into electing us to deal with the problem."

Andrea rubbed her forehead. Maybe Murray was right. And maybe there was something to being a professional politician after all. Though the thought did nothing to stop the acid in her stomach.

"Do me one favor," said Murray.

"What's that?" asked Andrea.

"Come to the election night party in Dallas. We'll have a suite. All kinds of food and drinks. Win or lose, I want you there for election night. Watch the returns come in with me and my team."

"I don't know, I can't leave my husband and the kids."

"Bring 'em."

"But the cost of the plane, the hotel—"

"The campaign will cover it," said Murray. "Any other excuses I need to shoot down?"

"No strings attached, right? You're not going to make me get in front of a camera or something, are you?"

"No strings," said Murray. "Just come and see what a presidential election night party is like."

Andrea could not hold back a slight smile. "You drive a hard bargain, Congressman." The thought of attending the party settled her pulse.

"I told you I was a car salesman," said Murray. "Top salesman in Dallas from 2012 and 2014."

"What happened?"

"I got myself elected to Congress," said Murray. "After that I couldn't sell water in the desert."

Andrea laughed. "Fine, Mr. Murray." His charm had won the day. "We'll come to Dallas for election night."

"Excellent. My assistant will call with all the arrangements. Talk to you soon."

"Goodbye, Congressman."

Andrea sat back and exhaled. *The election night party? With the potential president-elect?* Maybe she wasn't a suburban nobody after all. Maybe Murray really did take her seriously. She felt a surge of motivation and confidently took a big swig of her Diet Pepsi. As the liquid traveled down her throat, she could feel its caffeinated energy osmotically passing into her bloodstream. She dove back into revising her budget plans in earnest. She'd finally hit the big time.

CHAPTER 9

"**F**rank, so glad you made it!"

Lewis Mason, chairman of the House Debt Rebel Gang, greeted Acorn as he descended the stairs into the pub of the Capitol Hill Club, the elegant club the national Republican Party ran on Capitol Hill a block from Mason's office in the Longworth Building. Pictures of Republican notables lined the walls of the stairs. Eisenhower. Lincoln. Reagan. Taft. Bush. Icons of the Republican Party.

"Thanks for the invite, Mr. Mason," said Acorn.

It was a big deal to be invited to the Capitol Hill Club for the election night party. Other than being at the candidate's party watching the returns, the Capitol Hill Club was the place to be for a Republican.

The Club was once Acorn's domain. He'd made contacts and built his reputation here. His networking at the Club probably accelerated his career arc by a decade. The basement pub's low ceiling and dim yellow lighting practically screamed "smoke-filled room where politicians cut deals."

Now that the Ministry had activated him, though, the Club was the last place he wanted to be. He was terrified of saying the wrong thing and exposing his clandestine activities. But one didn't turn down an invite to the Capitol Hill Club for the election night party. That would have aroused suspicion. So Acorn swallowed hard and went.

It wasn't all bad. Cheeseburgers were on the buffet menu, and the Capitol Hill Club had one of the best burgers in the city.

He thought of his parents. "There's an engineer or doctor with no political power probably slaving away in a lab while the politicians enjoying themselves at this buffet control their lives with their decisions about health care, defense budgets, or the rest," his father would have said. He looked at the waiters busing the tables. Surrounded by political power while having none of their own. How could they stand it?

"Hey, Frank, you watching this? Murray is going to win this damned thing!" Mason roared.

There were five screens set up in the front of the pub. Each had a different network's election coverage. One by one they were calling the race for Murray.

"A stunning upset," the NBC anchor said.

"No one saw this coming," the CNN anchor echoed.

"What a win for Earl Murray and the Republican Party," said the Fox anchor.

Acorn's stomach churned. He was regretting having eaten that third cheeseburger.

Earl Murray was going to be the next president of the United States.

He had told Xu Li that Murray had no chance. *What am I going to tell her now? Is she going to disappear me?*

Acorn scanned the room. The chatter got louder as Murray's victory became clear. Attendees' faces glowed with the light of cell phones as they furiously texted. A few lit up cigars. In the middle of this growing celebration stood Acorn, aghast, wondering what Xu Li would say to him now. He had to remind himself not to look upset or disappointed and blow his cover.

"Frank, I bet you didn't expect this," said Mason.

"Did anyone?"

"Murray's going to be a pain in the ass to deal with."

"You're telling me."

"If he tries to cut the budget and entitlements the way he used to talk about in Gang meetings the few times he actually spoke, our voters will eat him alive," said Mason. "We're not going to break any promises President Roberts made to the voters."

"You know perfectly well that's what Murray's going to do," Acorn replied.

Mason pulled Acorn close to him. Amid the cigar smoke and drunken revelry, Mason whispered ominously in Acorn's ear. "Then we'll have to stop him, won't we?"

Acorn couldn't believe what he'd heard. He'd risen to become Mason's chief of staff by pretending to be a deficit hawk. Now that he needed to keep Murray from cutting the national debt, Mason agreed. He couldn't have picked a better member of Congress to serve. He might face Xu Li's wrath, but the task of manipulating Mason was as easy as could be.

Mason pulled away from Acorn and made his way to the stairs. He left, saying goodbye to no one. It wasn't like Mason to leave a party early, not when the drinks were flowing and there was free food to be had. Something was on his mind. Maybe he anticipated a showdown with Murray.

Acorn had his own showdown to contemplate. For Xu Li was no doubt waiting to hear from him. He dreaded her reaction to his now-disproven prediction that Murray would lose.

He looked over at the buffet. A new platter of cheeseburgers had just appeared.

One for the road. This might be my last.

CHAPTER 10

Andrea sat on a couch staring at a television in shock, goosebumps dotting her arms. The twelfth-floor suite in the Dallas Hilton that served as Congressman Murray's election night campaign command center was filled with people celebrating. Thrilled, stunned, excited, speechless—she was all of these and then some. Ryan was seated next to her with his arm around her and a broad smile on his face. Michelle was jumping up and down, shouting "Mommy's team won! Mommy's team won!"

A commotion exploded outside the room. The doors burst open and in walked a massive crowd of people, camera shutters clicking, television cameras recording, and microphone booms hovering over it all. The man who'd left the room two hours ago as Congressman Murray had now returned as President-elect Murray.

Over the last hour he'd acquired a massive entourage comprised of an army of Secret Service agents, aides, staffers, family members, celebrities, and who knew who else. The campaign staff swarmed President-elect Murray as he entered the room.

"Congratulations, Mr. President!"

"You did it, sir!"

Andrea stood up and watched but said nothing. Her head was on a swivel. Dignitaries, celebrities, staff, and hangers-on filled the room.

What am I doing here?

She retreated to the couch and sat down. She could feel her insides shriveling up, curling into a ball among the A-list social scene. She watched as Murray worked the room with ease. Working a room wasn't in Andrea's repertoire. She had trouble making conversation at her college reunion. How could she possibly hang with this high-powered crowd?

She shrank into the couch next to Ryan and nursed a Diet Pepsi through a half-hour of stage fright, saying nothing as she watched the crowd. Near midnight the crowd finally began to disperse to the hotel ballroom where more celebrations had begun. President-elect Murray did not join them. Instead, as the crowd thinned, he seated himself next to her. Secret Service agents took up positions around the couch.

"How about you and I head out to the balcony for a moment," said President-elect Murray.

Andrea nodded and stood up. As they walked to the balcony, she shot Ryan a questioning look. Murray saw it. "Your husband can come too if you'd like," he said. "He may want to be part of the conversation."

Ryan got up and the three of them headed out to the balcony. The lights of downtown Dallas shimmered in the background. The Secret Service took up their standard positions, one on the balcony and one inside the suite guarding the sliding door.

"We did it, Andrea!" A jubilant President-elect Murray embraced her warmly. "You and I, we need to talk."

"You did it, sir," Andrea replied. "I had nothing to do with it. You barely used my plans and policy papers."

"Nonsense," Murray said. "I used them quietly, in private, with people who truly care about the deficit. Just because I didn't splash them all over the airwaves doesn't mean I didn't use them. When you get more experience, you'll see the difference between the public and private campaigns politicians run."

"Get more experience?" asked Andrea.

"I want you to come with me to Washington," Murray said. "I need your help."

"For what?" Andrea's voice was a combination of excitement and dread.

"I want you to be my Office of Management and Budget director. Your job will be to write and manage the federal budget."

"Come again?" She took a step back and glanced at Ryan. "You want me to be your OMB director?"

"You know what that is, right?" Murray asked.

"You're asking me to be the most important accountant in the world?" Even as she said it, she couldn't believe it was happening. "Don't you have party poohbahs, donors, and apparatchiks to reward? I'd be perfectly happy to be an anonymous staffer at OMB."

"I'm the president-elect," said Murray. "I do what I want now. And thanks to SO MAD, you are the face of cutting the debt to the women of America."

"Mr. President, you need someone with experience in Washington," Andrea replied. Calling Murray "Mr. President" made Andrea feel as though she was in an episode of her beloved *West Wing*. "Making internet videos in front of empty rooms is one thing. Being out front, talking to crowds, talking to Congress? You saw how I failed in that Debt Rebel Gang meeting. You want more of that? I'm happy to keep writing budgets from my basement, but I don't want to be out front."

Murray shook his head. "I need you in Washington."

"I can't do this. I don't know anyone in Washington."

"If it doesn't work, I'll replace you."

"Maybe I could be the deputy, or the assistant, or something like that."

Murray leaned in close to Andrea and put his hand on her

shoulder. "That's not what I want. I want the person who spoke truth to the Debt Rebel Gang. You kicked their asses, whether you think so or not. I need the person who wrote all those draft budgets during the campaign. I need the person who rallied the SO MAD moms. You said it yourself. The country needs an accountant. And I am choosing you."

"Maybe I could talk to my family first?"

Murray pointed at Ryan, who'd been standing next to Andrea on the balcony listening to their conversation.

"Sweetheart, the president is asking you to serve the country." Ryan tilted his head and peered over his glasses at Andrea. "The president is asking you to serve the country. The *president*. The *country*."

Andrea looked at her kids through the balcony door. Aaron was plowing through what remained of the appetizer buffet, and Michelle was playing with the daughter of one of Murray's campaign aides, both still blissfully unaware of the debt bomb ticking in the background. The president was asking her to defuse the debt bomb and save their futures.

Andrea turned to Ryan. "What about the family?"

"We'll move to Washington," Ryan said. "It's fine. I can find a hospital to work at. The kids will find schools. We won't even have to sell the house. When we're done in DC, we'll come back home."

"The Virginia suburbs have some of the best public schools in the country," added Murray. "Your kids will be fine. And what an experience they will have. Not every kid has a chance to use the White House bowling alley for birthday parties. Yours will."

"That settles it," said Ryan.

Andrea nodded, sheepishly at first and then with growing conviction.

"Okay, Mr. President. I'll be your OMB director."

"I knew I could count on you," Murray said, smiling broadly. "Let's take on the debt and make history."

CHAPTER 11

A corn's four-hour drive to the cave felt more like eight. He'd kept the radio off. He didn't want to hear any more election coverage. What he needed to do was think.

How do I face Xu Li? What do I say?

He ran a few stories through his head. He could tell her most pundits had gotten it wrong, so he wasn't the only one. Or he could simply throw himself on her mercy.

Why waste your time thinking about what to say? You know perfectly well that the moment Xu Li appears on the screen you're going to forget whatever you planned to say and seize up tongue-tied. What's the difference what you decide to say now?

Acorn arrived at the abandoned drive-in theater. He looked around to see if anyone was there. The full moon provided enough light that he didn't need a flashlight. He'd come straight from the party and was still wearing his loafers. *Good. They make less noise.*

Acorn descended into the cave.

When he arrived, he tiptoed to the red button on the console beside the video screen. The acid in his stomach from the three cheeseburgers finally released and the reflux burned its way up his throat. He took a deep breath and pressed the button. Xu Li appeared on the screen.

"I see you misjudged the election results, Acorn."

Acorn momentarily stopped breathing. Xu Li had gone right for the jugular.

"Madame Xu, the American people are hard to predict. Too many factors at play."

"And you all think Chinese Communism is undesirable. Predictability is always preferable over mob rule."

"I know we need a strategy to respond to this," stammered Acorn. "I'll execute whatever plan you have."

"You are lucky you've burrowed as deeply into American society as you have, Acorn. If you were more expendable, we would not be having this conversation."

Was that meant to make me feel better? That I wasn't going to be liquidated? Or was she reminding me she had no compunction about liquidating failed agents?

"Is it the plan of Mr. Murray to cut the American debt and end the deficit?" continued Xu Li. "He spoke of it hardly at all during the campaign."

"All a ruse, Madame Xu. He had staff working on debt-cutting plans throughout the campaign to unleash if he won. But he knew he would not win if he let the American people know his plans before the election. So he said nothing."

"And you know this how?"

"I'm not a complete failure, Madame Xu. I know Murray. And I knew staffers on the Murray campaign. Including the staffer he had working on the debt-cutting plans."

"And who is this?"

"Andrea Gartner."

"This is the woman in the online videos?"

"Yes. She got the suburban moms all fired up about the debt, and Murray wanted their votes. So he put her on his campaign."

"Do you know her?"

Acorn saw an opportunity to show Xu Li he was a valuable, well-connected agent.

"She tried to run for Congress. I made sure she was nuked."

"Not completely nuked, obviously. She still seems to be a problem."

Acorn had miscalculated, forgetting Xu Li dealt only in absolutes. Success or failure. Life or death. She gave no partial credit. If Andrea Gartner was a threat, and Acorn had her in his sights and didn't take her out, he had failed in Xu Li's world.

"I don't think anyone expected Andrea Gartner to become the sensation she did. I thought the Debt Rebel Gang had broken her. If Murray had lost as expected, she would have been consigned to oblivion. But I am in a position to craft a new strategy." Acorn desperately wanted to stop talking about his failure to predict Murray's victory.

"We already have a strategy, Acorn. You may not plan for all contingencies, but you are an American. The Ministry thinks through every conceivable contingency. We have a plan."

"What is that?"

"We will speed up the timetable of Operation Pripyat."

The camera panned out from Xu Li slowly and behind her stood a man in an expensive suit. Even through the screen Acorn could tell it was a thousand-dollar, custom-tailored Ermenegildo Zegna suit.

"Study this man, Acorn. The next time you see him it will be the signal that Operation Pripyat has begun and it is time for you to move into action."

Acorn carefully studied the Russian-looking man. He looked wealthy in his pricey suit and perfectly folded pocket kerchief. But on closer inspection he was a brute. He had a thick build, large reddish nose, small, narrow eyes, and brown hair with a receding hairline and a beard. His supremely round, craggy, leathery face suggested he'd seen his share of combat.

"Have you a good sense of this man, Acorn?"

"Yes, Madame Xu."

"Good. The next time you see him, Operation Pripyat will have begun. And it will not be long before you see him again. I suggest you prepare now."

Acorn knew Xu Li didn't "suggest" anything. By "suggest" she meant "command."

"The wheels are turning now, Acorn. You must be ready to strike when you receive the signal."

"Yes, Madame Xu. I will be ready."

The transmission disconnected. Xu Li had not even said goodbye.

Returning to his car, Acorn finally turned on his radio. The local news station was replaying President-elect Murray's victory speech. Murray waxed eloquently about the bright future ahead. A smile crept across Acorn's face. He knew all of Murray's happy talk would soon come crashing down upon him. Operation Pripyat was about to explode the debt bomb.

CHAPTER 12

A little more than two months after election night, and one day after President Murray's inauguration, Andrea stared at the Eisenhower Executive Office Building, the "EEOB," as it was known, as she drove up to it for the first time as OMB director. She grabbed the lanyard from around her neck, flashed her badge with the White House logo, and followed the Secret Service agent's directions to the parking lot on West Executive Avenue, between the White House and the EEOB. Thick black security gates adorned with small gold stars guarded the West Executive Avenue parking lot. They began to retract when Andrea pulled up. She gazed in awe like Dorothy entering the Emerald City, the West Wing on her left and the EEOB on her right.

After parking in her reserved space, she headed to the EEOB entrance. The vaulted ceilings, marble floors and stairs, and ornate banisters and moldings inside the lobby took her breath away. It was a far cry from the nondescript suburban hovel where she did her clients' taxes.

Andrea made her way to her office on the third floor. She hoped her move-in to the White House went as smoothly as her family's move to their new home in Sterling, Virginia, the week earlier. Her neighbors, Paul and Ellen Frost, had brought over a small gift basket when the Gartners moved in. Paul was president of the local homeowner's association and officially welcomed new residents to the neighborhood. She had also moved her mother into a nearby assisted living facility in Springfield.

Three OMB office staffers came in and out of the office, bringing office supplies and computer equipment. She had never had a full staff retinue before. On any other day, Andrea would have worried about the cost of the move and this extensive staff and how it added to the debt, but even she was overtaken by the majesty of her surroundings. Out her window she had a view of the West Wing and the Oval Office. Her building oozed power from every pore.

Her personal office was twice the size of her private practice. Off to one side was a private dining room while on another side was a small study and library. Antique-style lamps softly lit the office, an upgrade from the harsh white fluorescent lights to which she was accustomed. The desk and furniture were wood, not cheap gun-metal-gray aluminum. It even had couches and a coffee table. A wood-carved OMB logo hung on the wall. This was no mere office. It was a command center worthy of the commander of the federal budget.

President Murray had told her the first thing she needed to do was hang her diplomas. He said the first thing the Washington elite would ask a rookie like her was where she went to school. Anyone ready to dismiss her as a lightweight would think again when they saw she was Ivy League. So Andrea went straight to the boxes with her family pictures and diplomas. Pulling out the hammer and nails she'd packed, she went to work hanging her Penn diploma on the wall.

"What's all that banging?" came a gruff cry from the foyer.

Startled, Andrea dropped the hammer. A rumpled, balding, bespectacled man about five-and-a-half feet stood in her doorway.

"Hanging my diplomas, sir," said Andrea sheepishly. "Is that okay?"

"We have people who will do it for you," he said. "Are you Andrea Gartner?"

"Yes, sir."

"So you're the D/OMB. I take it you already have your TS/
SCI clearance and you'll be able to attend the principals meeting
tomorrow in the Cabinet Room?"

"I'm afraid I don't understand a thing you just said, sir,"
Andrea answered. "Have we met yet?" She extended a handshake.

The man groaned. "Murray warned me about you. Said you
might be new to all this. I've been in this town and this game forty
years, and you don't know who I am."

Nice to meet you too.

"It's true, this is my first government job," said Andrea.

"First government job, and it's OMB director," he muttered.
"Unbelievable."

"I'm afraid you have the advantage," Andrea nervously replied.
"I don't believe we've met yet."

"Wally Flynn," he said. "The president's chief of staff."

Andrea took in his rumpled appearance. He was just how
she imagined a White House chief of staff would look. A little
disheveled, sleeves rolled up, tie slightly drooping as if he was
perpetually harried.

"It's good to meet you. I'm Andrea Gartner."

"You already told me that," grumbled Wally.

Andrea felt embarrassed. She'd promised herself she wouldn't
act nervous around all these high-powered people, and she'd
already blown it with the first person she'd met.

Wally glanced at Andrea's diploma. "You went to Penn, I
see."

"I did," said Andrea. "Majored in economics."

"I'm Princeton class of eighty-five," said Wally. "You'll find a
lot of us Ivy Leaguers around here."

So much for her Ivy League advantage.

"I'm looking forward to getting started," she said, hoping to take the conversation in a direction that didn't make her feel inferior.

"I'm sure you are," said Wally. "Now listen, I know the president brought you on board to fix the national debt, but let me make something clear to you right now. If you try to cut too much—you try to make big cuts to Social Security, Medicare, or anything else—I'll shut you down so fast you'll wish you never tried."

Andrea swallowed the lump in her throat.

"My job is to protect the president's political interests, and I'll be honest with you, you and your budget cutting are a threat to them. Especially since you're a rookie and don't know shit about government. Just keep your cutting blade dull and we won't have any problems. You cut too much, and I promise you, I'll unleash bureaucratic warfare that will have you begging to go home to South Carolina."

Andrea wasn't accustomed to people asserting hierarchy this aggressively.

Should I push back? Give in? I don't want to get off on the wrong foot. But what does that mean anyway? Would it be worse to push back or for him to think I'm a pushover?

Every fiber of her body was telling her to back down, to give in, to let Wally Flynn enjoy his moment of alpha male dominance. But then she thought of Cam Davis. He didn't become the Mattress King by backing down to bullies like Wally Flynn. He beat them and put them in their place.

I didn't uproot my family so Wally Flynn could marginalize me. I'm here to fix the budget. And that's what I'm going to do.

"Wally," Andrea paused a moment. "Can I call you Wally?"

"Sure."

"Wally, I came to do whatever the president tells me to do. If he wants me to make cuts, I'll make them. If you want to fight about them, we'll fight about them. If you win, you won't get any more trouble from me. But if I win, I expect the same."

Wally appeared taken aback, as if he'd been expecting Andrea to roll over. She cocked her head to one side, taking in his look of surprise. Wally must have noticed because he tried to regain his alpha male demeanor. "Glad we had this little talk. See you around campus."

Andrea took a deep breath. Her first real Washington conversation was over. She wasn't sure it was a success, but she was still alive and still OMB director, so it couldn't have been a total failure. She'd stood up for herself and lived to tell the tale. Maybe she could hack it in Washington after all.

No sooner had she turned back to setting up her office when another visitor dropped in. "You're doing all this unpacking yourself?" said the tall, slim man. "I'm Brooks Powell, the incoming Treasury Secretary. Would you like some help?"

Brooks looked like the consummate Wall Street banker in pinstriped pants, jacket with silk tie, and neatly folded kerchief in his jacket pocket. His mane of closely cropped and perfectly parted silver hair was held in place by the slightest dab of hair cream. He was a throwback who could have walked straight out of the drawing rooms of Brown Brothers Harriman in 1950s New York. Prior to becoming Treasury Secretary, he was the CEO of Goldman Sachs and a regular in the financial publications Andrea read. She recognized him immediately.

"Andrea Gartner," she replied.

Brooks walked into the office and offered a handshake. "You're the rookie Murray brought aboard," he said with a smile.

"I think so," said Andrea. "This is my first full week in Washington."

"I passed Wally Flynn in the hall," replied Brooks. "Did he come in and say hi?"

"Sort of." Andrea bit her lip. "He read me the riot act on cutting spending."

"Don't worry about him," said Brooks. "It's an old trick of his. Try to establish dominance the first time he meets someone new. I'm sure he doesn't want to cut spending. Might threaten Murray's reelection."

"We are going to have to cut spending at some point, Mr. Powell."

"Call me Brooks."

"Okay, but you would agree we need to cut spending, right?"

"Yes, certainly," said Brooks. "We'll cut spending when the time is right. And when it is, I'll be right there beside you."

Not bad, Andrea thought. *You've made your first ally.* It would be better if he wanted to cut spending now, but at least he was more supportive than Wally.

"You need any help unpacking?" Brooks asked.

"No, I'm okay, but thanks so much for the offer," replied Andrea.

"If you need anything, don't hesitate to call over to Treasury. You and I are going to be working together a good bit, so don't be a stranger."

"Thanks, Brooks. Looking forward to working with you."

Brooks headed out of the office.

Andrea turned back to unpacking. She'd just met the most powerful CEO in the country and he'd treated her like a peer. And she hadn't ended up tongue-tied. *You can do this*, she thought. *You can handle the big leagues.*

CHAPTER 13

A corn had dutifully read the *Express* every morning since President Murray's inauguration, but not once had he seen a message from the Ministry or Xu Li. A month had passed, and neither Xu Li or the Ministry had uttered a peep.

Had the Ministry given up on Operation Pripyat? Or on me?

He scanned every face on the Metro as he rode to and from work every day. Could a Ministry assassin be lurking on his commute to kill him because he hadn't stopped Murray's election?

Then he remembered something his father used to say: "The watched pot never boils, but the Ministry always has the gas on." Acorn buried himself in his office, shuffling papers daily and meeting with his staff as little as possible while trying to stay patient the way his parents had trained him.

Sure enough, precisely on the morning of the one-month anniversary of President Murray's inauguration, Acorn had just climbed the Capitol South Metro escalator when his special TAG Heuer watch began to vibrate. Acorn pushed the stopwatch sweep button and the small digital screen appeared with a message:

Receive the signal . . . Receive the signal . . . Receive the signal . . .

Acorn picked up his pace and briskly headed into Mason's office suite.

"Good morning, Mr. Palmer," said Mason's secretary as Acorn walked by.

"Morning, Sarah," Acorn said hurriedly. He had no time for small talk.

"Do you want your . . . usual coffee?" she asked as she followed Acorn. Before she could finish her sentence, Acorn had zoomed past her into his office with the nameplate on the door that read "Frank Palmer, Chief of Staff" and closed the door behind him.

Receive the signal. Acorn knew the message meant something was about to happen, something that would send him into action. He tuned his office television to CNBC, the business channel. Operation Pripyat targeted America's national debt. If something involving the debt were happening, CNBC surely would be reporting on it.

"Reports out of New York indicate an auction of US Treasury bonds is failing," the anchor stated breathlessly. "A consortium of governments and institutional investors has announced they will no longer purchase US government bonds because they do not believe the United States government will be able to pay back its national debt, which stands at forty trillion dollars."

CNBC cut to a news conference of one of the institutional investors. And there he was, the man Acorn had seen in his last meeting with Xu Li. He was wearing another tailored Zegna suit. Acorn was impressed. The Ministry made sure its agent looked good as it deep-sixed the American economy.

Zegna Suit unfolded a piece of paper, put it on the podium in front of him, and began reading. "We, the members of the Pripyat Consortium of international institutional investors, will no longer purchase United States Treasury bonds and fund the United States' government debt."

Acorn detected a hint of Russian accent. This guy had learned his English well, but his inflection was off. He was ever so slightly placing emphasis on the wrong words. And he was gruff. He was only reading the statement, which didn't surprise Acorn. Xu Li would not have left writing something so important to a field agent.

"We represent a large number of private and public institutional investors from all over the world," Zegna Suit continued. "While our members are anonymous, our concerns are not. The United States government debt is now forty trillion dollars. We no longer have confidence the United States government will be able to repay this debt. Therefore, until the United States proves its creditworthiness, the Pripyat Consortium of international institutional investors cannot and will not loan the United States money by purchasing United States Treasury bonds."

Zegna Suit left the podium, giving only a fleeting look into the camera. He'd made less than a second of eye contact with America. No glower or stare into the camera.

The CNBC anchor reappeared.

"There you have it, a group calling itself the Pripyat Consortium says they will cease purchasing American Treasury bonds." He turned to his guest, an American Fortune 500 CEO according to the caption on the screen. "Are you familiar with this Pripyat Consortium? And do you think this bond boycott will be successful?"

"I've never heard of any bond fund, or anything in the financial world for that matter, called the 'Pripyat Consortium.' But it will take more than one bond fund, especially one no one's ever heard of, to boycott American bonds to the point that the United States can't pay its debt. Our bonds are still the envy of the world."

That's what you think, bud. This is no mere bond fund at work.

CNBC's oblivious anchor nodded his head in agreement. "But what about today's bond auction failure?"

"It happens. The markets will be ready tomorrow and will correct. One person's boycott is another person's opportunity."

What fools, Americans. Always thinking the market is simply working as the market does. Didn't anyone wonder if maybe this was something more than just the market at work? That maybe someone out there had a motive other than making money?

Xu Li's opaque instructions were now coming into focus. The Ministry had made its opening move. Operation Pripyat was on. And if the Americans were oblivious, so much the better. It meant the first part of the operation had gone off without a hitch.

Acorn thought through how Operation Pripyat would play out. When the American economy collapsed, Americans would look at Zegna Suit and think the Russians were behind it. Knowing Congress, it would wrap itself around an axle trying to ferret out the Russians involved. They'd overlook the Chinese altogether.

Acorn had to hand it to Xu Li. Her strategy was brilliant. Classic misdirection against an enemy easily goaded into believing the worst about the Russians.

Acorn decided his first task would be to agitate and wind up his boss, Lew Mason, who was easy to manipulate when agitated. And Mason chaired the House Appropriations Committee. The committee would be ground zero in Congress for formulating a response to the debt crisis.

But *how* to agitate Mason? Surely Mason would want the country to respond swiftly to the crisis. But he was a pure political animal whose political thought process ran with the precision of a Swiss clock. First, he thought about how to ensure his reelection. Next, he thought about how he could screw his political rivals. When all that was done, if there was time, he'd think about what was best for the country. Acorn was convinced manipulating Mason all these years had been easy thanks to this one keen insight.

Mason couldn't learn about the bond boycott on his own. Acorn needed to break the news to Mason himself and spin it just right. If he did his job, by the end of the conversation Mason would have no interest in solving America's debt crisis.

Acorn went around the corner to Mason's office.

Mason was seated at his large wooden desk autographing some photographs for constituents. His jacket was off, his tie loosened, and his shirtsleeves rolled up. He'd moved his multiple awards, challenge coin collection, desk flags, and other trinkets to the edges of the desk to make room for his autographing. He liked to sign big, with a flourish, and it required a lot of desk space.

Acorn spotted Mason's prized baseball, autographed by the 2019 World Series-winning Washington Nationals, moved to the right corner of the desk. When the baseball moved, Mason was hard at work on something important. He wanted his autograph to be big and flawless on the photos he sent to his constituents.

"You see this?" Acorn asked.

"What?" Mason looked up.

"It's a bond boycott. Some investor consortium is boycotting American bonds."

"Say what?"

"An investor group calling itself the Pripyat Consortium has organized a boycott of American bonds. Sounds like a bunch of Russians if you ask me."

"Holy shit," said Mason. "The markets are going to tank."

"Forget the markets," Acorn replied. "The government is going to freeze up."

"Any thoughts on how we should respond?"

"Mr. Mason, you're the member. I'm just the staffer. You tell me what we should be doing."

"That's right, Frank. You are the staffer. And your job is to advise me. So advise me."

Acorn feigned thinking, placing his hand on his chin and

casting his gaze just over the seated Mason. But he knew what had to happen. *The Chinese needed Murray neutralized and Mason available to do my bidding. Use Mason to turn the country against Murray.*

"Mr. Mason, if I were in your shoes, I'd wait for Murray to make the first move. He's the president. He's the leader of the Republican Party. Let him decide what to do. That way, he'll get the blame for whatever goes wrong."

"That's nuts. Congress should design a debt-reduction package. If we do, we'll have more control over it. If someone starts making cuts, I want to decide what they are."

"Are you crazy? You want to have your fingerprints on the cuts? No sir. You want to be as far away from the cuts as possible. You want to outlast Murray and Andrea Gartner?"

Mason furrowed his brow. "What do you think? I want to see their favorable ratings in the single digits."

"Then you want to back off this and duck. Control equals blame, Mr. Mason. There aren't going to be any good ways out of this. Whatever we decide to cut, the person making the cuts is going to get blamed. I'm telling you, if you want Murray's favorable ratings in the single digits, make him make the cuts."

Mason narrowed his eyes and a sinister smile crept across his face. "A month into Murray's presidency and he has to deal with a fiscal crisis. Serves that asshole right. He spent all that time trashing my Debt Rebel Gang behind closed doors. Then he goes and hires that harpy Andrea Gartner as his OMB director. They think they're so much smarter than us? Fine. Let them figure it out."

"Exactly, Mr. Mason."

Acorn smiled. Mason was perfectly following the path Acorn laid out for him. Schadenfreude outweighed patriotism with Lewis Mason. It was hardly a contest. Mason had no problem seeing the American government seize up if it meant pain for his political rivals. He'd sell his mother for a political victory.

"What do you want to do?" Acorn asked.

"Turn the screws on Murray and Gartner," Mason said. "Hell, blame them for scaring investors and causing them to boycott American bonds. Let them take the hits when the country goes bankrupt. And maybe we put out a statement about how we have been pushing for a balanced budget for years."

A statement like this was obnoxious even by Mason's standards. Acorn loved it. "I'll get going on drafting that statement," he said with a smile.

CHAPTER 14

Across town, in the Old Executive Office Building next to the White House, Andrea Gartner's office phone rang.

"I think a bond auction is going to fail," said Brooks Powell. He hadn't even bothered with a "hello."

"What do you mean?" Andrea asked, confused.

"Some group of investors called the Pripyat Consortium has organized a boycott of US Treasury bonds."

Andrea dropped into her chair.

Murray's been president exactly one month and now this? And who on earth is the Pripyat Consortium?

Brooks's nine little words meant that all her strategizing for a gradual reduction of the debt that mitigated the country's pain went up in smoke. She had meant to reduce America's national debt on her timetable, not on the timetable of Goldman Sachs or European banks or whoever was running this mysterious Pripyat Consortium.

A favorite quote crossed Andrea's mind: "Events, dear boy, events." British Prime Minister Harold Macmillan had said that, his reminder that the best laid plans get tossed into the garbage when unpredicted events inevitably intervene.

One month. That was all it had taken for her to lose control of how the country would resolve its debt. Events and external actors were in the driver's seat now, starting with this Pripyat Consortium.

She stared blankly out her office window at the South Lawn of the White House, gripped by the horrific realization the

federal government might be about to run out of money and
unable to borrow more. Investors who used to lend the American
government money every day were now telling the United States
to pound sand.

"Jesus, Brooks, didn't you have any warning?" Andrea asked.
"A month into the job and the public up and decides to stop buying
bonds? Didn't you hear anything on the Street before now?"

"I'd heard nothing," Brooks replied, clearly irritated. "But so
what? It was only a matter of time before investors finally wised
up and decided to see if the United States would pay back some
of its forty trillion dollars of debt before they would continue to
lend the country money. You could build a stairway to the moon
with forty trillion dollars."

"You know what this means, right?" Andrea knew Brooks
understood the consequences of a bond auction failure, but for
some reason wanted to hear him say it.

"The government stops without borrowed money," Brooks
said tersely. "Social Security. Medicare. Medical research. Law
enforcement. Federal jobs. Ev-er-ry-thing. We won't even be able
to pay for mowing the goddamned White House lawn."

"It's the nightmare scenario," Andrea said. "I wish we'd had
time to do the budget cutting ourselves."

"Whatever governments and institutional investors are behind this Pripyat Consortium had other ideas," Brooks grumbled.
"They're about to trigger a full-blown American debt crisis."

The Pripyat Consortium.

Who were they? And why now?

Andrea had been an accountant for twenty-five years. She read
Bloomberg and the *Wall Street Journal* every day. She couldn't
remember one mention of any Pripyat Consortium. It sounded
Russian, though. The pogroms had driven Andrea's family out of
Russia just before World War I and she still remembered those

signs that used to be posted outside the synagogues in her native Baltimore: "Free Soviet Jewry." She didn't trust anything that sounded Russian.

"Have you ever heard of this Pripyat Consortium? Doesn't this seem a little fishy? A Russian-named heretofore-invisible investor consortium suddenly holding America's budget hostage?" she asked.

"I've been in finance all my life," said Brooks. "I thought I knew every bond fund that's come and gone. These guys? Never heard of them."

"Something's up, Brooks," said Andrea. "There's more to this than meets the eye."

Andrea hung up and sat there in shock. She was determined to figure out who this Pripyat Consortium was.

She did a quick Google search. "Pripyat."

Images of an abandoned town appeared. A rusted Ferris wheel in an empty amusement park. Crumbling classrooms in empty schools. Row upon row of rotting, abandoned apartment blocks. Feral animals roaming a ghost town.

What the hell?

Then she saw it.

A picture of the Chernobyl sarcophagus. A collapsed nuclear reactor filled with concrete. The monument to mankind's worst nuclear accident.

Who names an investment group after a nuclear meltdown?

This failed bond auction was no accident. It wasn't the markets tired of loaning the United States endless gobs of money. Whoever was behind the Pripyat Consortium wanted to hurt the United States. And they'd discovered the country's Achilles' heel.

CHAPTER 15

A ndrea had lost all focus after her call with Brooks Powell. Unable to relieve her tension, she decided to take a short walk around the White House complex. It turned into an hour-long hike up Connecticut Avenue to Dupont Circle and back, but it hadn't helped a bit. As she sat back down at her desk, she was as frightened as when she'd left.

This must be what a panic attack feels like.

She had to call the president and tell him the federal government had no money to operate. A year ago, Andrea was calling clients about tax deductions they could take. Now this? Had any American had to make a worse call to the president? Maybe the Navy brass at Pearl Harbor? This call would be right up there.

As she reached for the phone, she glanced at her Penn economics degree on the wall. Was there anyone she could call to salvage this situation before she'd have to call the president?

She walked over to her bookshelf, grabbed her Penn yearbook, and flipped through the headshots of her graduating class. Under each photo was a name and the person's major. Half these guys ran big Wall Street firms. Maybe they could save tomorrow's bond auction and help her beat the boycott?

It was a long shot. No fund manager or investment house chieftain was going to pour money into a bad bet out of warm patriotic feelings, and just because she had a Wharton business degree didn't mean she had some secret Skull-and-Bones handshake that would get her classmates to buy bonds and save tomorrow's bond auction. But it was better than having to tell the president the country was bankrupt. And if it worked, it would give the president some time to figure out a more permanent solution.

Andrea hurried back to her desk with the yearbook and pulled out a small dispenser with red and green Post-it tabs from the top drawer. She put a red tab on each economics major she knew from Penn. Then she searched online to find where each one worked. She put a green tab next to anyone who worked in a major Wall Street brokerage house. The ten classmates who got green tabs were getting a call.

After finishing her yearbook review, she leaned back in her chair, cracked open a Diet Pepsi, and took a swig. She'd been a Pepsi drinker since she won an "I Took the Pepsi Challenge" T-shirt at the Jewish-American Festival in Baltimore as a kid in the Seventies. She peeked into her recycling basket to be sure it had room for the several Diet Pepsi cans she expected to polish off while trying to recruit buyers for American bonds.

Now it was time to start calling.

All morning Andrea called one finance titan after another. None had any interest in buying American bonds. She'd appealed to their patriotism. She'd offered White House tours and pictures and dinner with the president, not knowing or caring if the offers were legal. After nine separate calls to nine different brokerage houses without getting a single commitment to buy bonds, Andrea was overcome with hopelessness.

She'd saved Buck Oates for last. He was her best hope.

William "Buck" Oates was one of her closest college classmates and a senior executive at Citicorp. They went back more than two decades. She'd helped him pass his sophomore macroeconomics class. If Andrea couldn't convince him to help, she wouldn't be able to convince anyone.

"It's good to hear from you. Been too long," Buck said. "But I had a feeling you'd be calling this morning."

"You've heard then?"

"It's all over the financial press. *Bloomberg* is reporting that the 'day of reckoning' is upon us."

"And what do you think?"

"I think I'm glad I bought those gold coins William Devane keeps pushing in those stupid late-night infomercials."

"Seriously?"

"No, not entirely seriously. But I'm not kidding, I did buy the coins."

"We have another auction in seventeen hours. If the government can't sell its bonds tomorrow, we're well on our way to not being able to pay for daily government operations."

Buck laughed. "Oh, woe is me! Are you trying to convince me not to buy the bonds? Whatever will I do without daily government operations?" His voice dripped with contempt.

"Come on, Buck. You don't really mean that. What happened to the guy I knew back at Penn? The guy who was in the band and was the last one home from the Locust Walk parties? You might be a finance titan now, but you used to be a pretty soft and sensitive guy."

"Yeah, well, soft and sensitive and a five-dollar bill will get you a grande latte at Starbucks on Wall Street. This is a tough business, Andrea, and I didn't get to where I am by taking pity on bond brokers and investing in their shitty bonds."

Andrea bristled at Buck's lack of sympathy in her moment of crisis but couldn't bring herself to beg for his help. "You know perfectly well even a Master of the Universe like you needs the government for something. Unless you don't mind pothole-filled rides to the Hamptons on the LIE or an uncontrolled free-for-all in the skies without any air traffic control, in which case tomorrow may be your lucky day. But not having air traffic control might make those helicopter trips to Southampton a little less safe than usual."

"I doubt things are that bad, Andrea."

Andrea reached for a sports analogy she thought would appeal to Buck. "Don't be so sure. It's like the Giants, right? Last year their offensive line was Swiss cheese. So they went out and bought a bunch of new O-linemen so the quarterback wasn't knocked on his *tuchus* every other play. We need to get our biggest financiers together, convince them of the urgency of the situation, and have them ensure that our bond auctions this week succeed. Otherwise, America will be knocked on her rear end in a way I can't begin to contemplate."

"Andrea, I'm a part-owner of the Giants. I could do something about the Giants' offensive line. I didn't run up forty trillion dollars in debt. I may be a well-connected financier, but I haven't the first clue how to convince someone that anyone is good for forty trillion dollars. I wouldn't buy debt from anyone forty trillion in the hole. I know a Ponzi scheme when I see one."

Andrea desperately appealed to Buck's liberal political sensibilities. "Buck, in twenty-four hours this country is going to have to stop funding Medicare and Social Security. Do you know what that means?"

"A lot of old people are going to die and I won't have to pay for their healthcare."

Andrea couldn't believe her ears. "Jesus, Buck, what the hell happened to you? You're a Democrat! You're not supposed to talk like that. In twenty-four hours, 'eat the rich' is going to go from a slogan to an operating principle. You think when most of the country's law enforcement officers lose their jobs and medical benefits, you and your four houses are going to be safe? Think again."

As she spoke, she realized she was articulating for herself the consequences she foresaw. She knew what budget cuts were coming.

"Listen, Andrea, we go back a long way, so I'm going to tell you this as gently as I can," Buck said, anger dripping from his voice. "Believe me, if we weren't friends in college, this conversation would already be over. Here's the deal: I'm not going to use my investors' money to prop the United States government up for a few more days. I can't do that no matter what the situation is. My obligation is to my clients. The money I invest is theirs, not mine. I can't be playing hero with their money no matter how much I might want to help."

"Fine, Buck." Andrea could see she was wasting her time. "We'll remember this the next time Wall Street needs a bailout."

Andrea slammed the receiver down in frustration.

Ten calls to Wall Street brokerage houses hadn't gotten her a single commitment to help salvage the next day's bond auction. Buck Oates had been her best shot. The jig was up. She would have to tell the president.

CHAPTER 16

"Andrea, what's going on?" President Murray said, sounding annoyed at the interruption.

"Mr. President, we have a problem," Andrea replied, her voice slightly catching.

President Murray paused.

Andrea swallowed. She should have started with some small talk, but it was too late now.

"I expect to get 'we have a problem' from SECDEF or the Secretary of State or a whip on the Hill telling me I've lost the votes on a bill," Murray said. "I'm not supposed to get it from the OMB director."

"Trust me, I wouldn't say it if I didn't mean it." Andrea couldn't lie or sugarcoat. Not because she was morally opposed to lying. She just couldn't pull it off.

"Well, what is it? A month in and you already have a problem at OMB? What could possibly have happened? Did a shipment of green visors get lost in the mail?"

Andrea didn't laugh. "Accountants don't really use green eyeshades anymore."

"All right, cut to the chase. What's going on?"

"Mr. President, a bond auction failed."

Silence.

"Mr. President, investors won't continue to lend us money to operate the government."

More silence.

"Mr. President, what this means is—"

"I damned well know what this means," President Murray growled. "Is there any way to salvage tomorrow's auction?"

"I tried, Mr. President," Andrea replied. "I called every finance titan I knew. They all told me the same thing. They didn't want the bonds today, they don't want them tomorrow. Not unless we can figure out a way to guarantee they will get paid back. And with a forty-trillion-dollar debt, they didn't believe any guarantee I tried to give them."

Silence.

"Mr. President?"

"I'm thinking."

More silence.

"Sir?"

"I think you know what this means, Andrea."

"Are you sure?"

"Get yourself over to the Oval. Bring the Nuke. I'll call Wally."

Then Andrea heard a dial tone. She leaned back in her chair, staring silently at the wood-carved OMB logo on her wall. *Maybe I could sell it and use the proceeds to buy a bond,* she thought ruefully.

Her eyes began to moisten as she stared at the Calvin Coolidge painting that hung next to the bookcase. Coolidge had always been one of Andrea's heroes. Her Republican friends loved the old standbys: George Washington. Abraham Lincoln. Ronald Reagan. The quirkier ones might admire Teddy Roosevelt or Dwight Eisenhower. But for Andrea, true to her accountant roots, Coolidge was king. Coolidge had met with his budget director, his Andrea equivalent, every day to review the budget. No budget crises for Calvin Coolidge.

When she learned she could get a painting from the White House's archives to decorate her office, she'd asked for a portrait of Coolidge. The archives had no trouble providing one. Coolidge portraits weren't in demand.

"What would you do, Mr. Coolidge?" she said under her breath. How absurd it was to think it might have some wisdom to convey.

But the portrait was as silent as its subject.

Andrea looked out her office window onto the Ellipse. The noontime sun illuminated interns and Hill staffers playing softball and Frisbee, tourists looking at the South Portico of the White House, and joggers on the Mall out for their daily runs. All seemingly blissfully unaware of the unfolding debt crisis.

Andrea willed herself from her chair and walked over to the Coolidge portrait. She looked at Coolidge's bland visage and wanted to apologize to him. Instead, she gently took the portrait off its hook and turned it over.

Taped to the back was a small key. Andrea removed the key, opened a drawer of a file cabinet in the far corner of her office, and pulled out a binder. She'd put the Nuke in the drawer when she'd moved in, hoping she would never see it again. Fearing leaks, she hadn't made paper copies or even saved an electronic copy on the White House computer system. It was bad enough having this document. She wouldn't survive its leaking.

She took a Kleenex from her desk and swabbed the sweat from her forehead and neck. She wiped her glasses clean of the sweat that had dripped onto them. Then she took two deep breaths, composed herself, and crossed West Executive Avenue, the Nuke in hand, to meet the president.

When she arrived at the Oval Office, President Murray was seated behind the Resolute desk. Wally Flynn was sitting across from him in one of the two armchairs, hunched over, elbows on his knees, sleeves rolled up, the lanyard with his White House pass dangling from his neck. They stared at Andrea when she entered.

Great, Wally Flynn. My good buddy. Mr. Reelect-the-President-at-All-Costs.

Andrea took a seat in the armchair beside Wally.

"Wall Street told me to pound sand," Andrea said.

"Greedy sons of bitches," Wally muttered.

"Would you loan money to someone forty trillion dollars in debt? I think that's what they refer to as a 'bad credit risk,'" she said.

Andrea's heart was racing again. Knowing the country had only one option was one thing. Telling the president was another. Her back tingled with sweat.

"Our only option is to use the emergency budget. The Nuke, sir." She held up the binder.

"What the hell is the Nuke?" Wally asked.

The president solemnly nodded, wordlessly giving Andrea the green light to bring Wally in on the secret.

"It's a budget that cuts what needs cutting to bring down the debt immediately," Andrea said. "Either we do the cuts on our terms or foreign lenders will do them for us. If we don't show some seriousness in cutting our budget now, foreign bond buyers will kiss us goodbye and we won't have any money anyway. We do it or they do it. Either way, it's getting done."

Andrea twiddled her fingers nervously. What if Wally got the president to say no? None of the other budgets she'd put together during the campaign cut the budget quickly enough to respond to the bond boycott. It was the Nuke or bust.

"Let me take another look at the Nuke." The president sat up in his luxurious leather chair. Andrea handed him the binder with the Nuke inside.

"You have a copy for me?" Wally asked.

"There are no copies," said Andrea. "Didn't want this to leak. Still don't."

Wally smiled. Andrea figured a wily Washington veteran like Wally would appreciate her paranoia about leaks. He got up from his seat and walked behind the desk to look at the Nuke over the president's shoulder.

"Other than what's written here, everything the American government spends disappears?" the president asked.

"That's how I drafted it," she confirmed.

Wally's eyes progressively widened as he scanned the Nuke. By the time he reached the bottom, his mouth was agape.

"My Lord, are you mad? You cut everything!"

"That's not true, Wally," said Andrea. "This is still a three-and-a-half-trillion-dollar budget."

"But half of it is going to pay down debt and pay interest on the rest of the debt," Wally exclaimed.

"What do you want me to do?" Andrea gritted her teeth. "That's what happens when you run up forty trillion dollars in debt. The payments go up."

"There is no way on this earth we'll get the emergency budget through Congress," said Wally. "They will eat us alive."

"Congress?" Andrea asked. "That's the least of our worries. This budget is going to kill people."

President Murray stood and wandered toward the fireplace on the opposite side of the Oval, seemingly lost in thought.

"Mr. President, we cannot make these cuts," Wally shouted. "We're completely cutting science, medical research, education? Pell Grants and student loans? Highway construction? The military budget? Have you lost your mind? Voters are going to kill us."

The president was slowly ambling around the Oval Office, looking at its paintings and sculptures, memorials to American power and strength, seemingly oblivious to Wally's caterwauling. He stopped at the bust of Lincoln on a small table to the left of the fireplace and rubbed it.

"Unbelievable," President Murray said. "Whenever there's a natural disaster or tragedy in the world, who's the first there?"

"Americans," said Wally.

"Exactly," the president said. "We transport supplies to earthquake survivors. We send doctors to Africa to treat Ebola patients. We send the FBI to help investigate foreign terrorist attacks and the NTSB to investigate plane crashes. No one has the logistical and technical capability to save human lives like the United States."

Andrea undid her ponytail and ran her hands through her hair. "Are you willing to tell a retiree she can't get her medicines because we're spending on earthquake relief in South Asia instead? Because that's the choice we face."

Wally continued reviewing the cuts. "The federal workforce? Contractors? You're slashing all that?" he exclaimed. "We'll lose Virginia for the Republicans for a generation!"

"I'm the OMB director," Andrea said, "not the chairman of the Republican National Committee."

"Laying off federal employees will be a shitstorm of the first order," said Wally. "We'll plunge the DC economy into a depression."

"You're not going to get any sympathy outside of Washington on that," Andrea snapped. "A lot of my small business clients in South Carolina went through some very lean times during the Great Recession. I saw it. I did their taxes. They know damn well Washington is the wealthiest region in the country. And this town doesn't make a thing."

President Murray returned to the Resolute desk where Andrea and Wally were facing off. "We can talk all we want about this small stuff, but it's a pimple on a gnat's ass. The real money is in entitlements. Medicare, Medicaid, Social Security. You all know it."

"There is no way on this earth I'm going to let you cut Social Security and Medicare." Wally banged his fist on the desk. "It's political suicide. Remember those ads the Democrats ran with Republicans pushing granny off a cliff in a wheelchair? That'll be you. Except this time, it'll be true."

"Strictly speaking, it's the international investors who won't lend the United States any money that are cutting Social Security and Medicare, not the president," Andrea said, rushing to President Murray's defense. "We can't make people lend the United States money, and we can't spend money we don't have."

"Strictly speaking, I'm sure the voters in Sheboygan won't give a shit about the international investors," Wally replied in a mocking tone. "They'll blame me, you, and every other member of this administration when Grandma doesn't get her insulin."

Just then, the phone on the desk buzzed. President Murray pressed the lighted button on the phone.

"There's a Treasury aide here to speak to you, sir."

"Send him in."

The thick door to the Oval Office opened. From behind it emerged an obviously terrified aide who couldn't have been more than thirty.

Bad news, thought Andrea. If this were good news, Brooks Powell would have brought it himself.

"What's the word from Treasury?" the president asked.

"Two things, sir. The major bond rating agencies have lowered the rating on American government bonds to junk. And the major industrialized nations—China, Britain, France, Japan, Germany— plan to dump the dollar as the reserve currency."

"English, son," said Wally. "What does that mean for us?"

"We won't be able to print money and inflate our way out of debt," Andrea said, doing her best to translate. "These countries know we've literally papered over our budget problems, printing trillions of dollars in new money backed by nothing but the full faith and credit of the United States. Which the bond rating agencies now consider junk. We'll have to pay astronomical interest rates to sell bonds."

"The United States is on the hook for forty trillion dollars, and someone else will decide the value of the dollars that will pay all that back," Murray added. The wrinkles between the president's eyebrows revealed just how stressed he felt.

The president turned to the aide. "Thanks, son. Appreciate it. Tell Brooks I say hi."

The aide nervously shuffled out of the Oval Office and closed the thick door behind him.

"Dammit, Earl, your presidency is on the line here," said Wally. "I told you not to bring in this neophyte who never spent a day in Washington." He spoke as if Andrea hadn't been standing there. "Even if we somehow manage to get this through Congress, you might as well forget reelection."

Andrea clenched her fists and heard her knuckles crack. She might not have had experience in Washington, but she had more than enough experience with ruinous debt.

"You're no better than the rest of the Debt Rebel Gang," Andrea fired back. "You can't think past the next election."

A tense silence filled the office. They'd all used up their respective arguments.

"Mr. President, are you going to make a decision?" asked Wally.

Finally, Murray revealed his thoughts. "All right, I've heard enough. You're both right. These cuts are political suicide. But we can't wave a magic wand, put money in the Treasury, and give it to the agencies to spend."

Wally sat down on the sofa. His plump cheeks were flushed and his bald head was red from arguing.

"Mr. President, we've been together in politics for twenty-five years. I knew you were going places the minute you gave your first speech on the floor of the House. I took a pay cut and demotion to come work for you. I've never regretted that decision. But you've just reached the pinnacle of American politics and you're about to annihilate your presidency."

Andrea seated herself on the couch across from Wally. He had his elbows on his knees and was leaning forward, resting his chin on his folded hands. President Murray sat next to Wally on the couch. Andrea looked at them and gave a last plea.

"Mr. President, you need to understand how serious this fiscal crisis is. If we don't implement this emergency budget now, we won't be able to borrow a dime and the government will come to a screeching halt. What do you think your reelection chances will look like if *that* happens? If you ask me, your only chance to get reelected is to pass the Nuke."

President Murray nodded forlornly. "I don't see any other way," he said. "Either we do the cuts on our terms or foreign bond-holders will do it on theirs. I know which I prefer."

Wally sank deeper into the couch, a Washington titan humbled by the accountant from the sticks. The titan was human after all, and he was finally awakening to the reality of the situation. Amid the gloom, Andrea felt a twinge of pride. She had achieved her first political victory.

The president was coming to grips with reality too. "I spent my whole political career planning, scheming, and plotting to become president," President Murray said. "Hell, every decision I've made since I was a freshman at Yale was meant to lay the groundwork for running for president. I finally make it, after all those bus rides and campaign stops, all those state fairs and fried food, and for what? I don't even have a chance to put my stamp on anything. I knew when I was in Congress the debt bomb would go off one day. I just never thought it would go off the minute I got into the big chair."

"Mr. President, the country handed you lemons," said Andrea. "Forty trillion lemons, in fact. But this can be your finest hour. You're being called on to solve the greatest financial crisis this country has had since the American Revolution. You have a chance to write your name in the history books."

Wally nodded, his face forming the slightest of smiles. The old political strategist was slowly coming to life. "How do you suggest we sell this shit sandwich of a budget to Congress?" he asked.

Andrea thought for a moment and then perked up. "An old accounting colleague of mine used to say, 'When all else fails, commit candor.'"

"What's that supposed to mean?" asked Wally.

"Just tell the country straight. These cuts are happening no matter what, so people might as well get the truth. The emergency budget is the only thing standing between the United States and full-on economic collapse. And I mean dumpster-diving, zoo-animal-eating, fleeing-to-Canada collapse."

"That makes sense. Though I'm not sure I'd put it quite like that," Murray said.

He stood up from the couch. Deciding on a course of action seemed to have energized him. His hangdog look was gone, replaced by purposeful pacing around the Oval Office. Now he was deep in thought, as if writing a speech in his mind.

Wally pulled out a notepad and paper and started scribbling notes.

"What are you thinking, Wally?" President Murray asked.

"It's all we've got," he replied. "Go for broke with the public. No pun intended."

"Okay. Wally, get some time on the networks for eight o'clock tonight and get a speech written. We need to get this emergency budget out there on our terms without creating mass economic panic."

"Yes, sir." Wally rushed out of the Oval Office to execute the president's instructions.

Andrea got up from the couch and headed to the door.

"Andrea?"

She turned to face the president.

"Yes, Mr. President?"

"Thank you. I needed that. So did Wally. We're going to get through this."

"No, thank you, Mr. President. You're the only one who can make this happen. It's us or bust."

CHAPTER 17

President Murray entered the Oval Office at seven o'clock, an hour before he was scheduled to speak. Cameramen from every major television and cable network were preparing their cameras and microphones in the Oval Office. The sun had just set, but its glow was still visible over the horizon through the windows.

He seated himself in the chair behind the Resolute desk. Andrea stood off to the side, taking in the magnificence of the Oval Office. The small bust of Winston Churchill sat on a table to the right of the fireplace. Above the bust was an oil painting of buffalo on the American frontier. Directly above the fireplace was the famous oil painting, *Washington Crossing the Delaware*. To the left of the fireplace was a painting of the War of 1812's epic Battle of Lake Erie. There was also an oil painting reproduction of the famous photograph of Buzz Aldrin on the moon and, beneath it, a small moon rock on loan from NASA.

The artwork and artifacts represented the pinnacle of American achievement, grit, and determination. Andrea's contribution to the long list of American achievements? Declaring national bankruptcy. She swore the artifacts were looking at her in disgust.

A makeup artist entered the room with his kit to prepare Murray for the speech.

Murray waved him away. "Lose it all. I'm not going to spend money on makeup and wardrobe when people are losing their

Social Security and health care. America is just going to have to get used to seeing me as I am."

The makeup artist glanced at the cameramen. One shrugged his shoulders. The makeup artist slowly left the room.

Andrea settled into a finely upholstered blue-and-gold chair in the adjoining television room as the on-site producer recited the countdown to the speech. When the producer said, "On the air," the somber-faced President Murray appeared on her television screen.

"My fellow Americans," Murray said in a somber tone. "For twenty years, this country has lived far beyond its means. Every year we borrow between five hundred billion dollars and one trillion dollars to meet our budgets. We borrow two million dollars every hour. In fact, it is hard to claim that the American government budgets anymore. The American government simply spends.

"We spend well over a trillion dollars a year on Medicare, Medicaid, and Social Security. We spend seven hundred and fifty billion dollars a year on defense and more on innumerable activities large and small. Disaster relief and recovery. Road and bridge construction grants. Education grants and loans. New federal buildings in the United States and abroad. School lunch programs. Foreign aid. Scientific and medical research. Rural internet programs. Urban housing programs. Grants to the arts. An ever-growing federal workforce. The government is so enormous, no single person could tell you everything it does.

"We've also spent enormous sums on investigations, impeachments, and all manner of other political circus stunts. They aren't free. Every time you see a congressional investigation, there are loads of lawyers, staff, and other expenses for which we are paying. Treating politics as sport and spectacle has costs.

"For too long, Congress has been unwilling to make any

spending cuts. We acted as if the American government had un-limited funds to do whatever it wanted. We blamed every problem on budget cuts or a lack of funding.

"In fact, the money was coming from you, the public. But not just the American public. The money was also coming from foreigners willing to loan the United States government money. Some of these lenders loaned us money because they thought the United States was a solid investment. Others loaned us money to gain leverage and power over the American government. Our political leaders on both sides didn't know or care where the money was coming from or why people were lending it to us. They were glad to have the money to spend it on whatever they wanted at the time. This cycle of borrow and spend has continued for over two decades. Our national debt currently stands at forty trillion dollars.

"My fellow Americans, the bill has come due. Those who once were happy to loan us money no longer are confident the United States can pay them back. Those who once loaned the United States government money by buying American bonds have made clear they will do so no longer.

"Without these borrowed funds, the United States can no longer engage in deficit spending. America can only spend what it takes in as tax revenues. Just as your family must make ends meet by paying your mortgage and credit card payments while paying your living expenses, so, too, must the United States government.

"This is not ideology. This is cold, hard mathematics."

Andrea was amazed by the president's demeanor. He seemed preternaturally calm. His arms were still. The wrinkles between his eyebrows were gone.

Only a pro could be this focused giving a speech this difficult and not reveal a hint of stress, she thought.

"Tomorrow I will send emergency budget legislation to

the Congress that will cut federal spending and ensure we will not have a deficit this year or in the coming years. The federal government has revenues of three-and-a-half trillion dollars. And that is exactly what we will spend. One trillion dollars will go to interest payments on federal debt. Another one-and-a-quarter trillion dollars will be used to begin to pay down debt principal. The rest will go to regular federal budget items.

"I have always prided myself on being straight and honest with you, my fellow Americans. Tonight is no exception.

"Federal spending in most major categories will be cut or frozen. We will immediately stop spending on federal grants and loans in all forms. This includes federal research grants and student loans. We will halt construction of federal facilities and all federally funded road and highway projects.

"We will substantially cut other government luxuries. We will not illuminate the Capitol, the White House, and the monuments in Washington at night. No more government-sponsored pageants and fireworks on the Fourth of July.

"Defense spending will be cut to the bare minimum. We will fund the military at an operational level. We will freeze development of new weapons systems. Even military flyovers of sporting events are out.

"We will furlough a substantial part of the federal workforce.

"Travel budgets will also be cut to the bare minimum. A single presidential trip overseas costs millions of dollars. Even foreign trips of other government officials and members of Congress cost enormous amounts of money. From now on, we will travel light. There is no reason we cannot stay in the airport Hilton instead of the downtown Ritz-Carlton.

"We will also significantly cut spending on immigrants entering the country illegally. The government has annually awarded multi-million-dollar contracts to companies to provide food, shelter, and basic necessities to immigrants who illegally cross our southern border. My heart breaks for them, but we simply do not have the cash to continue to pay for these expensive support contracts.

"Foreign aid will also be cut. As generous as America is, we have borrowed much of the aid money we have donated to other countries. The pledges of funds we have made after natural disasters all over the world have come from money borrowed from China, Japan, European countries, or the American public. In effect, the American government has served as the middleman for a transfer of aid payments to foreign countries.

"The government must also raise revenue quickly. Therefore, the emergency budget calls for an immediate tax increase to raise the highest tax rate to sixty percent for individuals making over five hundred thousand dollars, forty percent for individuals making between two hundred and fifty thousand and five hundred thousand dollars, and thirty percent for individuals making between one hundred thousand and two hundred and fifty thousand dollars."

The president hesitated. Andrea sat up in her chair and pressed the remote control to raise the volume on her television. It was a habit she'd picked up from her father. Whenever a ballgame announcer raised his voice to announce a "deep fly ball," Andrea would immediately reach for the volume dial and crank it up.

"Finally, we have no choice but to cut Medicare, Medicaid, and Social Security. Starting tomorrow, the government will drastically reduce Social Security checks. Medicare payments will be cut significantly as we restructure the program to cover only those who need it most.

"My fellow Americans, this is a crisis of our own making. For too long, politicians have used promises of a never-ending series of services and benefits to get elected and reelected, but no one ever told you where the money was coming from. Now, the money is gone.

"America has survived the toughest challenges. Civil war. World wars. The Great Depression. The Great Recession. September 11. Americans have always risen to the occasion, from defeating Nazis or Communism to conquering the world's deadliest diseases. We fight and win. This is just another challenge in our national journey.

"I choose to look at every new event as an opportunity. Getting our financial house in order will be painful. But it will be a truly priceless gift to our children and their children to bequeath to them a financially stable nation unburdened by debt. Together, we will overcome this crisis as we have overcome all others.

"Good night, God bless you, and may God continue to bless the United States of America."

The speech concluded, Andrea opened the door between her viewing room and the Oval Office a crack. President Murray looked out the window from the Oval Office onto the South Lawn and slumped in his chair, exhausted.

She had an ominous suspicion her roller-coaster ride was just beginning.

CHAPTER 18

Mason seethed at his table in the basement pub of the Capitol Hill Club as he and his Debt Rebel colleague, Congressman Quentin Stokely, watched President Murray give his speech on the big screen television. Acorn had advised him to let the president make the first move in dealing with the bond boycott and the budget crisis, but his natural instincts demanded that he be controlling the situation and driving events, not reacting to them.

"Who does Murray think he is, planning a budget without giving me so much as a courtesy call?" Mason grumbled.

"He *is* the president," Stokely replied.

"And *I'm* the chairman of the House Appropriations Committee," Mason roared. "The bastard doesn't even give me a heads-up before he foists this horrible budget on the nation? See this?" Mason pointed to the special congressional pin on his lapel. "This is my ring, and he's supposed to kiss it. If he thinks I'm just going to roll over and let him have his little emergency budget, he's got another thing coming."

Silently Mason recognized that this was his love of Russian strongmen talking. His American family had adopted him from Russia when he was only six, but he still remembered a little of Mother Russia. The harsh winters, his cold parents, and his tough older brother were some of his earliest memories, along with his family's hero worship of Lenin, Stalin, and Putin. Perhaps that was why although he was raised American, deep down he admired the most ruthless Russian leaders. The desire for absolute control. The totalitarian instinct. The consuming lust for power.

He had no love for Russia. It had abandoned him to America, wished him good luck, and dumped him in a place where good luck was in decidedly short supply. The midwestern American family that had adopted him lost their farm when the bank foreclosed. His adoptive mother had died in a factory accident a few years after the foreclosure. She was a farm girl at heart. She had no business being in a factory. She was inexperienced and poorly trained. That was what got her killed.

He remembered the family's struggles in the tiny apartment into which they'd been forced. No heat, cold water. Being teased at school for wearing hand-me-downs. His sister having to drop out of school and take care of the housework. He was keenly aware how no matter how bad the economy got for his family, politicians still wore their fancy suits and silk ties and enjoyed their lavish perks. He saw how businessmen kowtowed to them, hosting receptions in their honor and showering them with invitations to sporting events and glittering galas in the nation's capital. A thirst for power emerged along with an unquenchable determination to take advantage of the perks only afforded to the higher-ups.

People are going to toil on my behalf and beg for my favor, not the other way around.

"Murray has been screwing me since he joined the Debt Rebel Gang," Mason spat.

"He's a clever guy," Stokely replied. "He knows how to play the game. He didn't want you messing with his emergency budget. He wanted to present you a *fait accompli* and force you to swallow it whole."

"He'd better be ready because I'm about to flex my muscles."

Mason snatched his beer bottle and took a vicious swig. He squeezed the bottle, half wanting to break it.

Murray was better looking, more popular, and, most painfully, more powerful than Mason. Even at the height of his power, Mason always felt like an outsider. No one ever talked about him as presidential material despite his high rank. He was rarely the guest of honor at Washington's regular evening galas. And other power players graced the Sunday talk shows much more frequently. He was convinced others had an easier road than he did because of his humble background and his homely looks. And he was certain others were constantly plotting against him behind his back.

Mason's deep-seated anxieties formed the foundation of his decided ambivalence toward democracy. Another expression of his Russian heritage, perhaps. Americans loved to talk about their democracy, government by the people and for the people, but Mason knew better. Handsome, polished guys like Murray won popularity and acclaim, book deals and board memberships, while people viewed Mason as nothing more than a grubby climber of the greasy pole. He hated his Russian parents for giving him up, but more than once he thought he was more suited to Russian politics, where the people's opinions counted for far less.

Murray's speech and failure to even give advance warning of its contents ratified every one of Mason's conceptions about himself and his place in the political world. Mason's inner rage, like volcanic magma, bubbled to the surface.

This is my game. I dedicated my life to being the most powerful man in Washington. And here is Murray showing me up in front of the entire country. His family didn't get evicted. He wasn't forced to live in a tiny rodent-infested apartment. He's lived a gilded life while

I've scrapped and clawed for every bit of power I have. And now he's screwing me?

"How do you think the Gang should respond to this?" Stokely asked. "Murray is popular. He was inaugurated only one month ago. He's still in his honeymoon."

"I don't know yet," Mason replied. "But Frank Palmer and I are going to have a nice long talk tomorrow morning. I have not yet begun to fight. But I sure as hell will."

"Okay, John Paul Jones," Stokely wisecracked.

"Do you think this is some kind of joke?" Mason slammed his beer bottle on the table. "You think anyone would even know your name without the Debt Rebel Gang? Don't you forget who got you where you are. The Debt Rebel Gang made you. And I made the Debt Rebel Gang."

"Okay, take it easy, Lew," Stokely pleaded. "Don't be so paranoid. I'm on your team. Just let me know what you all decide to do."

"Believe me, I will," Mason seethed. "And you better damn well stand and salute when I do."

"Of course, Lew," Stokely reassured Mason. "You know you can count on me."

I count on no one. I trust no one. This emergency budget is going down, and I'm the one who's going to take it down.

"Let's get out of here," Mason said. "I have a couple long days ahead."

"I bet Murray does too," Stokely joked.

"You're goddamned right he does," Mason growled. "Just wait a moment. I need to send a text."

Mason pulled out his smartphone and typed a quick text to Frank Palmer. He needed Frank to get working on a response. Frank would know exactly how to respond to Murray. He was a pure political mercenary, one eye on helping his boss and one eye on his next job up the ladder. Frank would gladly do the dirty work for Mason today and against Mason tomorrow. Trust was purely transactional.

Mason pressed send and scowled at the smartphone momentarily. Then he and Stokely made their way up the staircase and out of the club.

CHAPTER 19

Acorn squeezed a foam stress ball as he sat at his desk awaiting Mason's arrival. Manipulating Mason always made him nervous. Would Mason ever figure out he was being led down the garden path by his top lieutenant? Acorn gripped the stress ball so tightly his knuckles were white.

For Operation Pripyat to succeed, he needed to kill the emergency budget. And if he wanted to kill President Murray's emergency budget, he had to get Mason into his raging irrational state. Because for the congressman, politics always came first. And when it came to politics, shivving his rivals and protecting his turf was his top priority.

The task before Acorn was clear: get Mason to forget about policy and focus instead on his political enemies. Make it about getting the upper hand on a rival. Then he'd dissolve into impulsive attacks, policy consequences be damned.

Mason had to be fuming. He had sent a short text after the president's speech—*That bastard. We are taking this emergency budget down*—and then gone silent.

Sure enough, at eight a.m., Mason roared into his office foyer in a fury, coffee cup in hand. Acorn kept the door to his office open in the morning just in case Mason wanted to talk when he arrived. But Mason rushed straight into his own office without saying anything and slammed the door.

Excellent. He's pissed off. He'll be pliable today.

Acorn put his ear to the wall that separated their offices and listened intently for any sounds coming through. He easily could hear Mason's purple rages through the cheap drywall. But today he heard nothing.

Then ... *boom!*

The wall exploded into a cloud of drywall dust and wood shards. Acorn shrieked, ducking and covering his head with his hand against the flying wall debris. Shattered drywall littered the floor.

A baseball rolled to a stop against the couch. Acorn could clearly see the signature on the ball's sweet spot: *Stephen Strasburg WS 2019 MVP.* Mason had thrown his prized 2019 Washington Nationals autographed baseball clear through the office wall.

Peering into Mason's office through the newly created hole, Acorn saw Mason pacing around, punching the air. "Jesus Christ, Lew, calm down! You could have killed me!"

"Get in here, Frank!" Mason shouted.

Acorn went over to Mason's office.

"I take it you're still steaming about the president's speech last night?" asked Acorn.

"What gave it away?"

"You came roaring in here like a bat out of hell and damn near killed me with a baseball that you threw through a fucking wall."

"Damn right I did. Goddamn Murray gives a speech like that without calling me first. I'm the chairman of the goddamn Appropriations Committee. The budget is my fucking sandbox! Who the hell does he think he is proposing this emergency budget without even calling me first?"

"Come on, Lew, you know perfectly well who was behind that speech."

Mason's eyes widened. Acorn had just lit the fuse on a bomb.

"Fucking Andrea Gartner! Fuck that fucking two-bit holier-than-thou schoolmarm. And fuck Murray for bringing her back from the dead!" Mason's red face clashed with his plain white shirt. The floor vibrated with every crash of his stomping feet. "I'm the goddamn chairman of the goddamn Appropriations Committee. I'm supposed to write the emergency budget, not Andrea fucking Gartner!" He slammed his fist on his desk, knocking the Legislator of the Year award he'd won two years ago from the Maryland Chamber of Commerce off the desk. It shattered into pieces on the floor.

"Lew, stop breaking shit and try to figure this out, okay?" Acorn needed Mason to focus if his plan was going to come to fruition.

"Did you hear what they put in that budget? Cutting Social Security? Medicare? The voters will kill us all."

Maybe so, but Acorn wasn't thinking about the voters killing Mason. That would be a nice bonus. No, he wanted a full-scale economic meltdown, and for that to happen, he needed the emergency budget to fail.

"Downsizing the government?" Mason shouted, the veins on the side of his head bulging. "I mean, what the fuck? I represent Maryland's DC suburbs! Half the people in my district are federal workers Murray wants to lay off. And the other half are federal contractors. And the other half are former government employees living on federal pensions! How am I going to face them and tell them the federal money spigot is off?"

"That's three halves, Lew."

"Oh, fuck off, Frank. You know what I mean."

"Well, weren't your voters hardcore Debt Rebels?" asked Acorn, continuing to egg Mason on. "They should be thrilled! Government spending is about to get a whole lot smaller."

Mason lowered his head, pulled off his glasses, narrowed his eyes, and looked directly at Acorn.

"Let me ask you something, Frank," he said in a low, con-spiratorial voice as he jabbed his finger at Acorn's chest for emphasis. "You ever wonder why the Debt Rebels stopped caring about the debt and carried water for President Roberts and his trillion-dollar deficits?"

"Not really, I hadn't. What are you getting at?"

"I'm getting at power, Frank. Some people just feel like political outsiders and glom onto the latest political rebellion movement, whatever it is. Yesterday it was about the national debt, tomorrow it'll be about something else."

Acorn opened his mouth, but Mason raised his finger as if to say, I'm not done. Acorn got the message and let Mason continue his soliloquy.

"Then along comes some politician who harnesses that rebellion, that anger. 'Follow me and we'll stick it to the insiders!' you tell them. You turn their anger into a virtue and others' willingness to build coalitions, make compromises, and achieve incremental successes into a vice. You tag your opponents with some pejorative name: 'Establishment,' 'RINO,' whatever. Now they're the villains. It's some serious jujitsu, and it's fucking magic. And the clever ones among them realize they can make money off the whole thing. Letters and histrionic emails to raise money against whoever is the Establishment quisling of the week. They may be supporting the cause, but they're making sure they get their cut. There's just one problem."

"What's that, Lew?"

"There's always going to be someone who comes along and gives a bigger and louder 'fuck you' to the Establishment. That guy steals all your oxygen. And then you realize you were never really driving the anti-Establishment bus. The people were driving. You just got in the front seat and steered for a while."

"Then what?" asked Acorn.

Mason narrowed his eyes again. Acorn recognized his cockeyed grin, with the left side of his mouth curled up, almost smirking. Mason was about to let him in on a secret.

"Then you've got two choices: you can become one of that guy's lieutenants and keep riding the tide or you can quit the whole business. You want to know why my Debt Rebel Gang dumped debt reduction and didn't say shit about Roberts's trillion-dollar deficits? Why the right-wing cable TV and talk radio guys fell in line? *That's* why. They realized they weren't driving the bus and quickly figured out how to at least stay in the front seats. They knew damned well what they had to do to keep their careers and their gravy train rolling."

"I don't know, Lew. That's a pretty cynical view of things. A lot of Debt Rebels really are worried about the debt."

Mason finally lost it.

"Jesus, Frank, have you been listening to a fucking thing I've been saying?" He pounded his fist into the desk. This is why I'm the congressman and you're the staffer. Isn't it obvious by now that my constituents don't give a damn about the debt? They dumped the fiscal responsibility shit the minute they found someone giving a bigger finger to the Establishment. So I stopped talking about the debt. And they kept reelecting me! So stop throwing the the damned Debt Rebellion in my face, dammit!

Mason had revved himself into a frothing, raging, irrational volcano.

Time to strike, Acorn thought.

"You need to kill the emergency budget, Lew."

"You're goddamned right I do."

Easy as pie. The selfish son of a bitch didn't even stop to think about the consequences for the country if the emergency budget doesn't pass. All he cares about is his political career. He's so damn shortsighted he doesn't even realize that if the emergency budget dies and the country collapses, he'll be out of a job too.

Acorn's parents were right. Politicians were capitalists on steroids. The capitalist would sell the Communist the rope to hang him; the American politician would vote to save his career even if it meant destroying the country.

"Hold a public Appropriations Committee hearing," said Acorn, rolling out his strategy. "Call Andrea Gartner up here and make her defend this budget. She won't be able to. You'll kick her ass and this emergency budget will never see the light of day."

"Yeah, let's haul her up here and make her tell America she's cutting their Social Security," Mason agreed as he rubbed his hands together spitefully. "Let her tell her Secret Service protection they're about to be laid off. Call the press. Tell the rest of the committee. We're having a hearing tomorrow."

"Yes, sir," said Acorn. His plan was working, and he'd barely had to lift a finger. It was almost too easy. He pictured himself in the new American government, the Communist government that would take power after the final collapse of American capitalism.

"Oh, and one other thing." Mason wasn't done.

"What's that?"

"Make sure the place is filled with angry voters. I want the Capitol surrounded by pissed off protesters."

"Gotcha. How about I set it for two? Give our protesters the whole morning to assemble."

"Good idea. I want that damned Andrea Gartner fearing for her fucking life."

Acorn smiled.

If Mason only knew.

CHAPTER 20

The morning of the hearing with the House Appropriations Committee, Andrea felt as though she was preparing for her own funeral. She had spent nearly an hour with Rachel practicing her testimony. When Rachel left to take a call, Andrea sighed to herself. She knew as soon as she repeated the president's insistence on cutting the budget, committee members were going to grandstand and either blame her for the cuts or pretend it was their idea.

Rachel rushed back into the office.

"I just got off the phone with the Secret Service. You need to look at this." She quickly typed something on her computer, then moved the screen so Andrea could see it.

"Take a look at my Facebook news feed," Rachel said. "It's saturated with ads from a million different groups all out to sink our emergency budget proposal."

One ad showed empty medicine jars and shriveled IV bags attached to people slowly dying in their beds and elderly nursing home residents being rolled out in their wheelchairs, unable to pay for their care and dying in the parking lot. Another featured a doctor yanking the IV out of a patient's arm and watching her slowly die.

"How long have these ads been running?" Andrea asked.

"The Secret Service says they've been running since yesterday. They've been viewed by at least a half-million people."

Andrea swallowed hard. "Who put these ads out?"

"The first ad is from a group called the 'Committee to Save

Medicare.' Some group called the 'Save Social Security Committee' did the ad with the IV."

"Who the hell are these people?" Andrea's eyes were wide.

"I have no clue," said Rachel. "And I've been in the political game for a long time."

"These groups sound phony," Andrea said. "Someone has to be behind them. Can we figure it out?"

"Not quickly," Rachel replied. "If there's one thing I've learned in all my years in politics, if you want to hide the tracks of your influence schemes, just put together a front group, give it a high-minded name, and set it loose. It'll take months to figure out who's really bankrolling the whole thing."

"We don't have months," Andrea said.

"These ads will go over great in the DC metro area." Rachel pointed at the screen. The first ad featured frozen defense production lines, empty seats, and silent IT systems in government buildings that couldn't even pay their electric bills. Beneath it was a video of agents boarding up federal offices and posting "For Sale at Auction" signs on their front doors. The second ad featured tumbleweeds blowing past the vacant, padlocked offices of Northrop Grumman, Boeing, and Lockheed Martin, America's largest defense contractors.

"Jesus, these ads have inundated your news feed," Andrea said. "Every other post is sponsored content trashing the emergency budget."

"I've never seen anything like it," Rachel said. "This has to be a coordinated effort."

Andrea got up and paced around the office, eyeing all the awards Rachel had received in her time in politics. Woman of the Year from the local Special Olympics for protecting their budget. A special commendation from the local food bank for securing an earmark they used to purchase a new warehouse.

"You like my awards?" asked Rachel.

"It's an impressive collection," Andrea said.

"Oh, please, sweetie," said Rachel. "It's all bullshit. These people gave me these awards for helping them get government money for whatever it was they wanted. You think these people really thought I was the top staffer on the Hill? Please."

It looked impressive all the same. Andrea had never won so much as a raffle at her local Rotary club.

"You were saying," Andrea said, returning to the original topic. "You wanted to go over the plan for today?"

"The Secret Service said these ads have been running all night on social media," Rachel replied. "People are riled up. They're expecting over ten thousand protesters to be on the Hill when we go up to testify. They're worried about your safety and want to send an agent with us."

"It's bad enough I have to go on national television to explain to Congress and three hundred million Americans why their Social Security and Medicare benefits are about to disappear. And one million federal workers are about to be laid off. You're saying my life is in danger?"

"Ah, don't worry," responded Rachel with a knowing smile. "Same thing happened to my old boss. You're not a real politico until you've pissed off enough people that they take a vacation day to come spew venom at you. Welcome to the club, sweetie." Rachel glanced at her watch. "Looks like it's about time to go up to the hearing. You ready?"

"I think," Andrea said, but she would have leaped at any excuse to postpone the hearing. *I'm not cut out for public debate. The committee is going to eat me alive, the same way the Debt Rebel Gang did. And it's all going to be on national television. They're going to expose me to the world for the weakling I am.*

"You'll be fine." Rachel offered an encouraging smile.

"I suppose. But my stomach's a mess. I feel like I chased some Taco Bell with spoiled milk."

Rachel was famous for finding humor in any situation. "When you get scared just try to imagine Mason in his underwear."

Andrea chuckled at the way Rachel said "underwear" in her sweet southern drawl. "Geez, thanks for that," Andrea said. "Just because my husband is a psychologist doesn't mean I get therapy for free."

They walked out of the EEOB to the parking spaces along West Executive Avenue. Rachel pointed toward a large, thick man in a dark business suit with a star-shaped lapel pin and sunglasses approaching them from the south end of West Executive Avenue.

"Here comes Jimmy now," said Rachel.

"I take it Jimmy's the Secret Service agent they're sending? I see the little cord in his ear."

Jimmy joined Andrea and Rachel on the sidewalk.

"Ms. Gartner, Ms. Samuels, I'm Agent Humphrey. You can call me Jimmy. I'll be protecting you today."

"Thanks, Jimmy. Definitely feel better having you along. My car is over there." Andrea pointed to her battered Toyota Camry.

"Jesus, Andrea, is that your car?" Rachel asked.

"Damn right it is. Just because the country can't manage a budget doesn't mean I can't."

"So we're taking this relic up to the Hill?" Rachel said.

"I'm not going up there in a motorcade. We're about to cut the medical benefits and Social Security benefits of millions of people and fire a million government employees. You think I'm going to take a limo up to the Hill? I may not be a politician, but even I'm not that tone deaf. Hop in."

Andrea got behind the wheel. Jimmy took the passenger seat, and Rachel sat in the back.

As they made their way up Independence Avenue to the

House side of the Capitol, Andrea could see a crowd blocking the street between the Capitol and the House office buildings in the distance. The shouting and chanting and drumming got louder as they approached.

By the time they reached the foot of Capitol Hill, Andrea realized the Capitol complex was swarming with angry protesters. It had to be at least double or triple the predicted ten thousand protesters. She could hear the cacophony of the protesters' chants and shouts over the car's engine. Jimmy's head swiveled like a turret, clearly assessing the situation.

Andrea saw signs that called for her and President Murray to be hanged, shot, starved, denied food and medicine, and worse. Other signs read "Down with the Emergency Budget" and "Fire Andrea Gartner." Twenty-four hours ago, no one even knew any of this was happening. The signs were too professional and there were too many of them. Something was up. The social media blitz. The preprinted signs. The Pripyat Consortium. It couldn't be happenstance. Someone had to be orchestrating this whole show.

But she couldn't focus on that now. Protesters were banging at her car. They were nearly surrounded when Jimmy grabbed the steering wheel, shoved Andrea into the back seat, and jumped into the driver's seat. He quickly shifted the car into reverse and pulled out of the crowd.

"Put your heads down!" Jimmy shouted.

Andrea and Rachel wasted no time complying. Cracks and pops that sounded like gunfire filled the air. Clouds of tear gas enveloped the car. Thumps against the side of the car echoed through the passenger compartment.

"Rubber bullets," said Jimmy. "It's the Capitol Police. Don't worry."

"Yeah, why would anyone be worried about flying rubber bullets?" Rachel muttered with her head buried on the floor.

Jimmy pulled the car out of the frothing mob, sped toward the waterfront on Maine Avenue, and pulled into a hidden underground tunnel.

"A secret entrance to the Capitol complex," Jimmy said. "Don't tell anyone."

"Your secret is safe with me," Andrea said.

"Of course, it is. We're flat on the floor and can't see a damned thing," replied Rachel.

A quiet came over the car as it entered a dark tunnel. It provided a respite from the braying mob. Soon the car came to a stop and Jimmy helped Andrea and Rachel out.

"The Capitol's secret underground garage," said Jimmy. "There's a special elevator we can use to get to the hearing room without facing any more crowds."

"You okay, sweetie?" Rachel asked.

"I'm a little shaken," Andrea said. "I wasn't expecting that."

"The mob can heckle all it wants, but it doesn't matter." Rachel put her arm around Andrea. "You've got mathematics on your side."

"And the math always wins," Andrea said. "Cold, remorseless, unrelenting math."

"Exactly," said Rachel. "Get in there and let those bastards know that if they don't pass your budget, they'll find out just how remorseless and unrelenting the math will be."

CHAPTER 21

S itting at the witness table in the hearing room, finally free
of the angry mob demanding her hide, Andrea felt a sense
of déjà vu punch her in the gut.

It was the same room where she'd met the Debt Rebel Gang
over a year ago. How much had happened in the year since! Her
congressional campaign ending in failure. Her campaign work
for Murray and his surprise election. Her improbable, nearly
unfathomable rise to OMB director. And now the potentially
catastrophic bond boycott.

Yet here she was, sitting in the very same chair at the very same
table she'd sat at when she first met Mason and his Debt Rebel
Gang. This time Rachel, now her deputy, sat behind her.

The members of the Appropriations Committee had already
taken their seats on the dais. Mason, the chairman, was in the
middle, with Frank Palmer behind him and Congressman Stokely
to his right.

Andrea sank further into her chair, shaken by the outside protesters and cowed by the angry gaze of the audience. She surveyed
the members of the committee. Her Debt Rebel Gang nemeses
were arrayed before her. There were Democrats, too, looking ready
to tear her apart for her proposed spending cuts. Her nervousness
began to give way to anger at the sight of the men responsible for
bringing her into this harrowing scene.

Mason banged the gavel to start the hearing.

"Members of the committee, we're here to deal with what the
administration is claiming is an American debt crisis. President

Murray now says, all of a sudden, a month into his presidency, he has to slash the budget. He's killing defense, he's violating our promises not to touch Social Security and Medicare, and he's firing our public servants. He is destroying the American economy and national security over a crisis he manufactured. Director Gartner, you had better explain why you are doing this without so much as giving this committee a courtesy call."

Andrea took a sip of water from the custom-made, private label "United States Congress" bottle. It annoyed her as much today as it had over a year ago. She thought back to Rachel's pep talk after that miserable encounter. About how someone needed to bang a gong about the debt. But this time, the gallery was full and the klieg lights were blazing down on her.

"Mr. Chairman, as you know, I may be the OMB director now, but more than a year ago I sat before your Debt Rebel Gang pleading for your support. I sat at this very table and told you we faced a debt crisis. Unfortunately, the debt crisis I warned you about is here. Investors won't buy our bonds. We can't borrow money. We have to cut the budget whether we like it or not. In fact, we—"

"You are going to kill seniors, hollow out the military, and ruin the economy with your thoughtless, blunderbuss cuts," Mason roared. "This so-called 'emergency budget' is heartless and cruel. If anyone had listened to me and my colleagues, we would have solved the debt problem a long time ago."

Rachel's hand gently landed on Andrea's shoulder and she whispered something in her ear, but whatever Rachel said barely registered. Andrea loved Rachel, but people like her just didn't understand. Rachel had gotten to be part of the game, tasted the power, enjoyed the spoils. People like Andrea weren't like Mason or even Rachel. They were the little people, the people who played by the rules. Nothing pained Andrea more than to live in the shadow of power, to be in Washington but not *of* Washington.

Except, perhaps, when one of these Washington power brokers looked her in the eye and treated her like a rube. Mason had just made that mistake.

"Now, Congressman," Andrea said, curling her mouth in a slight smirk. "Don't insult my intelligence. Over a year ago, I sat in this very room and told you we had a debt problem and demanded you end our trillion-dollar deficits. You told me to get lost because I was 'the Establishment.'"

"I have no idea what you are talking about," said Mason.

"Then you are a liar in addition to a Debt Rebel fraud," Andrea spat in disgust.

"How dare you," Mason bellowed. "I'm of a mind to hold you in contempt."

"That would make it a two-way street, Congressman." Andrea was feeling her oats. "I told you the day of reckoning would come, and I promised to point the bony finger of blame at you. Well, here we are and here it is." She glowered and pointed at Mason. "Just be thankful the finger I'm pointing is my index finger and not a different finger."

Murmurs from the audience filled the room. Andrea felt the gratification of revenge as she confronted the committee with its members' own words. She'd seized the scepter of control from Mason's grasp and was beating him with it.

"For once, I agree with my Republican colleagues," Democrat Congressman Brad Powers said. "Your budget will kill the elderly and destroy the social safety net."

"You should have thought of that when you spent trillions on infrastructure, expanded Medicaid, and gave away money for all sorts of green energy schemes," Andrea replied firmly. "You

Democrats have been no better than the Debt Rebels. Do you even know what money is? Money doesn't just exist. The government and corporations and rich people aren't bottomless pits of cash for your ideological hobbyhorses. There's a limit to everything. You can hit the wall gently or drive into it at one hundred miles an hour. Whatever you do, the wall is there, and it's not going to move."

Frank Palmer, seated behind Mason, leaned over his shoulder and passed a note to him. Mason nodded and resumed his questioning.

"How come you had no warning that bond buyers might stop buying American bonds?" Mason asked. "It's your job to know the market-borrowing conditions."

Andrea couldn't believe what she was hearing. "How was anyone in the administration supposed to know the precise limit of the world's tolerance for endless American borrowing? We're not mind readers, Congressman."

"President Murray is at the controls," Congressman Stokely interrupted, as if trying to run interference for the clearly flummoxed Mason. "This is happening on his watch."

"With all due respect, Congressman, he's been in office for a month," Andrea said, going in for the kill. "Look around you. Oil paintings. Custom water bottles with the logo of the United States Congress. Flat-panel television screens. Why are we buying all this stuff? There must be at least thirty staff members seated behind you. Why do you all need so many staff?"

The audience tittered, aghast. Andrea gathered herself, took a breath, and continued. "But Congressman Mason, you're correct. President Murray is at the controls. That's why we're going to pass our emergency budget to cut the deficit and reduce the debt. If you don't like it, I'm sorry. But you have only two options: pass this emergency budget or default on the debt."

Mason glanced around at the other members of the committee, as if hoping for a lifeline. His palpable frustration fed Andrea's confidence. She had the committee on its heels.

"If we pass this heartless emergency budget, people are going to die," said Mason.

"You think I don't know that?" Andrea shouted. "I know I'm taking away peoples' jobs and health care. Every night I can feel the ulcer developing in my stomach. But we don't have the money to pay for all the benefits we promised people. There's nothing I can do about that. Either you do it my way or you figure out some other way to spend money we don't have and no one will lend to us."

"If we don't pass your budget, Ms. Gartner, you'll have to come up with something else," Congressman Stokely said.

"No, if you don't pass our budget, *you* will have to come up with something else or we default," Andrea said, now in full command of the room. "If you don't pass my emergency budget, you can come up with your own balanced budget, just like you said you always wanted to. Revenue bills are supposed to start in the House under the Constitution, and I know you are the truest constitutional conservatives in America."

Suppressed guffaws rose from the audience at Andrea's sarcastic jibe.

Mason and the rest of the committee looked dumbfounded.

"Any more questions? Because I have work to do." Andrea shoved the microphone away with authority.

Mason shot a look of confusion to Frank Palmer, who shrugged his shoulders. Mason scratched his head and then turned back to his microphone. "Unless anyone objects, this hearing is adjourned."

No one objected. The committee members sat in stunned silence.

Andrea shoved herself away from the table and strutted out of the room, daring the gallery to touch her.

Jimmy and Rachel hurried behind her as they left the hearing room. The people in the gallery had come ready to destroy Andrea but were left looking at one another in silent bewilderment as she departed.

CHAPTER 22

I t seemed that everyone on the Hill had been watching the hearing. Mason had tried to kill the emergency budget, but after Andrea kicked his ass publicly, no one was listening to him. One day after the hearing, the emergency budget passed by huge margins, and an hour later it was on President Murray's desk to sign into law.

Default averted. Mission accomplished.

But it only took a day for the bushels of angry correspondence to arrive at OMB after the emergency budget's passage. Not long after, Andrea stopped reading opinion polls about how Americans felt about the emergency budget. Their letters were telling her directly.

One of the messages in the first batch had been comprised entirely of letters cut from magazines, serial killer-style, that read, "Your budget is killing us, but there are millions of us and only one of you." After reading it, Andrea asked Rachel to screen the incoming mail. Even without death threats, the letters told a frightening tale.

My son doesn't have his school lunch anymore.

I lost my job and my house because of your budget.

I'm eighty years old and can't even buy groceries without my Social Security check.

Your budget took away my mother's cancer drugs. You killed her.

This morning—a full month after the emergency budget went into effect and two months after her hearing with the House Appropriations Committee—was no different. Andrea's shoulders slumped when she entered her office and saw the latest pile of mail on her desk. She shoved it off her desk, put her elbows on the table, and rested her head in her hands.

Just then Andrea's personal cell phone rang. A photo of Andrea's mother appeared on the phone's display.

"Andrea?" said the voice on the other end.

"Mamie, is that you?" Andrea asked. As a toddler, Andrea couldn't pronounce "mommy"; it came out "Mamie" and the name stuck.

"Honey, they're kicking me out of the assisted living home," Mamie said. "They said all the Medicare patients have to leave."

Andrea raised her arms up to the sky as if to say, *Lord, what more do you plan to do to me?*

"They're kicking you out now?" Andrea asked. "Not even giving you a week to move out?"

"No," Mamie said. "They're moving someone into my apartment today."

Andrea looked out the window at the Oval Office. She wondered if the president was there. Maybe she could put him on the phone with the assisted living center's management. Scare them into keeping her mother for at least a little longer. As tempting as it was, she knew it was ridiculous.

"Okay, Mamie, stay there," Andrea said. "I'm coming to get you."

Andrea told Rachel where she was going, ran out of the office, hopped into her Camry, and sped across the Potomac to the assisted living facility off Interstate 95. Traffic was so light Andrea got there in twenty minutes.

When she arrived at the front driveway of the facility, a dystopian cross between a garage sale and a college dormitory move-in day greeted her. Furniture dotted the sidewalks. Armoires, chairs, and televisions were haphazardly strewn about. Suitcases were everywhere.

Scattered about this jumble of possessions were elderly residents, or perhaps now former residents, of the facility. Some sat in wheelchairs covered in blankets. Others on crutches leaned against the columns holding up the driveway cover. A few stood on their own, hunched over or holding one another up. Some were crying, others stared straight ahead with a faraway, bewildered look. It was as if a natural disaster had blown through the building and left everyone homeless.

Orderlies in white uniforms escorted residents out of the building in a miserable parade. An orderly would push an elderly person out of the building in a wheelchair, turn around, go back in, and push another poor soul out.

In the chaos, Andrea found her mother at the end of the driveway, surrounded by her furniture, her clothes—all her worldly possessions dumped right there by the side of the drive-way. The dining room table Andrea used to play hide-and-seek under. The ottoman where her parents hid the Passover Seder *afikomen* every year. The battered black leather rocking chair littered with strips of tape covering forty years of upholstery tears.

"Good lord, Mamie, what happened? Did they just throw you out?"

"Someone from the staff knocked at my door and said I'd have to leave if I wasn't going to pay out of my own pocket for my room," said Mamie. "I told them Medicare was paying the rent. As soon as they heard that, they brought some other old lady in. She looked out the window, said she liked the room and the view, and said she would take it. Next thing I knew two giant men were moving my stuff out and her stuff in."

"They threw you out because of the Medicare cuts?" Andrea asked.

Mamie looked confused, as if she didn't fully understand why this was happening. "The home said people who can pay their way out of pocket are like gold now. Nursing homes are fighting over them. The lady who took my room was paying completely out of pocket. The home said they couldn't afford to lose her. So out I went."

"Is this all your stuff?" Andrea asked.

"No, there's more upstairs," Mamie replied.

"Okay, Mamie, you stay here while I go up and get it."

Andrea charged into the building. Going up to get her mother's remaining things was just an excuse. She wanted to talk to the management. In the chaos of the lobby she saw a man in a sports coat and tie doing his best to direct the hordes of orderlies, nurses, movers, residents, and family members moving people out of the building.

"Excuse me, are you Mr. Ingram? The general manager?"

"I am, but I'm a little busy right now in case you can't see." Mr. Ingram didn't even look at Andrea.

"I'm Andrea Gartner," Andrea said. "You're evicting my mother."

Mr. Ingram stopped and looked Andrea up and down. "*The* Andrea Gartner?"

"Yes, that's me."

"Come here, I want to show you something." He gestured toward the window in the home's library. "You see this yard sale out here?" He pointed to the piles of household items strewn along the driveway with their hapless elderly owners standing around them in despair. "You created all of this with a stroke of your pen, Ms. Gartner. This is all your doing."

"I'm not going to get into a debate with you," Andrea said,

trying to resist taking the bait. "I'm here to get my mother, and you have no business throwing her out without so much as a day's advance notice."

Mr. Ingram laughed. "You're going to lecture me on what *I* need to do? Look at that woman by the curb holding the IV. She's got pulmonary disease. Next to her, Mr. Hays? He has Parkinson's. And that man next to your mother? Mr. McNally? Alzheimer's. When you cut Medicare, you cut off their ability to pay for medication, physician care, and their rent here." He jabbed his stubby finger at her. "All three of them will almost certainly die within the next two months. And those are just the first three I see. We're kicking out people with diabetes, heart disease, and cancer who will be dead in three months. Some of them have no family to take care of them."

Andrea put her hand to her forehead, aghast at her handiwork. She knew the emergency budget was the right thing to do, but to confront it with her own eyes shook her resolve. Until now, the consequences of the emergency budget were all abstract, statistics in a spreadsheet. For the first time, the individual consequences of the emergency budget lay before her.

The reality of what she had done had become inescapable: she had signed the death warrant for these poor souls. People were going to *die* because of her work. Years of budget indiscipline might have brought the country to this point, but it was she who had wielded the knife.

Feeling dizzy and faint, she reached for a chair to balance herself. Was she any better than the horrible monsters of history who'd killed millions? Mao's famines? Stalin's purges? She was condemning tens, maybe hundreds of thousands or even millions to death or lives of abject penury. And arrayed before her was exactly what these condemned millions looked like.

"Where are these folks going?" Andrea asked.

"Do you give a damn?" Mr. Ingram snapped.

"I wouldn't have asked if I didn't."

"We're sending the ones without family to a Red Cross shelter set up at Sudbrook Middle School."

"That abandoned school a few blocks from the subway?"

"The very one."

"No one has used that building for twenty years," Andrea said. "It's falling apart. I drove past it a few weeks ago. There's a tree growing through the left side of the building where part of the roof collapsed."

"That's not the half of it," Mr. Ingram said. "The Red Cross had to clean mold and rat feces from the gym. They couldn't get all the mold off the ceiling, but with time running out, the health department decided to let the Red Cross set up anyway."

"What about that guy?" Andrea pointed to a man in a military shirt and cap with a chest full of medals.

"That's Colonel Hurst," Mr. Ingram said. "Fought in Vietnam and Desert Storm. Wounded three times. He's got dementia."

"You could send him to the VA hospital downtown," Andrea said.

"Fat chance he'll get in," Mr. Ingram huffed. "Half its staff has been laid off. They've got a list of veterans a mile long waiting for months for their appointments, and they told me they had to cancel most of them because their doctors or specialists had been laid off. They said they can't even provide Colonel Hurst his medicines if he can't pay out of pocket."

"Does he have family?"

"No," said Mr. Ingram. "Thanks to you he might just curl up in the parking lot and die."

Andrea searched in vain for words, unable to find a comeback. "I'm going to get my mother's things," she said.

Andrea went up to her mother's apartment on the sixth floor. A tall woman in a white dress was visible through the open door. She was issuing commands to movers swirling about her, arranging furniture in the apartment. Three Louis Vuitton suitcases sat in the living room. The woman didn't seem to need assisted living services as she barked orders; it was the movers who seemed exhausted and barely able to stand.

The woman noticed her. "Are these bags yours?" She pointed to two large garbage bags on the kitchen counter.

"Those must be my mother's," Andrea replied.

"I'm sorry she has to leave," the woman said unconvincingly. "I'd been waiting nine months for a place to open up here. They told me I had to take it or they'd find someone else. Apparently, there are a lot of people willing to pay the full price without Medicare to live here."

"You could have said 'no', you know," Andrea said.

"They weren't going to let your mother stay no matter what. If it wasn't me, it would have been someone else."

Andrea was in no mood to talk and grabbed the two garbage bags. "I'll just take these and be on my way. Enjoy the apartment."

"I know I—"

Andrea let the door slam shut without waiting for the woman to finish her sentence. She made her way to the curb to meet her mother. The moving company the home had arranged had arrived and was loading Mamie's things into the moving van.

"Mamie, I got the rest of your stuff," she said. "Let the movers finish loading the truck. They can follow us home."

"I'm going to miss it here," Mamie said, her head hanging. "I was just getting comfortable and getting to know people. This was all I had."

"That's not true, Mamie," she said. "You still have your family."

Andrea helped her mother out of her wheelchair and into

the car. As she walked over to the driver's seat, she glanced one last time at the assisted living home. Confused elderly patients wandered the sidewalk aimlessly, tripping over the vases and furniture and suitcases at their feet, unaware the author of their misfortune was only a few yards away.

Andrea sped off, unable to look in her rearview mirror the entire way home.

CHAPTER 23

Acorn trembled as he descended the stairs to the cave. The narrow staircase was silent except for the metronomic dripping of condensation from two sharp points in the ceiling. The sinister *drip-drip-drip* felt like the ticking of a doomsday clock in an old war movie. Acorn could barely see in the darkness, broken only by a series of dim bulbs on the walls of the staircase.

The Ministry had given him twenty-two years, practically an eternity in the spy world, to burrow deeply into the United States government. And when the time came to finally cash in that twenty-two-year investment and engineer the overthrow of the American government, Operation Pripyat was failing. People were losing jobs and homes and yet somehow Americans weren't in the streets demanding revolution. Between families pooling resources, families simply learning to do without, and charities and philanthropists trying to fill the gaps, Americans were weathering the worst of the crisis.

It was a disaster for a spy agency as precise and as fastidious as the Ministry.

Acorn was certain Xu Li would be infuriated. He thought back to those times his father came home shell-shocked and his mother's stern warning: "One must never cross Madame Xu." But Acorn had done worse than cross Madame Xu. He had failed her.

A rustle of leaves came from behind him. Acorn fitfully turned his head to see if someone was following him into the cave but saw no one. All he heard was the dripping of the condensation and his own breathing, growing heavier with every step.

The cave was in its usual condition: spare and neat. Just the chair and the video screen and the small control panel on the wall to the right of the screen. The brown walls were damp from condensation, and the floor was swept clean of dust and debris. The single chair was perfectly positioned in its usual spot in front of the screen.

Someone had to be maintaining the cave, which meant someone else knew about it. He stopped and looked around again to see if anyone had followed him inside. Still nothing.

The red button on the control panel to the right of the screen was blinking slowly. Acorn had never seen it blinking before, and its slow blinking terrified him. It reminded him of the HAL 9000 computer's red light in *2001: A Space Odyssey*. It exuded coldness and purpose. It exuded Xu Li.

Acorn tiptoed toward the red button, terrified of what might happen when he pushed it. Would it release a message? Would it open a video communication? Would it blow up the cave?

He could barely control his trembling hand. He was on the verge of a full-body spasm, as if adrenaline had replaced the blood in his veins. Had the cave been larger, he would have run around it to burn off the terrified energy engulfing him. But the cramped cave offered little space, so he positioned his right hand in front of the red button and steadied it with his left hand. Then he closed his eyes, counted to three, and pushed the button.

The projector bolted to the ceiling of the cave whirred to life. Acorn opened his eyes and saw the image of the same spartan room from which Xu Li had given him his last instructions projected on the screen. The Ministry must want to speak to him. Acorn closed his eyes and exhaled deeply. He was still alive.

Acorn walked over to the wooden chair in the middle of the

cave, but it looked uncomfortable, so he stood in front of it. Within two minutes Xu Li walked into the camera's field of view and appeared on the screen. Acorn's hands shook again. He rubbed his temples and realized they were moist with sweat.

Xu Li looked no different than usual. Clad in her light blue Mao jacket, standing straight, expressionless, she remained the consummate inscrutable Communist apparatchik. Acorn had no idea if he was about to receive new instructions or die.

"How is the American government surviving our debt crisis?" Xu Li said. No greeting. No introductory banter. All business.

"Americans are somehow getting by and making due," said Acorn meekly, knowing he was admitting his understanding of the American public, which he'd provided the Ministry, was wrong. He braced himself for Xu Li's reaction.

"We anticipated that." Xu Li scowled. "You were supposed to make sure the emergency budget did not pass."

Thank goodness she can only see my face and torso, he thought. He could barely control the shaking in his right foot.

"Tell me, Acorn, how was the emergency budget able to pass?"

"Earl Murray and Andrea Gartner. They convinced Congress the country's economy would collapse and the potential for revolution would be real if the emergency budget didn't pass."

"Andrea Gartner is a mouse. Earl Murray is a weakling. Together they overcame your efforts with the senators and congressmen?"

"Everything I told them about what would happen from the Social Security and Medicare cuts happened. People *did* lose their medications. People *did* get evicted from their homes. People *have* died left and right. Hundreds of thousands."

"If this is true, why is it not bringing about a revolution?"

"I guess it's the American mindset. They dig in and survive."

Xu Li leaned directly into camera with a dark look. "You

allowed this operation to proceed knowing of the possibility Americans might not react as we expected?"

In a panic, Acorn looked over his shoulder toward the entrance to the cave, unable to shake the thought that someone was approaching him from behind. He knew how the Ministry worked. But no one was there.

"The American public is unpredictable. The American Congress more so."

Xu Li backed her head away from the camera. Acorn sensed she'd heard enough from him.

"Very well, Acorn. We will try again. Return home. You will receive further instructions."

"Yes, Madame Xu."

The screen went blank.

Acorn wiped the dripping sweat from his forehead. He peered at his hands to see how much sweat he'd wiped away and saw they were shaking badly. He looked around the cave. No flashing lights. No self-destruct countdown. He nervously looked up and down his body. No red dot from a laser sight.

Come on, you've been watching too many spy movies.

The brown rock of the cave walls was covered in its typical condensation.

Never stay in one place too long. It makes you easy pickings.

Acorn rushed out of the cave, still terrified the Ministry might initiate some self-destruct sequence.

As he emerged from the cave into the night, he spun his head back and forth, looking for any sign someone might be watching him. His breathing was getting heavier. He tried to control it by using a breathing exercise the Ministry taught him, frightened his terrified heaving might reveal his presence.

About fifty feet from his car, Acorn heard a rustle of leaves.

An animal? A bird?

He stopped and listened closely.

Nothing.

He resumed walking to the car and was about thirty feet away when he heard what sounded like a human whistle. His body shook as he turned his head frantically in every direction.

Then he saw it, a light directly in front of him and across the road where he had parked his car. It wasn't natural light, that much he knew. It was yellow, perhaps the glow of a sodium lamp or a flashlight. Acorn squinted and peered into the darkness.

The light flashed three times.

Jesus, there's someone there and they're signaling me!

Alarmed, Acorn walked as fast as he could to his car. He thought about running but didn't want his breathing to get louder. Leaves crunched under his feet, but he didn't care. *Someone* had already found him. He needed to get out of here as quickly as possible.

Finally, Acorn reached his car. He fumbled for his key fob. His hands were shaking so hard he dropped the fob as he pulled it out of his pocket. It hit the ground and he knelt to pick it up. On his knees, he very slowly turned one more time in the direction of the light, terrified whoever it was out there would now be right behind him.

Squinting, he saw nothing.

Then, just as he was about to turn back to his car, three more bursts of the yellow light appeared in the distance. Each burst lasted about a second and was separated by one second of darkness.

Dropping any concerns about noise, he pressed the key fob and quickly opened the car door, jumped in, and drove off.

After fifty yards or so he looked in his rearview mirror. There was a shadow of a figure he could not identify. Then he saw three more bursts of the yellow flashlight. Again, the pattern was one second on and one second off, three times.

Acorn floored his car and raced back to Washington.

CHAPTER 24

I
t was dark by the time Andrea pulled up to her house with her mother. The moving van followed her into the driveway. Andrea got out, walked to the passenger door, and opened it. Ryan was already on his way down the driveway.

"All right, Mamie, let's get you inside. I'll have them move everything to the upstairs guest room where we'll put you. Ryan, help me bring my mother into the house. We don't have a ramp and she can't climb stairs."

Ryan helped Mamie from the passenger side and escorted her into the house.

Andrea heard the television in the den and saw her kids watching it. NBC was broadcasting a special edition of its *Nightly News* featuring the effects of the emergency budget on the country. What Andrea had witnessed at her mother's assisted living home was happening throughout America. Seniors unable to pay for medicines or rent without Medicare. Hospitals discharging or turning away patients who could not pay out of pocket or with private insurance. Veterans denied prescriptions and appointments by VA hospitals. Immigrant processing facilities and their associated health care facilities shut down completely. NBC treated her children to a nationwide parade of misery, the same misery Andrea had witnessed with her own eyes a couple of hours earlier.

"Mommy, the kids in school are saying you did this," Michelle said.

"It's a little more complicated than that," Andrea responded.

Aaron chimed in, "That's not what the kids say. They say you forced them to do it because you are a cheapskate who wants people to die if it will save money."

"Aaron, President Murray told me not two hours ago he thinks we're doing the right thing. *The President of the United States.*"

"The kids say he's a cheapskate who's killing people too."

Andrea left the room and went into the kitchen, leaving Ryan with the kids and her mother. She stood over the sink, staring down into the drain, frustrated and exhausted from defending herself. Hate mail from strangers was one thing. But her son? Kids on a playground? Those kids were repeating whatever they heard their parents say. How could she even show her face in public if everyone thought she was a monster?

She slammed her fist on the countertop in frustration.

Couldn't someone explain to people what would have happened if she hadn't implemented this emergency budget? They were vilifying her for what was happening, but couldn't someone explain how much worse it could be?

From the kitchen she heard Ryan taking the children to task. "That's enough. Your mother is trying to save the country. Tell those little morons at school that."

Andrea caught her breath. Hearing Ryan defend her made her feel slightly less alone.

Just as she was getting back to herself, the doorbell rang. It was after eight. Who could possibly be wandering the streets at this hour on a weeknight?

Andrea went to the door and peeked through the window, expecting a salesman or reporter, but it was her neighbor Ellen Frost and another woman Andrea had seen around the neighborhood. At least it wasn't an angry mob.

Who knows, maybe they're here to give me a morale boost.

Andrea opened the door. "Hi, Ellen. It's good to see you."

"Do you have any idea what you have done?" Ellen's eyes were puffy and red.

"Come again? Are you okay?"

"No, I'm not okay," Ellen said. "Do you know what you have done to my family?"

"I have no idea." Andrea didn't know what else to say.

Then it hit her. Ellen was an auditor in the Department of Labor, and her husband Paul was an IT contractor there. They had to be losing their jobs.

Ellen motioned to the woman next to her. "This is Sarah Robinson. She lives across the street from you. She was a program analyst at the Department of Agriculture until last week. And her husband Steve worked as a real estate manager in the Department of Education."

"Hi, Sarah," Andrea said, offering a handshake. "I've seen you around the neighborhood."

"You've destroyed our lives!" Sarah shouted as Ellen began to cry uncontrollably. "We've all lost our jobs because of your damned budget. What are we going to do? How am I going to compete with a million unemployed federal workers for a new job?"

Andrea looked down at her shoes, then back at Ellen and Sarah. She wanted to run screaming from her doorstep. "I tried so hard, I did everything I could," she said. "When people stopped buying American bonds, we just ran out of money." Even as she was saying it, she wondered, *Did I really do everything I could?*

Andrea scratched her eyes, fighting the tears she felt coming. Once again, the raw reality of her handiwork was confronting her. Victims of her budgetary hardheartedness were literally laying the blame at her doorstep. Desperately trying to restrain her anguish, she tracked a moth as it flew around the overhead porch light and periodically grazed her cheek. Anything to avoid looking at Ellen and Sarah.

These women were just like her. Parents who had worked hard for a good life, for stability, to provide for their children. If her accounting practice had failed, Ryan wasn't making enough money in his job to keep things together. They would have to dip into their savings, sell the house, and put the family on a tight budget.

Andrea looked helplessly at her neighbors. She desperately searched for something to say, some way to help, but she came up with nothing. Her brain simply had no more capacity for creative thought.

"I wish I could do something to help," Andrea said. "I really do."

"You've helped us enough, thank you very much," Ellen seethed. Then she and Sarah turned their back on Andrea and left, not even saying goodbye.

Andrea went back into the house and sat down in the small family study. She buried her face in her hands and sobbed uncontrollably. "I've ruined the country, I've ruined everyone's life," she burbled over and over.

There was a light rap on the door. It was Mamie in her wheelchair, still covered in the blanket the assisted living facility had given her. Andrea gently wheeled her mother into the study.

"I take it you heard all that," Andrea said. She gently wiped her eyes and nose.

"Honey, the entire neighborhood could hear all that. Those people were speaking at the top of their lungs."

"Mamie, I can't take it." Andrea's voice cracked. "I'm getting hate mail every day of the week. People say they want me dead. My neighbors hate me. Maybe I've made a huge mistake. Three hundred million Americans can't be wrong." She sobbed and wiped her eyes with her mother's blanket.

"Yes, they can." Her mother calmly caressed Andrea's hand.

"These people who are upset with you probably don't understand everything going on. I don't really understand either. Let me ask you something, sweetie. Do you think you did the right thing?"

"I wouldn't have done it if I didn't think it was the right thing to do."

"And the president agreed?"

Andrea nodded. "He thought it was the right thing to do."

Mamie nodded. "Don't you think it's possible everyone else doesn't understand?"

"I'm sure they don't. But they are the judges of this."

Mamie shook her head in disagreement. "Honey, remember what your father used to say?"

"That people are idiots?"

Mamie laughed. "No, not that. He used to say, 'Nobody knows anything.' What he meant was that people are wrong. A lot. If you think it was the right thing to do, just forget it. You just go back in to work tomorrow and do your job."

"I wish I could."

"Well, what's done is done. You'll manage, they'll manage, we'll all manage. We've got no choice."

"We'll see, Mamie. We'll see."

CHAPTER 25

Acorn sat at his desk in his Longworth office in ominous quiet. For a week, his Ministry watch had told him only the time. No one from the Ministry had contacted him since his last meeting with Xu Li. She had told him to await instructions, but the Ministry's silence had grown deafening.

Acorn stared at the picture on his office desk of his parents and him on a trip to Niagara Falls. He remembered the trip like it was yesterday. He was ten. His best friend had just gone to Disney World and he had begged his parents to take him to no avail. "Playpen of the capitalists," his father called what everyone else called the Happiest Place on Earth. "Exploring nature and not handing over hard-earned money to exploiting corporate capitalist overlords is the kind of vacation a true socialist takes." They were that devoted to overthrowing the capitalist order and the United States.

Acorn held back tears as he looked at his parents smiling with the falls in the background. His father was wearing his usual plaid shirt and jeans, and his mother was in her typical dowdy dress. "We are workers and we wear the clothes," his father would say. Ten-year-old Frank had a sourpuss look. Acorn remembered thinking Mickey Mouse would have been a lot more fun than watching water go over a cliff.

He thought about his parents' sacrifices and his own. Never going to nice restaurants. Never taking a nice vacation. Dedicating themselves to bringing down capitalism. He felt a hole in the pit of his stomach. All that sacrifice and he'd failed. He'd failed his parents. He'd failed Xu Li. Despite the horrors of the financial crisis Operation Pripyat had created, the United States was still alive and still capitalist.

Twenty-two years he'd spent burrowing into American life. Twenty-two years he'd worked to get to the height of staff power in Washington. Twenty-two years of preparing to bring down the United States.

And he'd blown it.

Just as he was about to bury his head on his desk, Mason walked in. "Let's talk strategy," he said.

Mason's strategy talks were legendary among his staff. Walk or drive to a nice restaurant, sit, and listen to the old blowhard ramble about politics. Sometimes it was strategy. Sometimes it was politics. And sometimes it was just venting. You could never be sure which you were in for. Mason's strategy talks were more like strategy monologues. But the food was good.

"Sure, let's go." Acorn never said no to a strategy talk. Maybe Mason would pass along some nugget of information he could take back to Xu Li. Maybe he would have a chance to show Xu Li he wasn't a total failure.

They got into to Mason's BMW and drove west on Constitution Avenue, past the White House and Washington Monument, past the Lincoln Memorial, onto Interstate 66, and then onto the George Washington Memorial Parkway.

It was unusual for Mason to leave DC in the middle of the day. "Where're we headed, Mr. Mason?" asked Acorn.

"This new sushi place in McLean I discovered. Tachibana. Delicious stuff. You like sushi, right?"

"Sure, that sounds great."

Acorn hated sushi.

He noticed the silent construction sites along the parkway. Work had ceased under the emergency budget. Another monument to his failure to prevent the emergency budget from passing.

"We really fucked up that hearing, didn't we?" said Mason.

"Andrea beat us," Acorn said. "I've never seen her like that before."

"Why don't we talk strategy someplace a little more private before we get to the restaurant," Mason offered.

"Fine, but we have a three o'clock hearing, so we can't screw around and enjoy nature or anything like that," Acorn reminded Mason. "We have to eat and be back in the Capitol by three."

"I'll be there, don't worry." Mason seemed calm but distant, almost preoccupied.

He pulled the car off the parkway and into the secluded Fort Marcy Park between Washington and McLean. No one was around in the middle of the day. The park was a low-key, low-traffic destination, quiet on the weekends, desolate on weekdays. It was notorious in Washington for having been the site of Vince Foster's suicide during Bill Clinton's presidency.

"Walk with me, Frank." Acorn was getting nervous. Mason hated nature. He hated parks. And he hated leaving DC in the middle of the day. What the hell was going on?

"You know that failure comes with a price, don't you?"

"Of course, Mr. Mason. I know the hearing went badly. I have a plan—"

"Frank, that's not the failure I'm talking about."

"Then what gives?" Acorn asked nervously.

"You know the emergency budget wasn't supposed to pass. And I know it was your job to make sure it didn't pass."

Mason turned to Acorn.

"By the way, I have something I want to show you."

Mason opened the small satchel he often carried with him on the Hill. He pulled out a grainy photo with washed-out colors.

"What is this?" Acorn asked.

"It's a photo, Frank. I took this a week ago. Used a special camera."

"That's why the colors are weak?"

"That's right. The camera uses short bursts of light to help illuminate the subject. Three short bursts of light each separated by a second of darkness. But it hasn't been perfected yet."

Acorn did a double take.

Three short bursts of light?

He thought back to the mysterious bursts of light at the cave.

It couldn't be. Could it?

"What's in the picture, Lew?"

"Frank, I'm surprised you don't recognize it. See that little shadow in the center?" Mason pointed to a black image the height of a fingernail. "If you look closely you can make out the head and the arms and the legs. It's you, Frank."

Acorn glanced down at the photo more closely and his eyes widened. Thoughts rushed into his head like water after a dam break.

Did Mason know about the abandoned drive-in? Was Mason CIA?

Mason looked at Acorn with a slight air of contempt. "Did you really think I didn't know who you were and what you were up to, Frank? Or should I call you Acorn?"

Acorn opened his mouth to speak but his voice cracked and nothing came out except a light squeak. His world was crashing down around him and he stood paralyzed.

"There are penalties for failure, Acorn. Agents have to know the consequences. Examples must be made."

Holy living hell.

Mason wasn't CIA.

He was Ministry.

Acorn staggered backward in terror. "You mean you . . ."

"Frank, I'm sure you are a good agent. But did you really think you were so good you could work your way up to chief of staff in a congressional office? Did you really think I didn't know who you were?"

"All those years of constitutional conservatism, of railing against the deficit, of opposing the Establishment . . . all this time you were an agent too?" Acorn stammered.

"Come on, Frank. Like you weren't doing the same thing? Can you imagine deeper cover? Who could possibly think a Debt Rebellion-loving, boxing elephant flag-waving, cowboy boot-wearing constitutional conservative could be working for the Ministry?"

"Why didn't you tell me, Mr. Mason? We could have worked together. Imagine what we could have done."

"Compartmentalization, Frank. Ministry frontline agents like you are cannon fodder—the most likely to fail, and the most likely to be eliminated and replaced. Agents like you exist to protect agents like me. Surely you've figured that out by now."

Acorn's mind was racing and his limbs shook. He continued to backpedal slowly away from Mason.

"Now we can work together, right?"

"Come on, Frank. You know that's impossible. You failed. You're no good to us now."

I have to get out of here!

Acorn dropped the photo, turned, and began running away from Mason in the direction of the Potomac River.

Suddenly a gun went off behind the shrubs on the edge of the park. A bullet ripped through Acorn's abdomen. He crumpled to the ground, writhing on his back in pain.

"Shit, Pyotr, you were supposed to kill him dead," Mason shouted.

The shrubs rustled and a man in a black suit and tie emerged. Glancing up at his attacker, Acorn noticed he was about the same height and build as Mason and shared his round face and large nose. Unlike Mason, the man wore a beard of medium thickness.

"Do not complain, Crimson," Pyotr said, looking at his wrists. "You were supposed to knock him down for me to kill him quietly, not let him run away so I had to shoot him. And now I have blood on my suit. Ermenegildo Zegna suits are not cheap. The Ministry only gave me a few of these."

"I'll get it cleaned later," Mason replied. "Give him the tranquilizer."

Pyotr kneeled and opened a black bag that was by his feet. He quickly pulled out a syringe and a small vial of clear liquid and filled the syringe.

"Ohhh, Lew ... what are you doing ... why ... help me ... Lew, please don't kill me," Acorn pleaded.

Pyotr brandished the syringe, liquid dripping from its tip. Acorn raised his hands to protect himself. He smelled something awful, a combination of human sweat and rotten eggs, but he couldn't tell if it was the assassin or the dripping liquid.

"Shhh, Frank. This isn't going to hurt. It'll just slow things down for you." Mason turned to the assassin. "Now."

"Yes, Crimson." Pyotr then grabbed Acorn's left arm, pinning it to the ground, and jabbed the needle into his shoulder, pushing the plunger down quickly.

"Don't worry, Frank. This won't hurt much. This tranquilizer will just paralyze your muscles. You'll bleed out. It's a bit rudimentary but a very compact and clean way to kill someone."

Acorn struggled to move his mouth. The tranquilizer had quickly taken effect. His eyes froze wide open.

"I'm sorry, Frank. You know I have my orders just as you had yours. And if I don't follow my orders, what would happen to me is what's about to happen to you."

Acorn heard every word, but he was paralyzed and couldn't move even a finger to respond.

Mason glanced over to Pyotr, who nodded. Mason turned, walked back to his BMW, and drove off. Pyotr slung Acorn over his shoulder like a sack of potatoes and carried him to a black Subaru Forester parked in the woods one hundred yards away. As they approached the car, Acorn could hear its liftgate begin to open. Pyotr dumped Acorn into the rear of the SUV and wordlessly slammed the liftgate shut. Paralyzed, unable to speak, and his remaining blood draining out the wound in his stomach, Acorn silently watched the light coming through the vehicle's back window slowly fade to black.

CHAPTER 26

A ndrea was bleary-eyed. She'd barely slept. The events of the previous day, her neighbors berating her and all those elderly people standing on the sidewalk, consumed her thoughts. She would have done anything to stay home and hibernate for the next few months, but duty called.

On her way in to work she drove past the offices of one government contractor after another, all housed in shiny, new glass-and-steel buildings lining Virginia's Route 28 and Interstate 66. GovSoft, TechOps, iTech, CloudTech, the signs on the buildings read, meaningless mashups of made-up techno-speak.

She sagged in her seat thinking about all the people working at these companies. *They're all getting pink slips. And I might as well have signed them.*

She wondered if these names would still be on the buildings in a year's time.

As she drove, headlights crept up in her rearview mirror until they were practically on top of her.

Great, another annoying DC tailgater.

It was a black Subaru Forester with the special red-and-blue "Diplomat" plates. Diplomat plates always made Andrea nervous. Their drivers had diplomatic immunity and often took full advantage. Andrea changed lanes, wanting the Forester to pass and get as far from her as possible. But instead the Forester hovered at the rear corner of her driver's side, in the adjacent lane, exactly where he had been when he was tailgating her.

Why doesn't he just pass? Stay calm, don't look at him, think of something else.

As she drove past the exit for Poplar Tree Park, Andrea thought of her son's little league team that played on the baseball fields. The kids had no idea the debt bomb was ticking away while they played ball. She imagined the fields with missing bases, collapsed fences, and covered with weeds because there would be no money to maintain them.

A couple miles later, as Andrea approached the Capital Beltway, she looked in her rearview mirror again. The Forester was gone.

She breathed a sigh of relief and was about to go back to thinking about her son's little league when she stopped herself.

Enough. Enough of feeling sorry for yourself. Identify the problem. Work the problem. Solve the problem. Keep those baseball fields open.

What is the problem? People not buying American bonds.

And who instigated the bond boycott? This Pripyat Consor-tium.

What on earth is the Pripyat Consortium? No one ever heard of these guys before. How does some unknown bond fund, or group, or consortium, or whatever rally enough investors to torpedo an American Treasury bond auction? This can't be about finances. Someone is trying to harm the United States.

Her Google search on "Pripyat" had led her to pictures of the abandoned Chernobyl town Pripyat in Russia.

Could it be the Russians?

She had her doubts. Russia didn't have that kind of bond-buying power. And from her accountant days she knew Russian investors were buying overpriced Manhattan condos, not bonds. Put all the Russian buyers of American bonds together and form a boycott, and Americans would hardly notice. No, it couldn't be the Russians.

The Europeans? Sure, they bought American bonds, but why would they want to harm the United States? Even when the Europeans were angry about the Iraq War they didn't boycott American bonds. Europe seemed an unlikely culprit.

Japan? No, couldn't be. Relations with the Japanese were fine.

Come on, Andrea, think. Remember what you learned in that undergrad criminology class.

Means and motive. Means and motive.

Who had it?

Only one country bought enough American bonds that its engineering a boycott would threaten the United States' finances and had a burning desire to hurt the United States.

China.

But if it was China, why wasn't the guy who announced the Pripyat Consortium bond boycott Chinese? He looked Russian or Slavic or something.

Andrea dashed to her office after parking so she wouldn't lose her thought. When she arrived, she threw her coat on the couch, not even bothering to hang it on the door. She went straight to her computer and looked up "Pripyat Consortium." Links to news articles about the bond boycott appeared. She picked CNN's.

At the top of the article was a photograph of the man she'd seen on television announcing the Pripyat Consortium's American bond boycott. He looked Russian, just as Andrea remembered. But there was something familiar about the man. His face, his build. She could swear she'd seen him before.

Andrea called Rachel. Normally Rachel made sure she beat Andrea into the office, but Andrea's insomnia-fueled early arrival meant Andrea had gotten to the office first.

"Hello?" murmured a groggy Rachel.

"Rachel, are you up? I'm in the office. We need to talk. You have a moment?"

"Sweetie, it's six a.m. What are you doing in the office?"

"Something about this bond boycott is bothering me," Andrea said.

"Something? The whole thing is bothering us," Rachel replied.

"The Pripyat Consortium," Andrea said, nearly interrupting Rachel. "The guys boycotting the bonds."

"What about them?" Rachel yawned.

"The guy in the expensive suit who announced the bond boycott," she said. "He looks really familiar."

"Looked like a typical Russian oligarch to me," Rachel said. "Thousand-dollar suit and big red drinker's nose."

"No, no," Andrea said. "There was something familiar about him. His face, or his eyes. Something."

"I'm sure the FBI and the intelligence community are investigating it. Want me to check?"

"Yes," Andrea replied. "I'd really like them to look into that guy a little more. There's just something about him I can't put my finger on. Can we do that?"

"I have contacts all over this town," said Rachel. "I know people over at the FBI who can help." Rachel seemed awake now. Andrea heard a lilt in her voice. Rachel loved being a Washington insider. "I'm sure they didn't all get laid off. I'll call them."

"It's probably not every day that the OMB comes in with a request for the FBI, is it?" asked Andrea.

Rachel laughed. "There've been a lot of firsts lately."

"One more thing," Andrea said. "Make sure no one knows we're asking about this. Tell your FBI buddies to keep this quiet."

"Will do," Rachel replied.

As she looked out her office window to the White House lawn, illuminated by the morning light, Andrea continued to rack her brain.

What was so familiar about that Pripyat Consortium spokes-man?

It had rankled her since she'd first laid eyes on him. Now she was determined to find out who he was.

CHAPTER 27

Mason casually held his BMW's steering wheel with one hand as he turned into an alley behind an abandoned warehouse in East Baltimore.

All the years he'd been a Chinese agent and he'd never been part of a killing. He'd spent his life seeking political dominance over others, but political dominance was nothing compared to the feeling of having a man's life in his hands, of watching Acorn holding his stomach, blood dripping from his fingers, bleeding to death. Replaying it over and over in his mind gave him a nearly erotic frisson unlike anything he'd ever felt.

He slowly pulled his car up to a garage door on the side of the warehouse around nine p.m., lights off to minimize the chances of someone seeing him. The chipped and faded paint on the warehouse's side read "Gunther Machinery." The alley's broken concrete crunched under the wheels of his car. Some of the narrow plate glass windows were broken and filled with spider webs.

With Acorn gone, Mason was now the center of China's unfolding effort to bring down capitalism and the United States government.

As he put the car in park, he saw spots of dried blood on his index finger. Some of Acorn's blood must have sprayed him when Acorn was shot. Mason wiped the blood from his finger. He smiled at this initiation rite of an active agent.

He got out of his BMW and carefully navigated the broken driveway, avoiding the used needles the local junkies sometimes left behind. Quietly, he walked to the garage door, grabbed the chain attached to the door, and lifted it open. The mice and rats inside the building scattered, light reflecting off the eyes of the small rodents looking at him as they ran for cover. Mason inhaled deeply. The putrid smell of dead animals from the darkest corners of the warehouse filled his nose. He felt a tingling in his fingertips as the scent of death wafted through his nostrils.

He turned on a flashlight and led himself to the back of the warehouse. The dust and debris under his feet sounded like sandpaper. As he looked from side to side, he saw a few rusted machines and broken machine parts, perhaps left from the Gunther Machinery days. Incongruously, a broken piano sat in the middle of the old shop floor with missing keys and broken, tangled wires. Some old chairs were scattered about, their upholstery torn and stuffing strewn about, probably clawed out by the animals that infested the building.

He usually came to the warehouse from Capitol Hill dressed in one of his custom-tailored suits. He loved the filthy feel of his high-class slumming. He'd often fantasized about bringing one of his many flings here and going at it right there on the dirt-caked floor. But he knew revealing the warehouse to any of his one-night stands would mean certain death for them both.

Continuing to the back wall, Mason reached a small stairway, looked around to be certain no one was following him, and descended to the basement. Once there, he pointed his flashlight upward; a single light bulb and cord dangled from the ceiling. He pulled the cord and the light came on.

Against the back wall was a video screen and a small control panel. The walls were made of old, crumbling brick. The mortar between the bricks was cracked or missing altogether in spots. Rotted wood beams crossed the ceiling, thick enough that they supported the ceiling even with their surface rotting. A single small wooden chair sat in the center of the room facing the screen.

Mason took a seat in the chair, and at 10:01 p.m. the flat panel screen flickered to life. Xu Li appeared.

"Crimson."

"Yes, Madame Xu."

"Has Acorn been dealt with according to my instructions?"

"Yes, Madame Xu. He was suicided."

Expressionless, Xu Li simply nodded in acknowledgment. "His failures were grievous. How could he have misjudged the American public's reaction so badly? We spent years planning to bankrupt the United States and overthrow capitalism. But the US still stands."

Mason, supremely confident in his powers of persuasion, crossed his arms and angled his nose upward as he tried to convince Xu Li that Operation Pripyat had been a success. "Getting a million government workers fired and starving and killing millions of elderly and poor Americans by destroying the social safety net wasn't nothing, Madame Xu. Operation Pripyat might not have brought down the American government, but we've ruined millions of American lives."

"Nonsense, Crimson. Operation Pripyat is supposed to bring down capitalism and the United States government. Both remain. The mission has not been accomplished. It is up to you to complete it."

Mason's knees quivered slightly. Xu Li was impervious to his arrogant bluster. He couldn't buffalo Xu Li the way he had so many weak politicians. With Acorn gone, Mason began to realize that if capitalism and the American government didn't fall, he would be the next domino to tumble. If Xu Li wanted him suicided, he was as good as dead. He shook his arms and legs to rid them of their tension.

"You Americans may be reactive slobs, but we Chinese are careful, meticulous strategic planners," said Xu Li.

He hated when she waxed rhapsodic about how smart the Chinese were compared to the American brutes. He believed in socialism and exporting the revolution too, yet Xu Li treated him as an inferior second-class agent because he was American. If Chinese agents were clever strategists playing chess and American agents clumsy oafs playing checkers, why the hell did she need him and Acorn?

"We have a backup plan to destroy the United States government." Xu Li had moved on. "Though this plan is considerably messier, which is why I wanted to avoid it."

Considerably messier. Maybe there'd be more blood than the little bit he'd licked from his fingers. But as much as the thought of murder sent a thrill up his spine, Mason wanted to be certain the plan would succeed.

"Madame Xu, don't you think we might want to reassess our planning in the wake of the failure of our first plan?" he asked.

"You can be a part of the plan or you can be suicided too," came Xu Li's curt reply. Coming from Xu Li, it wasn't truly a reply. It was a threat.

"Madame Xu, I think whatever we do will work better if we wait for just a little bit to understand why Acorn's mission failed."

Xu Li stared into the camera. "Are you questioning my decisions?"

"No, Madame Xu."

"Have you forgotten what brought you into my service? How you were adopted from Russia by your parents in Kansas when you were six? How the bank repossessed your family's farm in Kansas a year later?"

"No, Madame Xu."

The Ministry almost certainly knew he hated thinking about his childhood. He'd spent years building his power and reputation as a political colossus bestriding Capitol Hill. As far as he was concerned, that six-year-old in Kansas was dead and buried. But Xu Li clutched his past tightly and deployed it when needed to stoke his rage.

"Remember that foreclosure agent telling you to look on the bright side, that you were going to get to move to a city? The auction, that bewildering recitation of numbers and raising of hands that represented the death of your happy life on the farm?"

"I know, Madame Xu." Mason tried to change the topic. "But I think we need to consider—"

"And you recall the fat, sweaty developer who purchased the farm and immediately subdivided it for custom-built McMansions? Your family's grimy first apartment in Kansas City? The roaches and ants in the kitchen and rats and mice as big as cats in the bathroom? The broken furniture strewn across the front lawn that passed for your toys?"

"Madame Xu—"

"And your adoptive mother's funeral after she was killed in the factory accident?"

Mason's cheeks flushed red. Madame Xu had fully exhumed that six-year-old Kansas boy. Mason balled his hands into fists of anger and clenched his jaw so tightly he was grinding his teeth. His eyes narrowed into an angry scowl.

"Enough, please, Madame Xu," Mason begged. "I hate them, I hate the Americans. Tell me the plan, Madame Xu. I want to see America die."

"That is better, Crimson. Are you now ready to implement the operation?"

"Yes, Madame Xu, yes."

Xu Li's psychological onslaught had physically broken Mason. His arms hung limply by his side.

"Very well. Within the next week we will set fire to the lake."

"Jesus," Mason whispered.

"When the lake begins to burn, the Americans will need money. Enormous amounts of money. Your job is to make sure the American government doesn't get it."

"That is why I worked my way up the Appropriations Committee, Madame Xu. I am perfectly positioned to execute your plan. President Murray will not get a dime." Xu Li's tour through Mason's childhood had stoked his thirst for revenge.

"For your sake," Xu Li said menacingly, "I hope you are right."

CHAPTER 28

The unexpected phone call at two in the morning from the White House put Andrea on edge. It wasn't as if she were in a deep sleep—that was no longer possible. But it was the tone of Rachel's normally cheery voice that sent shivers down her spine.

"There's a crisis in the South China Sea."

"Rachel, Hold on," Andrea said. She quietly got out of bed. Ryan was working the nightshift at his hospital, but she didn't want to wake her sleeping children down the hall. She stumbled over to the chair for a sweatshirt and then closed her door.

"Okay, I'm here," Andrea said.

"China's invading Taiwan and blocking the South China Sea," she continued.

China.

Andrea sat upright. Another puzzle piece snapped into place in her mind. The failed bond auction. The Pripyat Consortium. Now Chinese military aggression. All within a few months? No way was this a coincidence.

"Why are you calling me?" she asked. "The national security people should be getting the calls, not me."

"The national security team is meeting in the Situation Room in about thirty minutes," Rachel said. "You should be there."

"Why?" Andrea was now fully awake.

"If they decide to defend Taiwan or reopen the South China Sea, it'll cost money. Lots of money."

"Our budget is at stake," Andrea said.

"Exactly," Rachel replied.

"All right, I'll be there."

Andrea got dressed in record speed without waking anyone. She was leaving the kids and Mamie home without her or Ryan, but she didn't have much of a choice. Ryan would be home in a couple hours, so maybe no one would even know she'd left.

Interstate 66 didn't have traffic at this hour, so she was cruising comfortably down the highway when the lights of a car appeared about six car lengths behind her. She squinted in her rearview mirror. She could swear it was the same black Forester from the other day, with its high roof and red-and-blue diplomatic plates. This time it wasn't tailgating, and it was too distant to see the driver. Scared and in a hurry, Andrea floored her car, going eighty miles per hour all the way to the White House. She didn't look in her rearview mirror again until she crossed into DC. When she did, the Forester was gone.

President Murray's national security staff had assembled in the Situation Room. Principals sat at the long, polished mahogany table with gold metal trim. Andrea had taken a seat against the wall where the staffers sat.

This was her first time in the Situation Room. A carved wooden presidential seal hung on the front wall. Each leather chair had the seal of the president embroidered into its back. Custom White House water bottles and etched White House glasses were neatly arranged in front of each seat.

Andrea surveyed the assembled group and felt herself shrinking.

Secretary of Defense Todd Andrews sat to the left of President Murray's seat at the head of the table. He'd managed to get into a suit and tie for the meeting and his hair was perfectly parted and blow-dried.

Next to Secretary Andrews sat Chairman of the Joint Chiefs of Staff General Edwin Ogden. Even at this ungodly hour his heavyset frame was ramrod straight at attention. The general was in uniform, his left breast covered in rows of medals and bars.

Admiral Trey Wilkerson sat to President Murray's right. If General Ogden was the stereotypical army general, Admiral Wilkerson was the classic navy man. Tall and lean, his narrow frame extended well above the back of the chair in his pressed Navy whites.

And Vice President Matthew Campbell sat beside Wilkerson. He was by far the biggest person at the table, looking every bit the offensive lineman he was at the Naval Academy. He was in a crisp suit and tie, missing only the pocket square he favored.

The room exuded America's power and majesty. From the massive mahogany table, to the crisp military uniforms, to the sophisticated secure telephone, it appeared every bit the superpower nerve center it was.

Andrea began to regret crashing the meeting.

Here she was, Andrea Gartner, CPA, seated among the cream of the national security elite. All of them were dressed as if it was a normal morning while she had thrown on the first outfit she could find. These guys were used to the middle-of-the-night crisis call. She felt inferior, out of place, a dwarf among giants. It didn't take long for the military men to object to her presence.

"What the hell is she doing here?" General Ogden bellowed. "She's not a national security principal."

"OMB needs to be part of this discussion," President Murray insisted. "We may be about to spend a lot of money."

"Yes, Mr. President," General Ogden mumbled, making no effort to hide his disdain.

The president started the meeting. "Gentlemen, ladies, there is a crisis in the South China Sea. Todd, what is the current status?"

Secretary Andrews's grim mien said it all. "Mr. President, the Chinese have launched a full-scale invasion of Taiwan. They're cutting off all sea lanes in the South China Sea."

Andrea feverishly took notes, too intimidated to speak. She still felt as though everyone was looking at her, the interloper who didn't belong. Taking notes provided a distraction.

"Satellite imagery shows a Chinese aircraft carrier group positioned off the coast of Taiwan," Secretary Andrews continued. "Based on the imagery, DoD assesses Taiwan is completely blockaded by the Chinese navy. We've also confirmed with American diplomats on the ground in Taipei that Chinese aircraft are regularly flying sorties over Taiwan."

Andrea looked around the room again. A year ago, she was doing peoples' taxes. Now she was sitting in the White House Situation Room hearing about aircraft carrier groups and sorties over Taiwan.

Just keep taking notes. Look like you're following along.

"Has anyone on the diplomatic team spoken with President Chen?" Murray asked.

"No, sir," Secretary Andrews replied. "President Chen is missing. There are thousands of Chinese paratroopers dropping into Taiwan, and landing craft filled with Chinese soldiers are coming ashore on Taiwanese beaches."

Murray rubbed his chin. Andrea recognized he was resorting to his trick of stalling for time by thinking of additional questions.

"Has the Taiwanese military deployed?" Murray asked.

"Get Admiral Reboulet on the line, please," Secretary Andrews said.

A staffer in the rear pressed a button and Admiral Cal Reboulet, commander of the Navy's Pacific Command, appeared on a screen at the front of the room by secure conference call. He wore the close-cropped gray hair of a navy lifer.

"I spoke with General Tsai for about fifteen minutes before communications were interrupted," Reboulet said. "The Taiwanese Army is deployed in Taipei, and some Taiwanese fighter jets were able to scramble. But the Chinese took a lot of Taiwanese jets out before they could get airborne. I've been watching the explosions from the deck of my ship."

Murray nodded grimly.

"We've been getting reports saying Taipei has fallen and the Taiwanese president has gone into hiding," Reboulet continued. "We've confirmed the South China Sea is now completely blocked to commercial and international shipping."

"Anything else?" Murray asked.

"The Chinese Navy has completely blockaded Taiwan. And, Mr. President, you should know we have two ships with over one hundred sailors docked in Taipei and trapped," Reboulet said. "They're the ones who reported the fall of Taipei."

"Good lord," Murray spluttered. "How do you all see things playing out over the next few hours?"

"Mr. President, Taiwan could be overrun by the time the sun rises in DC," Andrews said.

Andrea noted the digital clock on the wall next to the screen. It read 03:37.

"Can you turn the monitor to CNN, please?" Murray asked an attendant. "See if they're broadcasting. You all remember Peter Arnett in the First Gulf War?"

Murmurs of agreement came from around the table. The screen split, with Admiral Reboulet on one side and CNN on the other.

The team gasped almost in unison.

"Good lord," said Ogden.

On the screen, Chinese soldiers were in the streets of Taipei firing at Taiwanese soldiers and civilians. Tanks crushed improvised barricades of cars, concrete bollards, and fencing. Fires burned halfway up Taipei's tallest skyscrapers where trapped civilians desperately waved their cell phones, hoping someone would come to their rescue.

The image of a dead civilian lying in the street, blood flowing like a river from him, turned Andrea's stomach. She slouched in her seat under General Ogden's glare. It was clear she wasn't wanted here.

"All right, folks, I need options," the president said.

General Ogden, Admiral Wilkerson, and Secretary Andrews exchanged looks and nods suggesting they had been discussing this for hours. They were experienced crisis managers. Big leaguers. Andrea could barely hold it together watching CNN.

"This is the gravest crisis since Korea." Campbell's chiseled jaw locked as he clenched his teeth. "It calls for a forceful response."

"We need to reopen the South China Sea," Andrews said.

"And how do you propose we do that?" Murray asked.

"A freedom of navigation flotilla," Wilkerson chimed in. "The USS *Ronald Reagan* carrier battle group is already in the South China Sea. We've got the *Reagan,* five destroyer escorts, and a handful of cruisers with anti-aircraft and Aegis anti-missile systems. They're in position and ready to run the Chinese blockade."

Andrea jerked her head back and forth like a tennis spectator as the four men volleyed ideas. All she could think about was the cost of what they were proposing. She stiffened. *Are you mad?* she chastised herself. *Worrying about finances when American lives are at stake?*

"And Taiwan?" Murray asked.

"Run that blockade too," Wilkerson responded.

"And put some troops on those blockade runners that can land in Taiwan and help the Taiwanese fight back," Ogden added.

Murray nodded in agreement with his military advisors. "We can't let this aggression stand. The South China Sea is too important to let the Chinese simply take it. The Koreans and Japanese will be shitting bricks."

"Besides," said Admiral Wilkerson, "the Chinese would never be dumb enough to shoot at our flotilla. They don't want a war with the United States."

"Exactly," Secretary Andrews agreed. "Running the blockade is a step short of going to war. We're not shooting. We're just restoring the status quo ante."

Andrea fidgeted with her pen, hoping someone in the room might disagree, or at least challenge the president and his military men. She was no foreign policy expert. *South China Sea, Taiwan, freedom of navigation* . . . none of it held much meaning for her. All she knew was that it sounded damn expensive.

"I think we're all in agreement," said President Murray. "Trey, order Admiral Reboulet to assemble two flotillas to run the blockades."

Andrea hadn't budgeted the hundreds of millions of dollars these flotillas would cost. Worse, what if the Chinese started shooting at them after all? She prayed someone might speak up and challenge the president and his military men, but all she heard was silence.

"We're settled, then?" Murray said.

"Wait," said Andrea feebly.

All eyes were on her. General Ogden's eyes widened, and Admiral Wilkerson's eyes narrowed. Secretary Andrews grimaced. They left no doubt: Andrea's comments were not welcome.

She hesitated and hunched her shoulders. The three most

powerful military men in America were glowering at her. She felt the entire combined force of the United States military trained upon her, trying to stare her into silence.

"Go on, Andrea," Murray said. "What's on your mind?"

At least someone wants to hear from me. Focus on Murray. Don't look at the military men. You didn't force your way into this meeting to be a wallflower.

"Mr. President, you asked for options, but it isn't options you need. What you need is cash. Any deployment of troops and ships will cost up to a billion dollars a day. We have enough reserve funds to last us about four weeks. After that—"

"Who do you think you are speaking in here?" Secretary Andrews thundered. "This is the Situation Room. The national security staff speaks in here. I don't care if you're new to government, we follow protocol."

"But this is important. A few weeks of ships and troops being deployed, and we'll be out of money." As she spoke, she looked at the president. He gave her an encouraging look. Fortified by the president's unspoken message, Andrea found her voice and spoke with conviction. "We'd need to borrow again or make even steeper cuts to Social Security and Medicare. We'll have to choose: save Taiwan or fund what's left of Social Security and Medicare."

Secretary Andrews scowled. Andrea shrugged her shoulders at him. She was determined to put the money issue on the table if no one else would, protocol be damned.

"Look, I'm just saying that if we somehow get ourselves in a war, we're going to go bankrupt in about four weeks. Not maybe ... we *will* go bankrupt."

General Ogden looked exasperated. "Are you saying the United States can't fight a war?"

Andrea could tell he was chomping at the bit to square off

against the Chinese and saw her as the only thing standing between him and his fight.

"That's exactly what I'm saying. Unless you plan to fight a war with volunteers swinging their fists, we cannot pay for a war. We can't even pay for your blockade runners without making more cuts. We just don't have the money."

President Murray sagged in his chair. Then his eyes widened, as if an idea had just popped into his head. "You think people might lend to us now to fight the war?" he asked. "Goodness knows Japan or South Korea are probably scared enough to loan us money."

Andrea shook her head. "I don't think so, Mr. President. No one was lending to us before this. I really doubt they'll lend now. Lenders will be scared out of their minds and put their money under their mattresses."

"What about war bonds?" General Ogden asked.

Andrea curled her face into a look of disdain. "Would you buy bonds from someone forty trillion in debt, General?"

General Ogden scowled but said nothing. Admiral Wilkerson was muttering to himself. She obviously had upended whatever carefully crafted plan the military men had prepared before the meeting.

"I don't think the Chinese are going to fire on us," Secretary Andrews said. "They don't dare fight a war against us." He flashed Andrea a look as if to say "checkmate."

General Ogden ominously fingered one of the medals on his uniform while Admiral Wilkerson crossed his arms against his chest, glowering intensely. But the president's willingness to listen to her had given Andrea confidence. "Mr. Secretary, if ever there was a time for China to start a war with the United States, this would be it."

Secretary Andrews wasn't giving up. "Mr. President, the ships are in position and ready to launch the blockade breakers."

President Murray sat back and looked at the ceiling. Andrea clearly had thrown a monkey wrench into his thinking too.

"We don't really have a choice," Murray said after a long pause. "We have to save the Taiwanese and free the South China Sea for international shipping." He looked at his military men. "I think you all are right. The Chinese wouldn't shoot at us and start a war."

Admiral Wilkerson shot a satisfied look toward Andrea. She slunk in her seat, realizing she had lost the argument.

President Murray nodded. "Okay, then. Run the blockade. Do it as soon as possible."

Admiral Reboulet saluted. "Yes, sir, Mr. President."

The president continued, "Edwin, have the Air Force begin sorties over Taiwan. Let's airlift food and medicine to civilians there. And put landing troops on some of those blockade runners."

"Yes, sir." General Ogden gave a crisp salute.

"That concludes the meeting," Murray said. "Anything else from anyone?"

Andrea felt compelled to reiterate her point. "Whatever we do, we have to get it done in four weeks. Otherwise, we're out of cash and either cutting more from Social Security and Medicare or stopping any military action cold. There's nothing anyone in this room can do about that." She exhaled. She'd said her peace. From the way the military men were looking at her, she thought they might strangle her if she said another word.

"Understood, Andrea," Murray said. "Cal, when will the blockade running flotilla launch?"

"Three hours, sir. 0700 Washington time."

"Good. Let's all reconvene here at 0700. I'm going up to the Oval to notify Congress."

He stood up to leave the Situation Room and the rest of the team stood up at attention as he left.

On his way out, General Ogden approached Andrea. "You find us the money to fight the Chinese, you understand?" He wagged his finger in her face.

"General, I'll do what I can. But get this over within four weeks so we won't have to find out if I've succeeded."

"You don't know a thing about fighting," General Ogden sneered as he headed for the door. "Stick to bookkeeping."

CHAPTER 29

A ndrea cursed the fates. She was physically exhausted and emotionally spent. Her confidence was already at a low ebb and the meeting had exponentially exacerbated her inferiority complex. She should have just stayed in bed.

She wandered outside to the South Lawn and walked along the perimeter fence, alone with her thoughts. The Washington Monument was darkened, its illumination cut under the emergency budget. She headed across Constitution Avenue to take a closer look.

When she reached the base of the monument, she looked east toward the Capitol and then west toward the Lincoln Memorial. Both were dark, their floodlights cut as well. In the distance, beyond the Lincoln Memorial, she could see Arlington Cemetery in the moonlight. Tens of thousands of American soldiers were buried there, killed in battle defending America's freedom.

Andrea thought of those soldiers and what they must have faced. The bullets whizzing by on the beaches of Normandy. Kamikaze planes crashing onto the decks of their ships. Ambushes in Korea and Vietnam. Roadside bombs in Iraq. What were her problems compared to those? Whatever happened with the budget, her life wasn't in danger.

What could the generals, the admirals, or the politicians do to you that was anything close to what those soldiers lying in Arlington went through? Who cares if you get dirty looks? Who cares if they tell you that you don't belong here? You are here. You got yourself into this position by banging the debt gong loud enough that someone finally listened.

A couple of lights were on in the House office buildings. They reminded her of her first encounter with Lewis Mason. If she hadn't fought back against Mason and his Debt Rebel Gang cronies, Murray would never have brought her onto his team. If that hadn't happened, she wouldn't have any chance to fix the debt. There wouldn't even be an emergency budget if she hadn't hoisted Mason on his own petard at that Appropriations Committee hearing.

Be the person who stood up to Lewis Mason. You have it in you. You did it then, you can do it now. The president needs you. You're all he's got on this.

Andrea thought about all her work to create the emergency budget. It was going to be ruined by whatever was about to happen with China. But now she had a small dose of confidence in her step. She'd survived losing the congressional race. She'd survived Mason's grilling at the Appropriations Committee hearing. And she'd survived America's reaction to the emergency budget.

You can play in the big leagues. Stay on the field.

She took a deep breath and appreciated the morning chill in the air. As she walked back to her office to get some rest before the seven a.m. meeting, she remembered she'd left Mamie and the kids asleep and alone.

"Dammit," she muttered as she scrambled with her cell phone and called Ryan. She hoped he was home from his night shift at the hospital.

"Jesus, honey, it's five in the morning," he said. "Where the hell are you?"

"Work emergency," Andrea said. "I'm downtown at the White House."

"Who's going to get the kids ready for school and onto the bus? Who's going to feed your mother? I've been working all night and need to get some sleep."

"Listen, honey, I don't make it a habit to come in to work at two a.m. Believe me, I'd rather be home and getting them ready for school."

"Really? Because lately you've been spending all your time in the office," Ryan said. "Your mother is practically an invalid. I have to do everything for her—cook her meals, walk her around, even give her baths. I don't have a moment for the kids. They're eating fast food for every meal and zoning out on video games. Social Services is going to haul me in for neglect. I've damn near had enough. If you don't start spending more time at home, this family is going to fall apart."

Enough of this. Tell him the whole thing straight and shut him up.

"Listen, Ryan, I came down here because the Chinese have started a war in Taiwan, okay? A *war*. I'm not sure I could have found Taiwan on a map two days ago." Andrea's voice cracked. "All I wanted to do was run numbers and balance the budget. I'm completely in over my head. When I say I'd rather be home, believe me, I mean it."

The phone went silent.

"Are you there?" Andrea asked.

"Yeah, I'm here," said Ryan. "I had no idea that was happening."

"Of course you didn't. One of the things about working in the White House is that you find out about things before anyone else. When I say something's a work emergency, it's a work emergency."

Tears began welling in her eyes. Where was that confidence she felt a few moments ago?

"Sometimes I think the president made a mistake appointing me to this position," she said, surprised that she was voicing her doubt.

"I think the president makes lots of mistakes," said Ryan, "but hiring you wasn't one of them. I'm no politico, but even I know the Pentagon budget is full of waste. Don't let them roll you, honey. You know what you are doing. You wouldn't be there if you didn't."

"I guess we'll see," said Andrea. She took a deep breath. "But thank you for helping me get through this. I needed to talk to someone. Just make sure the kids get on the bus on time, okay?"

Ryan sighed. "Okay, fine, but we're getting close to the red line here at home."

"Ryan, I can only handle one crisis at a time. I'll be home when I can."

Exhausted, Andrea made it back to her office in the EEOB. She only had a couple of hours before the team reconvened in the Situation Room. She laid down on the couch to get as much sleep as she could.

CHAPTER 30

T he Capitol building was a shadowy hulk filling the window behind Mason's desk. The west front glowed eerily in the moon's illumination. The usual red-and-blue lights of Capitol Police squad cars patrolling the streets were absent.

Alone in his office in the small hours of the morning, Mason was sitting at his desk with this tableau behind him quietly reading the decrypted message on his personal laptop.

"The fire has begun burning in the lake," it read.

He scoured the internet for news of events in Asia. The *South China Morning Post* had news of the events unfolding a world away. "The Liberation Has Begun" read the headline. The subhead read, "China Officially Reasserts Sovereignty Over South China Sea and Taiwan." Below the headlines were pictures of Chinese Navy ships patrolling the South China Sea and Chinese troops storming the beaches of Taiwan.

Mason stared at the screen and rubbed his chin with his hand. As deeply as he had been involved with the Chinese, it still was a shock to read these words and see those pictures. After a few moments' reflection, he quietly opened his desk drawer and took out a small notepad with the congressional seal and "Lewis Mason, Member of Congress" embossed at the top. He placed it on his desk.

Mason then reached toward the back of the drawer and pulled out a dull black handgun. He checked the magazine well to be sure it was empty, clicked the safety off, and pulled the trigger. The gun clicked and Mason smiled. It still worked. He slid the gun into the very back of the drawer and felt around until he found the gun's magazine. He nodded and closed the drawer.

Leaning back in his leather chair, Mason glanced at the flags and photographs from his political career that festooned his office. He laughed as he looked at decades' worth of awards on his desk and wall. "Congressman of the Year" from a defense contractor lobby. "American Patriot Award" from a hawkish foreign policy lobby. "Champion of Freedom" from a human rights organization. How he'd fooled them all!

He picked up a small Lucite globe from his desk. The inscription on its surface read "Son of Kansas, Friend to the World." His favorite professor at the University of Kansas Law School had given it to him when he was first elected to Congress. Mason thought back wistfully to those early days. He'd come to enjoy the adulation, the awards, and the attention that came with being a member of Congress. The feeling that he was needed, wanted, important. And all the work he'd put in to get where he was! He hadn't gotten the powerful chairmanship of the Appropriations Committee by waiting in line. He'd thrown some sharp elbows and pushed others aside to get there.

None of that mattered now. All of it was about to become a vestige of his past. He had come to Capitol Hill on a mission, and no amount of perks, power, and comfort was going to stop him from completing it.

Just then, he noticed the picture on the shelf of the House Debt Rebel Gang on the steps of the Capitol. There, in the back, stood Earl Murray. Tall and handsome, his perfectly coiffed silver mane standing out from the crowd. In the front stood Mason, stocky and rumpled, his bloated nose his most noticeable feature.

Goddammit, I created the Debt Rebel Gang. I was supposed to ride the Debt Rebel Gang to power, not Earl-fucking-Murray. I did all the work to make the Debt Rebel Gang a force in Congress and that son of a bitch backbencher glides into the presidency on his looks and his charm. I make the debt a path to power, Murray never does one goddamned thing to build the Debt Rebel Gang, and he's the one who gets ahead? One more reason to destroy American democracy.

His jaw clenched as he strained to overcome the urge to throw the globe at the photo. *Murray thinks he's got power over me? That bastard doesn't know the half of what's about to hit him. He's about to find out who's running this show. In the new era, pretty-boy show ponies like Murray won't stand a chance. When I'm through, the last thing he'll see before I ship him off to the gulag is me moving into the White House.*

Mason picked up his pen and scribbled the words "the guns are about to fire" on his notepad. Then, below it, he wrote: "CUT THEM OFF." He grinned as he imagined the humiliation he had in store for Murray.

The clock was ticking now. It was now only a matter of time before America came to know the real Lewis Mason.

CHAPTER 31

President Murray, Vice President Campbell, General Ogden, Admiral Wilkerson, their staffers, and Andrea reassembled in the Situation Room at seven a.m. Andrea had gone to the refrigerator in the rear of the Situation Room and pulled out two Diet Pepsis. She was exhausted and wanted to be prepared for another round of everyone ganging up on her again.

"What's the status?" President Murray asked.

Admiral Wilkerson gave Murray a quick briefing. "The *Reagan* carrier group is in position and launching the blockade running flotilla momentarily."

A staffer in the rear of the room tuned the monitors to special video feeds from the flotilla's escorts and overhead Air Force drones monitoring the flotilla. Live shots of the South China Sea and the *Reagan* carrier group greeted the assembled national security team.

The American blockade runners entered the South China Sea. The digital wall clock read 07:23 Washington time.

Within minutes a white trail appeared in the video from one of the airborne drones monitoring the artificial islands China had built in the South China Sea.

"What the hell is that?" Murray asked.

Admiral Wilkerson squinted into the television. Then he turned to the president. "It's the contrail of an anti-ship missile," he said. "Jesus H. Christ. The Chinese are shooting at the flotilla."

"Goddamn, Trey, what can those things do?"

"Mr. President, China's anti-ship missiles are big enough to take out a carrier."

Andrea couldn't believe how calmly Admiral Wilkerson announced what seemed like a deadly attack.

"Are you serious?" the president roared. "Are the Chinese trying to start World War III? Get those ships out of there!"

"Those missiles will be at the flotilla in two minutes," said Admiral Wilkerson. "The flotilla won't have time to maneuver out of the line of fire. We were banking on the Chinese not firing."

"What do we do?" Murray barked.

"There's nothing we can do." Admiral Wilkerson shook his head in disbelief.

"There are missiles flying toward our ships and we can't do a damn thing to warn them?" Murray asked.

"They're seeing what we're seeing," responded Admiral Wilkerson. "They know what's happening and how to respond. Their Aegis anti-missile systems should kick into action."

"What will that do?" Andrea blurted, terrified she was watching a war begin.

Admiral Wilkerson looked at her condescendingly, clearly annoyed by her ignorance. "The Aegis can take a shot at the missiles. Or throw up some chaff and force them off course."

"Will that work?" she asked.

"Maybe," said Admiral Wilkerson, frowning.

Images from another Air Force drone, this one monitoring the coast of mainland China, captured flashes of light.

"Anti-ship missile batteries on mainland China firing," Admiral Wilkerson declared.

"What do we do? What do we do?" Andrea exclaimed in a panic.

Admiral Wilkerson was blunt. "Hope and pray that the Aegis works."

"Jesus Christ," said President Murray, running his hands through his hair.

Footage from the Air Force drones showed a smoke contrail getting closer and closer to the Reagan.

"No!" Andrea gasped and covered her mouth with her hand.

The smoke contrail met the *Reagan*, and an enormous fireball erupted from her side. Fuel tanks and fueled aircraft began exploding, creating multiple secondary fireballs.

"Good lord," said Admiral Wilkerson, stunned.

The president watched stone-faced, muttering "Jesus" to himself.

The *Reagan* began listing badly. Aircraft spilled off the flight deck into the sea. The overhead drones caught sailors leaping into the water, some with life vests, some without. Sailors desperately fought the flames on the carrier's deck.

"She's gone," Admiral Wilkerson said. "She can't survive that."

"Those goddamned sons of bitches," President Murray fumed.

The drones then captured missiles striking three of the escort destroyers. One split in half immediately. Another sank within two minutes of the strike. The third was ablaze.

"We are at war, Mr. President," General Ogden said.

In the blazing and sinking American vessels, Andrea saw her carefully crafted emergency budget going up in smoke as well. She was terrified President Murray was about to jump into a shooting war he couldn't finish.

"Mr. President, we can't fight a sustained war without being able to borrow money," she offered.

The generals ignored Andrea and pushed ahead.

"We need to take out those Chinese missile batteries now." Admiral Wilkerson was so angry he seemed capable of destroying them himself. "A barrage of cruise missiles should do the trick.

The ships we have approaching Taiwan are loaded with Tom-ahawks."

Andrea froze. Balancing a budget was one thing, but this was war. Not only war, but a clash with the world's only other superpower. How could she possibly tell the president and the military not to fight? How could she tell Americans they could not avenge China's brutality? Americans would see the same images of sailors leaping overboard and flaming ships sinking. Who was she to tell Americans they couldn't fight back? She wanted to fight back just as badly. A real political pro might know what to do, but she had no idea. The feeling she had in the Situation Room, of being out of her depth among titans of state, overtook her. *What on God's green earth am I doing here?*

Still, she had to say something. If she didn't, the country would run out of money to fight anyway. And then she'd have no choice but to say something.

"Just remember, each one of those cruise missiles costs one million dollars," she told the group, almost apologetically. "Once you fire them, we can't buy more."

"Goddammit, are you watching this? American sailors just got blown into the goddamned sea. You find the goddamned money for this war, you hear me?" Admiral Wilkerson yelled. Her budgetary bleating had pushed him to the edge.

Too tense to think of a reply, Andrea could only repeat herself. "Mr. President, if you want more money, we need to make more cuts."

Admiral Wilkerson pointed at Andrea, his finger shaking in fury. "We have American sailors trapped in Taiwan on those two ships tied up in Taipei Harbor. If we can't get them out because you can't fucking pay for it, that's on you, and we'll be sure to make sure everyone knows it's on you."

"Oh, cut the 'blame the accountant' crap," Andrea snapped.

Your procurement system is so screwed up you spend billions buying the wrong stuff just to keep jobs in some congressman's district. Your next-generation warships have cost tens of billions dollars so far, and one of them doesn't even have working guns. And don't get me started on your next-generation fighter jet."

Admiral Wilkerson's face hardened into a scowl.

Andrea continued undeterred. "Yeah, that's right, Little Miss Washington Rookie Accountant knows all about that. If you hadn't pissed all that money away on your hopelessly expensive warships and jets, maybe I could pay for a real war now instead of keeping your contractors fat, happy, and voting in some damned key district!"

"Enough of this!" President Murray regained control of the meeting. "Andrea, you said we have enough funds to fight four weeks of war? Fine. That's what we do. Then we see where we stand. If we decide to keep going and need to make cuts, we make the cuts."

In four weeks, the American treasury would truly be empty. Andrea imagined herself standing in front of an empty bank vault explaining to the country how it had no money to fight the war. And what if things went badly? What if the country ran out of money in less than four weeks? Her natural pessimism was in overdrive.

General Ogden remained ready to go to war. "What now, Mr. President? We need orders."

President Murray left no doubt he had made up his mind. "Four weeks of war. Provide me plans. We fight the Chinese for as long as we can."

"Yes sir," General Ogden and Admiral Wilkerson said in unison. They got up and made their way to the exit.

Something was still on Andrea's mind.

"Before you go—"

President Murray turned to Andrea. "What is it?"

Admiral Wilkerson and General Ogden stopped just short of the door and turned to Andrea. Both appeared ready to strangle Andrea and get on with drafting their war plans.

"Isn't anyone wondering what a coincidence it is that China started a war just as we were implementing our emergency budget?"

President Murray threw up his hands in exasperation. "All I know for sure is this: China is blockading Taiwan, holding American ships hostage, and shooting at our ships in the South China Sea. Right now, I don't care if Martians are responsible for the debt crisis. We need money to fight the Chinese. And I need you to find it." He pointed at her.

"We're going to have to go back to Congress, which means we're going to have to ask Congressman Mason for the money," said Andrea. "After that hearing a few weeks ago, I doubt he'll give me the time of day."

"I've got no use for Mason, but we're stuck," the president said. "I'm not about to bring a war to a halt in four weeks because we ran out of money. Go meet with him. Bring Brooks Powell with you. Let Mason know this is serious, not political bullshit he can screw around with. This is life or death. If he won't appropriate money, he can explain to the American public why we can't fight back after the Chinese started sinking American ships."

Asking Mason for money seemed a dubious proposition, but after watching the *Reagan* go down, she was sure General Ogden and Admiral Wilkerson would spend America's last nickel to defeat the Chinese. And President Murray, for now, agreed with them. So back to Mason it would be.

CHAPTER 32

Andrea had lost most of her staff under the emergency budget, which meant Rachel was now doing the jobs of three staffers, including getting the morning papers ready along with the daily pile of mail. Every morning she made sure copies of the *Washington Post*, the *New York Times*, and the *Wall Street Journal* were on Andrea's desk when she arrived for work. Although Andrea got most of her news online, she still liked to see the morning papers in the flesh.

But this morning Rachel was nervously waiting for her in the small waiting area outside their offices. Today was already going to be bad enough having to meet with Mason.

"Morning, Rachel. How bad is it?"

"You'd better take a look at the headlines." Rachel pointed to the stack of newspapers on Andrea's desk. "We've got our work cut out for us."

Rachel followed Andrea into her office and to her desk.

"Good lord, Rachel," said Andrea as she scanned the front pages of the papers. "This is the worst thing I've seen since 9/11."

"AMERICA AT WAR" screamed the headline of the Washington Post above a picture of the burning *Ronald Reagan* in the South China Sea, sailors leaping off it in desperate attempts to save themselves.

"When was the last time Americans saw American ships burning in the Pacific Ocean?" Andrea asked. "World War II? This is probably the first time in their lives anyone's seen pictures of a sinking aircraft carrier in a newspaper instead of a history book."

"It gets worse."

Andrea looked below the fold of the *Post*. Pictured there were the two American ships in the Port of Taipei with a caption noting the ships had lost contact with the United States. The Chinese had severed or jammed all communication links to Taiwan.

The second page of the *Post* featured an article on American public opinion of the war. The country had quickly divided into two camps. The first demanded immediate retaliation. These Americans wanted to see something in China burn. "They messed with the wrong country!" a former Marine was quoted as saying. "We ought to wipe Shanghai off the map."

The second camp questioned why the United States was in the Pacific in the first place during the emergency budget's dramatic belt-tightening. "My parents just lost their Social Security," another interviewee said. "They can't pay for their medicines. They can barely pay their rent. Why are Americans halfway around the world protecting other countries while people are being thrown out of nursing homes and half the country is losing its health insurance?"

"The man has a point," Andrea said. "But we know where Murray stands, don't we?"

"That's why we have the pleasure of meeting with Mason today," Rachel responded. "Somehow we've got to get Congress to add the funds the president needs to fight this war by making cuts to something else."

Andrea grimaced. *It figures. I finally take a stand and it comes back to bite me.*

Just then Secretary Brooks Powell walked into Andrea's office. "Morning, everyone, ready to go?" he said in his commanding voice. The secretary delivered even the simplest comments with an air of authority.

"Yes, sweetie," Rachel responded sarcastically. "Andrea can't wait."

"Yeah, I can't," replied Andrea. "After I swallowed my pride and agreed to meet with Mason, I chased it with a swig of the Pepto in my desk." Rachel and Brooks both laughed.

"All right, let's go," Rachel said.

They left the office and walked to the West Executive Avenue parking lot and got into Andrea's ancient Camry.

"We're headed to Morton's, right?" Andrea asked as she put the car in gear. "Just a few blocks up on Connecticut Avenue?"

"Yup," Brooks said as he fastened his seat belt. "It's a Mason favorite. Though it's not really Morton's that is Mason's favorite restaurant."

"How's that?" asked Andrea.

"Years before Morton's took the space, the restaurant was Duke Ziebert's," Brooks replied.

"Ah, Duke Ziebert's," Rachel replied.

"What's Duke Ziebert's?" Andrea asked.

"Sweetie, back in the day Duke Ziebert's was the place where power brokers went to see and be seen. Practically invented the power lunch."

"Mason was a regular there," Brooks added. "He loved how people would point to his table and whisper, 'That's Congressman Mason.' He lived for those moments. Duke Ziebert's closed a while back, but Mason loves the Morton's that replaced it."

"You all and your inside baseball Washington-speak," said Andrea.

The drive was short and within ten minutes Secretary Powell, Rachel, and Andrea were at the maître d's station in the front of Morton's. They saw Mason sitting at a table in the back corner near a window overlooking Connecticut Avenue.

Mason spotted them and scowled. He got up from his table and walked toward them. As he approached, Brooks stuck his arm out for a handshake, but Mason didn't reciprocate.

"What the hell is this?" Mason asked gruffly. "This meeting is supposed to be me and Andrea. That's it. Whose dumb idea was it for you two to come along?"

Brooks dropped his arm to his side. "Lew, come on. We told you—"

"Nobody told me nothing," Mason growled. "This meeting is me and Andrea alone. You two"—he pointed at Brooks and Rachel—"get lost. Or there's no meeting at all and I'll go back to my lunch. Your call."

"What about Frank Palmer?" asked Brooks. "You bring Frank to every meeting I've ever had with you. Where's he?"

"Thanks to your budget cutbacks I had to let him go," Mason growled. "All we can afford for staff on the Hill are fresh-out-of-college kids."

"So where'd he land?" asked Rachel.

"He was so humiliated from losing his job to this political amateur's budget," Mason replied, pointing to Andrea, "that he went completely off the goddamned grid and took a job helping to manage a ranch in Montana. Chucked his cell phone and everything. Said he was done with politics and this whole town could rot in hell for all he cared."

Andrea's shoulders sagged as she looked at Brooks and Rachel.

"There's a nice little chocolate shop in the basement of the building," Brooks said. Andrea appreciated his sparing her the embarrassment of having to tell him to leave. Rachel nodded reassuringly, letting Andrea know she understood too.

Brooks and Rachel went down the stairs toward the retail

basement of the building. Mason turned sharply and began walking back to his seat, saying nothing and barely acknowledging Andrea.

She followed quietly, nervous about being on her own. The maître d' shoved a menu into her hand as she walked by. She sat down across from Mason at the two-person table. Mason had already ordered his lunch and eaten half of it.

What a jerk. Trying his little power move knowing I'm here to ask him for help.

Mason seemed to only care about one thing: power. Who had it, who had more of it, and who sat where on the totem pole.

Mason took a bite of a well-done filet and spoke, chomping vigorously and not even trying to hide the food in his mouth. "This place used to be full of lunchtime chatter and the clinking of glasses and cutlery on plates filling the air. Now it's three-quarters empty."

"What happened?"

"Your shitty emergency budget, that's what," Mason said. "Great work by your crack budget team."

Andrea could see the half-chewed piece of filet in his mouth as he spoke. The frosty reception was a sure sign he was still smarting from the televised humiliation she'd dealt him.

He's baiting you. Don't let him suck you into an argument.

She tried to change the subject. "Congressman, you know why I'm here. We need to amend the emergency budget to reallocate funds for the war. The president, the Joint Chiefs, they all want to fight, but we need to amend the emergency budget to provide them the funding. I'm a budget person, not a foreign policy expert, but the president and Joint Chiefs made it clear to me. If we don't fight, the Chinese are going to own Taiwan, control the South China Sea, and make us look like impotent fools. Have you seen the papers this morning? Americans are demanding revenge after the *Reagan*. Plus, we've got two ships and hundreds of sailors stuck in Taipei Harbor."

Mason looked around and then leaned into the table furtively. "Not so fast, Andrea. Who says we're at war? Last I checked the Constitution required Congress to declare war, and I'm a constitutional conservative, you know." He smirked as he took a big gulp of water.

Andrea dropped her menu on the table in disgust. "The *Reagan* is at the bottom of the South China Sea with untold dead American sailors. And you don't think we're at war? You're not going to authorize an amended budget to allow us to respond to this crisis?"

"Listen to me, and listen to me good," said Mason. "I'm not going to get any more Americans into any more foreign wars. Taiwan is six thousand miles away from the United States, and any threat to it doesn't pose a threat to the United States. I'm not sending Americans to fight and die to free Taiwanese." He theatrically grabbed a roll, slathered it with butter, jammed it into his mouth, and ripped it apart with his teeth. He made no effort to hide the chewed roll in his mouth. "After Iraq I'm done with that shit."

A waiter came over to the table. "Ma'am, do you care to order?"

Andrea was about to respond when Mason interrupted. "She's not ready yet. Give her a few minutes."

"Okay, I'll come back," the waiter said with a look of confusion on his face.

Andrea slapped her menu down on the table. *Who does this guy think he is? No sense ordering now.*

"Mr. Mason, if Congress doesn't amend the emergency budget to fight this war, and the Chinese keep Taiwan and assert complete control over the South China Sea, this is going to be on you. When the media and history books ask 'Who Lost Taiwan?' your picture will appear right there."

Mason took a swig of his water and laughed. "Don't try to scare me, Andrea. When people living on Taiwan can vote for me, then maybe I'll reconsider. Until then, I'm not fighting a war for them."

Andrea had had enough. "Then we have nothing more to discuss."

"Yes, we do."

"What's that?"

For the first time, Mason appeared to be taking the conversation seriously. He had been about to take a bite of a large morsel of filet but instead put his fork and knife down. He looked around as if to make sure no reporters were around. Then he leaned into the table and scowled.

"Don't you ever, ever, ever fuck with me like that again in a hearing."

Andrea shook her head and did a double take. After all that windup, it was that stupid hearing he was so upset about? She blurted her thoughts before she could catch herself. "You're going to sell Taiwan down the river because I made you look bad in a hearing? The global order is collapsing and all you care about is your image on TV?"

"No, I'm selling Taiwan down the river because my constituents don't give a good goddamn about it. But if that pisses you off, so much the better."

Andrea stood up and turned to leave. Then she turned toward Mason, searching for something to say. Her mouth moved but nothing came out. She was too disgusted. She turned away and stormed toward the door.

The maître d' saw Andrea rushing past. "Ma'am, is everything okay?"

Andrea didn't even look in his direction.

Zooming down the stairs, she went down to the retail shops in the basement to find Brooks and Rachel. She spotted them in the far corner of a small bookstore where they probably were trying to hide from the press.

"What the hell happened up there?" Rachel asked.

"Goddamn stubborn mule," Andrea said. "I go through how important fighting this war is to the president, and what does that damned egotist tell me? That he's still pissed about the hearing a few weeks ago and he's not going to give us a dime."

"That's not like Mason," Brooks said. "He used to be one of the biggest superhawks in Congress. Now he's all Mr. Restraint?"

"He's just a cowardly politician," Andrea said in disgust. "He'll do whatever's popular to save his own skin, and no one calls him on his blatant hypocrisy. He can RINO away knowing his Debt Rebel Gang cronies will provide him cover."

Still, Andrea was bothered by Mason's response. President Murray had told her the same thing about Mason—that he had been one of the foremost hawks in Congress and never met an international intervention he didn't support. The Chinese were presenting the most serious challenge to the global balance of power since the end of the Cold War, and now Mason wanted to sit on the sidelines?

Rachel and Brooks seemed confused as well. They looked at one another without saying a word.

"What do we do now?" Andrea asked, breaking the discomforting silence.

"We're in a race against time," Brooks said. "One of three things can happen. We can win the war in four weeks. Or we somehow get Mason to change his mind and fund the war."

"What's the third option?" Rachel asked.

Andrea knew the answer and said it before Brooks could respond.

"Surrender."

The word hung in the air. No one said anything.

The unspoken prospect of losing the war was now out of the closet and on the table.

CHAPTER 33

A ndrea's neighborhood was dark. There were no lights on at her house except for the one in the guest bedroom where her mother was staying. The place seemed dead as if no one was home. Andrea pulled into the garage. Her husband's car was there.

It had been a long day, and Andrea was still frustrated by her failed meeting with Mason. She was tired and starving. When she made her way inside, she bee-lined for the kitchen.

"Where's my glasses?" her mother shouted. The voice was coming from upstairs.

"Mamie, that you? I'll come up in a sec." Andrea put her satchel down.

The house had a different feel. The first floor was dark and silent. Back in South Carolina, when Andrea would come home later, her kids were at the kitchen table doing homework while Ryan made dinner. Aaron might still be in his baseball uniform from practice, and she'd tell him to take off his cleats because of the mud he was traipsing about. Michelle might be in the den reading a book or working on an art project.

"I can't see a thing," Mamie cried from upstairs.

"Mamie, I'll be there in a second. Just let me put my stuff down."

Where was everybody? I just walked in the door and I already have a crisis to deal with? Little help here, people.

Andrea hurried up the stairs. The kids' rooms were dark and empty. Ryan wasn't upstairs either. Her mother was all alone and the only light upstairs was coming from her mother's room. Andrea opened the door and saw her mother on her hands and knees on the floor.

"Where could I have put my glasses?" Mamie said, squinting at the floor.

"Here they are." Andrea rushed over. "They were just on your dresser."

"Oh," her mother said. She stood up and took the glasses from Andrea. "Thank you, sweetheart. How was your day?"

"I've never been through anything like this in my life. I don't know how politicians do it. I'm bouncing from crisis to crisis and meeting to meeting. China. Debt. Fixing our budget. I swear, I check my hair in the mirror every time I go to the bathroom to see if there is any gray."

"That's not so bad, honey," said Mamie. "Your father spent four years in Vietnam, and I was trying to raise you while he was gone."

Andrea's heart pounded. Home was supposed to be a refuge. She needed support, not her mother diminishing the stress of the monumental challenges she was facing. And she was exhausted and smarting from Mason's lunchtime barbs. Something inside her snapped.

"Come on, Mom, can't you just offer a little sympathy? All I get at work is grief. I need support too, you know. Did it ever occur to you that maybe, just maybe, my shit just might be a little worse than your back-in-the-day whatever?" Andrea's exhaustion was getting the better of her. After all her days of biting her tongue and being diplomatic at work, it felt liberating to be able to say exactly what she was thinking.

"Everyone has shit, honey."

"Yeah, everyone has shit. The guy next door needs a new roof, you've got arthritis, and I'm dealing with a shooting war with

China and a national debt crisis. All sounds like the same shit to me."

"Oh, give it a rest already."

Andrea snapped, "Give it a rest? What I wouldn't do for a little goddamned rest! Tell you what, as soon as I get a rest, I'll give you a rest. How about that?"

Mamie rolled her eyes. "You always had a temper. That's why I always said you're not cut out for politics."

"You don't understand me at all, do you?" Andrea shouted. "Maybe having you come stay with us wasn't such a good idea."

"Maybe cutting my Medicare and forcing me out of the assisted living home wasn't such a good idea," her mother replied.

Take a breath. Count to ten.

"Enough about me," Andrea said. "What is going on around here? Where is everybody? This place feels like a mausoleum."

"I hate it here." Mamie hung her head. "The kids won't even talk to me, and your husband hates having me around."

"What do you mean the kids won't talk to you?"

"They hide in the basement all day after school playing video games or watching TV."

"They don't even say hi when they come home from school?"

"They give me a nasty look and go straight to the basement," Mamie said. "And you're never here to give them any discipline."

"Where's my husband?"

"He's sick of me. He won't even look me in the eye anymore he seems so disgusted with having me around. Last night he set up this microwave, put this stack of Chef Boyardee next to it, and wished me good luck." She pointed to the microwave on her dresser.

"Unbelievable," said Andrea. "I work a few weeks of really long days and this family comes apart at the seams."

She charged down the stairs looking for her husband and children. The kitchen was still silent. The television in the living room, usually the family's evening background music, was off.

She'd never seen the house like this. It was unsettling.

Andrea opened the door to the basement stairs and went down. She could hear the unmistakable sounds of *Call of Duty*. It had to be Aaron, hard at work on his Xbox.

Sure enough, Aaron was sitting on a couch, feet propped up on a coffee table, fixated on his video game. Michelle was sitting next to Aaron, zoning out to some garbage reality television program on her laptop. It looked like the *Real Housewives* of who-knows-where.

She found her husband under the stairs in front of the washer and dryer. He was doing laundry.

"What is going on down here?" she demanded. "My mother is all by herself upstairs."

"So what?" Aaron grumbled from the couch.

"You don't talk about your grandmother like that," Andrea said.

"If it wasn't for her, I'd be at baseball practice instead of here," Aaron huffed.

"Excuse me?"

"All the money got spent on Grandma's medicines so they had to cut the school's baseball team. We just moved here and already my favorite thing in the world has been taken away."

"Okay, everyone upstairs," Andrea announced.

"But Mom—"

"No buts. Now. Everyone upstairs."

Ryan emerged from beneath the stairs. He looked beaten, with bags under his eyes and an overgrowth of stubble on his face.

"But I have to finish the laundry," he said.

"Nice try," Andrea said. "Everyone up, now."

Aaron slammed the Xbox controller on the small table in front of the couch. Then the three of them trudged up the basement stairs, Andrea following and herding them up like cattle. They all sat down at the kitchen table.

"Ryan, bring my mother down, will you?"

Ryan grimaced. "I've had enough. All I do is help her get around. And all she does is complain. She's *your* mother. Why don't you get her?"

"Dammit, Ryan, if you want to stay married, you get your ass up there right now and bring her down."

"Fine," said Ryan, irritated. He got up from the table, forcefully shoving his chair in, and went upstairs.

Aaron and Michelle laid their heads on the table, preparing to ignore the conversation.

A few moments later, Ryan came back with Mamie clutching his left arm. She winced in pain with every step from her arthritis. Andrea pulled out a chair from the kitchen table, and she and Ryan seated her mother and pushed the chair in. Then Ryan and Andrea sat down.

"Okay, what is going on in this house?" Andrea said.

No one answered.

"I mean it, someone better tell me what is going on, or I—"

"Fine, Mom, I'll tell you," Aaron blurted. "This is all her fault." He pointed to Mamie.

"What are you talking about?" Andrea had no idea what had gotten into her son. "What is all Grandma's fault?"

"All the kids are saying the school had to cancel the baseball team and the other sports teams because there is no more money to pay for them," said Aaron. "The kids say it's because we had to pay for old people's medicines and food and homes."

"Yeah," interjected Michelle. "And they had to cancel the after-school art classes because they said they didn't have any money anymore."

Aaron continued, "The kids at school say it's your fault, Mom, and the old people like Grandma. They said you took away the money for the school's baseball team to pay for all the stuff old people get."

Curse those little brats at school filling her kids' heads with nonsense. And curse their parents for feeding their kids the nonsense they took to school to torment her kids.

Except it wasn't nonsense. It was true, and Andrea knew it.

She took a breath. The kids deserved an explanation.

"Listen," Andrea said to Aaron and Michelle, "I know this is hard for you. It's hard for everyone. But this is not Grandma's fault. It's not any one person's fault. But things are bad for a lot of people. A lot of their parents are losing their jobs. Be thankful that's not happening to you. You've got a roof over your head and food on the table."

"Yeah, but big deal. Life sucks," said Aaron. "No baseball. And I'm losing all the friends I've just started making at school because they say this is your fault, Mom. It's not fair."

"You're right. It's not fair," Andrea said. "But no one said life was fair. And you're not the only one suffering."

"I don't care about anyone else's suffering," Aaron replied, annoyed.

Andrea froze, stunned by her son's callousness. She and Ryan hadn't raised their children to be uncaring ingrates. Had they really become this spoiled, this bratty, this selfish? Her first instinct was to unleash some unadulterated maternal discipline.

But she hesitated. Her son might be acting selfishly, but he was precociously perceptive. Andrea had lashed out at the American people for saddling the country with ruinous debt to feed their insatiable appetites. She'd stomped her feet about earlier generations of Americans leaving her with this mess to solve. Her son's anger was an unrefined and unfiltered reflection of her own feelings. The only difference was that he was thirteen and unable to restrain himself the way she could. How could she get angry with him? She understood him and, deep down, agreed with him.

No, scolding the kids wasn't the right approach.

"Aaron, Michelle, I understand what you are going through, believe me I do," Andrea said quietly. She took Aaron's hand. "You both are right. What we are going through is awful. And I am so sorry this is hurting you. This isn't your fault, and I don't blame you for being angry."

Unconvinced, Aaron shook his head.

Andrea had a thought. "Why don't you get the kids at school to go to the park after school and organize your own baseball game?"

"None of the kids at school want to play with me. I just started making friends and now they all hate me because of what you did. I'm locked out of all the games at recess. I sit alone in the football bleachers. And no one will eat lunch with me in the cafeteria. I sit all by myself."

"What about me?" asked Michelle. "I just made friends with Stephanie down the street, and now she's leaving school. I have no one to play with."

"Stephanie Brown left school?" asked Andrea.

"Yeah, she did."

"Why?" asked Ryan.

"She said her parents needed her to stay home and help around the house," said Michelle. "Her father lost his job and her mother is working at night so they can pay for things."

Andrea and Ryan exchanged a look. Stephanie Brown's father worked for the government. He'd probably been laid off. In addition to everything else, Andrea was responsible for forcing kids to quit school to work. She pictured ten-year-old Stephanie washing dishes and doing laundry like some Oliver Twist street urchin, her little fingers getting wrinkled and cracked as she scrubbed soap off dishes and folded clothes.

What have I done? thought Andrea. *I am despised. My family is despised. Everyone is in misery, all because of me.*

"We've had a major uptick in admissions for depression at the hospital," said Ryan. "I have double the case load I had two months ago. And half the pay. All these people are Medicaid or Medicare patients. Half of them can't pay a thing."

Her family's every word was another jab to her chest. She felt alone, even at home. She had no sanctuary from the horrors she'd unleashed on the country, on her neighbors, on her family. She wanted to crawl in a hole and hide from the world, never showing her face in public again. Maybe she could live like a hermit on some secluded beach off the grid.

"I don't care what you say," Aaron said. "All this has ruined my life."

Andrea could see she hadn't gotten through to the kids. It was once again time to commit candor.

"Aaron, Michelle," Andrea said. "Look at me."

"What, Mom?" Aaron replied, still moping at the table.

"I know exactly how you are feeling," she said. "I feel the same way. I do. But there are times in life where we have every right to be angry but we have to bear it. In fifty years, we will all look back and remember how we got through this horrible period of our lives. And, hopefully, we'll learn not to get ourselves into this situation again. Every generation of Americans has had its trials. The Civil War. The Great Depression. World War I. World War II. The Cold War. The COVID pandemic. This is your trial, and as hard as it is to understand now, someday you will look back on this as a shared experience that forged your generation."

As she spoke, she felt as though she was working to convince herself as much as her children.

"I wish I could make things better. Nothing pains me more than to see you suffering. But understand, we *will* come out of this, and someday it will be just a memory. I know it is hard for you to see that now, but you have to trust me."

Aaron exhaled. "I'm still angry," he said in a subdued voice. Andrea was getting through to him.

"Of course you are," Andrea said, still holding his hand. "I don't blame you. You have every right to be angry. But I don't want you to burn yourself up. Bottling up your anger will only hurt you. It won't fix what's making you angry. Keep your chin up. Things will get better, I promise."

"So what are we supposed to do?" Michelle interjected. "How can we have the right to be angry but not get angry?"

Andrea hesitated. "You know, you can help me save America. You can be part of the team that's working to get America back on her feet."

"How's that?" Aaron perked up.

"You and your sister have a chance to set an example for the kids at school and the rest of the country. What our country needs right now is to stiffen its upper lip and dial back the anger. So much of this country is angry. I see it every day. The talk radio and cable TV firebrands and their Debt Rebel Gang buddies that dumped me? They weren't worried about the debt. They were angry. And to be honest, they had a right to be angry. People called them racist, sexist, religious zealots, illiterate and uneducated hicks, and who knows what else. The smart set told them to sit on the side of the road and sip a Slurpee, laughed about their lack of sophistication, and called them troglodytes for trying to maintain traditions that had been uncontroversial for two thousand years. Thing is, anger doesn't pay back debt."

"So what are we supposed to do?" Michelle asked.

Ryan gestured to Andrea. "What we can do now is look forward, not backward. Your mother and I are making less money right now, so we need to make cutbacks around here. No more restaurants or going to the movies for a while."

Aaron sighed and Michelle put on her pouty face. "I can keep playing the Xbox, right?" asked Aaron.

"Yes, but we could take the opportunity to make some changes around here too," said Ryan. "More family time. We're going to start doing more things together. I'll teach you how to make a lasagna."

"Your father is a good cook," said Andrea.

"We can ride bikes," continued Ryan. "Read some books. We have five groaning bookcases full of books in the basement your grandfather left us. Work on some photo albums."

"And spend some time with your grandmother," said Andrea.

Aaron and Michelle both nodded. They were downcast—who could blame them?—but they were accepting. It was all Andrea could ask of them.

"All right, you two. Bedtime," said Ryan.

Aaron and Michelle dragged themselves up the stairs, heads hanging.

"We taught you well," Mamie said.

"I wish I completely believed what I was telling them," Andrea replied. "I'm not sure I convinced them. I'm not sure I'm convinced myself."

"You did fine, honey." Mamie gently rubbed Andrea's back. "I'm sorry I gave you a hard time before. I know you are stressed. We're all on a knife's edge."

Andrea gave Mamie a hug.

Mamie continued, "The kids are going through a very hard

time. I'm not sure your father or I could have calmed them down the way you did."

"Practice makes perfect." Andrea smiled ruefully. "And Lord knows I'm getting plenty of practice."

CHAPTER 34

"Where are we going?" Andrea asked as she ducked into the presidential limousine. Known as "the Beast," the multimillion-dollar custom Cadillac had armored plating, bulletproof windows, and fine leather seats. It even carried two pints of the president's blood in case of emergency.

"The Pentagon," President Murray responded. "We're going to try plan B to get Mason to give us the money we need to keep fighting."

"What? After he gave me the brush-off yesterday at lunch? There's no way he's going to come around. He's more than content to let us twist in the wind."

President Murray adjusted his glasses slightly.

"We're going to fight this war, dammit." He smacked his armrest for emphasis. "We simply can't let the Chinese sink American ships with impunity. And we can't sit idly by and watch the Chinese gobble up Taiwan. Every country in the world will conclude American security guarantees aren't worth the paper they're printed on. It will be open season for the world's worst actors."

Sixteen black cars, trucks, and vans made up the presidential motorcade. Some of them appeared to be carrying enough sophisticated equipment to land men on the moon.

Why do we need sixteen tricked-out vehicles to take the president five miles across the river to the Pentagon? she thought. *I bet this motorcade costs a million dollars.*

"Do whatever you have to do to convince him, Mr. President,"

Andrea said. "In four weeks, there will be no more money for the troops or the war. Unless you can convince Mason and Congress to amend the emergency budget to get more funds, this war will stop in thirty days. I'm sure the Chinese know this."

"I'll do everything I can to convince him." Murray's unsteady voice betrayed his uncertainty.

The little American flag and the flag with the presidential seal on the hood of the Beast, trimmed in gold braids, fluttered in the breeze as the limousine raced the five miles to the Pentagon.

Within ten minutes, Andrea and President Murray were walking through corridors of the inner sanctum of the American defense establishment. The corridors were lined with mahogany paneling. Portraits of past Defense Secretaries lined the walls. Every office was filled with large racks of commemorative coins, framed and folded ceremonial flags, detailed desk models of various weapons systems, statuettes of eagles and flags, and other knick-knacks. What Andrea wouldn't do to get the dollars spent on all those baubles back.

An army staffer led them into a conference room where Secretary Andrews, Admiral Wilkerson, and General Ogden were waiting.

"Jesus, look at this door," Andrea muttered. "It must be two feet thick."

"One and a half, ma'am," said the staffer.

"This must be the most secure conference room in America."

"They don't call it the Tank for nothing," he said. "It's got lead-lined walls, soundproofing, and a few other things I can't talk about."

The room wasn't just secure; it was downright opulent. The audio/visual equipment couldn't be more than a year old. Brand-new plaques of the seals of each branch of the armed services hung on the wall. The leather of the chairs, embossed with the seal of the different armed forces, still looked and smelled fresh. The Pentagon staff had placed the president's special chair with the presidential seal at the head of the long oak table. They'd even put out a special coffee mug with the presidential seal.

"You might be the first OMB director ever to set foot in here," Secretary Andrews said with a look of disgust on his face.

"I might be the first OMB director ever to dictate war strategy," she responded. "History I could have done without making."

"We could have done without it too," Admiral Wilkerson grumbled.

"Ease up, Admiral," President Murray said. "All of our nerves are frayed. Don't make things worse than they already are."

"My apologies, sir." The admiral nodded.

President Murray briskly went to his seat at the head of the table. "Everyone sit down. Is Mason on his way?"

"No idea," said one of the Pentagon staffers.

Andrea sat against the wall in the row of chairs set up for staffers. Only the military men sat at the table. Admiral Wilkerson and General Ogden seated themselves beneath the video screen at the other end of the long table opposite the president.

A knock at the door interrupted the awkward wait.

"Congressman Mason," President Murray said. "Glad you could make it."

A wave of anxiety flushed through Andrea when Mason walked in. She gripped her padfolio tightly to stifle her quivering hands.

"I appreciate the invitation. Sorry I'm late. Had a committee meeting that went overtime."

Lying jerk, she thought. Mason did a radio interview with the PureCon Radio Network every Wednesday morning. It had probably run long.

"I wanted Congressman Mason joining us today because it's important he understand the situation in Taiwan when we negotiate the budget," President Murray said.

"*If* we negotiate the budget," Mason chimed in.

Grumbles filled the room at Mason's rude rebuke of the president.

President Murray acted as if nothing had happened and started the meeting. "You all know why I've called you here. I know things are bad. But I want to understand exactly where things stand and our strategy for where we go from here."

Admiral Wilkerson began the presentation. An aide in the back clicked open the presentation on a laptop. A hush fell over the room as the picture of the hulk of a naval vessel appeared on the screen, its battleship gray charred to black.

"This is the USS *Florida*," said Admiral Wilkerson. "She was hit by a surface-to-surface missile. You can see the thirty-foot hole on its starboard side scorched at its edges. Somehow she managed not to sink and we towed her to the Philippines."

Jagged, twisted metal was visible inside the ship.

"Jesus," Murray said. "Did anyone survive?"

"I'm warning you about the next photo," Wilkerson said. "This one is graphic."

"I can handle it." The president gestured to the aide running the presentation. "Put it up."

Andrea wasn't sure if she could handle it, but she wasn't going to object. The less attention on her, the better.

The *Florida*'s control room appeared onscreen. Toppled chairs, shattered computer screens, and dangling wires littered the room. A severed arm lay on the floor, the now-dried blood that had emptied from it coating the floor. Three dead sailors, their faces bruised, bloodied, and swollen, were still strapped to their seats.

Andrea put her hand to her mouth. The pictures were graphic indeed. She tried to take her mind off the images by counting the number of stars on the service logos on the wall.

"Good lord," President Murray exclaimed. "Did anyone survive?"

"Not many. The command staff was all killed. Only the sailors in the bow or stern of the boat furthest away from the missile impact survived."

Andrea glanced over at Mason to see his reaction. He was chewing the ends of his glasses. The graphic photos had gotten his attention. Maybe the blunt presentation would change his mind about funding the war after all.

Admiral Wilkerson continued. "This next photo is the sunken wreckage of the USS *New York*. A surface-to-surface missile hit her broadside in her stern."

The *New York*'s stern had been blown to pieces.

"Here is a picture of the *New York*'s engine room," the admiral said. "This one's graphic too. We sent divers to look for survivors. What you're about to see is all they found."

In the flooded engine room of the *New York*, the bodies of two drowned soldiers bobbed silently. Their bloated faces stared hauntingly, the shock of their last moments on Earth fixed upon their frozen countenances. Broken metal shafts and turbine blades littered the scene. The camera flash reflected off the oil-stained water, giving the scene an eerie greenish hue.

Andrea turned away, her hand covering her eyes. She thought about Aaron and Michelle. These dead sailors were somebody's children.

She glanced at Mason. He was jotting on his notepad. From his hand motion he was underlining something emphatically. He must have sensed Andrea looking at him because he lifted his head and his eyes met hers. She looked away, embarrassed he'd caught her watching him.

"Do you want me to continue?" Admiral Wilkerson asked. "I've got at least thirty more photos like this."

President Murray put his hand to his temple and exhaled. He looked around the room at the other attendees, as if to silently gauge their thoughts.

"Do you really have thirty more photos like these?" said Mason. Even he seemed aghast.

"Yes, sir, at least thirty more. And I started with the least gruesome ones. The next ones are worse by orders of magnitude."

Andrea's mind raced with plausible excuses she could give to leave the room.

"I've seen enough." Mason put his pen down and wiped his eyes. "I don't need to see any more."

"Maybe just give us the bottom line," President Murray said.

Admiral Wilkerson cleared his throat and straightened his posture. "Mr. President, the first two weeks of the war have been a bloodbath. We've lost fifteen ships. Seven have been sunk, including the *Reagan*. The other eight are so badly damaged they won't be usable for at least a year."

"Casualties?" Murray asked.

"Over two thousand. Nine hundred dead, eleven hundred wounded. Many badly," said Admiral Wilkerson, folding his arms in front of his waist.

General Ogden weighed in. "And the Chinese have kept the Air Force from taking the Chinese air defenses out. We've lost seven F-35s and ten F-15s."

"How about the situation in Taiwan?" the president asked.

"It's no better," Admiral Wilkerson reported. "Our Army and Marine detachments have suffered two thousand casualties, including five hundred deaths."

Admiral Wilkerson gestured to the staffer in the back of the room. The staffer clicked a mouse a few times until he reached a photo of two large building complexes.

"These are the Taiwanese parliament building and presidential palace, Mr. President. Both are flying Red Chinese flags."

Mason pulled his glasses off his face in astonishment. "I never thought I'd see the day Taiwan fell to the Chinese," he said. "The Chinese have wanted to take back Taiwan for nearly a century. They're probably dancing in the government compound in Beijing. If we lose this war, the post-World War II international order will end, and China will be the predominant global power."

"That's exactly right, Lew," Murray replied. "But it doesn't have to end this way. We need funding to fight back and avenge our soldiers and sailors, funding only you and the Appropriations Committee can provide."

Mason nodded. "I've never seen pictures that gruesome. I know what my constituents would want me to do about this. I'll need to convince the Appropriations Committee, especially the Debt Rebel Gang members."

"I'm glad you've come around, Lew," the president said. "After Andrea told me how your lunch went, I thought you'd made up your mind."

Mason sneered at Andrea. "You shouldn't have sent her to talk to me. After her antics in that televised hearing, I needed to put her in her place and remind her who runs appropriations in this town. Now that I've gotten that taken care of, we can get down to negotiating."

Andrea was on the edge of her seat poised to defend herself when President Murray shot her a look. She understood. The president had gotten what he wanted from Mason. He didn't want her to say anything that might upset his hard-won victory. Andrea grimaced but nestled herself back into her seat.

"I can send Andrea and a team up to the Appropriations Committee to hash out a deal on funding if you want," President Murray said.

"Don't even think about that," Mason replied. "She's *persona non grata* with my committee."

"I'm willing to go up personally if that's what it will take," the president offered.

"No, let me talk to the committee," Mason said. "Trust me, I have more credibility with the Debt Rebel Gang members than any of you do. The only way they'll be convinced to fund the war is if I can assure them the Debt Rebellion won't excommunicate them as heretics."

"Okay, Lew, let us know how it goes," President Murray said.

"We stand ready to help in any way," Admiral Wilkerson added.

The budding lovefest left Andrea cold. She couldn't tell if President Murray was feeling the same discomfort she was. Mason had already screwed her once when he denied her his endorsement in her congressional race. She was uncomfortable having her fate in Mason's hands once again. But the president appeared at ease.

"Gentlemen," said Mason, standing from his seat and preparing to leave, "when I have an answer for you, I will be sure to communicate it to you and to the public. I want to rally the public to my position."

"Thank you, Lew." The president walked over to Mason, followed by Admiral Wilkerson and General Ogden. They each shook Mason's hand as he left the room.

"Gentlemen, thank you for the briefing," President Murray said to the admiral and the general. "Please keep me posted on war developments, and I will let you know if we need your help getting funding from the Hill."

"Thank you, sir," Admiral Wilkerson said. He and General Ogden saluted and left the room.

Driving back to the White House complex in the Beast, Andrea couldn't hold her doubts back any longer.

"I don't trust Mason," she said. "Do you really think he'll be able to convince the rest of the Debt Rebel Gang and the Appropriations Committee?"

"Don't worry about them. They're probably just worried they'll be disinvited from next year's TrueCon Fest if they vote for the war funding." President Murray laughed. "I'm sure once Mason promises they can vote for the war funding and keep their anti-Establishment cards they'll fall in line."

"Just remember what he did to me when I was running for Congress," said Andrea.

"You still have PTSD from your congressional race, don't you?" He chuckled. "Don't let it overwhelm your judgment now. He didn't have any problems screwing you back then because you were a nobody accountant from Bumblefuck, USA. I'm the president of the United States."

If you say so, Mr. President.

CHAPTER 35

A ndrea felt cautiously optimistic after the Pentagon meeting. Maybe President Murray was right. Maybe once Mason came around the country would be able to fund the war. But the sight that greeted her when she arrived at the EEOB the following morning snapped her back to her default pessimism.

"What is going on out there?" she asked as she walked into her office suite. "The whole place is surrounded by police and metal barricades. And there are a ton of people out there. I could barely get in."

"There's a big anti-war protest this morning in Lafayette Park," said Rachel. "Can't say I'm surprised. Our polling has gone into the toilet."

Andrea flipped through the *Washington Post* and *New York Times*. Rachel was right. Seventy percent of Americans now opposed the war.

"I guess the American public didn't react well to the sight of sinking American ships and outgunned landing forces," Andrea said. "Anything else to brighten my day?"

"There's a report Mason might break his silence and go public with his position on the war today in a speech on the House floor," Rachel said.

That was quick. Maybe Mason had no trouble getting his Debt Rebel Gang cronies in line. And maybe what he says will calm the protesters.

"When is he speaking?"

"Not sure yet, but I'll keep you posted. The protest will be starting in a little bit if you want to hunker down somewhere."

Andrea looked down at the papers and thought for a moment. "Actually, I might go out there and see how people are feeling for myself. Us non-political types don't always believe the polls. You think it'd be safe for me to go out there and see how people are feeling?"

"You're the OMB director, not the Beatles," Rachel said. "I think you'll be okay."

Andrea made her way outside onto the stretch of Pennsylvania Avenue in front of the White House. It was barely nine and Lafayette Park was already teeming with protesters. They had completely stopped traffic on H Street at the north end of the park. People were streaming in from Sixteenth Street and Connecticut Avenue to the north, New York Avenue to the east, and Pennsylvania Avenue to the west. There had to be at least five thousand people crammed into Lafayette Square and the surrounding streets.

The massive throng held a dizzying array of signs. "Taiwan is a Western Colony," read one. Another said, "America Is Not the World's Policeman" on one side and "Let Someone Else Protect the South China Sea" on the other. A protester with a bullhorn shouted about "nation-building at home, not three thousand miles away." Chants of "gut the military, not Social Security" and "pay for Medicare, not war," echoed off the stately façades of the nineteenth-century townhouses lining Lafayette Square.

What member of Congress is going to vote for more Medicare cuts to fund this war now?

Andrea's worst fears were coming true. President Murray had started a war he might not have the money to finish.

She lowered her head, undid her ponytail, and waded into the crowd. She thought letting her hair down might help hide her as she wandered through the protest.

It was a strange mix of aging hippies with guitars and tambourines, young millennials with iPhones Instagramming the protest, feminists with pink anti-war shirts, even some shirt-and-tie professionals who looked like they were on break from one of the local law firms.

Counter-protesters had made their way into the crowd and mixed uneasily with the protesters. A few "Don't Surrender to the Chinese Commies" signs dotted the landscape. It didn't take long for Andrea to run into two protestors arguing.

"It's not America's job to keep ships going through the South China Sea," shrieked an older woman who appeared to be in her sixties. "We're spending all this money and watching our soldiers die for other countries. If it's so important to keep the South China Sea open, let other countries fight for it."

A middle-aged man in a leather bomber jacket and crewcut shouted back, "Did you see what the Chinese did to us? They killed thousands of our troops, and they had a right to be there. They're holding American ships in Taiwan hostage. We should fight those bastards to the death!"

The anti-war protesters had formed a circle about six feet in diameter around the arguing counter protestor and the others with him.

"You fucking warmongers!" an anti-war protester on the circle's perimeter yelled.

"Chicken hawk bitches!" yelled another.

Andrea didn't like where this was heading. She scanned the crowd for Park Police or Secret Service.

"Fuck you, you wannabe Vietnam anti-war protest play actors," another man bellowed as he rolled up his sleeves. "If you don't want to fight the Chinese, American blood is on your hands!"

He lurched toward the crowd and started swinging. The protesters mobbed the counter-protesters.

"Stop it, stop it!" Andrea shouted.

Andrea found herself in the middle of a scrum of protesters and counter-protesters. She was feeling around her pocket for her cell phone to call for help when a group of Park Police in full riot gear moved in, slammed several people to the ground, and handcuffed them. Andrea was knocked down in the melee.

"You all right, ma'am?" An officer outstretched a hand to pull Andrea up.

"I think so," Andrea said. "Just a little jostled, that's all."

"Miss Gartner?" The policeman recognized her. "What are you doing out here?"

"Wanted to see what people were saying up close and personal."

The officer shook his head disapprovingly. "It's not safe for you to be out here during protests. They should have gone over that when you started. If you really want to come out here like this, you need to call the Secret Service first and get an escort."

"All right, *mea culpa*," Andrea said. "I've learned my lesson."

The morning had left no doubt in Andrea's mind. Americans were at each other's throats. And time and money were running out.

The policeman led her back to her office in the EEOB.

"Good lord, Andrea, what happened to you?" Rachel exclaimed. Andrea glanced in her office mirror and saw her jacket was covered in dirt, her hair was a mess, and her lipstick was smudged on her face.

"Are you her assistant?" the officer asked.

"I am."

"Do me a favor and don't let your principal go running around protests again by herself, okay?" he said.

"Okay, okay." Rachel turned to Andrea. "Let's get you into your office and on the couch. You look dazed."

Rachel seated Andrea on the couch and brought her a bottle of water.

Just then the phone rang. Rachel went to Andrea's desk and picked up the phone. "It's Stanley Marshal."

"I'll take it."

Rachel pressed the speakerphone button so Andrea could take the call from her couch. "Stan, what's up?"

"Congressman Mason has scheduled a speech on the House floor this morning. The president would like you to join him in the Oval Office to watch."

"Of course, Stan. I'll be there."

"So it's true Mason's finally going to take a position," said Rachel. "I guess he was able to get in touch with his TrueCon Network buddies to find out what the anti-Establishment position is so he could take it."

"You're more of a cynic than I am." Andrea smirked lightly.

"I've been in politics longer than you, sweetie," Rachel replied.

"Mason was supportive of more funding when we left the Pentagon yesterday." Andrea's voice betrayed uncertainty. "He said it himself that if we lose this war, China will become the preeminent world power. That seemed to change his tune."

"Like that'll mean anything to Mason and company," Rachel grumbled. "If you ask me, it'll all depend on what his voters are saying."

"For once, I hope you're wrong," said Andrea.

The energy in the Oval Office was tense. Vice President Campbell, Brooks Powell, Admiral Wilkerson, and General Ogden were already there when she arrived. The protestors in Lafayette Park remained in full throat. President Murray seemed focused on the television in front of the Oval Office fireplace. It was tuned to

C-SPAN's coverage of Mason's speech. Lawmakers were shuffling into the House chamber, murmuring greetings to one another.

The lawmakers' gathering lacked the jocular atmosphere of a State of the Union Address. A sense of foreboding filled the air. Yet the president seemed unusually confident. Perhaps he knew something they didn't.

"Thanks for coming, Andrea," the president said with an assured smile.

"I'm worried about this speech," Andrea replied. "That was awfully quick for him to convince the Debt Rebel Gang."

"Relax, Andrea. Mason said he'd get the Appropriations Committee and his Debt Rebel Gang cronies in line," Murray said. "He hasn't called to report any holdouts. If there was a problem, we'd know by now."

"As soon as he announces the additional war funding, we can implement some of the additional attack strategies for dislodging the Chinese from Taiwan," said General Ogden.

Mason took to the floor. C-SPAN's cameras panned the House chamber. The House, usually empty for these floor speeches, was filled with members awaiting Mason's comments. What Mason said in the next fifteen minutes would determine the course of the war, the course of the Murray presidency, and the course of world events. Andrea's pulse quickened.

The cameras cut to the ornate rear doors of the House chamber made famous in every State of the Union speech. They flung open and in marched Mason, speech in hand.

"He's in his element now," said President Murray. "A packed house and all of America watching. He's about to work his 'no-one-is-more-conservative-than-me' shtick for all it's worth. At least he'll be using it to help us for once."

Mason strode to the well of the House. A hush descended over the chamber. Mason unfolded his speech and began.

"For two weeks now, Americans have been fighting and dying in Taiwan. The war costs America a billion dollars day. Hundreds of billions of dollars in military equipment has been destroyed. For what? To protect *Pax Americana*? Why should we be the ones to keep the world's peace? Every time Republicans talk about defending *Pax Americana*, there is never any *pax* involved. No, always shooting and war and imposing America's will on someone else. All of this is paid for by the American taxpayer. Why?

"Meanwhile, President Murray is slashing Americans' Social Security. He's taking away your Medicare benefits. Seniors are being thrown out into the streets with no money and no way to get the prescription drugs they need to stay alive. The poorest Americans have seen their social welfare safety net cut away. They are without food. They are without shelter. They are without medicine."

"What the fuck is he doing?" President Murray shouted, horrified.

That goddamned momzer did it again, Andrea thought. *And this time he's screwing over the president of the United States.*

Mason took a breath and surveyed the crowd, a malicious smile creeping across his face. He looked directly into the camera.

"President Murray would rather save an island of foreigners than feed, clothe, and provide medicine to Americans. He would rather fight a war in Asia than provide retirees their hard-earned Social Security. I categorically reject this and say:

"Come home, America.

"Come home and care for your parents and grandparents.

"Come home, America, and provide for your children.

"Come home, America, and let other countries pay for their own defense.

"Come home, America, and support the troops by keeping them out of war.

"I will not let my committee or my party vote to amend the emergency budget to pay for the president to fight half a world away."

President Murray glowered at the television screen, his hands balled into fists. "That goddamned two-faced backstabbing son of a bitch," he snarled through gritted teeth.

"If the president wants to save money, he doesn't need to write a new budget. He just needs to stop spending on a war in Taiwan," Mason continued. "How hard is that? I have been watching President Murray's war and it has become clear to me. This war is lost. We will not defeat the Chinese in a few more weeks of fighting, and Congress will not approve one more nickel for this war. That is my solemn pledge.

"It is time to end 'Murray's Chinese Theater.' The president should apologize to China, negotiate a withdraw of American troops and vessels from the area, end this madness, and bring our troops home."

The House chamber erupted in applause. Only a handful of the most hawkish Republicans sat on their hands. All the Democrats and two-thirds of Mason's fellow Republicans were on their feet cheering.

"What the hell just happened?" President Murray jumped from his seat and swung at the air. "They're treating him like he just won the Battle of Normandy. We're going to lose this war because of him!"

He grabbed the vase from the coffee table and hurled it against the wall. It exploded into a thousand pieces, with Andrea, General Ogden, and Admiral Wilkerson ducking for cover from flying ceramic shrapnel.

"Did you see the way Congress reacted?" the president roared. His face flushed red as he paced the perimeter of the Oval Office. "What the hell was Mason thinking? He promised me he would get the Appropriations Committee onboard. He lied straight to my face. That goddamned son of a bitch!"

"Mason may be an opportunistic jerk, but what about the rest of them?" Andrea said. "Was anyone not giving him a standing ovation? There's no way we're going to be able to amend the emergency budget to fund the war."

She resisted the urge to let fly an *I told you so*. Having been on the business end of Mason's duplicity had sensitized her to his antics in a way President Murray hadn't experienced. Until now.

President Murray stopped and stared intently at the picture of Andrew Jackson on the wall. Andrea knew her history. Jackson probably would have challenged Mason to a duel. And he would have kept fighting until the war was over or he was impeached and removed. Or shot dead on the battlefield himself. Earl Murray might be tough, but he was no Andrew Jackson. And it wasn't 1830. Presidents didn't saddle up and ride onto the battlefield. Mason's speech and the reaction to it told the tale. Murray was going to have to pull the troops from Taiwan and the South China Sea.

"These spineless weasels are pathetic," General Ogden growled. "Congress is going to leave our soldiers to die at the hands of some damned Communists. Are we seriously going to acquiesce in the worst territorial land grab since Hitler invaded Poland? Because we're broke?"

General Ogden's words were a gut punch. He might as well have tossed the blame right at Andrea's feet. She thought about resigning right then and there. Just get up and walk out. Go home to her kids.

But it was too late for that. If she'd resigned before the war started, she might have kept President Murray from starting the war. Now she was responsible for all the American lives lost in vain. She walked to the window and stared at the landscaping outside, trying to keep her emotions in check.

"There is no way at all I'm going to sit and let some finger-in-the-wind bullshit artist like Lew Mason let the Chinese get away with sinking our ships and killing our sailors," Admiral Wilkerson shouted. "This is nuts. You think Andrew Jackson or Teddy Roosevelt or Ronald Reagan would have cowered in the face of a chickenshit Congress? Hell no. He'd tell Congress the war was happening and grab the money from someplace and do it. How many divisions does Congress have? They want to stop this war? Over my dead body!"

The yelling was getting to be too much. Andrea imagined herself riding a centrifuge spinning so quickly it was disintegrating, flinging parts in all directions. Desperate for calm, she turned to Admiral Wilkerson.

"Look, Admiral—"

"I've heard just enough out of you, you goddamned bean counter," Wilkerson shouted. "You're the one who got us into this mess."

"You're blaming me?" said Andrea. "I didn't send that flotilla into the South China Sea to be sitting ducks for China's target practice. You're the one who said the Chinese would never be dumb enough to shoot at our flotilla. This flotilla, this whole war, all of this is on you, not me."

"Why you goddamned—"

Admiral Wilkerson lunged at Andrea and shoved her backward into the Resolute desk. Her upper back hit the desk and she fell to the floor. She stared up at the admiral, stunned.

"Get a hold of yourself!" General Ogden shouted. He grabbed the enraged Wilkerson and shoved him over to the couch in the middle of the room.

"You disgrace!" Murray shouted. "How dare you physically assault someone in this office! Your resignation! Now!"

Red-faced and huffing, Admiral Wilkerson ripped the ribbons from his uniform and slammed them on the coffee table. Then he ripped off his medals and slammed them down so hard the glass on the table cracked.

"You are leaving over a hundred dead American sailors at the bottom of the South China Sea and doing nothing to avenge them. And you call me a disgrace?" He flung his hat like a Frisbee across the room, and it slammed with a thud against the wall. "You make me sick. Never spent a day in harm's way in your life, and now you're cutting the military off because you are too cheap and too chickenshit to pay to defend them. Rot in hell, all of you."

Wilkerson stormed out of the room. His ribbons and medals, a lifetime of service, sat in a disheveled pile on the broken coffee table.

General Ogden helped Andrea up from the floor. "You okay?"

"I'm fine. I'm sure worse has happened in this office."

"Why don't we all settle down for a second," Murray suggested.

Fisticuffs with Admiral Wilkerson wasn't how Andrea had intended to bring calm to the group, but she appreciated everyone settling down all the same.

Just then the president's phone rang. The president placed the call on speaker.

"Senator Stover on line one, Mr. President," said the operator.

Senator Justin Stover was a calm, even-keeled Senate ally of President Murray's to whom the president spoke regularly. Andrea hoped he might be able to restore calm to the Oval Office.

"What's the good word, Justin?" the president said.

"Mr. President, I'm sorry to say it, but there is no way we'll have support in the Senate for amending the emergency budget to fight this war. You are going to have to find a way to end it."

The president looked down at the plush carpet with the

embroidered presidential seal. His look said it all to Andrea. She knew Stover was a straight shooter. If Justin Stover was delivering bad news, the news genuinely was bad.

"Thanks for the update, Justin," Murray said, and hung up.

"The Senate has bailed on you too, huh?" said Andrea.

"It's over," said Murray sadly.

Andrea feared that no matter how responsible Mason was for ending the war, the country would see her emergency budget as the instrument of defeat. Her head drooped as she imagined herself joining the long line of American villains and turncoats: Benedict Arnold, the Rosenbergs, Aldrich Ames, Robert Hanssen, Edward Snowden, and now Andrea Gartner.

In the quiet that had descended upon the Oval Office, Andrea carefully thought about the country's options. She desperately didn't want to pull the plug on the war with the Chinese, knowing what that would mean for the country and for her personally.

"If we just had a little more time," General Ogden suggested. "See if we can improve our position on the ground before calling it quits. A few more weeks."

Andrea realized time was something she could provide. Even if the United States didn't have time to win the war, she could find money to prolong it and get America better terms for ending it.

But the time she could provide would come with a painful catch.

"Mr. President, I have an idea," she replied. "But I hesitate to bring it up."

"Speak," Murray ordered.

Andrea glanced out the window. She could see the Washington Monument and thought about her earlier late-night walk.

"We could move some funds," she continued. "I think there's at least ten billion dollars in the Pentagon's budget I could reallocate for a few more weeks of war. But there's a problem."

"What's that?" Murray's eye twitched.

"The problem is it's fucking unconstitutional!" Ogden shouted. "You can't rob Peter to pay Paul to keep this war going. You take something from a different Defense Department account, someone's going to suffer."

"General Ogden is right," said Andrea. "Congress appropriated the money for something else. I think it's probably unconstitutional to grab the money. Mason and his constitutional conservatives will scream to high heaven, and they'll be right."

"Mason is dead to me," Murray growled. "I don't give a damn what that bastard and his damned Debt Rebel Gang thinks. Can you get me ten billion dollars to fight the war?"

"Mr. President, we could take from the construction and maintenance budgets," Andrea said. "And we could cancel the Pentagon's free summer concerts in Washington, the Blue Angels air shows, the Marine Corps Marathon, and all the other frills the Pentagon funds. I'd hate to have to do this, but we could take funds from the veterans' and family benefits accounts as well. If you let me squeeze every last bit of fat out of the Pentagon budget, I'll get you ten billion dollars to fight with. Maybe more."

President Murray rubbed his chin. "Ten billion dollars. How long can we prolong the war with that?" He turned to General Ogden.

"The war costs about a billion dollars a day," said General Ogden. "If we are careful about how we fight and spend the money, we probably can get up to two more weeks of fighting. I'm not sure it's worth it."

"Can you make those weeks of fighting painful for the Chinese?" the president asked.

"Mr. President, I can nuke Beijing if you want," said General Ogden.

"How about we not do that?" President Murray sighed. "I want

China's nose to be bloody enough that they want the war to end too. But leave nukes out of this."

"We can probably destroy China's bases on their artificial islands in the South China Sea," said General Ogden. "But two weeks probably isn't enough to dislodge the Chinese from Taiwan."

"Every little bit counts," said President Murray. "Andrea, what do you think?"

"There's a risk the courts could stop our reallocation of funds, but if I was a betting woman, I'd say they don't. Would a court really tell the president he can't fight to get those sailors out of Taiwan? After the Chinese sank all those ships? No way."

"Andrea, move those funds," President Murray said. "Two more weeks of war it is."

CHAPTER 36

T he next morning, Mason was seated at his Longworth office desk writing notes to supporters and basking in the glow of his dramatic speech the previous morning when the news banner scrolling across the TV screen caught his attention.

BREAKING NEWS:
President Murray announces $10 billion to be moved
from Pentagon projects to fund the war

Mason furiously smashed the point of his pen into his desk repeatedly. The point finally broke and blue ink gushed onto the desk and his hands. "Goddammit!" he shouted.

Mason grabbed his sports coat and dashed out of his office.

"Mr. Mason, where are you going?" asked his one remaining staffer as he bolted past her desk.

"Not now," roared Mason. "Cancel my schedule. I have a personal matter I need to attend to."

He understood that ten billion dollars meant the war would continue for at least a couple more weeks. Xu Li was not expecting that. If Xu Li found out before he had a chance to tell her and put his own spin on it, she might replace him the same way she replaced Acorn.

Mason hustled down the Longworth building hall to the parking lot angrily muttering to himself. "Who the hell does Andrea Gartner think she is? Did she miss the day they taught

appropriations law? *I* am the goddamn appropriations committee." He kicked at the air. "If I don't appropriate it, the Pentagon
can't spend it!"

When he got to his BMW he pressed a small button on his
watch. A digital keyboard appeared and he typed "entering the
temple: 3.0." He anticipated it would take him about an hour to
reach the warehouse in Baltimore, but he wanted an extra two
hours of cushion in case of traffic and to prepare to face Xu Li.

Message sent, he started the car and screeched out of the
Longworth parking lot, tires peeling against the pavement. Every
traffic light seemed to turn red as he drove along North Capitol
Street to the parkway to Baltimore. At the third red light his
impatience overcame him and he furiously pounded the steering
wheel. "Andrea Gartner! When this is over and the Chinese have
me running the country you will be Prisoner Number One in my
fucking gulags!"

Driving up the parkway Mason steadied himself in preparation for meeting with Xu Li.

*If all Andrea can find is ten billion dollars, she'll only be able to
cover a couple more weeks of war. America's war effort is running
on fumes. If China can hold on for two more weeks, we're going to
succeed.*

Halfway to Baltimore he ran across a four-car accident on
the parkway. There were no police or EMS anywhere in sight.
All probably slashed by the emergency budget. Accident victims
were tending to one another while motorists struggled to navigate
around the accident without any police direction. Normally he
would have exploded in road rage for being stuck in traffic, but he
was enjoying the chaos of the accident scene. The missing police
and EMS, the pathetic bystanders desperately trying to admin-
ister first aid to the bloodied victims, and the tangled, unmanaged

traffic gave him confidence heading into his meeting with Xu Li. This chaos was his creation, and he would make sure Xu Li knew.

Mason finally arrived at the abandoned Baltimore warehouse after dark. He slowly drove his car up the alley beside the building. He had to go slowly; drug addicts had been known to shoot up there at night. He'd once nearly run one over. In the distance he could see fires burning in oil drums of homeless encampments. There were twice as many fires now since the emergency budget went into effect.

Mason went down to the warehouse basement and pressed a red key on the control panel beside the screen. A Chinese agent appeared onscreen, greeted Mason, and disappeared down a hallway off-camera. When she returned, Xu Li was with her.

"This war was supposed to be over by now, Crimson."

"Give it time, Madame Xu. Murray and Andrea Gartner are piecing their war budget together with duct tape and bailing wire. In a couple weeks they'll be out of money."

"You told me the war would last less than four weeks. How is it that the chairman of the American Appropriations Committee does not know how much money is left for the war? I want answers, Crimson."

"It's Andrea Gartner. She's playing games with the budget. Sneaking money from other accounts."

"Ah yes, Andrea Gartner. Your budget director. She is a hardheaded one. But very practical and creative." Mason detected grudging admiration in Xu Li's voice. It wasn't like her to heap praise on anybody, much less an enemy. He felt betrayed. It wasn't as if Andrea Gartner was doing such a great job. Americans were unemployed, deprived of medicine, and dying.

Why is Xu Li holding me to an impossible standard while praising our enemy?

"I know what she has been doing with the budget numbers." Xu Li didn't elaborate. "And I know she humiliated you in those hearings you promised would bring down her government. She is a bit more formidable than you give her credit for."

Shit, she already knows about the extra money. Stay calm. Don't let her think she's got you nervous.

"She's a self-righteous, arrogant know-it-all. A scold. Americans hate that," said Mason.

"Maybe, but she's also a tough and principled lady. Very American. We would have a difficult time recruiting her as an agent."

He was getting tired of all this Andrea Gartner praise. *You're lucky I have my own reasons for hating the United States, otherwise I'd tell you and the Ministry to pound sand. And then I'd tell the CIA all about our little project.*

"Do not worry, Madame Xu. I have this under control. America will only be able to fight a couple more weeks with the money Andrea Gartner has found. She won't be able to find any more, I can assure you that. And then we'll be able to proceed with our plan for America."

"I hope for your sake you are right," Xu Li said coldly.

"What are my instructions, Madame Xu?" Mason wanted to change the subject.

"You are to decapitate Denali."

Mason knew who Denali was. Decapitating Denali would be checkmate for the United States.

"What about Andrea Gartner?" he asked.

"Leave Andrea Gartner to me," said Xu Li. "You worry about Denali. The plan is and remains to complete Operation Pripyat. To do that, you must decapitate Denali. Make that happen, and you will have made up for your failures."

Mason felt a weight lift off his shoulders. Xu Li might admire

Andrea, but she hadn't forgotten he was her ally and Andrea Gartner their common enemy.

"When should I decapitate Denali?"

"Chinese agents will soon enter the United States. When they do, the time will be right."

"How will I know when the agents are in the United States?"

"You will know when you are supposed to know. Until then, do not do anything that will compromise your ability to decapitate Denali."

"Yes, Madame Xu. I will be ready."

"For the downfall of the United States and the glory of Communism."

"Yes, Madame Xu. For the downfall of the United States and the glory of Commu—"

Xu Li ended the transmission before Mason could even finish.

Fuck her. Her stupid Ministry head games aren't going to work on me. I'm Lewis Mason. The chairman of the House Appropriations Committee. She can't get rid of me; I'm the highest-placed agent she has. She needs me to decapitate Denali. And when I do, she's going to need me to run America. Then we'll see who's the real boss of this operation.

Mason left the basement and walked toward the garage door to leave the warehouse. The stench of rotting animal corpses and feces was overwhelming. He breathed in deeply, savoring the smell. After he collapsed the country, every American would have to learn to enjoy the smell of death.

Mason confidently strode out of the warehouse, looking forward to his new task: decapitating Denali. It would be the capstone of his career.

CHAPTER 37

B y the fifth week of the war, Andrea had come to dread the latest news. Every update on her smartphone was grimmer than the last. Crashed planes, burning ships, flag-draped caskets. Catastrophic news rolled in unrelentingly. There was no respite. Every news website and every blog saturated their readers with bad news. The grim truth was clear: America was losing the war.

This morning she scrolled to the Major League Baseball website to check on her beloved Atlanta Braves. The pennant race was heating up, and the Braves were surprise contenders. Following their chase for the World Series provided a welcome respite from the chaos enveloping her.

Rachel poked her head into the office. "Sweetie, you mind if we have a chat?" She walked into the office and took a seat across from Andrea.

"We're coming up on the end of our two-week extension of the war, and things aren't looking good." Rachel's sweet manner of speaking somehow made bad news seem less bad.

The *Washington Post* website's headline read: "Stalemate in South China Sea Continues." The subhead: "No end in sight." Words like "stagnated," "stalemate," and "slog" jumped off the screen.

"So I see." Andrea sighed.

"There's more," said Rachel. "Keep reading."

"The United States has yet to dislodge China either from the South China Sea or Taiwan," Andrea read aloud. "The Navy continues to lose ships at a blistering pace. And the Army is having difficulty resupplying and reinforcing the soldiers it had landed in Taiwan."

"It's not all bad news," said Rachel. "Keep reading."

"The Chinese military's momentum has stalled too," Andrea said. "American resistance is degrading and destroying China's carefully built South China Sea defenses. Many more Chinese troops are being killed than the Chinese admit they expected."

"You always wanted to get into politics," said Rachel. "To paraphrase my main man, Toby Keith, how do you like it now?"

Andrea moved to the the *New York Times* website. "American Public Resoundingly Opposes War Effort" read the headline. Andrea's shoulders slouched in resignation.

"Wow, look at this paragraph," she said. "Americans have soured on the war, demanding an end to the war to free up funds for Medicare. Over eighty percent of Americans would rather end the war than make cuts to Social Security and Medicare to keep fighting. Americans we spoke to do not understand why the country is sending ships to the South China Sea to be devoured by China's vicious anti-ship defenses. A TrueCon Network host thundered that 'Taiwan was a renegade province that China was entitled to bring back into line and the United States should respect China on this. Sometimes a country's leaders need to crack some skulls and roll some tanks.'"

"We're screwed, aren't we?" Rachel's honeyed voice clashed with her depressing conclusion.

Andrea shrugged her shoulders. "We were screwed from the beginning. And you know perfectly well everyone's going to blame us for it."

"Quit feeling sorry for yourself. You took this job, remember?"

"I took this job to pay down the debt, not defund a war."

"Sweetie, this is politics. If you don't want to deal with the unexpected, you're in the wrong business."

"If I defund this war, people will hate me."

"People hate us for fighting the war! When will you realize you can't win? This is politics. Everybody hates everybody. It's like *Wargames*. 'The only winning move is not to play.'"

Andrea's office phone rang, interrupting the argument. She was grateful for the rescue from Rachel's grief.

"The Chinese Foreign Ministry and Ministry of Finance are holding a joint press conference at nine a.m." It was Stanley Marshal. "The president would like you to join him in the Oval Office to watch."

"That's a half-hour from now."

"Yes, ma'am."

"I'll be right over."

Andrea turned to Rachel. "That was Stan Marshal. Some Chinese government press conference is happening. The president wants me to watch it with him in the Oval."

"Don't you go bringing any of your whining in there, okay? Stuff's bad enough as it is."

"You're right," said Andrea. "Thanks for keeping me grounded."

"We go back a long way, sweetie." Rachel put her arm around Andrea. "We're going to get through this, even if I have to drag you across the finish line."

CHAPTER 38

A ndrea left the EEOB and walked over to the White House. Anti-war protesters were again filling Lafayette Square to Andrea's left, screaming about imperialism and who knew what else. A group of retirees was protesting Social Security cuts. By now the protests had become the background music of her workdays.

Andrea quietly slipped into the West Wing. President Murray was waiting in the Oval, seated on one of the two couches in the center, facing the flat-screen television set up in front of the fireplace to show the press conference. Vice President Campbell and Wally Flynn were seated on the couch opposite the president.

"It's about to go on," President Murray said. "All the networks are televising it live."

Andrea wasn't surprised. "They know something big is about to go down."

The screen flickered to life. A Chinese conference room appeared with a small lectern at its center. A painting of Mao Zedong hung above the lectern, flanked on both sides by the familiar red logo of the Chinese Communist Party. A small, wiry man with a bony face and thin, dark hair took the stage.

Andrea recognized him from the newspapers as Xiao Shuang, the Chinese foreign minister. Camera shutters clicked and flashbulbs flashed as he took the podium.

Xiao exuded arrogance despite his slight frame. He looked like a goody-two-shoes mediocrity who got ahead by being the class kissy bottom, sucking up to his teachers and, later, his Communist Party bosses. Mamie would have called him a twerp. To Andrea he appeared way too triumphant for a representative of a country in a shooting war with the United States.

Xiao began speaking. A government translator voiced over the broadcast in English.

"Ladies and gentlemen, thank you for being here today. As you know, the United States has taken aggressive and unwarranted action in Chinese territory. The United States' behavior is unacceptable and greatly destabilizing. The Chinese people will defend their sovereignty.

"For centuries Western nations have imposed their will on the Chinese people. From the Opium War to the territorial concessions in Shanghai, from the theft of Hong Kong and Macau to the imperialistic support for the renegade province on Formosa, the Chinese people have been subjected to the most ignominious treatment by the West."

Xiao's cocky demeanor and the emotionless translations coming through the television gave the press conference a threatening feel. He had something up his sleeve.

"But as Chairman Mao correctly pointed out, the West is decadent, corrupt, and dissolute. Its politicians have borrowed China's money to buy trinkets designed to win them votes. All the while China bided her time." Xiao tilted his head upward, his nose pointing arrogantly in the air. "Our people have endured great hardship and sacrifice to put the Chinese nation in a position to humiliate the West and allow China to take its rightful place as leader among the nations."

President Murray turned to Andrea. "You warned us the Chinese would say this."

"Except he looks like he's enjoying it," she responded.

"Today Western nations purport to tell China what it can

and cannot do in its own South China Sea," continued Xiao. "The United States has its Monroe Doctrine, telling other countries they cannot meddle in the affairs of the Western Hemisphere. Yet America dictates to China about the South China Sea and Asia. Even as it depends on China to fund their own government and allow their leaders to buy the frivolous baubles that keep them in power.

"If there was any doubt that China's governing system is superior to the United States, the events of the last week should erase all doubt." Xiao's voice dripped with disdain. "While the Chinese government remains on solid financial footing, owing to the careful planning of our economic experts, the American government must beg for money to perpetuate its imperialist control over Asia." Xiao radiated satisfaction as he belittled the United States. "Still, it gives me no pleasure to be speaking to you today."

"Lying sack of shit," President Murray seethed. "He's loving this. Typical Communist Party apparatchik. The guy can't go ten minutes without lying through his teeth."

Xiao continued, "For years, China, her allies, and bond funds quietly aligned with the Chinese government have kept the American government afloat by purchasing and repurchasing American Treasury bills. Collectively, we now hold four trillion dollars of these Treasury bills.

"These last few weeks have proven that the United States is no longer a worthy investment partner. The American government has seen fit to make war on China. China and her allies are no longer going to finance the American government by holding its debt. If the Americans want to impose their imperialism on us, they will have to borrow money from someone else."

"Enough windup, you windbag," said President Murray. "Throw your goddamn pitch already."

"Therefore, the Chinese government, its allies, and its aligned bond funds will no longer hold our four trillion dollars' worth of American government securities. When this debt matures over the next several months, the Chinese government will demand repayment of the principal."

Andrea dropped into the couch. Xiao had thrown a pitch, all right. A fastball right to the earhole.

China and her allies held four trillion dollars in United States bonds.

Four *trillion* dollars.

On top of everything else—slashing the budget, fighting a war— she was now going to have to find four trillion dollars to pay off the Chinese-held bonds coming due in the next six months?

The United States couldn't default. The government would collapse. The country would never be able to borrow a dime on the international markets again. Worse, if the American economy collapsed, it would take Europe, Japan, and the rest of the West with it. The Chinese were threatening a global financial catastrophe.

But where was Andrea going to find four trillion dollars? She'd barely been able to scrape ten billion dollars together to keep the war going for two weeks. Four *trillion* dollars? It didn't exist.

"We hope and expect the United States to honor its debts to China and her friends and pay the principal and interest on its bonds in short order," Xiao said. "The Chinese government will immediately contact its counterparts in the United States government to begin to negotiate the terms of this repayment. We hope this process goes as smoothly as possible, but we retain all options for obtaining repayment. We trust the United States will honorably settle America's debts to China."

Minister Xiao swaggered off the stage with an unmistakable air of satisfaction, having put America in her place.

President Murray stared at the screen.

"Mr. President?" said Andrea.

He snapped out of his daze. "Yes?"

"We're hosed."

Murray stood up and walked over to the fireplace, then paced back and forth in front of it. "What a smug son of a bitch," he growled.

"Paying back four trillion dollars is utterly impossible, Mr. President, emergency budget or no emergency budget."

"Print money?" He was grasping at straws.

"That'll ruin every saver's retirement fund. And the world has already announced it's dropping the dollar as the reserve currency. It won't work."

"Is there a way out of this mess? We have to end the war, right?"

"The war's a few billion dollars, Mr. President. Pocket change compared to the debt. Ending it now won't find us four trillion dollars. We need four trillion dollars in revenue, stat."

"Get people to send in their taxes early?" Campbell suggested.

Andrea shook her head. "We collect about three trillion dollars a year in taxes. If we use every dime to pay off the debt to China and the bond funds, we won't be able to spend a thing on keeping the government or military operating at all. And we'll still owe the Chinese a trillion dollars."

Campbell's shoulders sagged. "What a bloody mess."

"My nightmare scenario was not having enough money to operate the government. But having to find four trillion instantly to pay back China, while we're in the middle of a war with China? This is like my nightmare had a nightmare." Andrea was at a loss.

Then President Murray looked directly at her. There was something in his eyes, a look she hadn't seen before. Fear, determination, anger.

"If that little shit wants his money right now, he's going to have to pry it from my cold, dead hand," Murray growled. "If we don't have the money, he'll just have to wait until we do."

CHAPTER 39

Andrea slumped into her couch. She hadn't felt this debilitating, delirium-inducing cocktail of exhaustion, hunger, and worry since she was a first-year accountant at a large accounting firm during tax season.

She was twenty-five at the time and had just passed her accounting exam. Her boss, Derek Williams, was arrogant and demanding. He didn't give instructions; he shouted them. He expected his associates to be available every minute of every day, weekends be damned.

"Get in here, Amanda!" Derek had bellowed.

Andrea, already beaten down by Derek's abuse, stepped into his crowded office and said, "It's Andrea."

"What?" Derek said without looking at her. "Why haven't you completed the assignment I sent you last night?

"I'm working on it now, but there are two other assignments you've got me working."

"We're paying you big money to get things done by the time we need them," Derek thundered. "If you're going to survive as a big-time accountant, you need to be able to walk and chew gum at the same time."

Andrea had spent the next three days living in her office, working all night and all day, sleeping only briefly, and showering in the office gym. But she began counting the days until she could find a less frenzied job.

Nothing since that first job compared to how overwhelmed Andrea felt now. She envisioned herself the gravitational center of a meteor shower. Navy admirals screaming at her about American sailors trapped on ships in Taipei Harbor. Army generals bellowing about the inability to reinforce the American soldiers futilely trying to dislodge the Chinese army in Taiwan. Mason refusing to give her any money for the war. Her family disintegrating into warring camps. And now, the Chinese demanding four trillion dollars to pay off America's debt to China.

She stared blankly at her desk, the piles of paper mocking her. The mess on her desk meant nothing. All of it, every bit, represented a speck of dust compared to four trillion dollars. She desperately wanted the world to know just how angry she was, but she couldn't find the words. Her verbal paralysis simply added to her growing rage.

Boiling with frustration, Andrea slammed her fist on the desk, hitting it so hard she dented it slightly. She realized the desk made for an easy target. She slammed her fist three more times, turning the dent into a miniature crater. Then she took her feet and kicked the metal support bar at the back of the desk four times, bending it out of shape.

Rachel poked her head into Andrea's office. "What's going on? Everything okay, sweetie?"

Andrea was too tired and too angry to lie. Besides, why bother? No lie would have worked. "Just burning off the anger. Don't worry. I'm only taking it out on inanimate objects. At least it's not Mason or his damned Gang or any of those military guys that hate my guts."

"Okay, sweetie. Just don't hurt yourself."

Her knuckles were still throbbing in pain from her destructive exertions when her computer chimed to an arriving email. She sat down at her desk, saw it was from the State Department, and hit "print." The printer behind her desk spat out a ten-page document, written in its original Chinese with a State Department translation. It was China's comprehensive settlement proposal.

She snatched the papers from the printer and, forsaking her dented desk, sat on the couch, propping her feet up on the coffee table.

For once, the Chinese government hadn't lied. Xiao's ministry had contacted the United States almost immediately to negotiate a cease-fire and the terms of America's debt repayment. The Chinese must have prepared it long before now, just waiting for the right time to release it. More evidence of some larger strategy at work.

Andrea's pulse inched upward with every word she read. The cease-fire proposal was humiliating.

The document said it would allow American naval vessels trapped in Taipei Harbor to leave and let the American forces on Taiwan to honorably retreat from the island. China would retain control of the South China Sea but would allow a corridor under international control to permit international trade through the waterway.

Her eyes grew wide at the next paragraph. China would get to keep Taiwan and give it the Hong Kong treatment. One country, two systems. The Chinese government, her allies, and affiliated bond funds required repayment of the debt in American government property.

"Holy shit," she muttered. China wasn't proposing a payment plan. It was proposing a bankruptcy repossession! China would adjudicate America's bankruptcy the old-fashioned way: by repossessing collateral. It was going to seize American government property.

She quickly read the next paragraph out loud: "'China requires representatives of the Chinese government enter the United States to personally identify the collateral.'"

"Rachel!" Andrea shouted.

A moment later, Rachel rushed in looking flushed. She quickly shut the door behind her.

Andrea held up the document. "Have you seen this?"

Rachel nodded. "Not yet. I—"

"The Chinese are demanding to come onto American soil and take four trillion in American government property to repay the debt. They want PLA soldiers traipsing around the United States, taking federal government property until they've grabbed four trillion dollars' worth," Andrea said in disbelief.

"Chinese soldiers? On American soil? Taking American government property? What the hell?" Rachel sat down on the couch. "Do the Chinese really want to go down to Alabama and start pulling up monuments and see what happens? They obviously don't know about our Second Amendment. Our people pack heat. And my granddaddy shot at their sorry asses in Korea. They try to come here and take American property, he might start shooting at them again."

"Your grandfather's been dead for twenty years," Andrea said.

"I know. It wouldn't stop him."

Rachel stood, reading glasses affixed to her nose, eyes looking over them at Andrea. Rachel remained in disbelief. "What are they thinking?" she asked.

"They want to rub our noses in it. Humiliate us. It's a Bob Gibson."

"A what?"

"A Bob Gibson. You know, baseball Bob Gibson. The Cardinals. He hit his old roommate Curt Flood with a pitch the first time Flood came up to bat against him after Flood went to the Phillies. It was his way of telling Flood 'we're not roommates anymore.' The Chinese are telling the world the United States isn't running things anymore."

"Can't we just auction stuff like a normal bankruptcy?" Rachel asked.

"Guess we can ask the Chinese when we beg them to end the war," said Andrea. "They're in the driver's seat now."

Andrea stared at the OMB seal on her wall. All the targets of China's proposed repossession—from the brand-new Smithsonian museums to the new state-of-the-art FBI headquarters to the TSA metal detectors to the renovations of the Capitol—were paid for with money borrowed from China and other foreign countries. If China demanded repayment, China had to be repaid. And if the United States didn't have the dollars, the only currency left was government property. How else could the country repay the debt?

Andrea didn't have a good answer.

Which was a problem, because President Murray needed one.

CHAPTER 40

Mason leaned back in his chair and smiled. The Capitol dome visible from his window looked so small and insignificant. That it had fallen into his lap because of the creativity and ruthlessness of his Chinese masters mattered little to him. He was winning. The United States was losing. The capitalists who had ruined his adoptive family's life were getting their comeuppance. Now all of America would know the humiliation he felt when his family was foreclosed off its farm. Now Americans would experience the pain of not knowing if or when their lives would ever be the same, just as he had. Americans were about to learn about life in a world order dictated by another country.

And that show pony Earl Murray would know what it was like to lose to the unpopular workaholic in the back of the class.

He thought about Acorn and felt a twinge of regret. Maybe he'd knocked off Acorn too quickly. Things were now going better than expected and, deep down, he knew Acorn had helped set it all in motion. Acorn probably didn't deserve having his guts sprayed across Fort Marcy Park. But more than anything Mason felt triumph. He was a man among boys, a political colossus, getting the job done where weaker men like Acorn failed. He was in control, and President Murray and Andrea Gartner were dancing to his tune.

The office printer started to whir. Mason got up quickly and pulled the incoming document from the machine. The document was in Chinese, with an English translation. At the top it read, "Ceasefire proposal from the People's Republic of China."

The first page bore a Ministry stamp. Xu Li must have arranged to provide him a copy.

Mason grinned as he read the peace offer. The balls on his Chinese masters! Demanding American property? Coming to the United States to pick it up? This was some next-level chess. If Americans weren't fuming before, they were going to be fuming now. The seeds would be ripe for an overthrow of the American government and its capitalist economy.

With the proposed ceasefire terms, Minister Xiao had thrown the ball up to the rim for the alley-oop. Mason needed to slam it home. He called his one remaining staffer into his office.

"Get a press release ready and a press conference set up. I need to respond to the Chinese peace offer that just came in."

Mason handed his staffer the document. She scanned it and looked up at Mason in horror.

"You can't agree to this," she said.

"The hell I can't."

"You're going to let Chinese soldiers come into the United States and just take whatever American property they want?" She looked dumbstruck.

"Only government property. We owe them four trillion dollars. We have to pay it back somehow."

"What has gotten into you? Four years ago, you were Mr. Anti-Communism. Now you can't stop caving to these commies."

"I'm a debt hawk, and we're repaying our debt," said Mason, struggling not to look like the cat who ate the canary.

"You can't be serious."

"America wants this war to end. They'll take any bullshit excuse I fling out there. Why not make it sound plausible?"

"I agree. You should make it sound plausible. But the shit you're spewing so far? It's not plausible."

"You follow this stuff. The Debt Rebel Gang? They don't give two wet farts about the debt. As long as the Establishment is squealing in pain they'll be happy."

His assistant appeared aghast. Mason didn't care.

She thinks I'm cynical? This is Capitol Hill, sweetheart. Take a number.

"Fine," she said. "It's your presser. I'll notify the media. You write and say what you want."

"Oh, I plan to."

"Where do you want to have it?"

"Right here, in this office."

His assistant left shaking her head to prepare the media alert fax and organize the press conference.

Reporters piled into Mason's office around two p.m. Mason was behind his desk, the American flag on one side, the Kansas flag on the other. There he was, Lewis Mason, lion of the House, chief appropriator extraordinaire, in all his glory.

Don't let them see you relishing this. Any hint of glee and people might suspect something.

Mason tried to scare himself straight. *Xu Li is watching,* he thought. He put on his best more-in-sorrow-than-in-anger face. His assistant stood silently in the back of the room.

Sunlight shone into the office from the window behind Mason. As the House appropriations chairman, he got the choice of nearly any office he wanted. He'd picked one with a clear view of the Capitol dome. He wanted to see that dome every day. It reminded him of his mission: to bring that dome down. Or, at least, under China's heel. He imagined the day when they wheeled out the statues of George Washington and Thomas Jefferson and wheeled in Chairman Mao or Lenin. Hell, maybe they'd let Lenin's embalmed corpse lie in state in the Capitol rotunda. Talk about sticking it to the capitalists.

The press throng assembled in Mason's office, encircling his desk. Mason spoke with the arrogance of a lord of all he surveyed.

"Thank you for coming, ladies and gentlemen. I have a very short statement to make. As I indicated in my floor speech earlier this week, I will not, under any circumstances, allow legislation to come out of the Appropriations Committee that provides any further funding for the war with China. Andrea Gartner's scrounging for dollars in the dark corners of the Defense Department budget is completely unconstitutional. A true conservative would not tolerate such violence to constitutional principles."

Reporters jostled to get their recorders closer to Mason. Camera shutters whirred as they photographed him.

"Nevertheless, Andrea Gartner can scrounge for money for only so long. She knows it, I know it, and the president knows it. They can creatively cobble together war funds for now, but the only real way to fight a war is with a dedicated funding stream. I'm here to tell them no such stream will be forthcoming from my committee.

"If the president wants to unconstitutionally search for pocket change to fight his war, so be it. But he is fighting a war he cannot afford, and one day in the not-too-distant future it will come to a screeching halt when he can't find any more money. When that happens, American service members will be stuck overseas in harm's way, unable to defend themselves."

Mason meant to terrify the country and soften it up for the news he was about to deliver. He interrupted his speech with one of his famous pregnant pauses. Then he dropped his bombshell:

"China has made us a peace offer."

The gathered reporters scribbled furiously. He was breaking news to make Murray appear as though he was not only stealing money to fight the war, but also keeping information from the American people. He was going to kick President Murray and Andrea Gartner's asses into next week. They wanted to embarrass him in a televised hearing? Two could play that game. And Mason hadn't become Appropriations Committee chairman by accident. He could play the game well.

"China is offering to return our sailors trapped in Taiwan and our soldiers fighting there. That is what we want. All China wants is for us to acknowledge its sovereignty over areas over which it traditionally had sovereignty. It will protect the rights of the Taiwanese and permit international shipping in the South China Sea. What more do we want?"

Mason theatrically took a drink from his coffee mug emblazoned with a "Mason for Congress" logo.

"I urge the president to make peace, save the country, and take the deal China is offering. As the Chinese government has made clear, they want us to repay our debt as well. If the shoe were on the other foot, we would want the same. Would you lend money to anyone and not expect repayment? Especially if someone owed you four trillion dollars and was asking for more? Seeing as the Murray administration cannot pay its debts with money, the Chinese want in-kind payment and are willing to come to the United States to get it.

"As a conservative and a deficit reduction supporter, I urge the president to accept the offer and clean the debt slate with China."

Reporters were writing furiously. Mason could see the reporters processing what he just said and slowly realizing the humiliation in store. Mason smiled. It was a moment of pure political ecstasy. One of those moments that comes once, maybe twice, in a political career.

The crowd erupted into murmurs and questions.

A reporter shouted through the din, "You mean allow China to come to the United States and take property?"

"Yes."

"Why not sell property at auction and give China the money?"

"China wants the property, not the money."

"What property?" another reporter asked.

"Any property it wants, within reason. I have it on good understanding the Chinese won't take classified information or sensitive military hardware or anything of that nature."

Mason was shaping the battlefield. If the Chinese didn't get any sensitive property, what was the big deal? In fact, he didn't give a damn about the property, and, he figured, neither did China. They wanted the imagery. It would be pure propaganda gold.

"Do you think the American people will accept this deal?" another reporter asked.

"Why don't you ask me if the American people want to get their soldiers and sailors home and out of this messy, unfunded war? What do you think? The answer is yes."

Mason nodded his head toward his assistant in the back of the room. She piped up. "Any more questions?"

It was three o'clock, and Mason knew reporters were on deadline and wouldn't have many more questions. Some had already left to file their stories.

"Thank you for coming," said Mason.

Reporters rushed out of the office. Several stopped in the hall outside the office suite and were dictating stories on their cell phones.

Once the room cleared, Mason's assistant closed the door, leaving her and Mason alone in the office. Mason was still sitting in his chair. "I hope you're happy with yourself," she said. "You've just handed China a victory. This might well be China's most glorious hour."

No, sweetheart. It's Lewis Mason's most glorious hour.

CHAPTER 41

Andrea had watched the Mason press conference on C-SPAN with her jaw open in shock. He had just slammed the ball back at her in their ongoing ping-pong match. She rubbed her forehead, completely flummoxed. How could he man who called himself the Chief RINO Hunter be advocating surrender to China when not one year ago he didn't care one iota about deficits and was an unabashed China hawk?

Rachel poked her head into Andrea's office. "The president has called a meeting in the Oval, Andrea. He wants you there ASAP."

Andrea sighed. The last few weeks had been nothing but circular motion, an orgy of trips to the Hill and the Oval Office, without having made a shred of progress on anything.

"I'll be there, of course. Help me get ready."

Andrea and Rachel pulled together a folder of budget documents showing where things stood with the war and projections out for the next several weeks. Prepared for the meeting, Andrea made her way to the Oval Office.

Walking past a mirror in the hall, she saw her unbrushed hair sticking in all directions, a visible manifestation of her physical and emotional exhaustion. Her neighbors blamed her for their eviction. Millions around the country blamed her for the destruction of their Social Security. The military blamed her for keeping them from fighting a proper war. And now she might be about to preside over America's liquidation sale.

I didn't sign up for this, Andrea thought. She was slipping straight into her familiar feeling-sorry-for-herself zone, but she caught herself.

You did sign up for this. You knew the debt was a mess. You knew a crisis was coming. You wanted to be the hero. You want to save America? No one else is going to solve the problem. Pull yourself together and solve this.

President Murray was seated behind the Resolute desk when Andrea arrived. Vice President Campbell and General Ogden were seated on one couch, padfolios open on their laps. Brooks Powell and the Secretary of State were seated on the couch facing the general.

Andrea walked in sheepishly. "Everyone is here already? I thought I was on time."

General Ogden shook his head and glowered at her with his heavy-lidded eyes. She had a feeling he'd come loaded for bear. She felt her blood pressure rising and patience dropping. She told herself to stay calm. If she was going to pop off, she was going to do it strategically.

"You're fine," said President Murray. "Take a seat."

Andrea sat down on the couch beside Brooks Powell and opposite General Ogden.

"We need to respond to the Chinese offer and Congressman Mason's endorsement of it."

"Yes, sir," the assembled group said in unison.

"Let me start by saying I'm tempted by the Chinese offer," said President Murray. "Anything to end this war and get our soldiers and sailors out of there and home."

Andrea couldn't believe her ears. She had expected the president to dig in and demand she find more money. General Ogden pursed his lips and began turning red.

Murray reviewed the situation. "We have one week of war funds left, right?"

"Yes sir," Andrea replied.

"Congressman Mason is off his meds and won't appropriate any more funds under any circumstances, even if Americans remain trapped in Taiwan," the president said. "Is there any way we are going to get a better deal than this?"

Andrea sensed an opening. "This deal is absolutely the best we can get. Otherwise we're going to have to nickel-and-dime our way through funding this war, and that is no way to run a railroad. If this war is still on when we run out of money, China wins completely. This way, we get a little something and we buy time to straighten out our finances and be prepared if there is a next round."

"This is surrender!" General Ogden roared. "Why are we talking surrender just when we have China on the ropes?" His round face was now beet red. Andrea could swear he was physically swelling. "Do you think they would have proposed this if they thought they were winning?"

President Murray cocked his head slightly, as if thinking the general had a point. "If we really do have the upper hand in this, how long would it take for us to defeat the Chinese?"

"At the current rate, unless we really take the gloves off, several months, probably." Even General Ogden knew the Chinese were no pushovers.

Andrea figured as much. "I hate to keep bringing this up, but we don't have several months. We have only one week of money left."

"Enough of your damn excuses," General Ogden shouted. "Find some more money, dammit!"

"I did my part!" said Andrea, more comfortable raising her voice to the general. "I found as much money as I possibly could. This is it without Congress."

"Screw Mason," General Ogden sneered. "What I wouldn't do

to get that guy out of Congress. Screw the Hatch Act. I'd campaign against his sorry ass tomorrow."

President Murray turned to Andrea. "There's nothing else you can do?"

"I've found what I could." She pulled her pockets inside out for effect. "There is no way I'll be able to find the several months' worth of money General Ogden just said he'll need. We have to take this deal. Our finances won't get better, and neither will our position in the South China Sea. If you don't take the deal, you are going to have to end the war in a week and you won't get even a fig leaf of a concession."

"General?" the president asked.

"This is absurd. Do you know what we could let fly into China from American shores?" General Ogden slammed his fist on the coffee table. "You want to end this war in a week? I'll end this war in a week."

Andrea nearly blurted out her horror, but President Murray beat her to it. "And what's going to land in California before it's over? You don't think the Chinese will be able to respond in kind? They have nukes too, you know."

"We've got more."

President Murray was aghast. "If we lose Los Angeles and San Francisco, it's okay if they lose Beijing, Shanghai, and Hong Kong? Bombs Away Ogden?"

"That nickname's taken," said Andrea.

"The bean counter speaks again," said General Ogden, still red-faced and swollen with fury.

"You can call me any names you want," Andrea retorted. "We don't have the cash to keep paying the expenses to be shooting at the Chinese. Mr. President, take the deal."

"You think that's going to solve our problem?" General Ogden was boiling. "Every two-bit tinpot dictator is going to look at this surrender and think it's open season."

Andrea raised her arms in frustration. "What do you want me to do about it? The government can't borrow money. I can't conjure money. What part of there is no money don't you understand?"

"I don't understand any of it! America has three hundred and fifty million people. We have three trillion dollars a year in tax revenue. Take the damn money and fight the damn war!"

"You are going to get us all impeached by the end of this, General." Andrea knew it would be her and President Murray and not General Ogden getting hauled up to the Hill for impeachment hearings.

"Maybe you deserve it," General Ogden hissed.

"Maybe we'll fund the impeachment hearings with your war money," Andrea blurted.

She nervously looked around the room, wondering if she'd crossed a line.

"All right, that's enough," President Murray interjected. "I'm taking the ceasefire. Our boys in Taiwan have to come home."

Andrea swore steam was coming out of General Ogden's ears.

"What's really got me worried is paying back that four trillion dollars in debt with collateral," the president continued. "Fighting the war with unconstitutionally obtained funds might get me impeached. Allowing Chinese solders to come to America and take government property might get me shot."

"Do we really have a choice?" asked Andrea. "The alternative is defaulting on that debt. And if we default, the world economy will collapse."

"The world is going to collapse if we surrender Taiwan and the South China Sea to the Chinese," General Ogden barked.

Andrea wasn't going to be the first OMB director to preside

over an American default. "My collapse will have Americans selling apples on street corners for a nickel again. The consequences of a United States default would have the Chinese coming to take property look like a Sunday picnic. You think things are bad now? Wait until no one will loan the US money ever again. Talk about belt-tightening. That would be gastric bypass surgery."

"Print money!" General Ogden bellowed.

Andrea rolled her eyes. *Didn't anybody ever listen to her?* "The dollar's no longer the reserve currency. China and the Europeans saw to that. We can't inflate our way out of debt. How many times have I been over this? We've already killed Social Security. You want to kill peoples' retirement accounts too? You want people to pay for food with truckloads of dollars? Why don't you go online and search 'Weimar' and 'wheelbarrows' sometime?"

Silence.

The president turned to Brooks Powell. "Any ideas, Brooks?"

"No sir. I hate to say it, but take the deal. We won't get better terms."

The president looked at the group with a blank stare, then nodded mournfully.

Murray looked at Andrea, then turned to General Ogden. "Accept the cease-fire," he said.

CHAPTER 42

T he thought of the humiliating surrender—President Murray called it a "cease-fire" but it was a surrender—sickened Andrea and kept her awake all night. She sat at her kitchen table—the family asleep upstairs—and wondered what the next day would bring. Surrender on top of Medicare and Social Security cuts might move the protesters in Lafayette Park from holding signs to burning effigies. Thousands of American soldiers and sailors dead. Billions of dollars of the most sophisticated military machinery up in smoke or at the bottom of the sea. All to watch the Chinese flag fly over Taiwan and the South China Sea.

A car slowly drove by outside. Then the thud of the Washington Post landing in her driveway. She looked up at the clock. It was 4:50 a.m. Even though she got the papers at work, Ryan wanted the Post for the crossword puzzles.

She opened the front door, collected the paper, brought it inside, and pulled it from its plastic sleeve. The headline left no doubt as to the outcome of the war:

Ceasefire Reached in Dramatic End to War; Funding
Crisis Forces Peace; Taiwan to Stay in Chinese Hands

Andrea first felt relief. The death and destruction were over. American soldiers would be out of harm's way. But she was surprised the headline said nothing about the repayment of the debt to China with American assets. How did that not make it into the headlines? Andrea wasn't about to complain, though. That might be the most unpopular aspect of the whole thing. For now, the less said, the better.

More surprises were in store. According to an overnight poll, over seventy percent of the American public supported the cease-fire. The Post quoted a TrueCon Network anchor gushing over President Murray bringing the troops home and making Taiwan fight its own war.

Good grief. Did they miss the part about China coming to the United States to grab property to repay the debt? But Andrea stopped herself. For the first time in forever, she felt like she'd been a part of something people liked. Or didn't hate, anyway. TrueCon Network hosts weren't branding her an Establishment lackey for once. Andrea didn't know whether to be happy or worried. She had no frame of reference for the bouquets TrueCon Network hosts seemed to be throwing her way.

Andrea went upstairs and quickly dressed and showered. She wasn't dreading going to work. In fact, she felt like a damned hero. All hell broke loose around her, and she was the calm amid the storm. The glue holding the place together. For a moment she fancied herself the rock of the administration. She'd given Murray the extra weeks of war he needed to get the best terms possible for ending the war. And doggone if Americans didn't think he had.

On the drive to work, she turned on the radio to the local news station, WTOP. There were no more ads for government contractors with all her budget cuts. The hosts were talking a lot more than usual to fill the air.

And who should they be interviewing this morning but her nemesis, Lewis Mason.

"If it wasn't for my cutting off the funding, we'd still have our boys getting shot at by the Chinese," said Mason. "It was never our fight. And we shouldn't be going into debt to support some foreign country."

That goddamned jackass. Mason had done everything he could to make it impossible for her to deal with the debt and then used that very problem to end the war. All of a sudden, he was in touch with his inner isolationist and rediscovering his worries about the national debt. Still, it was a nice change of pace from him beating the snot out of her and President Murray.

"If it wasn't for the Pripyat Consortium international bond boycott, could the United States have continued to fight the war?" the interviewer asked.

"We'll never know, will we," said Mason. "I deal in reality, not hypotheticals."

What a smug, arrogant son of a—

The Pripyat Consortium!

She hadn't heard a thing since she'd asked Rachel to have the FBI look into that Pripyat Consortium spokesman.

Andrea pulled into her parking space on West Executive Avenue and rushed up to her office. She ran straight in and grabbed Rachel.

"Come into my office, quickly," Andrea said.

"Good morning to you too, sweetie," Rachel said sarcastically. "What's going on?"

"With all the craziness I'd totally forgotten about how you asked the FBI to check into that Pripyat Consortium spokesman."

"I did ask," said Rachel. "They told me they'd been working it from the moment the guy appeared on the television screen. But they had no idea who he was. I haven't heard a thing from them since."

"Let's get them on the phone and get an update."

Rachel leaned over Andrea's desk and dialed a number on the speakerphone.

"FBI, Agent McClain," said the deep voice.

"Hey, Gus, it's Rachel Samuels."

"Rachel, I was wondering when you'd call," Gus said with hesitation.

"My boss wanted to see if you had anything new in your investigation into that Pripyat Consortium spokesman. I have her on the line with me."

"Hello, Ms. Gartner," said Gus. "We looked in our databases and asked our financial crimes contacts around the world. We haven't found a thing so far about the Pripyat Consortium or the spokesman."

"What does that mean?" asked Andrea.

"That the Pripyat Consortium probably is a front for someone else, some bad actor that wants deep anonymity. It's a ruse of some kind. Quite possibly a foreign cutout doing the dirty work for a government that wants plausible deniability."

Andrea shook her head. "What about the Pripyat Consortium spokesman? The guy in the fancy suit. Do they know who that was?"

"We looked at every database we have," said Gus. "We talked to Interpol, MI5, GCHQ. No one has a clue who this guy is. It's like he doesn't exist."

"What is he, a hologram? I saw him with my own eyes on TV. And doggone if he doesn't look familiar," said Andrea. "Doesn't the FBI have every surveillance tool in the world at its disposal?"

"He's probably working for a hostile government," said Gus. "Russia, China maybe. Pripyat was in the Soviet Union, you know. And we just got done shooting at the Chinese. If I was a betting man, I'd say one of them is the likely culprit."

"Yeah, I know about Pripyat. Chernobyl. Doesn't that seem weird to you?" Andrea asked.

"Naming an investment group after an abandoned nuclear-contaminated town is some kind of sick joke," Rachel interjected.

"Or a message," Andrea said. "Agent McClain, keep us posted on what the FBI finds. Someone must know something. We've got to figure out who's behind this."

"Absolutely," Gus replied. "Our director has made it our top priority. When we figure this out, we will be sure to let you know."

CHAPTER 43

"Enter the temple tonight," the message read.

The Ministry must be pleased, Mason thought. *Tonight, I receive the spoils of my victory.*

And what a victory it was! China owned Taiwan and had turned the South China Sea into a Chinese lake. America had been humiliated. Vietnam, the Philippines, even Australia and South Korea were adjusting to the new reality and coming to Beijing to beg for mercy. If Beijing wanted to tighten the screws on any of them, who was going to come to the rescue? The bankrupt Americans?

As he drove to his Capitol Hill office the morning after President Murray announced the cease-fire, Mason surveyed his handiwork, wishing he could publicly claim credit for the misery he'd unleashed. The domestic effects of the emergency budget were everywhere. Half-built bridges and construction equipment sitting idle. Crowds of angry people surrounding pharmacies, unable to pay for their prescriptions because of Medicare cuts. Kids aimlessly wandering the streets because the federal grants their school programs depended on had been abruptly cut.

But when he turned on his office television to watch the morning news programs after arriving at the office, he was shocked to learn snap overnight polls on CNN had President Murray's approval rating at sixty percent. Sixty percent! For a guy who had cut people's Medicare and Social Security? The headlines were brutal. The *New York Times* webpage called the surrender a "dark day for freedom," and the *New York Post* ran a headline of

"Choker!" with President Murray's picture. And yet Murray was becoming *more* popular, not less.

How was it possible the country was reacting this way? The budget crisis and war were supposed to trigger revolution, not strengthen the president. Acorn had misread the American public. Mason now wondered if he himself had misread the public too.

What am I going to tell Madame Xu?

She had to be happy, didn't she? The Chinese had achieved their eighty-year-old dream of reunifying Taiwan with the mainland and taking control of the South China Sea. The United States had been humiliated and exposed as a paper tiger, unable to afford fighting a war and defending itself. It was open season on the United States. And he'd made it happen.

Having reassured himself Xu Li would appreciate his handiwork, Mason spent a quiet day in his office doing phone interviews and signing more pictures to send to constituents. As evening approached, he departed his office for the abandoned Baltimore warehouse. Night had fallen by the time he arrived.

The stench of death still hung over the place. Dead animals, animal droppings, abandoned furniture, that broken piano. He loved the contrast with his immaculate, ornate Capitol Hill office building, his Capitol Hill clothes absorbing the scent of the filth like pungent cigar smoke. He was no effete trust-fund-baby radical, no Brooklyn hipster protesting the Man by day and eating farm-to-table tapas and drinking craft beers by night. He got his hands dirty and enjoyed licking them clean.

He slowly descended the darkened staircase to the basement. A small flashing red light from the console beside the video screen pierced the darkness. He tiptoed into the basement, flashlight on, and found the solitary working lightbulb. He pulled its chain and turned it on. The bulb lit the middle of the room, but the rest remained in the shadows.

He made his way to the red button and pressed it. The ceiling projector whirred to life. The same room from which Xu Li had communicated with him previously appeared on screen. It was empty.

Where was the Ministry? They called him all this way and no one was there? Mason fitfully looked around the basement. Was someone lurking in the shadows? Was the Ministry about to suicide him like it had Acorn? Mason felt the urge to run.

But before he could, Xu Li appeared on the screen. She said nothing at first, but her furrowed brow and intense scowl left no doubt about her view of Operation Pripyat's status.

"You have failed, Crimson." Xu Li intensified her scowl.

Surely she couldn't be *that* angry, could she? He'd struck a mighty blow for Marxism, the oppressed peoples of the world, the Third World, the Left. The capitalist hegemon was crawling on its hands and knees begging for money just to stay afloat. Lenin dreamed of it. Stalin dreamed of it. Mao dreamed of it. And he, Lewis Mason, who grew up in Nowheresville, Kansas, had done it.

Mason's thoughts went back to Acorn, how he was dumped in the trunk of the Forester and left to bleed to death. A shiver crawled down his spine. Was he next to be suicided?

"Madame Xu, I do not understand. China is ascendant. America is reeling. What more is there to be done?"

"America exists, and as long as America exists, she will be a threat to China."

"America can't buy a ham sandwich."

"Not today. But you are like all the other Americans. You can't think a hundred years into the future."

"With all due respect, Madame Xu, no one can."

"*I* can," Xu Li replied angrily and arrogantly. "As long as America exists, it can recover. It can grow more food, extract more oil and gas, and catch more fish than any country in the world. A country like that will not stay down forever. A weakened America is not enough. America as we know it must cease to exist."

"What more can we do?" Mason asked.

"Operation Pripyat was intended to topple the American government and its capitalist economy and replace it with Chinese Communism. Neither of these things has happened yet."

"But how do you plan to accomplish this? The bond boycott didn't do it. America losing the war didn't do it. We're running out of tools in the toolbox."

"Never mind the details. You know perfectly well no agent knows all the details of any mission. Compartmentalization. We can't have one of you weak Americans spilling his guts in fear. You still have one remaining task: decapitate Denali. The rest will fall into place."

There was no going back now. Mason could decapitate Denali, or he could fertilize Fort Marcy Park. Decapitate Denali it would be.

CHAPTER 44

After weeks of endless meetings in stuffy conference rooms, being in the fresh air of Poplar Tree Park was a welcome relief. With the war over and the emergency budget still in place, President Murray had given Andrea a week off. She'd begged for some time to reacquaint herself with her family before the Chinese repossession teams arrived. The president gladly gave it to her. There was nothing to do but wait for the Chinese repossession teams to arrive.

"Come on, Michelle, let's have a catch!" Aaron shouted, ball and glove in hand. Michelle and Aaron trotted onto one of the baseball fields.

Andrea helped her mother onto a bench. "Can you watch the kids? I'd like to take a walk."

"Sure, honey, I'll keep my eye on them," Mamie replied.

"Your grandmother is watching you," Andrea shouted. "Don't get out of her sight!"

"Whatever, Mom." Aaron rolled his eyes in mock disgust.

Andrea and Ryan walked the trail that circled the park.

"It is so nice to breathe real air again," Andrea said.

"It's nice just to have a little family time," Ryan responded. "I hardly see you anymore."

The park was quiet and empty. Chirping birds and the wind rustling tree leaves made the walk a Zen-like experience.

"Remember when we used to take walks by the riverfront in Columbia?" Andrea asked.

"Of course." Ryan smiled and took Andrea's hand. "I knew you were special then. Always so observant. You could spot a rare bird or a sailboat from a mile away."

Andrea exhaled calmly at the pleasant memory. The tension of the last several weeks were draining out of her, at least temporarily.

Andrea glanced back at the kids and smiled. They'd moved on to the little playground beside the baseball field and were climbing the jungle gym.

"I suppose if we could survive them, we can survive anything," Andrea said. "Remember the time Michelle made a mural on the wall with crayon after she learned about the Sistine Chapel in art class?"

"Oy," Ryan groaned. "It took me a week to repaint the wall."

They continued walking along the path. They passed a large tree that had a carving of a heart with "Melvin + Sara" inside.

"You know we'll make it through all this, right?" Ryan asked. "I mean, we made it this far."

Andrea snapped back to reality. Tomorrow was the day the Chinese repossession would begin.

"The next few days are going to be some of the worst in American history," Andrea replied, her head shaking.

"Maybe so, but remember when Aaron accidentally threw a ball through that window and knocked over that armoire of heirlooms?"

Andrea nodded. "He destroyed the whole thing."

"Remember what I said?"

Andrea nodded again. "You said it's just stuff."

"Exactly. Whatever the Chinese take, it's just stuff. Would you rather be living in China? They have cameras everywhere, and they arrest people for saying the wrong thing. I don't want to live like that. Wondering if the government will take me or the kids for looking at someone the wrong way."

Andrea listened, expressionless.

"Let them take statues, relics, furniture, whatever. I'd still rather live in the United States any day of the week and twice on Sunday," Ryan said.

"You realize people are going to hate me."

"I won't," Ryan said emphatically. "And isn't that all that really matters? Who cares what other people think."

"I do," Andrea said.

"Well stop," Ryan replied. "You're in politics. Everybody ends up unpopular in politics."

Andrea laughed. Ryan always had a way of making her feel better.

They'd nearly completed circling the park when Aaron and Michelle came running up to them. "Can we go to Ledo's for pizza and then ice cream?" Michelle chirped.

Ryan glanced at Andrea. She smiled.

"Sure, sweetheart, get your grandmother and we'll meet you at the car."

The kids ran over to the bench where Mamie was sitting, lifted her by her arms, and began making their way to the family minivan.

"Tomorrow is going to be terrible," Andrea muttered.

"Forget about tomorrow," Ryan said. "Just enjoy some pizza tonight. Ledo is your favorite."

Andrea put on a smile as they made their way back to their minivan where the kids and Mamie were waiting.

CHAPTER 45

Andrea awoke at five a.m. Her holiday was over. The other shoe was about to drop. Chinese soldiers were on their way to claim property to pay back America's debt to China. The country was about to find out what that part of the cease-fire agreement meant. It would be one of America's greatest humiliations and, in her mind, she had authored it.

She dressed quickly, drove to work, booted her computer, and read the online headlines. Then she glanced at her smartphone. Her email had filled with alerts from every major news outlet.

The headlines and alerts were as bad as she feared.

"China to Begin Claiming Government Property."

"Chinese Soldiers, Statesmen Arrive to Collect on Debt."

"CHINESE REPO MAN" screamed the New York Post, complete with a photo of the poster from the movie, *Repo Man*, and the Chinese premier's face superimposed on the image of Emilio Estevez.

Andrea streamed NBC's morning coverage to see what people were saying while she brewed some coffee.

NBC had supplanted its usual programming with coverage of the arrival of the Chinese repossession teams. Reporter Chuck Reed was broadcasting live from Lower Manhattan looking out toward New York Harbor.

"I'm reporting from New York City, where any moment now the Chinese repossession teams will be arriving. Thousands of Americans have come to watch this historic event."

The camera panned the crowd of New Yorkers gazing out toward the harbor in the mist of the early morning.

"There! There they are," said Reed. "If you look just beyond the Statue of Liberty, you can see the silhouette of several Chinese warships."

The figures of the ships in the Chinese flotilla grew larger and clearer as they approached and then docked at New York Harbor, the Statue of Liberty standing watch in the foreground.

"The people who have come to watch this unfold are in shock," Reed reported. He turned to one of the spectators. "Sir, what are your thoughts as you watch the Chinese Navy entering New York Harbor?"

"It's a damned disgrace," he said. "I had to see it with my own eyes to believe it was really happening."

Andrea slammed her fist on her desk. The humiliation of the Chinese arriving and the blame she could already hear coming her way were too much. She needed to vent.

Footsteps approached her office.

"Andrea, you here?" Rachel said. She must have arrived in the last few minutes.

"Yes, looks like I beat you in this morning," Andrea replied. "Come in and watch this with me."

Rachel pulled a chair next to Andrea's so she could see her computer screen.

Two of the Chinese ships made a left turn away from the flotilla toward Liberty Island. One of the ships had an enormous crane on its deck.

"Where are those two ships going?" Andrea wondered.

The ships dropped anchor next to Liberty Island. The ships were side-by-side with the Statue of Liberty. The crane of one ship slowly deployed its hook and harness over the Statue of Liberty. Chinese soldiers swarmed from the other ship to the base of the statue, clambering up the stone pedestal to the base of the statue. Bright lights and sparks began to appear at various points at the base.

"What is that?" Andrea asked.

Rachel leaned forward and squinted at the computer screen. "It looks like they're cutting the Statue of Liberty off its pedestal!"

Andrea leaned back from the screen, mouth agape and eyes bulging.

"Good lord, they're taking it," she replied.

The ignominy left her speechless. The Statue of Liberty had greeted generations of immigrants to the United States. It was the first thing her great-grandparents and Ryan's grandparents had laid eyes on as they sailed into the United States for the first time. It was an indelible family memory, passed down to them just as it surely was in millions of American families. The Statue of Liberty represented their families' very freedom and victories over the worst regimes in human history. Andrea and Rachel sat dumbstruck as they watched the army of one of the world's most odious totalitarian regimes set to work removing the statue.

"It looks like the Chinese are using welding torches to remove the Statue of Liberty!" Reed shouted into his microphone.

Onlookers covered their mouths in shock and disbelief as they realized what was happening. A small girl buried her face in her mother's stomach as her mother gave her a tight hug. Some turned away, unable to bear the sight. An elderly woman dabbed her eyes with a handkerchief. Two burly men gestured obscenely at the Chinese. A group of teenagers threw stones angrily but helplessly into the harbor.

"Jesus." Rachel scanned the NBC video library. "Play that one." She pointed to a video titled "Chinese Arrive in Baltimore." Andrea clicked on the link.

"I'm Anthony Givens, reporting from the Dundalk Marine Terminal in Baltimore," the reported said.

Three loud booms exploded from the video.

"Chinese ships have entered Baltimore harbor," Givens said. "The lead Chinese ship just shot three cannons into the air to announce its arrival. The ships are festooned with Chinese flags and red banners. Chinese sailors in their pressed whites are standing at attention on the bows. Large loudspeakers are playing what I think is the Chinese national anthem. The ships will be docking here in a moment and disembarking their crews to begin the repossession."

"Go to NBC's live feed," said Rachel, mesmerized by what she was seeing. Andrea clicked on a link.

"The Chinese repossession trucks are driving along Broening Highway," Givens reported breathlessly. "They appear to be making their way to Interstate 95, but we don't know where they are going. Our choppers and news trucks are following them."

One of the cameras surveyed the crowd of locals lining both sides of Broening Highway as the Chinese repossession convoy drove past. Many held American flags. Others held signs reminding the Chinese that they were "Commie scum."

The camera captured a young girl with pigtails holding a small American flag with a hangdog look on her face. American soldiers lining the road were restraining onlookers from charging the convoy with bats and hurling projectiles at it.

Cameras from overhead news helicopters captured the convoy emerging from the Fort McHenry Tunnel heading south on Interstate 95 in the direction of Washington.

"One of the trucks is getting off," Rachel said.

"At the Fort McHenry exit?" Andrea felt as though her eyes were going to pop out of her head.

The Chinese truck rolled up Fort Avenue. Andrea had ridden

that road a thousand times as a kid. Givens followed behind in his news van. The Chinese truck rumbled past the brick-wall-lined gate at the entrance to Fort McHenry and into its empty parking lot.

Andrea hadn't been to Fort McHenry in years, but from the broadcast images it was just as she remembered it. Her father used to take her to the fort when she was a child growing up in Baltimore. She was always so fascinated by the oversized fifteen-star flag that flew over the fort. She liked to run in and out of the reconstructed buildings and along its ramparts. She'd sit on the large green space outside the walls, eat a corned beef sandwich from Jack's or Attman's or Weiss's, maybe a Baltimore-style hot dog wrapped in the traditional slice of fried bologna, maybe a coddie or Western fries too for good measure, and watch the ships going in and out of the harbor.

The truck parked and two Chinese soldiers briskly got out. The National Parks Service employee who was sitting at the entrance to the small passageway leading in reached his hand out to shake hands with the soldiers, but they walked straight past him without even looking.

"Assholes," Andrea muttered. "Such disrespect."

The two soldiers walked along the small dirt path under the brick archway entrance and directly to the flagpole. They began untying the halyard from the cleat at the foot of the pole.

Andrea watched in horror as the Chinese began lowering the flag. No ceremony, no salute, nothing.

"Has there been a lower moment in the history of the United States?" Andrea asked. "We've let a mortal enemy waltz in and take the Star-Spangled Banner. People died to keep that flag flying over that fort, and now we just let these bastards walk in and take it."

Givens and his camera crew had followed the Chinese

soldiers into the fort. "The flagpole is bare for the first time in two centuries," he reported, astonishment on his face. "Not since 1814 has a flag not flown on this pole."

Andrea felt the weight of over two hundred years of history as she watched the flag come down. She sensed the eyes of ghosts on her, of Francis Scott Key and James Madison, of Sam Smith and George Armistead, the heroes of the War of 1812 and the Battle of Baltimore. She imagined the flag surviving through the night, illuminated by the Congreve rockets the British mercilessly fired at the fort in their failed bid to capture it. An entire squadron of British troops and ships couldn't defeat the Americans. And now, two Chinese soldiers were helping themselves to the sacred artifact the Americans defended to the death that night.

Rachel shook her head in disbelief. "This country will never live this down," she said. "I'm telling you, people will never, ever forget this image. They might as well have opened our skulls and branded it on our brains. 'O say does that star-spangled banner yet wave, o'er the land of the free and the home of the brave?' Not anymore it doesn't."

As the flag descended the flagpole a heavy gust of wind began to blow, unfurling it in all its glory for one last time. It was as if Mother Nature herself was unwilling to accept America's fate and wouldn't let the flag go down without a fight.

But the Chinese soldiers, pulling harder to overcome the wind's resistance, continued to lower the flag.

Not even Mother Nature can save the country now, Andrea thought.

The bottom of the flag began to hit the ground; the Chinese soldiers weren't bothering to catch the flag to keep it from touching the ground as American soldiers would. The flag slowly piled up, folding over itself in a heap, until all that remained of the Star-Spangled Banner was a red-white-and-blue pile of cloth. The soldiers didn't bother folding the flag. They each took a corner, dragged it along the dirt path out of the fort, and tossed it, covered in dirt, into the back of their waiting truck.

A combination of anger, sadness, and sheer helplessness left Andrea numb. She watched, mesmerized, as the Chinese drove out Fort McHenry's gates with their first piece of repossessed property.

Just then Andrea's cell phone chimed. Stanley Marshal was asking if she could come to the Oval Office.

"POTUS is calling," Andrea said. "He wants me to join him in the Oval to monitor events."

"I'm sure he does," Rachel responded. "Let him know we're all here if he needs anything." Rachel patted Andrea on the shoulder. "And one more thing: don't forget, we are doing the right thing. It sucks, but just remember that, okay?"

"Will do." Andrea got up and wearily made the trek back to the West Wing.

CHAPTER 46

The EEOB wasn't nearly the beehive of activity it normally was, with so many staffers furloughed by the emergency budget. As Andrea walked through the lobby, she heard her footsteps echoing off the lobby's vaulted ceiling. The din of conversation that usually obscured these echoes was gone.

President Murray was seated on the couch in the Oval Office with his jacket off, tie askew, and his chin resting in the palm of his hand as he watched the Chinese repossession on the television that was set up in front of the fireplace. He looked like a stockbroker who'd lost it all in a market crash.

"Thank goodness someone is here." President Murray sighed. "I don't think I could take watching this alone. I sent the vice president up to the Hill to monitor events there."

Andrea dejectedly seated herself next to the president and joined him in silently watching the television.

Stanley Marshal entered the Oval Office and pierced the gloomy silence. "Mr. President?"

President Murray shook his head quickly, as if shaken out of a reverie. "I'm sorry," he said, turning to look at Stanley. "What is it?"

"The Chinese Embassy has advised that the repossession team will be arriving at the White House within the next thirty minutes."

President Murray looked shell-shocked. "You want to leave?" he asked Andrea.

"Desperately," she responded.

"Me too," Murray said. "I can't bear this."

"But we have to stay, Mr. President," said Andrea. "We need to try to retain as much dignity as we can." Her conversations with Ryan yesterday and Rachel this morning had fortified her resolve.

"Dignity left town a long time ago," Murray said. The morning's events seemed to have left him in a daze.

Images of Chinese representatives making their way down New York Avenue toward the east gate of the White House complex appeared on the television.

"Stan, call State. Get someone who speaks Chinese down here," the president said.

"Will do, Mr. President," Stanley said, running off to make the call.

NBC's camera on the North Lawn picked up two Chinese soldiers in their dress whites and gold braids, with red stars on their hats, holding ceremonial rifles with gleaming gold bayonets, taking up positions at the front door to the White House. Tourists snapped photos in disbelief as Chinese soldiers, not American Marines, stood guard at the West Wing entrance in full dress uniform.

Two massive flatbed trucks pulled into the White House driveway. Andrea was jarred by the sight of these dirty, utilitarian vehicles with their roaring diesel engines and industrial-sized tires driving along a driveway ordinarily the province of the highest-end limousines.

There was a knock at the Oval Office door. The door slowly opened and Stanley Marshal poked his head into the Oval.

"Mr. President?"

"Yes?"

"The Chinese are here," Stan said.

President Murray looked at Andrea, still standing beside him.

She nodded mournfully. He nodded, then turned to Stan. "Escort them in, Stan," he said with a resigned sigh.

Six Chinese representatives entered the Oval Office. Four were armed soldiers in fatigues. Two appeared to be bureaucrats in dark blue suits and solid red ties. A Chinese television correspondent and her camera crew followed behind.

President Murray stood ramrod straight and tightened his tie. "Welcome to the Oval Office, gentlemen," he said in the strongest voice he could muster.

One of the Chinese bureaucrats in a suit nodded toward him. The rest said nothing. They didn't even look in the president's direction. For all Andrea knew they didn't understand a word the president had said.

The bureaucrat pointed to the north wall of the office to the left of the fireplace and gestured for President Murray and Andrea to move there. The Chinese soldiers circled the room like predators closing in on their prey, inspecting their booty. One of them began taking photographs with his smartphone.

President Murray gritted his teeth. "That guy is taking selfies with his iPhone. I'd like to knock his block off."

"Dignity, Mr. President," said Andrea, gently restraining him with her arm. "We need to maintain a stiff upper lip for the country."

The Chinese soldiers laughed, joking around as they rummaged through the Resolute desk. One eyed the red telephone on the desk, fascinated. He picked it up and put it down repeatedly, perhaps wondering who was on the other end. It had been an emergency line to the Pentagon. President Murray had it disconnected when the Chinese arrived in the United States.

Andrea's stiff upper lip began to waver. She wished that for once, just once, she had the physical courage of an Andrew

Jackson or Teddy Roosevelt. To be able to walk right up to one of those Chinese soldiers and lay them out cold, right there in the Oval. Her jaw clenched and she felt pressure rising in her head and the muscles in her arms tensing. All the energy she wanted to unleash on the Chinese soldiers had nowhere to go.

The Chinese yanked the Gilbert Stuart painting of George Washington from the wall and carelessly tossed it into a cart. Bits of plaster fell to the floor. Dolley Madison had saved that painting before the British burned the White House in 1814. Andrea imagined herself pictured in a history book next to Dolley Madison.

Here's the hero who saved the picture, and here's the failure who lost it.

The Chinese bureaucrat screamed at the soldier. The soldier bowed before the bureaucrat apologetically.

"What was that about?" President Murray asked the interpreter State had sent.

"He told him to be careful, the painting is worth millions," the interpreter replied.

As the soldiers continued their work, the Chinese television correspondent took up position in front of the fireplace and began prattling away in incomprehensible Chinese.

"What's she saying?" President Murray asked.

The interpreter quietly responded, "She is saying that this is the end result of democracy—voters' demands bankrupting the country and politicians too cowardly to stop them. She said China's system is far superior, with experts providing economic stability and no elections requiring politicians to promise voters outlandish and unaffordable spending."

"Fuck these assholes," President Murray said. He clenched his fists so tightly his knuckles turned white and his fingertips a dark red.

Four Chinese soldiers stationed themselves at each corner of the Resolute desk and lifted it onto a waiting dolly. Two of the soldiers rolled the desk out of the Oval Office.

"That desk has been in this office for over a hundred years," Andrea said. "I'm going to be sick . . ." She covered her gaping mouth with one hand and held her stomach with the other.

The Chinese continued to loot the rest of the contents of the Oval Office. The bust of Winston Churchill. The painting of Andrew Jackson. The flags of each military service with the ribbons clipped to the top of the flagpole honoring their every battle. All unceremoniously grabbed, loaded onto hand trucks, and rolled to the cargo trucks in the White House driveway.

Finally, all that was left was the Oval Office carpet and the coffee table with the broken glass top Admiral Wilkerson had cracked with his fist.

"What happened here?" the Chinese bureaucrat asked in English.

"None of your goddamn business," President Murray said.

The Chinese bureaucrat laughed. "You can keep this. We do not want broken furniture. Now move yourselves, please."

"Don't you talk to me like that," President Murray protested, pointing at the bureaucrat.

The bureaucrat said nothing and shooed at the president.

President Murray raised his fists and began to move toward the bureaucrat, but Andrea stepped between him and the Chinese soldiers. A donnybrook in the Oval Office would do the country no good. Seeing the president in a fistfight with Chinese soldiers would only add to America's debasement. Especially because there were more Chinese than Americans in the Oval Office and the president might well lose that fight.

"You goddamn sons of bitches!" President Murray shouted over and over.

Andrea gripped the president's arms tighter. She imagined herself a coach restraining the irate Oriole manager Earl Weaver of her youth. She slowly backed the president off the carpet and toward the wall as the Chinese bureaucrat snickered.

The Chinese soldiers rolled up the carpet and loaded it onto the last waiting dolly. The Oval Office stripped bare, the soldiers marched out of the office. The lead bureaucrat gave President Murray a mock salute and left. The president lunged forward, but Andrea restrained him again.

Now they were alone in an empty Oval Office. The office was so white. So plain and empty. All that remained was the coffee table with its broken glass top in the center of the room.

President Murray slowly walked around the empty room, looking at the walls like someone inspecting a new house. There were circles on the floor where the military services' flags used to stand; sunlight had faded the floor around the bases. He ran his finger over the hole in the wall where the painting of President Jackson had been mounted. A small bit of plaster fell from the hole. The grandfather clock was gone, its outline still visible from having protected the wall from being faded by sunlight for a century.

Andrea bit back tears. She checked her watch. It had taken the Chinese nearly four hours to complete their repossession work in the White House.

The president's smartphone chimed. It was a text from Vice President Campbell on the Hill. "The Chinese are taking everything here," Murray read aloud.

He called out into the foyer where Stanley Marshal was still on duty. "Can you get me a computer? I want to see what else the Chinese have been doing."

Stanley brought in a small laptop computer and set it down on one of the Oval Office's built-in shelves.

"Go to C-SPAN's website," Murray said. "See what's happening in the Capitol."

The C-SPAN homepage featured a series of videos from Capitol Hill chronicling the Chinese repossession team's work in the Capitol complex. There was a video link that read "Statuary Hall repossession." Andrea clicked on it.

The video captured Chinese soldiers rolling small trucks, cranes, and other heavy lifting equipment into Statuary Hall. The soldiers were loading the statues onto rolling dollies and removing them. Samuel Adams. Dwight Eisenhower. Thomas Edison. Helen Keller. The Chinese even removed the beautiful deep-red curtains with the bright gold trim that served as the backdrop for these marble American heroes. All they left was an empty rotunda, the Corinthian columns at its perimeter and the decorative ceiling the only hint of the hall's former grandeur.

"I used to take tour groups to Statuary Hall when I was a congressman," the president said. "Beautiful room, the old House of Representatives chamber. With every state's two statues of their native sons and daughters who became American heroes. I'd walk the tour groups all the way through each of the statues to be sure they appreciated the richness of American history. One of the most American rooms in America. Every one of them represented something great about this country. People are watching this at home, probably wondering if we're about to become a Chinese colony."

"This is what it must have looked like when the Visigoths sacked Rome," Andrea said. "I'd do anything to go back in time to cut something from the budget, anything, just so we didn't have to watch this."

Andrea clicked on the next link, titled "House and Senate Chambers repossession." The studio anchor was speaking in a quiet golf voice. "We're now getting live shots of the House and Senate floors.

The cameras in the House and Senate chambers captured Chinese soldiers pulling up the desks and chairs on the floor of both chambers. Two Chinese soldiers pulled down the flag behind the Speaker of the House's seat. That flag had served as a backdrop to some of the most memorable speeches in American history, from FDR's "a date which will live in infamy" speech in the wake of the attack on Pearl Harbor to a century's worth of State of the Union addresses. The methodical stripping of the two chambers reminded Andrea of the end of a funeral, with gravediggers unfeelingly dumping dirt on a freshly laid coffin.

C-SPAN had even captured Chinese soldiers taking the American and state flags outside each member's office suite and pulling off the bronze name plaques adorning the front door of every door. The same plaques Andrea saw when she'd first come to the Hill seeking the Debt Rebel Gang's endorsement. Her political adventure had come full circle.

President Murray sat stone-faced and numb as he witnessed the Capitol Hill repossession. He appeared emotionally unable to react further.

The country couldn't see the president like this. As long as he stayed strong for the country, it would survive, Andrea thought. But a shell-shocked president might end any hopes of surviving the debt crisis. The president didn't have much of his staff left under the emergency budget. Only Stan Marshal was around now, and he was a functionary. It was up to her to restore the president's strength.

"Pearl Harbor and 9/11 were dastardly. The Kennedy assassination was horrific. But this?" President Murray's eyes glistened with tears. "This is *humiliating.*"

"What about when the British burned Washington?" Andrea asked.

"At least we were fighting then," he replied. "Not surrendering."

He walked over to the windows facing the South Lawn, fixing his vacant stare on the Washington Monument.

Andrea thought about her discussion with Ryan the day before. She might be feeling the same humiliation as the president, but she knew why she was putting herself through it. President Murray needed her to recalibrate his equilibrium and confidence the same way Ryan had recalibrated hers.

"Mr. President, what do you think America is?"

The president turned to her. His nose was red. "What do you mean?"

"I mean, why are we working so hard to solve this debt crisis? What are we putting ourselves through hell for?"

"What are you driving at?"

"America is an idea and an experiment in self-governance," Andrea said. "A test of whether a nation can create a government of specific, enumerated powers that maximizes human freedom and gives each citizen a voice in their governance."

"Experiments can fail," President Murray replied.

"Experiments don't wait two hundred and fifty years to fail," Andrea said. "Our people are made of strong stuff. How do you think they got past five years of killing each other in the Civil War and got on with the business of building the country? We owe it to our ancestors to get past this."

"Times are different, Andrea."

A small flame had lit inside her. "Mr. President, you and I took very different roads to get to where we're standing right now. But I think we're motivated by the same thing: to leave the place better for our children and their children. Lord knows we didn't ask to implement the emergency budget or fight this war. But we're seeing it through. And so are Americans. They're looking at all this trauma and helping their neighbor in need, not rioting."

The president, head bowed, slowly circled the spot on the floor where the Resolute desk had sat. "We'd better hurry it up and see it through, because I'm sure to be a one-term president."

"It may not look like it now, but when the debt slate is clean, we will have done what we set out to do," Andrea said. "I said it before and I'll say it again: I think this will be your finest hour. But if you lose reelection, history will be kinder to you than the electorate."

"I wish I had your confidence, Andrea."

"You can, and you should, Mr. President."

CHAPTER 47

T he chiming of an alarm clock awoke Mason in his Capitol Hill office. Normally he slept in his apartment uptown, but he was not going to miss the sun rising over the Capitol the day after the Chinese had ransacked it. Mason got up from his couch and went to his desk chair, seated himself, and turned to face the window with anticipation.

As sunlight began to peek over the horizon, the Capitol dome came into view. The fifteen-thousand-pound Statue of Freedom that had sat atop it since 1863 was gone, hauled off by Chinese soldiers the day before.

What could be more demoralizing for Americans than to watch a totalitarian Communist dictatorship pull down the Statue of Freedom?

The flagpoles atop the House chamber stood bare. The parking lot, usually buzzing with black Suburbans shuttling members of Congress to work, was empty.

Intoxicated by the sight of the stripped Capitol exterior, Mason turned back to his desk to see what the Chinese had done to the rest of the country. He browsed through news media on his laptop, smiling at the sheer number of videos chronicling America's humiliation.

In one video, Chinese soldiers methodically emptied the Air and Space Museum, hauling off John Glenn's *Friendship 7* capsule and the *Apollo 11* capsule. In another, Chinese soldiers carted away copies of the Declaration of Independence, the Constitution, and the Emancipation Proclamation from the National Archives.

A third video showed Chinese bureaucrats taking the tea sets and furniture from the Diplomatic Reception Rooms in the State Department and the massive bronze bust of John F. Kennedy from the Kennedy Center.

A video of New York showed the Statue of Liberty's empty pedestal standing powerlessly on the island with the Statue of Liberty lying on its side on the deck of a Chinese barge steaming out of New York Harbor. Shock, sorrow, and hopelessness were written all over the faces of the New Yorkers watching it sail away.

Mason never thought he would see a video like this in his wildest dreams.

I, Lewis Mason, pride of the Kansas heartland, succeeded where the Nazis, Japanese, and Soviets all failed. I defeated, humbled, and sacked the United States.

Mason now understood what Xu Li meant when she said he would know when to make his move. Any Ministry agent worth his salt would know the iron wasn't going to get any hotter. Chinese soldiers were on American soil. And if the faces of ordinary American citizens were to be believed, China had stunned Americans into a mortified paralysis.

After a shower in the Longworth building gymnasium, now shorn of its exercise equipment, Mason called the White House.

"Congressman," President Murray said coldly.

"Mr. President."

Mason sensed the curtness and anger in the president's voice. *So much the better. His judgment will be off.*

"I saw the Chinese were in the White House yesterday. Did they not take your phone?"

"We all brought in old phones and furniture. I'm sitting at a card table Andrea Gartner brought from home on a folding chair she found in her garage."

Mason feigned concern. "My goodness, Mr. President."

"What do you want, you duplicitous son of a bitch?" asked the president, still fuming from Mason's double-cross. Mason decided to get right to business.

"Mr. President, we need to decide where we go from here. Budget-wise, I mean."

"You fucked me, Lew," the president shouted. "You think I'm going to negotiate anything with you now? You're lucky I don't come up there and wring your neck. And even if I was inclined to meet with you, my team has got a long way to go before it's ready to talk to Congress."

"Respectfully, I disagree, Mr. President. I think we ought to work together from the beginning. From the ground up. It'll help the country heal to see us working together."

"*Now* you want to work together?" President Murray shouted. "Fuck you, you cynical bastard. You get up in the well of the House, trash the war, embarrass me, and now you want to work together?"

Mason persisted. He wanted his meeting with the president. "We need to at least give people the feeling that mature heads are working together to solve the problem. Let's just meet. One-on-one. Air it all out and get back to work."

"Lew, once I get done pulling out the knife you stuck in my back, maybe I'll meet with you. Until then, I'm not interested."

Mason changed tactics and decided to appeal to President Murray's sense of patriotism. "Mr. President, remember your speech? Remember how you said we owed it to our children to solve this problem? Forget what you think of me. I'm here and ready to solve the problem for them."

President Murray hesitated.

Good. I've hooked him. Now reel him in.

"I've got Andrea Gartner in the Oval with me," said President Murray. "Hang on."

President Murray put the phone down. But he forgot to

press mute. Or maybe the old phone didn't have a mute button. Whatever it was, Mason could hear everything.

"It's Lewis Mason," the president said. "He wants to meet. I'd rather leap into a pile of manure."

"Maybe you should do it," said Andrea. "I know Mason's a turd, but Appropriations is Appropriations. We've got to work with him to solve the debt crisis, whether we like it or not."

Mason smiled. Andrea was doing his work for him.

"I don't trust that lying sack of shit for a second," said the president.

"Me neither, but we can't solve the debt crisis without him," she said. "You know that. It's no worse than when you sent me to go beg for war funds from him."

Thank you, Andrea, Mason thought. *I couldn't have made a better argument.*

After a long pause, President Murray said, "All right. If you think it's worth trying, I'll meet with the bastard."

The phone jostled, and the president returned to the call. "Lew, I talked to Andrea, and she's convinced me to meet. Which is remarkable, considering what you did to her and to me. But I swear, you stab me in the back again, and I will make it my mission in life to destroy you."

"Thank you, Mr. President." Mason grinned. "I'll do everything I can to make sure you don't walk out of the meeting disappointed."

"Where do you want to meet?"

"I'd be happy to host the meeting," Mason said. "I still have some furniture in my office, and I saw the Oval Office was pretty well ransacked." Now that President Murray had agreed to the meeting, Mason couldn't resist twisting the knife further.

"Fuck you, Lew. You're not the only member of the Appropriations Committee. I'm sure I could find someone who's less of an asshole to deal with."

"I'm sorry, Mr. President, I didn't mean to insult you," said Mason disingenuously. "Trust me, I really do want to solve this problem."

"Ha. Trust you?" President Murray laughed. "No fucking way. But we can meet in your office. You're in Longworth, right?"

"Yes, I am. Office 4946. There's one more thing."

"What's that?"

"I'd like to meet one-on-one. No Andrea Gartner, no other Debt Rebel Gang members, just you and me, if that's okay."

"Fine. Whatever," the president said, annoyed.

Mason smiled. He was on his way to decapitating Denali.

CHAPTER 48

Twenty-four hours ago, Chinese cargo trucks had loaded up their booty from the White House. Now the halls and rooms were empty, stripped of their contents and shorn of their grandeur. The solid red, blue, and green of each room's wallpaper, uninterrupted by the colors of paintings, curtains, and furniture, was blinding.

Andrea was in the Oval Office preparing some notes with President Murray for the meeting with Mason when she felt her cell phone vibrate.

"Pls call me ASAP emergency," the message read. It was from Rachel.

"Mr. President, could we pause for a moment? I need to call Rachel. She says it's urgent."

"Not now, Andrea," Murray replied. "The car to take me up to the Hill should be here any minute. We need to get these notes done."

"Understood, sir."

Andrea continued typing talking points on her laptop. Her cell phone was vibrating non-stop. Rachel had texted four messages. She ignored it.

"This look good?" she asked Murray, turning her laptop screen to him.

"Perfect," Murray replied. "I imagine I'll go off-script at some point. It always happens."

"You'll do fine, you always do," Andrea said to give him a little confidence before leaving. She emailed the talking points to Murray.

White House staff pulled up two sedans to take President Murray up to Mason's office on the Hill. The seventeen-car motorcade convoy was no more. The Chinese had taken the limousines.

"Good luck, Mr. President," Andrea said as President Murray climbed into the back of the waiting car. He nodded, smiled, and closed the door.

Andrea watched the president's car drive off until it disappeared along Pennsylvania Avenue. She then turned her phone on and finally reviewed Rachel's texts as she hurried back to her office. They were progressively more urgent:

I need to speak with you!

Call me now!

WHERE ARE YOU?????

When she reached her office, Andrea was surprised to find it untouched. The Chinese apparently spared it in their White House looting.

Andrea called Rachel. "I got your texts. What is going on?"

"Are you sitting down?"

"Why?"

"You aren't going to believe what I have to tell you. This is some deadly serious stuff."

Andrea dropped into her office chair and stared at the West Wing outside her window. "All right, I'm sitting." She could practically feel the adrenaline secreting into her bloodstream, delivering a confounding mixture of dread and excitement. "FBI called me this morning. They brought in some experimental facial recognition technology from MIT, and they think they've finally solved the Pripyat Consortium mystery. Pull up a picture of that Pripyat Consortium guy."

Andrea opened her laptop and pulled up the Pripyat Consortium press conference online.

"Okay, I have him on my screen now."

"Take a good look at him. You said he looked familiar, right?"

"Yes."

"The FBI thinks his name is Pyotr Dzerzhin Mesorovsky."

Andrea frowned. "Who the hell is that? Should I know?"

"He has a brother," said Rachel.

"Get to the point already!" Andrea bellowed.

"His brother's name is Lavrenti Mesorovsky and he lives in the United States."

Andrea went through her mental Rolodex without success. "I've never heard of anyone named Lavrenti Mesorovsky."

"That's because he Anglicized his name."

"To what?"

"Lewis Mason."

"Excuse me?"

"You heard me. Lewis Mason."

"*The* Lewis Mason?"

"Look at Zegna Suit, the Pripyat spokesman, and then look at a picture of Mason."

Andrea quickly typed into the search engine and pulled up some pictures of the House Appropriations Committee chairman.

Lord almighty.

Andrea knew Zegna Suit looked like someone familiar to her, and now she knew why.

Lewis Mason.

The resemblance was uncanny. The same thick build. The same short arms and stocky legs. The same vaguely Russian features—the narrow eyes, the bulbous nose. Zegna Suit wore a beard, probably to conceal his identity.

Rachel finally dropped the bomb. "Zegna Suit is Mason's brother."

"You mean—"

"Mason's a Russki."

"What about that whole story he loves to tell? The farm in Kansas? The foreclosure? The apartment with all the rats in Kansas City?"

"That part of his story is true. But here's what he doesn't tell people. He didn't leave Russia because he was an orphan. His father worked for the Soviet government. The FBI thinks there's a good chance the Russians planted him here in the United States decades ago and planned to activate him as an agent when he became an adult. They probably put him in a situation where he was sure to grow to hate the United States."

Andrea's mind flooded with thoughts too quickly to process. Was this a dream? Lewis Mason? A Russian spy? Sure, he was an unmitigated jackass, but never in a million years would she have ever thought he was a Russian spy. The guy made his political living trashing people who he thought weren't conservative enough, excommunicating them from the Republican Party for their sins. How could Mr. Debt Rebel Gang, Mr. Chief RINO Hunter, be a Russian operative?

Yet at some level, she knew it was true. All these unexplained events—Mason's attempts to kill the emergency budget, his double-cross that ended the war with China, his lack of concern for Taiwan—were starting to make sense.

"Andrea, you there?" Rachel said, concern in her voice.

"You have to be kidding me," Andrea whispered.

"The FBI thinks it's all true. It's a classic deep-cover spy story. And it gets worse. Mesorovsky's middle name is Dzerzhin."

"So what?"

"Dzerzhin is a shortened form of Dzerzhinsky. It turns out that Zegna Suit and Lewis Mason are the great-grandsons of Felix Dzerzhinsky."

"Who the hell is that?"

"The founder of what became the KGB."

Andrea couldn't believe her ears. "The *KGB*?"

"Yes, the KGB."

Andrea could feel the blood draining from her face. She thought she must look white as a ghost. The *KGB*, the old Soviet Union's state security and intelligence agency.

"Jesus, Rachel, Mason called a few hours ago and asked the president to meet with him to discuss the budget. Murray didn't want to do it, but I convinced him. The president is heading over to Mason's office as we speak."

"You have to stop that meeting and get the president the hell out of there. Radio the Secret Service. Call the Capitol Police. Get someone to pull the fire alarm. Anything. Just get the president the hell out of there!" Rachel sounded frantic.

Andrea hung up and immediately called the Secret Service using a special number programmed into her cell phone. "This is OMB Director Andrea Gartner. You need to put me through to the president now. It's an emergency."

"Slow down," the operator said. "I need you to follow the protocol. Can you give me your Cabinet code?" Every Cabinet member had a special code to confirm their identity.

"This is Andrea Gartner. Emergency code 755220."

"Okay, let me just confirm your code—"

"We don't have time to confirm my code!" Andrea shouted. "The president is meeting with Lewis Mason. He needs to get out of there now. Do you understand?"

"Ms. Gartner, the president has his security detail. Whatever it is, they can handle it. I'll radio them to let them know," the Secret Service agent said, annoyance in his voice. "I'll let them assess the situation."

"But Lewis Mason is—"

A dial tone interrupted her. The Secret Service agent had hung up.

Andrea slammed the phone down. There was a good chance the president was in mortal danger and she hadn't told them about it soon enough.

There was only one thing left she could do. She raced out to her car to try to save President Murray herself.

CHAPTER 49

Every muscle in Andrea's body was taut as a piano wire. She was the only thing standing in the way of President Murray walking into Mason's office a sitting duck.

As she pulled her car out of the White House complex onto Washington's crowded streets, she thought of those Seventies' cop show reruns she watched when she was home sick from school. The ones where Detective Hunter would pull out a police dome light, slap it on his car, and zoom toward the crime scene. What she wouldn't do to have that awesome power right at this moment. Without police lights, Andrea waited at every red light along Pennsylvania Avenue. She thought about running the lights but was afraid of the cross traffic.

She wondered if she should have found a Secret Service agent willing to drive her up to Capitol Hill. But she'd already struck out calling the Secret Service. Plus, she'd have to find a Secret Service agent with a car. Most of the Secret Service had been laid off, and most of its motor pool was on a ship bound for China. She'd make it to the Hill faster on her own.

Her left foot twitched impatiently at the red light at Fifteenth Street as she waited to turn left onto Pennsylvania Avenue. "There are two streets here!" she screamed helplessly at the traffic light, stuck on red. That was when she saw the black Forester again.

It was two cars behind her, but it was unmistakable. Andrea stared into her rearview mirror and could just barely make out the driver. That same pale, almost pasty complexion, the full, bearded cheeks, the balding head, and the suit. Mason's brother.

The Pripyat spokesman in the Zegna suit. The man she now knew as Pyotr Dzerzhin Mesorovsky.

Terror gripped her. She turned her radio off to remove any distractions. She needed to be sharp.

The light turned green. Andrea made the left turn onto Pennsylvania Avenue and looked again in her rearview mirror in time to see the Forester making the same left turn. Behind the Forester she saw an ambulance.

When she reached Twelfth Street, she turned left. Two cars behind her, the Forester made the left turn without signaling. Andrea drove past the Hotel Harrington and up to the intersection of Twelfth and F Street. This time, a right turn toward Capital One Arena. Sure enough, the Forester made the right turn, still two cars behind her.

Now Andrea slowed down, just like she'd seen in the movies, and waited for the light at Eleventh Street to turn yellow. The crosswalk signal counted down to red. Six ... five ... four ... When the crosswalk timer reached three, Andrea roared across the intersection, leaving the Forester stuck behind the car between them, which had stopped at the light.

Lost him.

At the next block she turned down Tenth Street to get back to Pennsylvania Avenue and resume her race to the Hill. To her left was Ford's Theatre, the site of President Lincoln's assassination. The feeling of doom crept over Andrea again. She wasn't superstitious, but driving past the site of the first presidential assassination as she raced to prevent what might possibly be another assassination jangled her nerves. She stepped harder on the gas.

At Tenth and Pennsylvania, she made a left turn and was back to impatiently waiting at red lights to go the remaining ten blocks to Capitol Hill. She ignored her rearview mirror, focusing instead on the traffic ahead of her. Who was slow, who was fast, who could she get around? She looked for beat-up old cars and out-of-state plates, the slowpokes she'd need to get past, and plotted her path around them like a NASCAR driver.

Stopped at yet another red light on Sixth Street near the National Archives, Andrea glanced into her rearview and shook in fright.

There was the black Forester, looming like a monster she couldn't kill. It was right behind her now; she didn't even have the protection of a car or two between them. Had he seen her turn back to Pennsylvania Avenue? Was he tracking her with some GPS device?

Her left leg twitched faster.

Should I make a run for it? Should I drive to a police station? Should I try to call the Secret Service again?

Her brain was overloaded with options. She couldn't finish a thought before it was overtaken by another.

In a panic, Andrea whipped her head left and right, looking for oncoming traffic, and then floored her Camry to try to get through the light and leave the black Forester behind. Her tires squealed. Then, out of the corner of her eye, she saw motion. A red blur. Then an explosion.

The Camry spun wildly as shards of glass exploded across her face and arms. Andrea screamed as the left side of her head collided with the beam separating the front and back driver-side doors. She could no longer make out shapes; all she could see were blurred colors, a rainbow of reds and blues and greens passing before her eyes.

Another loud bang and the spinning stopped as abruptly as it had started. Another shower of glass flew past her face, this time from her right. Her head jerked wildly to the right, her body twisting against the resistance of the seat belt.

Then all motion stopped, the sounds of exploding glass and collapsing metal replaced by silence. Her left temple throbbed and warm liquid trickled down her face and onto her neck.

She opened her eyes just enough to confirm she was alive and stared forward, dazed. The sunlight seemed brighter, almost blinding. Light entered her eyes but no images registered in her mind, as if the light was passing through her without stopping. Looking down, she could make out lacerations, bright red with blood, crisscrossing her forearms. When she moved her feet, she felt layers of broken glass shards beneath her shoes.

Just as she began slipping into unconsciousness, the sound of a siren pierced her ears.

Paramedics? Police? How could they have gotten here so quickly?

A red light flashed, illuminating the interior of her destroyed car.

It must be an ambulance.

She heard voices at the car door. They weren't speaking English; it sounded like Russian. The car shook as the people outside tugged at its door. With a pop and the squeal of creaking metal, the door swung open. Shards of glass fell from the window onto her left arm.

"*Dermo!*" shouted a man she still could not see. Andrea was no expert on languages, but she recognized the Russian accent. "If she's dead, so am I. Xu Li will see to that," said the invisible stranger.

Andrea's lightheadedness, bordering on delirium, gave the encounter an unreal, dream-like feel. She didn't know who was talking—there were two voices—and couldn't follow the conversation at all.

A large weight pressed her into her seat. The smell of an unbathed man mixed with gasoline filled the air. She could make out a round, bearded face and a bulbous nose. He was wearing a necktie and the glare of sunlight shone off his business suit.

It was the driver of the Forester. Zegna Suit. Pyotr Dzerzhin Mesorovsky, Lewis Mason's brother.

Still in shock from the accident, she opened her mouth slightly and tried to lift her arms, but she could neither speak nor move. She could only watch helplessly in terror as the large, stinking Mesorovsky leaned over her.

She heard the snap of the seat belt unfastening. She listlessly slumped forward, her head hitting the steering wheel. She bounced off the wheel, groaned, and fell sideways out of the car's open door.

"Dermo!" Mesorovsky shouted. "Help me lay her down."

Andrea groaned again as Mesorovsky and someone else pulled her the rest of the way out of the car and laid her on the street. Mesorovsky applied bandages to her temple. The flow of blood down her face abated.

"Please . . . please . . . help me," Andrea whispered.

"Don't worry," Mesorovsky said. "I don't want to kill you. I need you."

The talk of death began to bring Andrea to her senses. She opened her mouth to speak but could only gasp sounds. It was as if the accident had severed the link between her brain and her tongue.

"Load her into the ambulance," Mesorovsky said in a commanding voice. "And give her the sedative."

They grabbed her by ankles and under her arms. Everything smelled of gasoline. She heard what sounded like counting in Russian—"*raz, dvah, tree*"—and then she was lifted onto a stretcher. She felt the pinch of a needle in her shoulder and something being injected into her veins. Moments later, the stretcher slid into the rear of an ambulance. Everything appeared blindingly white. White walls, white sheets, white equipment.

The ambulance horn blasted, and she lifted her head slightly, barely able to control her body. Her brain was issuing commands, but her body independently was deciding whether to respond. To her right she saw Mesorovsky seated against the ambulance wall. Out the open rear ambulance doors she could see a man beside her wrecked car leaning over some sort of small device. After another blast of the horn, the man dashed toward the ambulance. Flames began to erupt from the device as the man leaped into the open rear doors.

"Ekhat, ekhat, ekhat!" Mesorovsky shouted "Go!"

The man slammed the rear doors shut. The ambulance jumped to life, zooming away from the scene, siren blaring.

As the ambulance sped off, Andrea heard a massive explosion. The ambulance shook violently from the explosion's compression waves.

"Go!" Mesorovsky shouted.

Mesorovsky leaned over Andrea menacingly as she lay on the gurney. Even in her semi-conscious state, Andrea was overcome by his pungent odor.

"The president, the president," Andrea slurred, barely able to form the words as the sedative took hold. "I need to get to the president."

"No, we have other plans for you, Miss Gartner," Mesorovsky said. "Do not worry. Nothing will be left back there. By the time the police put the fire out and figure out what has happened, you will be long gone."

"Where are you taking me?" Andrea whispered.

Mesorovsky smiled. "There is someone special who wants to meet you."

CHAPTER 50

Mason was sitting at his office desk when he heard the echo of President Murray and his shrunken Secret Service detail coming down the Longworth Building's hall. The sound of the static from the Secret Service walkie-talkies was unmistakable. With most of Congress's staff laid off and congressional business at a standstill, Mason could hear almost any sound in the hall.

He jumped from his chair and walked out to the entrance foyer. His left hand repeatedly squeezed a spongy stress ball while he bit the fingernails of his right.

Staring at the white of the bare walls, stripped of their paintings by Chinese agents, Mason felt sweat beading up on his forehead. He took out a handkerchief and wiped his face dry.

Everything he'd done in the United States, from law school to politics, had been designed to set up the approaching moment, his chance to write his name in the history books, to go down in posterity with the heroes of the Revolution. Lenin. Stalin. Mao. Ho Chi Minh. He simultaneously felt exhilaration at the chance to fulfill his destiny and abject terror that he would make a mistake and fail.

Mason sensed his pulse and breath rate rising. He thought back to his poverty-stricken apartment in Kansas to steady his nerves and build up his anger. It was an old trick the Ministry taught its agents. Convert the energy of fear into directed, purposeful rage.

The president's shadow appeared on the hallway floor outside the entrance to the office suite. Mason knew the pinnacle of his career was moments away.

"Mr. President, thank you for coming." Mason outstretched his hand.

"Congressman," the president said, accepting the handshake coldly.

Mason turned to the Secret Service agents. "I'm sorry I don't have any chairs for you. The Chinese took them all."

"They understand." President Murray looked around the empty foyer. His face was filled with disgust. All that remained in the foyer was tattered carpet with imprints of where furniture used to sit. Holes and hooks on the wall stood as silent reminders of the pictures that used to hang there. All the stuff of a congressional office, from the plaques, to the flags, to the souvenir coins from trips to this or that agency, had been hauled away.

"The Chinese did a number on this place too," President Murray grumbled. "It looks like a vacant storefront."

When they reached the door to Mason's personal office, the president turned to his security detail. "All right, fellas, I'll see you when we're done," he said.

Mason knew the president had a habit of leaving his security detail outside of private meetings with senior government officials. He was counting on it.

"Have a seat." Mason pointed him to the plush leather chair facing his desk.

Murray grimaced again. "How come the rest of your office is stripped clean but you still have your stuff?"

"I dead-bolted the door," Mason replied. "I heard the Chinese come by and try to get in. They must have decided not to bother breaking down the door and moved on."

As President Murray walked toward the chair, Mason closed his office door and quietly turned the deadbolt.

"I hope you and Andrea realize I want to solve the debt crisis." Mason calmly took a seat behind his desk.

"Lew, I'll be blunt, you fucked me hard, and I'm of a mind to jump across this desk and kick your ass," President Murray said. "But Andrea convinced me to work with you on a long-term plan to solve our debt crisis and salvage what's left of the country. You're lucky you didn't succeed in exiling her from politics."

"Huh?" Mason mumbled, distracted.

He'd been so overtaken by anticipation of this moment that he'd forgotten to put the magazine into the dull black handgun in his desk. His hands fumbled in the drawer as he tried to slide the magazine into the gun without President Murray noticing.

"When we make more Social Security and Medicare cuts, you might tell the country that the Debt Rebel Gang supports it and take some of the heat off me and Andrea."

"What?" Mason was still fumbling.

"Lew, what's going on? Are you listening?"

"Uh . . . yes, yes I am. You were saying something about Andrea Gartner."

Got it!

Mason gently opened the gun's magazine chamber and silently slid the magazine into the chamber. The sweat dripping down his back tingled his skin. His pulse was rising.

"Mr. President, do you know why I called you here?"

President Murray furrowed his brow. "What kind of question is that? We're in the middle of a budget crisis, and you are the House Appropriations chairman."

"Mr. President, I need to tell you something." Mason felt a rush of adrenaline. The moment was upon him.

"What's that?"

"Mr. President, isn't it clear by now that Chinese economics are superior to ours?"

"Come again?" President Murray squinted and shook his head in confusion.

"The Chinese economy and government. They are superior to ours."

"What the hell are you talking about?"

"Mr. President, I hope you don't mind my saying this, but our government is decadent and corrupt, spending billions of borrowed dollars on wealthy and middle-class retirees while the poor get nothing."

"Lew, are you okay? What the hell has gotten into you?"

"Mr. President, I think the time has come to acknowledge Chinese supremacy in the world. Their economics are superior. Their military is superior. And their special operations are superior."

"Wha—"

Mason whipped the gun out of the drawer, took aim at the president of the United States, and fired four times.

Blood exploded from President Murray's chest and head, spurting onto the desk, and spraying Mason's shirt and glasses. Murray sagged backward and then dropped off the chair to his left, two bullet wounds in his head and two more in his chest.

Commotion exploded in the waiting area outside Mason's office. The office door shook against the deadbolt as the Secret Service agents struggled to get in.

Mason calmly stood up from his desk, confident in the deadbolt. There, on the floor in front of him, was the president, lying face-up in a pool of blood. He watched the blood flow down the president's tie, crawling up its white stripes and staining them red. A pool of blood bloomed in the carpet beneath his body. Blood dripped down the wood back of the chair President Murray had been seated in seconds ago, staining the seat cushion.

Mason dropped his gun at the sight, the smoke still emanating from the gun barrel. His palm tingled from the heat of the freshly fired weapon.

He knelt beside the body and checked for a pulse. There was none. He dipped his right index finger in the blood on the president's chest and smeared it on the president's white shirt. The bright red of Murray's blood clashed with Mason's pale white skin.

Lavrenti Mesorovsky, alias Lewis Mason, code name Crimson, had decapitated Denali.

History would now know the name Lewis Mason. And the Ministry would forevermore know the name Crimson.

He turned away from the murdered president, certain the deadbolt would keep the Secret Service out long enough for the Chinese agents hiding down the hall to come to his aid. In this single moment, he was surrounded by everything he'd worked for his entire career. He looked out his window at the Capitol dome, shorn of its statue of Freedom. On the street below, Chinese soldiers were still loading the contents of the Longworth building into trucks. Behind him lay the dead American president. Seeing the symbols of his triumph calmed his nerves.

His office door continued to vibrate from the pounding of the Secret Service, and with each kick the wood around the deadbolt and hinges splintered a bit more. The door was only a few more kicks away from falling.

Where are they?

Unnerved, he thought about what he would do if his Chinese protectors arrived too late. He only had one bullet left for the two agents about to blast into his office. If it came to a shootout, he was a dead man.

With one final kick, splinters exploded from the wall as the deadbolt separated from it and the door fell inward. The president's security detail charged into the room with guns drawn.

"Secret Service!" they screamed. "Hands in the air!"

Mason complied.

This was not supposed to happen. I did my job. Where are they?

The agents seemed utterly confused, unable to wrap their heads around what they were seeing.

"Stand right there and don't—"

Gunshots rang out from outside Mason's office, spraying the office with a hail of bullets. Mason shrieked as he watched the Secret Service agents fly sideways, blood spraying in all directions. His white office walls were instantly splattered with blood.

Several large Chinese men entered the office from the entrance foyer. They looked down expressionless at the lifeless bodies at their feet. Their still-smoking guns left a trail as they entered.

"Where were you?" Mason asked, still shaking. "Another thirty seconds and I would have been dead on the floor."

A small, officious-looking Chinese woman in a baby blue Mao-style suit followed the Chinese men into his office.

"Madame Xu . . ."

Seeing Xu Li in person stunned Mason and he took a step backward to the windowsill. "It is an honor to be in your presence," he said, regaining his balance and bowing deeply.

Xu Li smiled wanly as she looked at President Murray's body. "I see you have decapitated Denali."

"Yes, Madame Xu, I have," Mason said, regaining his composure. "I've done what generations of Communist agents have only dreamed of doing." He looked over his desk and pointed. "Look out this window. Look at what we have accomplished."

Xu Li walked around the desk and stood beside him.

Mason folded his arms behind his back, standing at attention. He towered over Xu Li by more than a foot but felt like a scared child in her presence.

"Do you see that, my heroic leader?" Mason said. "The Capitol dome's statue of Freedom is gone. Your agents are taking every statue, every painting, every symbol of freedom and democracy out of the building. Come tomorrow there won't be anything left here to keep the government running."

"You have indeed done your duty, Crimson," Xu Li said quietly.

"I've done more than that," Mason replied. "I've altered the course of world history."

"*We* have altered the course of world history," Xu Li boomed. The fully exposed whites of Xu Li's eyes betrayed her chilling fanaticism.

"It is time for us to establish the new regime," said Mason. "I stand ready to serve."

"That won't be necessary, Crimson," Xu Li said.

"What do you mean?" Mason was taken aback. "I've devoted my life to making this happen. I've succeeded beyond your wildest dreams. You owe me."

"Crimson, you have indeed succeeded. We never could have gotten close enough to the president alone to kill him as you did. But our plans for the United States beyond this point do not involve you. Your help is no longer needed." Xu Li turned toward Mason, her eyes still wide. "*You* are no longer needed."

Mason shuddered and took a step away from Xu Li.

'You' are no longer needed?

Mason turned toward his office door. Two Chinese agents stood guard, blocking the exit. One menacingly rubbed the gun slung over his shoulder, eyeing Mason the way a lion eyed its prey.

"We cannot have you involved in the post-capitalist government," Xu Li said. "I need someone who is thoroughly obedient and trustworthy. How can I trust someone willing to betray his own country? No, Crimson, your work is done."

Mason could feel the terror building within. He looked at the gun he'd dropped on the ground. He didn't think he could reach it before one of the Chinese agents shot him.

"Take this." Xu Li handed him an envelope. "These are your new instructions."

Mason took the envelope. He pulled a piece of paper from the envelope, slowly unfolded it, and began reading.

Agent Crimson is awarded the Order of Mao, the Ministry's highest honor. Agent Crimson completed Operation Pripyat by killing the president of the United States, the leader of the world capitalist faction. His obedience, devotion to duty, and willingness to sacrifice himself for the Revolution shall be an example to all Ministry agents. We honor Agent Crimson's memory with the posthumous awarding of the Order of Mao. He will forever hold a place in the history of the Revolution.

His eyes widened as he reached the end of the paper.

"But Madame Xu, I didn't die," said Mason.

"Yes, you did," Xu Li said, a sinister smile creeping across her face.

One of the Chinese agents walked toward him slowly. He grinned sadistically and caressed his gun like a baby.

Mason turned to Xu Li. "You can't do this to me. I've completed the most important mission in the history of world Communism."

Mason frantically looked for a way out. The office door was still blocked by one of the Chinese agents. He surveyed the room for another exit, but all he saw was the window. The approaching Chinese agent was now in front of the desk, his gun still draped over his shoulder. Mason watched as he began to remove the safety on the gun.

"I *have* to do this to you, Crimson," Xu Li said emotionlessly. Her clinical indifference terrified Mason more than her sinister visage. "I cannot have this story told."

"How can you—"

Mason saw the flash of the Chinese guard's gun out of the corner of his eye and felt a puncturing of his stomach. The note he had just read fluttered out of his hand, followed by the sound of glass shattering and thousands of stabbing pains in the back of his head as his skull crashed into the window behind him. He crumpled to the floor and felt warm blood gushing over his hand as he futilely tried to cover his stomach wound.

"You have served your purpose, Crimson," Xu Li said.

The Chinese agent, still grinning sadistically, sidled up to Xu Li.

"But . . . but . . ." Mason whispered.

"I need this." Xu Li snatched the note and envelope from the floor.

Mason coughed up blood while Xu Li carefully folded the note, put it back in its envelope, and slid it into the pocket inside her jacket.

"If you'll excuse me, Crimson, I have to get to a meeting."

"A meeting?" said Mason in barely a whisper, gurgling blood as he spoke.

"Andrea Gartner is waiting for me." Xu Li looked down at him. "Farewell, Crimson." Then she turned to the soldier and nodded.

The soldier stood over Mason, his smile broadening. He cocked his gun, aimed for Mason's head, and fired.

CHAPTER 51

A ndrea awoke in a dark basement tied to a chair. Not one of those expensive ergonomic chairs in the White House, but one of those old-fashioned wooden chairs with the flat bottoms and stiff backs that doubled as a treatment for scoliosis. A single lightbulb hung over her head. The walls were damp, and she could hear the drip of water through cracks in the ceiling and walls.

Her head throbbed in pain. A bandana or bandage of some kind had been wrapped around her head. She tried to raise her arms to feel the wound, but her hands were bound to the back of the chair.

"Where am I?" she rasped.

She groggily recalled the events of the day. The accident. Driving down Pennsylvania Avenue, heading to Mason's office. The call with Rachel. Mason . . .

Omigod!

Andrea jolted into full consciousness. She desperately tried to free herself from the chair. She kicked, shook, rocked, everything she could do, to no avail.

"Help! Somebody help me!" she shrieked at the top of her lungs. "The president is in danger!"

A loud buzzer pierced the room. A door opened and a tiny bit of light entered. She heard the footsteps of someone approaching her, but the darkness obscured the person.

"Help! Get me out! I work for the president! He's in danger!"

The stranger responded quietly, "I know."

"Get me out of here so I can help him!"

"That is not part of the plan."

Andrea had nearly screamed herself hoarse as she struggled in vain against her restraints.

The stranger drew closer to Andrea and into the glow of the bulb. The light revealed a short, slight Chinese woman dressed in a baby-blue Mao jacket and pants.

"Do you know who I am?"

"I don't give a hoot who you are," said Andrea. "If you don't get me out of here, someone is going to kill the president!"

"Oh, my dear, he's already dead."

Andrea felt time slowing down, almost as if she could feel the signal traveling across her neurons in slow motion as she processed what she'd just heard. How could the Secret Service have ignored her? She'd tried to save the president and instead ended up helplessly imprisoned in some godforsaken basement, unable to warn anyone else about what was unfolding. She raged at her impotence.

"Goddamn you," she shouted as she violently struggled against the cables binding her wrists and feet to the chair. "Who do you think you are?"

"I am the person who engineered the destruction of your government and soon will establish its replacement." The woman walked around Andrea's chair slowly. "You don't know who I am, do you?"

"No, I don't," said Andrea.

"You should never have invited Chinese troops onto American soil," the woman said calmly.

"That's pretty obvious now, you damned commie."

"But you had no choice because you made such a mess of your budget. Now how about I tell you who I am so you can stop calling me a 'damned commie'?"

"You can tell me your name, but it won't stop me from calling you a damned commie."

The woman slapped Andrea across the face.

"That is enough of your disrespect, you bankrupt American failure."

She leaned down, her nose inches from Andrea's.

"My name is Xu Li. I am the head of Chinese State Security."

"How did you get into the country?"

"Our aircraft carriers and destroyers are very large and I am very small."

"Who else have you grabbed?"

"Oh, it's only you, my dear. We killed the president."

Andrea tried to kick her legs, but her feet were bound too tightly to the chair. "Why don't you just kill me, then?"

"Because I don't want you dead . . . yet. I just want you here."

Andrea was confused. *Who kidnaps the OMB director? All the targets in Washington, DC, and China picks the OMB director?*

"Who are you, anyway?" Andrea was so dazed Xu Li's introduction hadn't registered the first time.

Xu Li walked directly under the light, then turned and faced Andrea.

"You did not hear me before? I see the sedative hasn't worn off yet. My name is Xu Li. I am Minister of State Security of the People's Republic of China."

China.

It *was* China all along.

"Tell me, Xu Li, why is the Chinese Minister of State Security interested in America's OMB director? Don't tell me you couldn't find anyone with more sex appeal."

"Because you are the biggest threat to me."

Andrea wondered if her head wound included a concussion.

"*I* am the biggest threat to you?" she responded in amazement. "I command exactly zero divisions, zero aircraft, and zero ships. If the OMB director is your biggest threat, you're living one weird life."

"Again with the derogatory comments," replied Xu Li calmly. "I would think someone in your position, bankrupt, tied to a chair with a bleeding head wound and a dead president, might be a little more respectful toward me. Me, who has put you in this position."

Xu Li continued to slowly circle Andrea's chair.

"We Chinese have been patiently planning to use your national debt to bring America down. For years we watched you borrow money to spend on capitalist baubles. The bread and circuses for your masses whom you allow to vote. You must listen to them. And what do they say? 'More, more, more for me.'"

Xu Li pulled out a silver chain, thicker than a necklace, and swung it menacingly.

"Your people, they do not care where you get the money," she continued. "How is it you say? Robbing Peter to pay Paul? As long as they aren't Peter, they are happy, yes? You have to give in and give them their free goodies or else they won't vote for you."

"What's your point?" Andrea spat.

Xu Li's slow footsteps crunched against the broken concrete. "You Americans are proud of your so-called democracy. But it isn't a democracy. It's a bribe-ocracy. In China, we have corruption and bribery, too, but only among a small few. You Americans, you must bribe a whole nation. That is not good for one's fiscal health, now is it?"

Xu Li continued to spin the silver chain around her finger as she walked. The threat of violence hung in the air.

"China and her allies were only too happy to lend you money for all your domestic bribery. You Americans didn't even realize you were borrowing from banks and countries secretly allied with

China in her fight against the United States. And now here you are, forty trillion dollars later, all frittered away with nothing to show for it. The only thing better than an America hopelessly in debt is an America hopelessly in debt to us. To *me*."

"What do I have to do with any of this?" asked Andrea.

"You, my dear, thwarted my plans at every turn. Who do you think was behind the Pripyat Consortium? I picked a Russian town just to throw you off. And not just any Russian town, but the one synonymous with disaster. But your emergency budget kept the country from ruin, and for some reason your people didn't revolt as we expected."

Andrea recalled what she'd said to President Murray about how America was an idea, an experiment, whose goal was to maximize human freedom. "Totalitarians like you don't understand us at all," she said.

"And how is that?" For the first time Xu Li seemed off balance, her voice tinged with a hint of uncertainty.

"Because Americans are survivors," said Andrea. "That's what makes us great. Free people find ways to survive. We buckle down and bear hardship because we are confident better days are ahead. Free people can correct their mistakes and control their own destiny. Totalitarians like you treat your people like commodities. Like so many cans of beans."

"That is no explanation," Xu Li said defensively. "You are the bankrupt one, not me."

"If you want to delude yourself into thinking your totalitarian government will last, go right ahead," said Andrea. "You totalitarians perpetually have your finger in the dike. You think you can solve every problem by the government just pulling on this economic lever or suppressing that political speech. The pressure builds up and you have to take ever more extreme measures to keep people content. The more you push off the inevitable, the worse the explosion when it finally comes. And it always comes."

"Oh my, you are much feistier than Mason warned me." Xu Li smiled and regained her cockiness. "How China treats her people is beside the point. It is your bankruptcy that has brought us together. But even though you thwarted our plans with Pripyat, you hopelessly weakened yourself to do it. You provided China an opportunity to rectify some historical wrongs."

"Taiwan and the South China Sea," Andrea muttered.

"Now you are catching on, my dear," said Xu Li, still circling Andrea, swinging the chain a bit faster. "With the United States impotent, we took back China's rightful inheritance."

"Except we weren't as impotent as you thought," Andrea said.

"So it was. And again it was you who thwarted us by keeping the war going with your budgetary gimmicks and tricks. When your people failed to revolt after we took Taiwan, sank your ships, and confiscated your most valuable national heirlooms, there was only one way to end capitalism and topple the American government."

"And what was that?"

Xu Li stopped circling and leaned closer to Andrea. Her slight smile disappeared. Andrea could feel and smell her breath, so foul it seemed Xu Li hadn't brushed her teeth in weeks. Xu Li stared directly into Andrea's eyes with a fanaticism Andrea had never seen.

"Brute force."

"This is what it's all about?" asked Andrea. "Toppling the American government? Ending capitalism?"

"I should say those are rather lofty goals, wouldn't you? Should it be about something else?"

"World domination? More territory? Middle Eastern oil? How should I know what else you might want?"

"All that will come, my dear. With America a bankrupt shell of itself, all things are possible for China."

"What is it you want from me?"

Xu Li smiled and laughed faintly. "I want you right here, unable to come up with your clever and creative budget schemes to thwart my plans. I cannot have you interfering any longer."

Andrea paused as she momentarily felt relief that Xu Li had said nothing about killing her. She had been so focused on parrying Xu Li's rhetorical attacks she hadn't realized she was starting to become light-headed. She couldn't remember the last time she had eaten. Her hunger, the pitter-patter and squeaking of rats scampering in the darkness, and the musty smell of rodent feces, dust, and mold were making Andrea delirious.

"I'm starving," Andrea said.

Xu Li went to a dirty sink by the wall and filled a filthy plastic cup with brownish water. She reached into her pocket and pulled out a small packet, tore it open, and poured a white powder into the cup. She then pulled a straw from her pocket, dropped it into the cup, and stirred.

"I see the worry on your face," Xu Li said. "You must be a very poor card player. Do not worry. This powder is only a nutritional supplement. I want you alive, but I can't waste food on you. I have soldiers to feed. But you have created problems for me. People who create problems for me do not die easy deaths. The last thing you see will be the collapse of your country and the new People's Republic we put in its place."

Andrea was so desperately hungry and thirsty she was willing to take her chances with the filthy drink.

Xu Li leaned over and placed the straw under Andrea's lips. "You are not like the other Americans I have dealt with in my time."

"Is that so?" Andrea asked. She sucked a deep sip of the cloudy water through the straw.

"Yes, it is. I've never dealt with anyone quite as feisty and without pretense as you."

"I'm glad I lived up to your high standards," Andrea replied. "I'll bet you didn't expect that from an OMB director." Still parched, she took another sip of the water. It might have been dirty, but Andrea savored it going down like Pellegrino.

"I expected a sniveling, terrified prisoner willing to tell me anything," replied Xu Li.

"A year ago, you might have gotten that. But now, with the entire country hating me, politicians on both sides hating me, and even my neighbors hating me, I'm not that person anymore. I'm actually quite dangerous." Andrea sucked air through the straw loudly as she took the last remaining sip of the drink, making sure the slurping at the end was pronounced.

"And why is that?"

"Because I have nothing to lose."

"I doubt that. Surely you're worried about me killing you. Or your children?" Xu Li paused. "Oh yes, I know all about them. Where they live, where they go to school."

Andrea jerked her hands and feet wildly trying to escape. Xu Li was relishing this moment of weakness with a wicked smile on her face.

No, stop. Don't show you're scared for the kids. Maybe then she'll leave them alone.

"If my emergency budget saves the country and preserves their futures, it will have been worth it," Andrea replied.

"Even if I were to kill you?"

"You don't think I'd take a bullet for the United States?" Andrea was revived and relieved that the powder probably was nothing more than a nutritional supplement. "Just because I'm an accountant and not an Army veteran doesn't mean I wouldn't give my life to save the country from its debt problem. Congratulations. You took a shrinking violet CPA homebody and turned her into a lethal patriotic weapon ready to die to save her country."

Xu Li folded her hands across her chest and smiled. "You'd fit right in at my Ministry," she said.

"I'd rather you just kill me." Andrea couldn't believe she'd said it.

"Why are you Americans so cross? Your country is bankrupt, your president is dead, your country blames you for the mess, and now you are our prisoner. Why wouldn't you want to join us?"

"All your spying and you know nothing about me," Andrea said. "Here's a history lesson for you. The czars drove half my family out of Russia, and the Nazis drove the other half out of Germany. Totalitarian governments have been singularly awful to my family. I'm not about to roll the dice on another one."

"I'm sure we could arrange a much better reception for you in China."

"You mean the Chinese government would treat me better than the czars and Hitler? Don't hurt yourself trying to do *that*."

Xu Li drew her right arm back and sharply struck Andrea's neck. Andrea toppled forward and her forehead smashed against the dirt-caked floor. She looked up, expressionless, and saw Xu Li hovering menacingly over her as if gloating about her strength. Xu Li righted her chair and stared into Andrea's eyes.

"Enough of your insolence!" Xi Lu shouted.

Andrea merely groaned and winced in pain.

"You are like all Americans," Xu Li spat. "Your bullying ways get you in nothing but trouble. How do you say it? Writing checks with your mouth that your body cannot cash?"

This is nothing, Andrea thought. *Remember those graves in Arlington. Every blow she lands on you is a blow she's not landing on the country. The more time she spends torturing you, the less time she's spending torturing the country.*

Xu Li turned her back to Andrea and walked toward the door.

A thought crossed Andrea's mind. *Don't let her leave. If you keep her in this basement, she won't be able to direct whoever she has working for her.*

"You know this whole scheme of yours isn't going to work, right?" Andrea shouted.

Xu Li stopped and turned to Andrea. "What scheme?"

"The whole topple-the-American-government scheme."

Xu Li cocked an eyebrow. "And why do you say that?"

"Because Americans will sell their organs before they capitulate to foreign invaders. By now, Vice President Campbell has already been sworn in as president and is hunting your sorry ass. Someone will come to get me out of here, you know that, right?"

Xu Li laughed. "Oh, my dear, you really are quite precious. Your president is dead and your government is doomed. It is only a matter of time before we end capitalism and put a People's government in place."

"I suppose you don't see the irony in all this."

"Irony?" Xu Li responded.

"I'm only one person," Andrea said. "But this one person, given the freedom to speak and challenge the party line, has thwarted the grandest plans of your entire Communist machine. Someone like me would get thrown in your gulags. But in the United States, a simple accountant like me can speak loud enough and long enough that they make a difference. Freedom might have gotten us into this mess, but freedom is going to get us out of it."

The chain reappeared in Xu Li's hands as she slowly rolled it between her fingers.

"You don't know when to quit, do you—"

Two explosions followed by gunfire from upstairs shattered the quiet of the basement. Xu Li whipped her head around to the door. Then she glanced at Andrea, eyes widened. For the first time Andrea saw surprise on Xu Li's face.

"You hear that? That's the sound of freedom," Andrea said, hoping it was true. "The cavalry is here."

Xu Li stared at Andrea, searching for something to say, but nothing came out of her mouth.

"Look at you now," Andrea continued. "Where is your vaunted army now, huh? Anyone coming to save you like they're coming to save me?"

Xu Li was frozen, uncertainty written on her face.

Shouting in Chinese and English pierced the darkness as the gunfire upstairs continued.

Xu Li screamed in frustration as she violently pressed a button on her large wristwatch over and over and looking toward the door. But the door remained closed.

Xu Li then came back to Andrea with a small pocketknife, frantically trying to cut off the cables tying Andrea's hands, feet, and waist to the chair.

"You don't have all day, honey. You could build a bridge with these cables they are so strong. Why don't you—"

Xu Li smacked Andrea's face so hard that the chair fell over again. Andrea's jaw connected with the concrete floor and she screamed in pain. Her ears rang and black spots danced in her eyes.

"There!" a voice shouted. "She's down there!"

Boots stomping against the stairs echoed through the basement, followed by pounding on the door. Deep male voices shouted, "Open up!" and "Don't shoot! No dynamite! Gartner may be in there!"

The calm, collected Xu Li, the epitome of secret agent sang-

froid, had made a grievous mistake letting her emotions overcome her. The rescuers upstairs must have heard Andrea hit the
floor and scream.

Xu Li frantically whipped her head back and forth in des-
peration. She appeared to have completely forgotten about
Andrea. The banging at the door was pushing Xu Li over the edge.

"There's no way out for you," Andrea sneered. "You'd better
give up now if you want to live."

Xu Li reached into her jacket pocket as panic appeared to
overtake her.

Andrea's muscles tensed.

What is she grabbing? A gun? A knife?

Xu Li pulled out a small cardboard paper pouch with a red
stripe that looked like a single-serving portion of instant oatmeal.
She tore it open with her teeth and emptied a white pill into her
hand. Still strapped to the toppled chair, Andrea watched from
her side as Xu Li shoved the pill into her mouth.

"No one came for you, did they?" Andrea said.

White foam oozed from Xu Li's mouth.

"You're expendable to your totalitarian masters. Even you,
the great Xu Li, the spymaster nonpareil, was just another can
of beans to them. My country came to rescue me. Your country
expects you to kill yourself rather than be taken alive."

Xu Li's eyes widened as if she was about to speak, but before
she could utter a word, she dropped to the floor unconscious. The
white foam now gushed from her mouth and was coursing through
the cracks of the broken concrete floor.

Seconds later, the light of a welder's torch appeared on the
bottom left corner of the basement door and began tracing its
edges. When the light had traced the entire perimeter and reached
the bottom right corner of the door, boots began kicking it. With
a squeak, the heavy metal door toppled inward like a domino

and men in SWAT gear charged into the room. Behind them ran Rachel, also in SWAT gear.

"Get down!" a SWAT team member shouted as red laser sights crisscrossed the basement. "Get on the ground!"

Rachel went directly to Andrea's chair and righted it as the agents fanned out.

"Andrea?" she said.

"Rachel . . ." Andrea eked out. Rachel looked so small in the bulky SWAT uniform. "Oh, mercy, am I glad to see you."

"Me too," Rachel said.

The agent who'd entered the room before Rachel still had his gun drawn as he surveyed the scene for danger.

"Over there." Andrea pointed to Xu Li's collapsed body. "She's the mastermind of it all."

The agent walked over to Xu Li's body, kneeled beside it, and took her pulse. "This chick's gone," he said.

"How did you find me?" Andrea asked.

"Never mind that now," said Rachel. "We need to get you out of here."

"Where are we?" asked Andrea.

"East Baltimore," said Rachel.

Andrea's emotional nervous system froze as if some internal fuse had blown. Fifteen minutes earlier she thought Xu Li was about to kill her. The events of the last week had simply overloaded her emotional circuitry. The ransacking of America. The assassination of President Murray. Her family's breaking down. Hours in the darkness of a fetid basement tormented by Xu Li. Now, suddenly, it all seemed to be over.

Andrea couldn't cry, or laugh, or cheer, or scream. A torrent of emotions was pulling her in every direction, leaving her numb and emotionless.

Two soldiers cut Andrea's wrists and ankles free.

"Get her out of here," said Rachel.

Each soldier put one of Andrea's arms over his shoulder and carried her out of the basement and up the stairs, her legs too weak to move, her toes dragging on the floor.

Rachel followed.

As the agents carried her up the stairs and out of the warehouse, Andrea saw dead Chinese soldiers, the collapsed walls, and the tanks, covered in shattered brick fragments.

"My Lord," said Andrea. "What happened here?"

"You rest." Rachel gestured to the two SWAT officers to keep hustling Andrea out of the warehouse. "There'll be plenty of time later for me to fill you in."

The cool night air slapped Andrea in the face. It was a welcome relief from the stultifying, unventilated basement. She took a deep breath. The SWAT agents took her to a waiting ambulance and paramedics helped seat her in the back. Rachel jumped in for the ride to the hospital.

"Just tell me, Rachel," said Andrea. "Is it over?"

"It's over," Rachel said. "It's over."

"And my family?" asked Andrea. "Are they all right?"

"They're fine. I got them hidden in a secure location right after our call. I had a hunch something was going down."

"Boy do I love you." Andrea's eyes filled with tears.

"They're safe and sound," Rachel said, smiling with relief. "And very, very proud of you."

CHAPTER 52

A ndrea hated hospitals. The sterile fluorescent white lights. The antiseptic yet mildly nauseating smell. The barely edible food on plastic trays, plastic plates, plastic everything. The insistence on serving Jell-O at every meal. Even the food seemed to be made of plastic.

Andrea was just about to tuck into a breakfast of powdered eggs and a muffin when the door of her hospital room opened.

"Mind if I come in?" Rachel asked.

Andrea barely had energy after two days in the hospital, but she offered a weak yet warm smile. "Rachel," she said wearily. "It's so good to see you. I'm about to go stir crazy in this place."

"You were lucky," said Rachel. "The doctors found swelling in your brain when you got here."

Andrea slowly lifted her arm and gently touched her left temple. She felt the bandages covering the wound and the surgical opening. "Feels like they did some work up here," she joked.

"It was probably from the car accident, though they don't know for sure. The doctors said another two days in that basement and you probably would have had a fatal stroke."

Andrea widened her eyes a bit.

"You're lucky your Chinese kidnappers took you to Baltimore," Rachel continued. "We took you to Hopkins. There's nothing left of the government medical facilities in DC. The Chinese ransacked Bethesda Naval Hospital. They took everything except the walls and doors."

Just then, a commotion stirred outside. A small Secret

Service detail took up positions at the door. President Campbell and Brooks Powell followed them into the room and went to Andrea's bedside.

"Andrea Gartner," President Campbell said, smiling and putting his hand on Andrea's. "What a relief it is to see you."

"Mr. Vice President," Andrea said wearily. Rachel and Brooks exchanged a look. Andrea realized her mistake. "I mean, Mr. President, sir."

"You know about President Murray?" Campbell asked.

"I think so," Andrea said. "Xu Li said he was dead."

"It's true," Rachel said. "Congressman Mason murdered him."

"We're quite sure from the forensics that Mason killed him," said Brooks.

Andrea shook her head in disbelief.

"How on earth does the FBI and the CIA miss that the chairman of the House Appropriations Committee is a Chinese spy?" Andrea was baffled.

Campbell smiled wryly. "The Debt Rebel Gang is now trying to explain how one of their leading lights turned out to be a Chinese mole. They're finding it's not a lot of fun to be on defense. A Debt Rebel Gang tied up explaining how a Chinese spy infiltrated its ranks won't have time to excommunicate heretics from the Republican Party."

"Where are the Chinese now?" Andrea asked. "Did you kick them out of the country?"

"Gone," Campbell said. "They were already nearly gone when you had your accident. They took their property and skedaddled. No more Chinese soldiers on American soil."

"And President Murray?" asked Andrea. "Aren't they going to pay a price for that?"

"We don't have anything to fight the Chinese with," Campbell said. "The Chinese took too much government property and we have no money. We couldn't fight a war if we wanted to."

"What happened to me?" Andrea asked.

"You were kidnapped by Chinese agents," said Rachel.

"The guy in that SUV who was following me?" Andrea asked.

"The Pripyat spokesman," Rachel said. "Zegna Suit. He really was Mason's brother. The FBI confirmed it. He took you from the accident scene to the warehouse in Baltimore."

"How did you find me?"

"The Chinese murdered Congressman Mason after he assassinated President Murray," Rachel said. "When Zegna Suit found out Xu Li had killed his brother, he turned himself in to the FBI. He said he wasn't going to let Xu Li discard him like she discarded his brother. He told us everything. Operation Pripyat. Xu Li. And the location of the warehouse where they were holding you."

"We sent in a SWAT team, two FBI counterterrorism units, and half of what was left of the Maryland National Guard," Campbell said.

"But why did the Chinese murder Mason?" asked Andrea.

"Mason thought he was going to be president, or chief commissar, or whatever the Chinese planned to install after they toppled the American government," said Rachel. "But they washed their hands of him after he assassinated the president. Shot him dead in his office."

"Did the Chinese really find four trillion dollars' worth of stuff?" Andrea asked.

"I think so." Campbell sighed. "Those oil and gas leases on federal lands are going to put them over the top, probably. Thirty years of oil and gas profits? That's a tidy sum."

"Don't forget the ritual humiliation," interjected Brooks. "The pictures of them hauling the Resolute desk out of the Oval Office and the *Apollo 11* capsule out of the Air & Space Museum are in the papers all over the world. Everyone thinks the United States is done. They think China is the superpower now."

"Did they leave anything behind?" Andrea asked.

"Yeah," said Brooks. "They left your desk. They didn't like the big dent in it."

Andrea smiled sheepishly. "Maybe I should have gone nuts on some more stuff in the White House," she joked. Finally, a valuable use for her temper. Imagine all future government property being issued with the "Andrea Gartner dent" to prevent creditors from seizing it to pay government debts.

"How about the country?" asked Andrea.

"Well, my polls suck." Campbell shrugged his shoulders and smiled.

"You know what I mean," Andrea said.

Campbell and Brooks exchanged glances. "Andrea, things are grim and okay all at once."

"How's that?" she asked.

"People are still dying from the emergency budget," said Brooks. "Still no Medicare or Social Security for most people. Can't afford it. Lots of kids not eating enough without complete school lunches."

"What's okay about any of that?" She tried to sit up but felt a little dizzy.

"What's okay, shocking really, is somehow the country is holding together," President Campbell said. "Surviving. A lot of corporations and wealthy philanthropists are trying to pick up the slack to provide medicines and food to people who need it. It's not perfect. But there's no rioting or shooting in the streets."

Brooks agreed. "People are angry, but there's no revolution. Unless you consider their demands that Congress pass balanced budgets a revolution. Even your old friends in the Debt Rebel Gang are now saying they supported balanced budgets all along."

"Brings to mind the old quote from that French revolutionary Ledru-Rollin: 'There go the people. I must follow them, for I am their leader,' or something like that," President Campbell said. "You could put that quote on the Debt Rebel Gang's tombstone and make it the TrueCon Network's slogan."

"They all thought they were driving the anti-Establishment bus," said Andrea. "They were really only riding the tide."

"Don't get too worked up," Brooks said. "Docs say we need to control your blood pressure."

"We can't have you dying on us," Campbell said. "We need you back at OMB. You've been on the debt issue from day one. Besides, everyone hates you already. Who's going to come in and take this job knowing we have years of emergency budgets ahead of us?"

"You make it sound so appealing," Andrea replied sarcastically.

"So you'll come back?" Campbell asked.

Andrea hesitated. She thought of her kids. She'd taken the OMB job for them. But she nearly had gotten killed doing it. She wanted to be home more than anything in the world. Her husband, her kids, her mother, all of them needed her. Her work was done; the emergency budget was on autopilot now. As long as it remained in place, the debt would slowly be paid off. The country was on a glide path back to normal. It would take a decade, at least, but it would get there.

"Mr. President, I greatly appreciate your confidence," Andrea said, "but it's time for me to go home."

Campbell nodded, disappointed but understanding. "You did it, you know."

"Did what?" Andrea perked up.

"Saved the country," Campbell said.

Andrea scoffed. "Hardly. We're not a superpower anymore.

Lost Taiwan, lost the South China Sea, probably lost the respect of the rest of the world. And the Chinese stripped the country clean."

Campbell looked down at her, gently patting her hand. "Yeah, but we're still here."

Tears welled her eyes. "Barely," she whispered.

"Barely still counts, doesn't it?" Campbell smiled. "We can replace property. It's just stuff. We're still here. The sun will rise, the sun will set, and the United States of America will go on. And it's because of you. Don't let anyone ever tell you you're just an accountant. You're the accountant who saved the country."

EPILOGUE

On the fifth anniversary of President Murray's election, Andrea Gartner stood on the lawn of her South Carolina home, watching Aaron playing catch with Ryan while Michelle rode a bike with her friends around the cul-de-sac. Her mother sat on a rocking chair on the front porch reading a book.

Andrea rarely thought about Washington anymore.

After leaving OMB, she'd returned to South Carolina and her CPA practice. Leaving Washington had been easy; fortunately, the Gartners had only rented their DC home. The Washington real estate market had collapsed in the wake of the emergency budget and homes sold for pennies on the dollar. The Gartners had just terminated their lease and headed home to Columbia.

Andrea's old landlord had given her back her old office space. The faded "Jake's Doggy Day Care" in the background of the "Andrea Gartner, CPA" sign on the front door of the office was still there. She'd never been so happy to see it. And the hot buffet on the first floor never tasted so good.

Business was good; she was famous now. People thought with her Washington experience she had a special connection with what was left of the IRS. She didn't, but if people wanted to think that, who was she to stop them? But that fame was a double-edged sword. Plenty of people still hated her. Wally Flynn never talked to her again after President Campbell replaced him with one of his longtime staffers.

Everyone wanted to see the letter from President Campbell awarding Andrea the Presidential Medal of Freedom she displayed in her waiting room. He had awarded it to her just before she left Washington. There was no medal; the emergency budget had cut purchases of medals and other such swag. All President Campbell could give her was a handwritten letter on plain white printer paper. But she'd framed it with the Office Depot ballpoint pen the president had used to sign it.

"Mom, I'm hungry!" Aaron shouted. He sounded like a boy, though he was now about to graduate high school and planning to study engineering in college. Even though NASA had been forced to close up shop, private space companies were sprouting up, hoping to pick up the slack.

Andrea smiled. "I got some stuff to make a lasagna tonight."

"Dad and I can make it," Aaron said excitedly.

"I was hoping you'd say that."

Andrea gazed at the neighborhood. "Michelle, come in, it's getting dark and you need to do your homework!" Andrea shouted across the cul-de-sac.

"All right, Mom," Michelle said, and she pulled up on her bike.

Andrea turned to her mother. She was in her best health in years, pain-free and able to walk and move about the house. "How about we go inside now?" she said. She lifted her mother up, took her by the arm, and walked her across the porch and into the house.

Andrea was about to close the door when she noticed the flag on her porch. It was the flag from her old EEOB office. President Campbell had given her the flag as a keepsake.

The orange glow of the South Carolina sunset brightened the flag. Every day for the five years since she had left DC the sun had risen and set over that flag. The colors hadn't faded a bit. It was the same red, white, and blue as it was the day she walked into the White House for the first time. Nothing had destroyed that flag. Not the emergency budget, not the war, not the Chinese repossession.

Andrea smiled as she stepped into the house and closed the door.

ABOUT THE AUTHOR

Michael E. Ginsberg is an attorney in Washington, DC, practicing in the field of national security law. He spent a decade in private practice at Arnold & Porter LLP in Washington, DC, and then worked several years in the US government as a Senior Associate General Counsel in the Office of the Director of National Intelligence (ODNI), where he served as legal counsel for the Intelligence Advanced Research Projects Activity (IARPA). He serves as Vice President and Deputy General Counsel at a Virginia-based defense contractor.

Ginsberg has also served in senior leadership positions in the Republican Party of Virginia and is the cofounder of the Suburban Virginia Republican Coalition.

A 1997 graduate of Harvard College and 2002 graduate of Harvard Law School, he also holds a master's in aeronautics and astronautics from Stanford University (1999). A native of Baltimore, Maryland, Ginsberg lives in Centreville, Virginia, with his wife and two children.